Mistress

of

Mayhem

Book 1

iMAGITECHMEDIA.com
3708 E 29th Street #381
Bryan, TX 77802

The story, all names, characters, and incidents portrayed in this production are fictitious. No identification with actual persons (living or deceased), places, buildings, and products is intended or should be inferred.

Editor Armando G. Mendive
Editor Belle Manuel
Editor Dr. C. Ramirez
Ship 3D Modeling Gabriel Ramirez
Book Cover Design J.A. Ramirez

ISBN

Mistress of Mayhem Book 1 (Paperback)
978-1-964667-00-3

Mistress of Mayhem Book 1 (ebook)
978-1-964667-01-0

First Edition
0 9 8 7 6 5 4 3 2 1

To my sons, you are my greatest creations,
and I hope I inspire you
to always follow your dreams.

Acknowledgment

Writing a book is a journey—a solitary endeavor that is made possible by the support and encouragement of countless individuals along the way. As I reflect on the completion of Mistress of Mayhem, I am filled with deep gratitude for those who have walked beside me on this remarkable path.

A story born in the middle of a graveyard shift as I ascended the metal grated steps of a dark warehouse in the very early hours of a cold winter morning. I could hear the echoes of my steps and the shadows of the trucks that rested quietly beneath me, and that's where this journey started.

This work would not have been possible without my wife Ivette, who provided me with the time to hone my craft and considerations that elevated me and my inspiration. Your belief in me and your endless support at my side into the late hours of the night have been my greatest source of strength and inspiration. Your input and feedback have made this the best version of this book, and I am glad we did it together.

I would like to express my heartfelt appreciation to my family for their unwavering love and encouragement throughout this journey, in particular to my parents and my sister, for their constant positivity.

To my friends, thank you for your guidance, your insights, and your unwavering belief in the power of storytelling. Your words of encouragement and constructive feedback have shaped me and this book in ways I could never have imagined.

I am indebted to my editors and the publishing team for their guidance, expertise, and unwavering commitment to excellence. Your dedication to bringing this book to life has been nothing short of extraordinary, and I am profoundly grateful for your tireless efforts.

To the readers who will embark on this journey with me, thank you for your curiosity, your open hearts, and your willingness to explore the worlds I have created. It is my sincerest hope that Mistress of Mayhem brings you joy, inspiration, and a renewed sense of wonder.

With anticipation and excitement, I invite you to join me on this extraordinary journey—a journey into the heart of Mistress of Mayhem.

~J. A. Ramirez

Mistress
of
Mayhem

Book 1

By:

J. A. Ramirez

Chapter 1

Ophelia sat on the floor with her back against the cold steel of the ship's inner wall. Her head hung low in resignation, taking a deep breath and slowly lifting her head until it touched the wall. She banged her head softly four or five times in frustration, forcing herself up and noticing the grease and grime on her hands and coveralls.

"Look at me. I'm a damn mess. I've got more grease on me than there is on this entire ship."

A deep female voice responded from overhead, "Madam, that would not be efficient, nor would it be profitable. May I remind you that for the fourth month in a row we are running over budget and our reserves are being depleted at a high rate? We cannot sustain this, and my systems are currently running at sixty-four percent efficiency. It would be more cost effective to find ah... A more talented technician to put their hands on me. It may be a little more fun, if you found one for you, too."

"What! Mistress, please. What was I thinking, installing that programming into your systems?" the young woman protested.

"Clinically speaking, you were going through a rebellious phase. Your official statement was, 'mother said father spends more time with the ship than her. I thought it was only proper.'" The AI paused for a moment, then spoke almost wistfully. "That being said, I miss him, your father. He had firm hands. I miss those hands working on me. He was an amazing engineer and mechanic. His piloting skills were average and` his programming skills abysmal, but oh my, those hands. Makes a girl just quiver," Mistress stated, accompanied by a loud whirling noise of a servo revving up in the background.

Rolling her eyes, the young woman replied, "For all that is holy in the galaxy, please contain yourself. We don't have any more spare servos."

"Speaking of which, the left servo on the bay doors needs replacing. How am I going to let anyone inside, to leave their cargo if I can't open myself to them?"

"Is that all you ever process? A girl's got to work. If they can't come inside, we can't get paid. Plus, I like to be in good shape," Mistress retorted.

The young woman just shook her head and sighed. "Enough!"

"Very well. You used to be fun. I will start you a bath, so you don't dirty anything else. It's hard enough to clean up after you. I have also plotted an alternate course that will save on fuel," the ship replied.

"Do I even want to know?"

"Probably not, but you'll find out, anyway. There are cargo tankers headed towards section Delta 5. We should be able to piggyback off them for almost half of the trip. It will add a day but save us a ton in fuel. Now go take your bath and get some rest. You have been running yourself ragged lately. I will call when it's time," the ship said in a more concerned tone.

"Fine," replied the young woman, standing and moving off.

Ophelia removed her overalls, dropping them to the floor and setting them next to her boots. She first scrubbed and rinsed them with a cleaning agent that would remove the grease from everywhere before relaxing in a bath. Feeling the warm water raining down on her, she finally broke down with tears that were hidden by the rushing water from the shower. She leaned against the shower wall and clenched herself tightly, silently crying.

It had been over three years since the disappearance of her parents, and still she didn't know if they were alive or dead. The scene she found inside the ship showed a possibly darker fate. They had gone off to test the ship's new systems as they prepared for their family expedition.

Ophelia was finishing up finals before she graduated and would join them on their trip to see and explore the galaxy. Instead of a fantastic journey through the stars, she encountered a troublesome scene aboard the ship and later a betrayal by the company her parents had built from scratch.

Inside there were no bodies to be found, but the signs of a battle remained. The ship was poorly cleaned because of her not having completed the cleaning programs installation prior to her exams. Chemical solvents used to clean the interior of the ship contaminated any evidence that could've been found. The ship was empty, and Mistress's memory core had been wiped as if she had never left. The Mistress of Mayhem was highly advanced and customized in almost every fashion, built on a prototype frame, but still no evidence could be obtained.

Law enforcement in the sector was overloaded with work. A missing person case with little to no evidence was not very important to them. Her life crumbled, she missed her own graduation, her boyfriend and friends eventually stopped calling or passing by.

Little by little, they cut her off from everyone and everything, while she spent every waking moment watching dozens of technicians from Knightforge Technologies as they scoured the ship, all the while being vilified by the company's lawyers and government entities. The family lawyer worked diligently to keep them at bay, but suffered a sudden stroke and was remitted to the hospital. He was in a coma for months, and his company did a much less effective job than he had against the many entities that were now coming after her. His last advice, before his sudden heart attack, spurred her to scour the ship for any clues of tampering, whether it was physical or digital.

Six months passed before she got her captain's license, finishing the courses she had begun earlier on with her father. She needed to get away to escape the madness and became a transporter, seeing if she had better luck getting information from the different ports that the ship may have been, too. That venture proved to be no better. She had one charge on a credit account that provided her some hope, but it turned out to be nothing.

Slowly, things degenerated. With few clues, her parent's company's board freezing and limiting her access to the family assets, dwindling resources, and finally being boarded by raiders, she was almost at her breaking point. Those marauders stripped various components from the ship, killed the small crew she had aboard, and beat her so badly it almost cost her own life. Mistress had taken some damage and not all of her systems were functional, not to mention the loss of the stripped or damaged components. Every day she was losing a little more and her sanity was next.

Dad, Mom, I miss you. Please be safe, she thought as she held her arms close to her body. She was scared, and for all her education, training, and intelligence, she could not deny that she was alone and on the verge of losing it all. She shook her head and clenched her fists in defiance to the darkness that loomed over her.

Ophelia, get ahold of yourself. You are going to find them. I will find them! She argued back in her own mind, hoping with all the conviction she could muster.

The young woman noticed she was shivering under the hot water of the shower and began applying the breathing techniques she had learned. The water suddenly shut off, and the deep, sensual voice came over the intercom.

"Madam, we are under water restrictions. The scrubber systems are missing or damaged, meaning that we cannot recycle the water. I have allotted you all that I can for today. If I eliminate your bath, you can shower again in four-point-three-seven days."

"What! Is that all the water we have?" she asked incredulously.

"Captain, you have been in the shower for almost an hour. Our luxury fittings use three gallons per minute, meaning you have used up one hundred seventy-two gallons. All that and sadly, you were alone," the ship responded.

"I can shower myself just fine, Mistress!" Ophelia retorted.

"I am aware of that, madam, but why would you want to? I love it when other hands are on me, giving me a nice scrub down. It makes my sensors tingle. Those hands can be biological or mechanical. It's all the same to me. Makes me quiver just to process it," Mistress replied as the entire ship suddenly shimmied.

The young woman sighed. "I am going to bed. Wake me when we arrive at the tankers.

"Yes, madam. Would you like for me to play you some music to sleep?" the ship asked.

"Yes, please. Level 7," the woman replied.

"Very well, madam. Good night," Mistress replied.

After a pause, the young woman took a deep breath, placed a hand on one wall as she walked towards her bed. "Mistress. Thank you."

"Of course, Madam. It's my pleasure," the ship replied.

"Madam Ophelia?" the ship said.

"Yes, Mistress?" Ophelia replied.

"I will always take care of you, Madam. Now get some rest," the ship replied softly.

The young woman continued caressing the ship gently, to her Mistress was much more than a ship, she was family. That thought gave her solace, knowing she was not alone and allowed a wisp of a smile to touch her face as she reached her bed, looking forward to getting some long overdue sleep.

Almost a day had passed when Ophelia heard the alert, followed by Mistress's voice. "Captain, we are approaching our target."

"Thank you, Mistress. I'll be right there," the young woman replied groggily as she slowly rolled out of her bed, pushing her dark hair from her eyes, sighing.

Rubbing her face, she yawned once more while the lights slowly brightened, filling her quarters with a gentle glow. Her quarters were larger than any suite on travel liners and had so many more amenities.

She donned her normal attire, which was composed of a VESA long sleeve shirt with a slim protective vest and Spacefarers cargo pants with small chain accessories. Though these items looked like general clothing, they had specific functions.

The VESA Garment was skintight and made up of various layers that temperature regulated the body, and provided some padding. It would also provide some protection from the harshness of space. The pants and vest would protect the body from any space debris and seal itself in case the wearer found themselves in a vacuum or harsh environment. The vest also had optional circuitry that provided a basic force shield around the wearer's head in case of emergencies.

A full suit of either product would protect the wearer in case they found themselves in space for twenty-four to forty-eight hours. In her particular combination, the wearer would have closer to twenty-four hours than forty-eight.

Her grunge style appearance mixed with a gothic flare was one of the few things she kept from her school days. Fortunately, companies like Spacefarers and VESA made an extensive selection of garments suitable for the extremes of outer space and many other environments, yet suitable for many fashion styles. Her garments paired with her I.D.P.A.D.D. or Individual Data Processing Assistant and Data Director, a crucial piece of electronics in most people's lives, but most people called them a datapad or IDP for short.

Her model augmented her outfit and allowed her to customize certain aspects of her suit for fashion or function. It also provided an air keyboard and Heads Up Display if paired with proper accessories, such as glasses or contact lenses. The IDP was sturdy and programmable, with the ability to do countless functions and connect to a wide variety of devices, with thousands if not millions of applications available in cyberspace. Something that she rarely took off, even if it took up half of her forearm.

Finally, being dressed and making her way to the lifts, she paused as her eyes drifted towards an ornate door down the hall with her family crest engraved on it. It was her parents' room and though she had been in there countless times; she had not entered inside for months. She never moved to her parent's quarters, though it was a much bigger area, she did not need it, but that wasn't the only reason, and she knew it. She left it as it was, hoping to find her parents. Even if she avoided not wanting to dwell on her failures, but lived with and thought of them constantly, being in their room was more than she could bear.

Finally arriving at the bridge, she strode to a raised dais with three chairs covered in fine plush embossed orangish material with dark stitching on the dais. Each had illuminated arm rests and a series of consoles that could shift to any of the seats, but the center captain's chair was the most prominent. There were plenty of other seats, enough for an entire crew in the rest of the bridge, but they had programmed Mistress to assume almost all functions on the ship. Allowing a person to effectively fly the ship by themselves.

"All right, Mistress, let's see what we have. Display the target on the viewing screen," the captain ordered.

Millions of microscopic lights came on, displaying the infinite number of shimmering stars as the ship pivoted upwards, bringing the large tanker into view. Massive behemoths of metal that carried an enormous amount of cargo from different planets or sectors, sometimes called trains. These large vessels were named such because of the large numbers of sections that were referred to as cars in honor of early 19th century steamed engines that would go in a line over long distances.

Each tanker carried its own security, whether it be as completely automated drones and gun turrets, which were normally seen with high value cargo, or a fleet of pilots and short-range fighters. The latter being the most common since pilots and second-rate short-range fighters were so inexpensive compared to the better trained maintenance crew and upgraded facilities that are required with a large high-tech drone fleet.

Tankers provided a haven to many spacefarers, the vastness of space provided very little of anything in-between sectors. Tankers all had port cities that were an absolute necessity to the companies and governments that were invested in them, as much as to the privateers and freight ships that received contracts to deliver merchandise to other areas outside the normal routes of the cargo ships. Those goods provided much needed resources to remote territories of the outer rim and opportunities to everyone involved.

The lights on the tanker flickered and then again sent warning flags to the young captain. She zoomed the image closer on the viewing screen and confirmed her suspicions; the tanker was in distress. Smoke piled out of the large cargo ship and quickly dissipated in the vacuum. Sparks of electricity exploded in various areas along with shards of metal in all directions.

"Mistress, are you registering this?" the young woman asked.

"Captain, I am picking up no radio signals on any channel. Makes a girl think she's not wanted. But there are various short-range fighters approaching us at a high rate of speed. Five, to be exact, and they're coming around the belly of the beast. Visual in 30 seconds. Should I raise shields?" the ship asked.

"Not yet. If we can identify them as tanker security, I don't want them to think we are hostile. Will we have enough time to defend ourselves and escape if they are threats?" Ophelia asked.

"That's unlikely," Mistress responded.

"Then slow down, plot an escape route and be ready to run. Maybe one quick jump from the drives should get us far enough, but let's try hailing the fighters," the young woman commanded.

"I have been, madam, and that jump will burn out the rest of the fuel, leaving us stranded in space, but I'm calculating the best spot," the ship replied.

"It may not be the best option, but we will be away from here and then pray for the best," Ophelia stated nervously understanding the grim fate of what she suggested.

Ophelia felt a knot in the pit of her stomach suddenly grow. She had heard of raids on cargo trains, but was doubtful of the validity of those claims. One thing was certain: something had happened to that cargo train, and this could be a problem or an opportunity for her.

She tried to calm herself. She had run into pirates before and had been fortunate that a passing Galactic Defense Force cruiser came by when it did. Having heard horrible stories of pirates for most of her life was bad enough, but living through the experience was worse than any story.

Her mind wandered to that day, feeling her palms getting sweaty, she closed her eyes and took a deep breath. She did not want to feel how she did that day, almost a year ago. She truly felt vulnerable and scared. She had lost two crewmates and friends, along with some cargo and various parts from the ship, leaving her only a dark reminder of the possibility of her parent's fate.

The ship provided words of comfort. "They will not touch you, Ophelia. I promise. I will ready the guns."

"Don't make promises you can't keep, Mistress. Hold off on the guns, let's just see how this plays out and be ready. We don't have the firepower or the fuel, and we may need the extra energy to escape. The Capacitors that we have left may not hold the strain of combat," the captain replied.

"Yes, madam," the ship confirmed.

The ships approached quickly in a V formation. A common formation for ship security. Mistress identified the ship class displaying it on the screen. Fortunately, they matched the database of the type commonly used for tanker security. Ophelia could make out the lights flickering in unison coming from the lead ship. "Is that ship's lights flickering in a pattern?" she asked.

"Yes, madam, it's old Morse code. It says..." The shipped paused, deciphering the message. "They are identifying themselves as GDF Tanker security forces and that most communications are down. They are approaching to use short range comm systems."

"It took you that long to decipher the message. Are your functions compromised?"

"Always when pilots are approaching, just look at those sleek ships," the AI said in a flirtatious tone, then continued more seriously. "But no, madam, my processing is just fine. They are relaying the message at a speed to be deciphered by a life form," the ship replied.

As they closed the distance, four of the ships slowed down to almost a stop, spreading out to provide maximum coverage of fire as the lead ship slowly approached. Once in range, she heard a young man's voice through a static-filled channel.

"Mistress of Mayhem, this is Lieutenant Sherps of the Defense force for CT-109. Please identify yourself and your intentions for your visit. Over." The voice quickly cut out.

"Lieutenant Sherps, this is Ophelia Knight, Captain of the Mistress of Mayhem. Our intentions are friendly. We seek to refuel and pick up a contract. Over," was the reply.

Ophelia could see the large tanker with a series of flashing red lights indicating an emergency. The launch bay was filled with commotion as people tried to fill their ships with cargo and people. The young woman was concerned about the squadron in front of her and the scene transpiring on the viewscreen.

"Captain, you are clear to land. Please pilot your ship to Docking Bay 47. We will escort you to your destination. Under no circumstance will you approach the launch area. Failure to comply will be dealt with harshly. If that is not to your liking, you must depart the area at once. Over," the officer instructed.

"Thank you, Lieutenant. We will continue to Docking Bay 47. Over."

"Captain of the Mistress of Mayhem. Once you dock, please wait in your ship for further instructions. Now move along. Lieutenant Sherps, out," the man finished as the radio cut out.

"Did you hear that authority in his voice?" Mistress said, in a playful tone, "I mean like grrrrrr."

"I did, and that is not the usual welcome. Let's be ready for anything. Keep the escape route handy, in case we need a quick exit," Ophelia instructed.

"Yes, madam. The course has been plotted," replied the ship.

The copper-colored ship made its landing, and the docking area was practically empty of ships except for various security force ships. The cargo tanker was on high alert. Vast groups of security squads patrolled the area and seemed heavily armed. Two squads surrounded the Mistress of Mayhem after landing, as a third group escorted an older gentleman with what seemed to be his aid.

Loud servos echoed in the cargo bay, Ophelia released a heavy sigh as she waited for the complaining mechanism to finish it's task, then noticed the older officer as the bay door finished opening, exposing the inside of the ship and its captain. The man and his aide waited with irritated expressions as Ophelia made her way down, the guards eyeing her carefully, ready to attack. Approaching the man, she smiled, recognizing his face.

"Greetings, Admiral Palios, it's so good to see you again," she said, her voice filled with genuine warmth.

The older man gazed at her, trying to place her face, but it was not his action that concerned her, but that of his aide. The woman was much older than Ophelia, and at first what seemed like an anxious personality changed to an icy-cold stare, with a subcompact pistol in her hand instead of a stylus.

The Admiral glanced at his aide, his agile mind searching his memories as his eyes fell on Ophelia, who put her hands up, wanting no quarrel. The young woman's eyes widened as various muscles clenched seeing the light gleam off of the aide's weapon. Ophelia's eyes darted towards the older man nervously before returning her gaze to the pistol that was pointing at her face.

"Young lady, listen to my words. How is it you know the Admiral? Be honest, I'm easily agitated," the aid warned.

"I've known him for many years," she said, then with all the calm she could muster, turned her head towards the man. "You and my father worked on many projects together back on Karmier," the young woman replied.

"Karmier? That was almost a lifetime ago. Who is your father, dear?" the man asked with great curtesy.

"Knight. Harris D. Knight. Sir," the young woman replied, her eyes never leaving the pistol.

"Knight... Ophelia?" the older man asked in feigned surprise.

"Yes, sir," she replied with the meekest of smiles.

"Cynthia put that gun away. This is my longtime friend Harris Knight's daughter. Come here, child, it's been too long," the man said, opening his arms. "You've grown so much." He embraced the young woman with a genuine smile, taking in her appearance. "I'm so sorry, my dear. I tried contacting but there was no one answering. Please tell me you at least got my messages," the man asked.

"I did, Admiral, and I am sorry I didn't reply. It was a difficult time," she stated.

"Understandable, did they ever?" he asked hesitantly, not wanting to sadden the young lady with thoughts of her parents' situation.

She just shook her head sadly. "With no evidence, there was nothing to be done."

"Bastards!" he muttered a little louder than he intended.

"Sir," his aide said, trying to bring the Admiral back to the matter at hand.

"Yes, thank you, Cynthia," he said, taking a deep breath and straightening his overcoat with a stiff tug to compose himself. "Well, we shall talk about that more later. Right now, we have more pressing matters. CT-109 has taken some damage. And we have been using every available resource to make deliveries of the cargo. Most of the best cargo has been taken, so no easy runs left," The officer sighed as he scrolled through the data that was being displayed on his glasses. "Let me see here what kind of run we can put together for you."

The Admiral turned to his aide, delegating the job that was better suited for her. "Cynthia, find her the best of what we have left and get it on her ship," he instructed, then turned back to Ophelia. "So, the Mistress of Mayhem, hmmm. Who named her?"

"I did."

"Sounds fitting." The old man smiled reassuringly.

"You know, your parents were amongst my closest friends, and amongst the smartest, too. They put that ship together using an alpha class patrol cruiser frame. It was hard to get, but I pulled a few strings. It was a prototype by a company that went bankrupt making it. Highly modular and with an insane amount of flex, tested to handle an extreme amount of stress. In the end, it was too expensive for the fleet to put into mass production. Too bad, they would have been so much better off had they gone with it. Your dad had integrated several unique ideas and features to the ship, not to mention guns," the officer continued.

"Those would have been nice, but I had some system failures and got boarded about a year and a half ago, taking some major losses. I was fortunate to escape, thanks to her back-up systems and a GDF cruiser that happened by," Ophelia stated.

"Fortunate indeed. I am glad you are okay. It is good to see you dear," he said with a smile. "Let's get you loaded up and off this boat just in case it goes up," the older man jested.

"Sir!" the aide interjected, surprised at the sensitive information being relayed to someone she considered a stranger.

"Relax, Cynthia, this young lady has attended more top-secret meetings than you. She was always in my office as a kid. She was a quiet one and those almond eyes of hers made me pay for more ice cream than I could count."

"I was not aware that Mr. Knight had a daughter," Cynthia replied.

"She shipped out for school just prior to your arrival, and we maintained a privacy protocol for her safety," the Admiral added.

"Oh," the aide said surprised, then stared at the young captain and her ship in a new light, her face never changing from her stoic expression. A loud crashing sound near one of the remaining ships redirected everyone's attention.

Nearby, a series of containers had collided, and canisters were rolling in all directions. A group of soldiers, along with a cargo ship's crewmen, were arguing with each other. The Admiral turned to his aide.

"Cynthia, deal with that, please," the man ordered.

"Yes, sir," she replied and moved off.

The older man waited a moment before turning to Ophelia. "You need to get off this ship as quickly as you can. There have been too many coincidences in the last few years, and they have been escalating. This was more than just a freak raid. I believe sabotage or help from inside the tanker was involved. Quickly, what is your status and that of the Mistress?" he asked with a discrete sense of urgency.

"I'm fine, sir, as for the mistress, she'll hold. Her main guns are mostly operational, shields are at 75%, structural is sound but there are several ghosts in the system since we got boarded. The worst thing is I'm running on fumes. I was planning to hitch a ride," she responded.

"Hmm, that's not good," the older man said as he scratched his chin, nodding to himself as he formulated a plan. "We need to talk, but now is not the time."

"Uh, okay," Ophelia responded, her tone full of concern and apprehension.

The man nodded and cleared his throat as his aide arrived. "Let's get you fueled up, and we'll dispatch you with a few of our remaining orders. Hopefully, we can get you back on your feet. Are your long-range capabilities functional?"

"Mostly," she replied meekly.

"Good lord," the admiral said as he stood there shaking his head and rubbing his eyes. "Nonetheless, you will take these shipments and get them to their locations at all costs. You need a crew."

"I really don't want one. I had one and lost them during that boarding," the young captain interjected, not wanting to be responsible for anyone else.

"I understand, Ophelia. Losing people is hard, but it's part of the job and you don't have an option here. This cargo needs someone to oversee it," the admiral firmly instructed.

"But Mistress can..." she tried to protest but was cut off by the officer.

"She may be a remarkable ship and AI, but you need a Cargo Specialist for this run. I won't hear another word about it, young lady," the admiral said in a firm tone. "Cynthia, who do we have available?"

The aide hesitated, glancing back in the direction where she had just come from to a young man picking up containers. "Uh..."

"No!" the admiral quickly replied, cutting the aide off. "Absolutely not. I am trying to help her, just find someone else."

"That's it, sir. Right now, with the damage and the failing systems, we're all hands-on deck. There is no one else."

"How about in the tank?" he asked.

"The tank, sir? Um..." she replied hesitantly.

Scrolling through her digital files on her visor, searching for something to offer her commanding officer. Making a series of quick motions in the air as she interacted with her data unit and visor. She moved her head from side to side as she swiped, touched, and expanded the virtual images only she was seeing.

Admiral Palios stood there impatiently staring across the deck toward the copper-colored ship, stopping for a moment considering his plans as he eyed the ship. He could see some of the damage she had taken from the encounter with the pirates and the asteroid field, but it was mostly superficial. The armor seemed intact, and the ship was much nicer than he had originally expected from what he had been told.

"Sir, the options are not very good. You have the deserter, a drunk, two unknowns that the systems have not yet identified, and cricket. We have evacuated the others."

"Cricket? What is she doing in the tank?" the man asked, surprised.

"The report says it had something to do with her breaking a planter over the drunk's head," the aide replied.

"Wow, I didn't think she had that in her, but the drunk?" Palios replied and shook his head.

"That's it," the aide said.

"Give her Cricket," the man instructed.

"What about the deserter—Crewman Billy Williams? He's a good hand and knowledgeable. Never had any actual problems, he just wanted out of his contract, and it's almost up anyway. We can offer him a termination status on completion of the run to guarantee his loyalty. All he wants is out. It could be a win-win and save us tons of paperwork," Cynthia commented.

"Your logic is sound, Cynthia. I just don't like a person who doesn't meet his commitments," the officer replied.

"Agreed, sir, but he's young, and she could use an experienced hand on board. We could use one less person to deal with in the tank," she hinted.

"Fine, make it happen. Ophelia, you will take off in less than an hour, or possibly sooner. I will assign you your manifest. You will have to make multiple stops, but you will be refueled here and will be provided and an advance for fuel. This is not normal, but it's allowed during emergencies. Contracts are all paid upon completion. We will provide you with any additional supplies you may require. Now, come on, let's go get you your crew."

"Sir, with all due respect. I can handle that. Your presence is more needed here or on the bridge," Cynthia protested.

"You're right, Cynthia. Please take good care of Captain Knight." She then turned to the young girl. "Ophelia, my dear, take good care of yourself and Godspeed. I'm here if you need anything." Embracing her warmly, she then moved off, giving instructions to his entourage.

Cynthia made more motions in the air as she shifted through the data and moved files, arranging all of the Admiral's instructions. Despite constant interruptions, she remained focused on her task of communicating with others and giving orders dealing with the emergency that was happening on the tanker. Ophelia was in awe at the commander's high levels of organization and multitasking capabilities. The woman was managing various groups on multiple levels and seemed in complete control of the situation and did it with composure.

Walking quietly behind the commander trying to process everything that was happening, she noticed her IDP flashing. She tapped on the screen to see that the commander had sent her the files on the two crew members that were joining her on the trip. An idea she did not like at all. She had been traveling alone since the attack on her ship and had become accustomed to the dark solitude and the freedom of not being responsible for others.

"The admiral seems very fond of you? I have not seen him react with such warmth in years. Do you have a lot of history?" Cynthia asked, clicking and swiping, but never losing her stride.

"I guess. I slept a lot on the couch in his office," Ophelia mused.

"The blue one with the embroidered service logo on it," the woman asked.

"That's the one." Ophelia chuckled. "He still has it in his office? Wow, that was a gift from my family when he got his command on Karmier..."

Ophelia began, but was interrupted by Cynthia's erect finger telling her to wait a moment. The woman then gave orders over her comm unit. Ophelia just followed quietly as they boarded an accelerator pod, which worked much like a lift or an elevator, but used magnetic force on a rail and was much faster.

It had been many years since Ophelia had been on the command side of a tanker. Tanker trains were owned and maintained by the core planets, which meant the military operated it, being considered a sovereign territory of the core planets. The Galactic Defense Force oversaw ship maintenance and overall security and storage of precious resources like ore, fuel, or any other commodity that was in large quantities being transported between systems.

Each tanker train had a port city attached to it, which was run by the many individuals or companies that invested in it. With its own governing body, like any other city. The tanker side was maintained to the high standards of the GDF, but port cities differed from train to train. It was highly advanced and well taken care of, unlike the docking station portion of the ship. Which was maintained by individuals or the local authority which eventually reported to the fleet side. The biggest difference was seen from port city to port city, depending on the Admiral of the tanker and his view or desire as to their involvement in the city.

It was clear from the port that the Admiral allowed the city their own identity, seeing the less than stellar conditions of the port. That was currently being commandeered by the GDF because of the emergency on the tanker.

Finally, approaching their destination, which was the detention cells, their lift glided over a promenade which was used for various activities, one of which was a food court for all the service members. The area was vacant except for two soldiers quickly picking up chairs that were overturned and littered the hall. A series of screens flashed a red light with a LEVEL 4 ALERT written across the screen.

"Level 4?" she inquired.

"Yes. We are fighting to save the train at this point. A torpedo that hit us punctured the hull. Fortunately, it was a dud and did not explode, but we must get to it. It is still live ordinance and its partially embedded in a tank with a lot of fuel. That is why you must hurry and get out. If it explodes, even if your shields were at 100% you might not make it, even at a range of 1000 miles," the commander explained.

"Wow, that bad," Ophelia replied, shocked.

"Normally, maybe not a big deal. Most of these cargo trains carry anywhere from six to twelve storage cars or tanks. One tank can hold a million tons of cargo. We have ten cargo areas, half of which are loaded with fuel, and the other half are filled with explosives, most of which are headed to Minos 4-6 for mining operations. In others words, we are sitting on a very large bomb and it's ticking," the commander said in a very calm voice.

"And how much is that equal to in barrels of fuel?" Ophelia asked trivially.

Cynthia had her eyes focused on her task and didn't even look back, when she quietly answered, "Ten million barrels."

Ophelia stayed quiet as she digested the information, they said no other words until after the doors of the pod opened, at which it seemed they both took a breath. They passed a few sets of security doors until they reached the detention center. The doors opened and the sergeant on duty stood immediately and saluted.

"Officer on deck!" the man announced, then stood and saluted.

"At ease, sergeant." The woman saluted back. "Status?" the commander asked.

"It's all quiet here, ma'am. We're just babysitting," the sergeant responded.

"How many in your detail?"

"We had ten, but with the alert and these being low risk cells. We are down to five people, including myself."

"Well, you have new orders, sergeant. Captain Knight will take Cricket with her. I will speak with the deserter. Then you'll have two guards go with the deserter to his new destination. You plus your two other guards will escort these other prisoners to the gate so that they may reach the launch bay for evacuation, then get yourselves to your designated areas," Cynthia instructed.

"Yes, ma'am," the sergeant responded quickly, then immediately started typing and giving instructions to the others, who quickly moved into action while the two women waited. A screen came on, displaying the names and location of the detainees, along with a map of the area.

"Captain Knight, if you would please place your hand on the screen and proceed to cell number seven. Once there, place your hand on the palm reader on the adjacent wall and the door will open. Upon your return, cricket can get her belongings and you may depart."

"Thank you, Sergeant."

"You are welcome, Captain Knight. Commander, the deserter is..."

"In cell three. I am aware, Sergeant. Just carry out your orders," the commander said, cutting him off.

"Yes, ma'am," the sergeant replied and continued his work, then paused. "Ma'am, is this order accurate? The deserter is being released, but he hasn't been arraigned or signed any documentation?"

"Yes, Sergeant. Just process the order. He will take the deal. I'm sure of it," the woman replied.

Ophelia moved down to cell seven and paused as she stared inside, feeling empathy for the inmate on the other side of the barrier. Inside sat a nervous young woman, about her age, curled up against the wall, her knees tucked in close. She was slender and her hair seemed somewhat unkept and hid her face from view.

"Excuse me, are you the one they call Cricket?" Ophelia asked.

The young woman glared up at her, eyes peering through a curtain of golden hair. She had a slender face with eyes that were red and puffy from crying. She mumbled something that was inaudible and continued to stare at Ophelia with a hint of bitterness.

"Can you repeat that again? I could not hear you?" Ophelia asked again.

"That's not my name!" she said much louder and visibly annoyed.

"My apologies. Let me see here..." She examined the file on her HUD, seeing images of the young woman along with historical data. "Emily. Doctor Emily Kricay. Well, Emily, I am Captain Ophelia Knight, and I am here to inform you that you've been assigned to my ship."

"Assigned! What do you mean assigned? I'm a private citizen on contract with a company, not the fleet. I am not with the GDF," she protested, perplexed.

"True, but you assaulted a man with a flowerpot and gave him a concussion, possibly a skull fracture. Assault and battery are still illegal offenses. Admiral Palios has interceded on your behalf and has assigned you to my ship for this run, in exchange for dropping your sentence and keeping your record clean. Is that acceptable to you?" Ophelia asked with a warm smile.

"YES! Yes, that is very acceptable," the woman said excitedly, wiping her face.

"Let's go," Ophelia instructed, placing her hand on the wall and opening the cell. The young scientist was already standing and approaching the door in disbelief. She gaped at Ophelia with skepticism, but Ophelia only smiled back casually.

"Is this for real?" Emily asked.

"Yes. Now let's go get your gear. We need to hurry," Ophelia responded.

"Yes, Captain, right away," she said and hurried to the duty officer. Less than five minutes later, she returned. Her clothes and demeanor had changed. The sergeant handed the woman her backpack and wished her luck. With a wave of her hand, Dr. Kricay rushed out of the detention center. Ophelia grinned sympathetically, having had some issues prior to her departure to space for the first time.

Entering the acceleration pods and beginning their trip to the docking bay. The alarm still sounded and flashing lights blinked all over the promenade as the two young ladies glided over the area.

"Want to tell me your story and why you got stuck in there?" Ophelia asked.

"Not really."

"Since you are coming on my ship, it's not really a request."

Cricket sighed with resignation. "The man I hit was a jerk. He was the first person I met when I arrived here. He was part of the train's immigration team, and we were in front of a large group of people, including new recruits. Maybe he was trying to be funny, but he read my name as Cricket. It stuck since then and I hate it, it is not my name. I have suffered with that name for two years. It became a running joke for a group of them, then other civilians jumped on that bandwagon."

The young scientist shook her head and kicked the side of the lift. "It bothered me so much. I know it's stupid, but it did. Some people would make chirping noises when I was at places or do some other stupid thing like that, since that day, and haven't been able to shake it."

The lift slowed down while it was passing by some unspecified area, making the two women shift their balance, but then accelerated again. Emily ran her fingers through her blonde hair, scratching her head in frustration, before facing Ophelia, who carefully listened to every word.

"A few nights ago, he was stumbling down the street and called out to me and said some stupid comment about crickets and mating sounds. I know he was drunk, but I just got so angry at that moment, all my studies, everything that I have worked for so many years for nothing because of what that asshole did. I lost it and hit him with a pot over the head and then kicked and screamed at him a bit. Not my finest moment, I admit," she finished, hitting the window of the lift lightly with the bottom of her fist.

"Definitely not. But we've all been there, in one way or another. It's where we go from here that matters," the captain declared.

"Go! Oh, no. I need to pack. I will go get my stuff and be back in two hours," The young botanist said, a bit frazzled.

Ophelia chuckled. "Two hours? We take off in less than forty minutes. That gives you thirty-eight minutes to get back."

"Thirty-eight minutes! Oh, shit! I can't... Think, Emmy, Think... um." The young woman paced around, trying to solve the problem.

"So, it's Emmy? Is that what you like to be called?" Ophelia asked.

Emmy stopped and starred at her new captain. "Yes, please," she said with a smile. It was the first time in almost three years that anyone had cared to ask for her real name. *Maybe it is time to get off this train,* she thought, considering her things, even if they weren't many. She had a transient pod and though not a very big one, she'd been living there ever since she arrived at CT-109. Then an idea occurred to her.

"Captain, if it's all right with you. I have a fully automated transient pod that I can have here in thirty minutes if we can fit it on the ship. It's not huge or anything, only about eight meters long and three meters wide. Everything I have is there," she said hesitantly, but hopeful.

"Emmy, I don't even know what cargo we are getting... You know what? Bring it. We will find space."

"Thank you, Captain," the young woman replied humbly.

Ophelia turned back to the transparent wall on the accelerator pod, observing in silence at the disarray below as they left the promenade behind. She, more than most, understood what losing everything was like and only having a small sacred space could mean everything to a person. Mistress was that for her and it was as sacred and lifesaving as it could be. It was her small space of sanity in the universe. She was not about to take Emmy's away.

Ophelia just nodded as Emmy began touching buttons on her datapad. Removing the visor glasses from her vest, Ophelia put them on and transferred all visuals to the glasses. She had received her manifest and was reading over the contents and their destination. Each woman typed away on their IDP quietly for the duration of the ride.

The doors on the pod slid open, and before them was the vastness of space with various ships in the process of departure. The glow from the ship's thrusters or drives flashed as they moved away from the tanker. The glow from propulsion engines blinked in the dark backdrop of space. Dozens of short-range fighters hovered defensively around the tanker or flew in squadrons patrolling different sections.

"Wow," Emmy said, as she followed a group of fighters as they crossed her view.

Ophelia briefly removed her glasses, pausing to stare at the dozens of ships in a well-coordinated dance around the cargo tanker. The two women just gawked at the sight that was truly spectacular when a voice broke the silence from behind them.

"Quite the show. Enjoy it ladies, you will not see this very often," Cynthia said as she approached them. "Your cargo is being brought now and will have to be loaded quickly. We are beginning preparations for Phase 1 separation of this section. So, get your loader ready. Your cargo will be here shortly. I need you off my flight-deck," the commander instructed.

"Um... I don't have one. The pirates took it in the raid," Ophelia responded hesitantly.

The commander let out a sigh, shaking her head. "That is going to be a problem for you. I can load you up, but two of the sites have no loaders there. How will you get those containers out? It's a full-service contract."

A few moments passed as they moved toward Mistress, when Cynthia stopped, noticing something across the deck. Adjusting her visor, she peered off into the distance. "I think I may have a solution for you. There is an older unit in our possession. I don't know what's wrong with it. All I know is that it's not functional. It worked when we took it offline. Maintenance was then using it until it crapped out. There is a crate with leftover and secondhand parts that will go with it. The catch is you are going to have to bid for it. This is fleet equipment and can only be sold in public auction."

Ophelia was perplexed as she stared in the direction the commander was previously focused on, but could barely make the loader out. When an invitation came up on her visor. Noticing the invitation, she placed the visor back on. Clicking the link, it immediately took her to an auction site. A picture of the equipment and a price of 50 credits. She glanced back at the old loader and the timer was already on 10 seconds and counting down.

"I would click on 'Bid' quickly, before someone else finds the site. Ms. Knight," the commander said.

Ophelia was shocked at how quickly it had all happened and clicked on the bid button as the time counted down. The item closed, and she received various emails saying she had won and her payment had been processed.

Another message followed shortly, sending her the documentation to the equipment. The young captain scratched her head and referred to the commander with a confused expression. "Commander?"

"Ms. Knight, this is a sophisticated military operation. Most things run at a steady pace, but when things require operational speed, I can make it happen. This is the admiral's ship and his command, but it's my job to make it work." The woman winked. "Congratulations. You now have a loader; I hope you can get it to work. Now hurry up and get off my deck."

"But it said I paid it?" the young captain asked, confused.

"You did. I took it from one of your contracts. Is there a problem with that? Or can we finally get you off my deck?" the woman said in an irritated tone.

"N-no, commander. Thank you. We will leave as quickly as possible," Ophelia said, still trying to grasp everything.

"The deck crew is fueling you up as we speak, and I will have the cargo brought to you. I have also added one more order to your manifest, which needs to be handled with the utmost care and attention. We have sent details to your account." Turning to the young scientist, the officer continued without missing a beat. "Dr. Kricay. We have a transient pod at the gate with your information on it. Can you verify that, please?" the commander asked.

"Yes, ma'am. That is mine. I am trying to facilitate our prompt departure," the young woman replied.

"I thank you, Ms. Kricay, and would like to remind you that your amnesty is on the condition that you finish the deliveries with Captain Knight as her cargo specialist. Best of luck to you," the commander's answers were to the point with little emotion.

"Captain Knight, your other crew member is being brought to you by security. He will be here shortly. Billy is an experienced deckhand and can handle himself well. I have advised him of the conditions for his separation from service and is free to leave after your last delivery.

My condolences on your loss and wish you and your mission the best of luck. I knew Mr. Knight; he was a good man." The officer's voice was level, but genuine.

The commander extended her hand and shook Ophelia's, then turned and moved off, giving orders to other members on the deck.

Turning to Emmy, Ophelia pointed to the ship in a grand gesture. "There she is. That's my ship. The Mistress of Mayhem. Welcome aboard Emmy."

The young woman let her eyes take in the ship and grinned, seeing the exotic picture of the pin-up girl painted under the name. It was an erotic, red-haired vixen dressed in clothing that was too tight for her body. One hand held a finger to her lips as if she was shushing you to secrecy, while the other held various cards fanned out.

Her provocative pose, that exposed her legs as she sat on some sort of satellite, a pose that enhanced her other features, and as you went up the picture, taking in the woman's voluptuous form reaching her slightly exposed bosom and pale skin, but it was her deep purple eyes that caught the eye of any onlooker and held their attention.

The detail of the drawing was so lifelike a passerby almost expected her to walk off the ship at any moment. If that wasn't enough, the copper paint with black lines augmented the ship's allure, mystified by the occasional passing smoke of exhaust or steam that exited the ship.

"I like her. She has attitude," Emmy said.

"Yes, she does," replied Ophelia with a grin, as she winked at the ship.

"I saw that," Mistress said over the earpiece in Ophelia's ear.

"Emmy, let's put your pod in cargo bay two, along with our new loader. That way, we can try to keep it separate from the cargo. We have some rooms on the third floor. You can have your pick," Ophelia told her new crewmate.

"If it's okay with you, can I connect my pod to the ship and stay there?" the young scientist asked.

"Sure, that would be no problem. Mistress can interface with your pod and just about any other tech out there," Ophelia replied.

"Oh, I get to interface with something else. I can't wait," the sultry voice said over the comm.

"Behave!" Ophelia said.

"Huh? Oh, I will, I promise," the young scientist answered.

"Not you Emmy. Well, I expect you, too. But I was talking to Mistress. That's the name of the ship's AI. and she has quite the personality," Ophelia explained.

"Oh," Emmy replied with some concern towards her new captain.

Ophelia picked up the sentiment and felt a little embarrassed. "Don't worry, Emmy, I'm not weird or have any odd fetishes. The Mistress has a long story. I actually wrote a lot of her programming," the captain said with pride.

"Not weird at all," Emmy said, a little defensively.

Ophelia dropped the conversation before it became even more awkward. She began giving instructions to the ship, so Mistress could prepare for incoming cargo and monitor the refueling. Mistress had received the manifest and had already begun plotting a course for the Calicos system, as well as calculating a series of configurations for the cargo to load and unload with greater ease.

"Ophelia, have you seen the last manifest and what we are transporting?" Mistress inquired after a few minutes.

"Yes, it is some sort of stasis pods. Why?"

"This is not your average cargo. Those stasis pods are carrying prisoners. We are acting as a prison transport. And not just any prisoners, these are space faring pirates, with actual bounties. One of them is a captain and a very notorious and deadly one at that," the ship said with some concern.

"So, he's in a stasis pod. No one is going to be doing any pirating. As for his history, it's not a big deal. He will sleep the whole way and then some. Now just finish plotting the routes. We need to leave," Ophelia said dismissively.

"Also, I saw that bucket of bolts you got. I am a pretty young lady. I can't be seen with that old garbage can inside me. What will the others say? All it's going to do is spill lubricant and who knows what else over my clean, shiny floors. It's disgraceful," Mistress complained.

"You are the one that said you wanted some powerful arms to work on you," Ophelia shot back.

"Strong yes, but also functional," the ship retorted. "No one is going to take us seriously with that thing, a broken cargo bay door and all my other missing parts. I feel violated," the ship continued.

"Well, we have another hand coming onboard. Maybe he can patch you up a bit," Ophelia responded.

"I noticed he used to work in a scrap yard. Do I look like scrap to you?" Mistress continued.

"You will be if you keep it up. This is what Admiral Palios gave us and we are going to do it right. Now cool your thrusters. And that's an order," Ophelia commanded.

"Fine," Mistress replied and then stayed quiet.

Ophelia continued her preflight check as she awaited her last crewmate and the remaining cargo. Emmy had carefully situated her pod through the damaged door and into its new home for the time being. She then continued to assist the GDF crewmen in placing the loader Ophelia had gained on the other side of the bay just to give herself some room, since Emmy was worried about leaks and a foul smell that came from the old over used machinery.

A young crewman approached, reporting that the refueling was complete, along with topping off of any other fluids, including her water tanks. Ophelia thanked the deckhand, then looked past him as two GDF guards escorted a man, who she suspected was the deserter. More cargo followed, causing Ophelia to shift her attention to her IDP and wondered. *Where is all this cargo coming from?* Even as she reached the call button to see if there had been a mistake, she received an incoming call.

"Yes, Commander," she said as she saw the woman on her visor.

"I see you are still on my deck, Ms. Knight," the woman stated.

"Yes, Commander. The cargo just arrived, but it seems more than what I have on the manifest," Ophelia replied.

"That's because there is, Ms. Knight. I added another two orders to your manifest, since they did not fit on any other vessel. Their loss is your gain and the paperwork will come through shortly. One thing though, your loading time has not changed, something that is unavoidable. Please hurry Ms. Knight. You do not want to be on that deck when separation begins. Good day," the officer said and cut off the communication.

"Shit!" was Ophelia's frustrated response.

"Captain Knight?" asked a guard.

"Yes," she answered as she rubbed her eyes.

"This is prisoner 183749. We are relinquishing him into your custody. Do you accept?" asked the guard.

"Yes," she replied again.

"Please sign on the datapad," the guard instructed.

Ophelia made her mark on the datapad, while the guards removed the restraints from the young man's hands and neck. They dropped a backpack with whatever belongings pertained to him and pushed him forward. The man stumbled but caught himself within two steps and turned about to react, but contained himself.

"This is better than a piece of crap like you deserves," one guard said.

He was almost two meters tall, with light brown hair and eyes. They dressed him in a basic orange jumpsuit with a large D spray-painted on it. It had been two weeks since he had tried to escape, which also coincided with the last time he had shaven his face. The prisoner had a disheveled appearance, with a mop like haircut and a scraggly beard that didn't suit him. He still maintained a unique charm that immediately caught the attention of both young women.

He paused, taking in the ship, then shifted his gaze towards the two women and grinned. Turning slightly, he glanced back at the guards, shrugging slyly. "I guess I'll just have to make the best of it boys."

One guard took a step forward and was stopped by Ophelia, who stood between them. "Thank you. I'll take it from here."

The guard rolled his eyes and shook his head before addressing the captain. "Do yourself a favor and push him out of an airlock."

As the guards left, Ophelia smiled as she turned to study the young man. He was ruggedly handsome which added to his overall charm. The deserter smiled back and raised his eyebrows, displaying an interest in the young captain. "Anything I can do for you, Captain?"

Ophelia provided a coy smile and took a step closer, whispering, "Why yes. Get the cargo on the ship and be careful, or I'll take the guards' advise and push you out of an airlock."

Grabbing his bag from the floor, the man moved off, shrugging off the rejection. Ophelia took a deep breath as she turned to the next set of guards. Her heart raced a little, not having dealt with a crewmate in a longtime and never one, that was so easy on the eyes.

"Captain Ophelia." A heavily armored guard approached with a datapad in hand. "Sergeant Warrant with GDF Security. I got here a transport pod with eight stasis pods. Each pod contains a convicted criminal in it. Have you ever used one of these stasis pods before?" the guard asked.

"No, I have not, sergeant," she replied.

"Nothing to it," the man said encouragingly, tapped the keypad, opening the transport's door and allowing them access.

He showed her each pod for verification of the inmate held in stasis inside, then showed her how to activate, deactivate, and monitor vitals of both the inmates and the pod. After they had verified the prisoners, he locked the door and gave her the pad to sign.

Placing a thick metallic key in a slot and turning, he said, "This is a security override in case of an emergency. Keep it safe or leave it in the security compartment. We have sent security clearance for your biometrics to your ship for syncing," He motioned the other soldiers forward, directing the transport pod into the ship.

"Best of luck to you. Now, you be careful out there and under no circumstance let these animals out of their cage. These are very dangerous people. Godspeed to you," the man said in the voice of a concerned friend.

"Thank you, sergeant," she said with a tired but grateful smile.

The man nodded and turned around, giving orders to his men, who uniformly turned around and began back for the interior of the structure. That last remaining cargo pods followed, filling up the space in both cargo bays pretty tightly.

"You two secure the cargo and prepare for launch. We need to get off this tanker," Ophelia yelled, then made her way around the ship, making a quick final inspection before their departure.

Emmy waited by the last bay door. "She's a lovely ship, Captain, and that copper exterior is beautiful, but you are missing an important coating on the outer shell, which can be a safety issue when entering an atmosphere."

Sighing, Ophelia replied as she entered the ship, "I know." Taking one last look around, then instructed, "Mistress. Get us out of here."

"Yes, Captain," the sultry voice replied.

Chapter 2

Far away near the edge of the spiral arm of the galaxy is a planet called Tersa 4, known for its main crop of a starchy like vegetable called a Taidar. There were no Taidar fields in the southeast region of the planet, just miles of unforgiving desert. It was somewhere in this desert that an operative of a special operations group had glided in under the cover of darkness using the latest stealth flyer suit technology available. Landing on a large rock formation that centuries of wind and sand had smoothed. This formation was special; special enough to receive a name and it was 3T.

A person could say many things about the Spec Ops group called THE RAVAGERS, but creative nomenclature was not one of them. 3T was just that, Three T words put together: Taidar Terrorist Tower. Though not known by many, at one time it was the home of a local warlord and space pirate. That warlord had spent a small fortune carving out the base underneath using slaves to dig and the plunder to upgrade his base. That man had been killed decades earlier and now someone new had taken over the base in the last few years, only known to the GDF as the Warlord.

Deep inside this stronghold was Corporal Jo'su, the smallest member of the Ravagers, having made his way through the base with a degree of silence that would have made a mouse envious. Being the smallest made him the likeliest candidate for many of these infiltration missions, given that some of his counterparts were well over two meters in height and he was short of the two-meter mark.

The mission was a simple nighttime snatch and grab: break into their base, go down a few levels to the holding area and recover some unknown item that was being stored in a centurion security container that weighed almost 50 kilos for something that was slightly larger than a shoebox. It was all simple until he arrived at the storage room and noticed various other items and Alpha boxes of various sizes.

Matching the item to his IDP, he grabbed it. Then a familiar Alpha box nearby caught his eye. Verifying that it was more than familiar, he punched in a security code and it opened, allowing him to verify a prototype he'd stolen almost three years prior. Seeing the other items around the room, he realized other things that were familiar.

Why are these here? These should be back in a GDF secured location. All these things should be.

Putting the designated item along with a few others into a class 9 Alpha box, he knew the items would be well protected and not missed by anyone until it was too late. He had chosen the box for more than its familiarity. He chose it because of its reinforced handles and straps that would make it easy to carry as he made his way out of the tower.

Sticking to his pre-planned exit strategy and moving cautiously, expecting more resistance but encountering none. The lack of personnel in the base was concerning to the corporal, keeping him alert. Moving stealthily and taking no chances as he made his way through the compound's stone hallways. Each step emphasized the emptiness of the base and compounded his worry. Adjusting the Alpha box on his back brought his mind to the rule he was breaking of not taking anything not on the list, but how could he pass it up, knowing what it was.

Why are we being called for a mission like this? So many other regular teams could have done this? And why are all these things here? He kept asking himself as he considered all the items back in the secured storage. So many questions, along with the nagging feeling that the entire operation felt wrong.

He suspected his selection was because he was the smallest person in the unit and was normally picked for stealth missions for just that reason. Now with the lack of personnel and security, he was considering the hesitation by his immediate superiors suspicious. His captain had offered various other suggestions, but the high command selected him despite his superior's protests and recommendations.

The Ravagers were not ordinary operators. They were part of an elite prototype special operations unit and though they were given a lot of leeway, they still had to obey the chain of command. Being a member of the Ravagers was not something that a person could opt for. There were a series of criteria that had to be met for selection and none of them were well intentioned.

After surviving the operations, the tortures, and the training, keeping in top physical condition was just the beginning. It had been three years of specialized training and constant monitoring by doctors and scientists, which to him, it all felt like torture.

They had altered those selected or kidnapped all the way down to their DNA. They all appeared human, or mostly human, but their physical attributes had all been exponentially increased. For six months the scientists broke their bones, tore their muscles, and stressed their organs, all for the purpose of increasing the density of bones, fibers, joints, and every other part of their body in order to make them the ultimate killing machines.

They continued for six torturous months; then they ordered the augmented soldiers to make contact with an enemy. They continued placing their subjects in the worst of conditions against a vast array of enemies just to continue testing them and pushing their physical limitations further with the penalty of death or insanity always lingering close by. To the Ravagers, it seemed as if they were on the front lines every few weeks for more than a year.

They gave those that survived more specialized training and then continuously sent them out on specialized missions or raids. Somehow, those missions always seemed to be a bloodbath, something he accredited to the commanding officer's bravado or stupidity. Things degraded from there, when one Private Brooks got promoted to lieutenant. Brooks was a gargantuan man, who seemed capable, but ended up being a little more than a blood-thirsty savage.

Fortunately, his reign of terror ended when Sergeant Corinth, a tall and cunning woman, stabbed him with a pipe. She stuck the pipe right through his chest and was the first to gain rank through ascension. It really had turned into something primal, a true survival of the fittest scenario, where only the strong survived. But then again, that was the Ravagers model. "The strong survive and the weak will perish."

It amazed the corporal every day, having survived so long, being the youngest and the smallest of the group, or at least the one that had shown the least gains. Being the runt of the litter wasn't easy, but his advanced technical ability gave him a unique opportunity that caused the others to leave him alone, but it wasn't the only reason. Corporal Jo'su had been challenged by others in the group.

Twice he had fought and lived to see another day. Those attacks taught him to always be alert. The military taught that a unit is a family, but when that family tried to kill a member while they're eating or toweling off after a shower. Those actions don't build much faith in that family. He had survived those attacks, but was forced to kill another member of his company, not because he wanted to, but because he had to.

This is madness. I should not be here. We should not be here, he repeated in his mind.

Reaching a junction in the corridor, Jo'su pressed himself against the roughly cut out stone wall. Listening for breathing or any sound at all that would have confirmed his opponent's presence, but found none.

Glancing around, he saw a fairly short corridor leading to another T Junction. Again, he approached quietly, noticing the wall at the end of the corridor had a sign under a light. It was the first sign he had seen since he exited the secured storage chamber, but this was a peculiar sign. It appeared like a crown roughly cut into the stone.

"Royalty, huh?" the corporal mumbled to himself and clicked a button on his scanner, disabling him from being tracked.

Turning down the corridor towards the crown instead of the exit was probably not the smartest thing, but he felt the need, too. Reaching an archway at the end of the hall and pausing, it was not a precaution this time; he knew there were people there and stopped, staying just out of sight of anyone inside. Pushing a button on his IDP ejecting a small disc-like object no larger than a small coin that took flight entering the room and quickly soaring upwards. He could see everything his nano drone could see on his helm's visor.

The room had at least five people in it, four of which were sitting in front of a console retrieving data from their screens. The fifth person in the room seemed to be some sort of leader, moving from screen to screen, skimming through the information. Tapping twice on his IDP, Jo'su focused the drone's camera, making it zoom in on one screen. The information was familiar to him. He had come across it on one screen back on the ship, a screen that was quickly shut off by another member of his unit. Now, studying it closely, it seemed like a bounty, when a hand filled in the area of the camera as the leader pointed to something on the screen and spoke in a garbled language that was altered by a device to avoid spying.

Seeing the tattooed armed surprised him, because of its familiarity more than its appearance on his visor. *Those markings are identical to that guy we captured a few months back, and what's he pointing at? That's a bounty on the screen and it's the same one that was back on the ship, something to do with a coup and a planet on the edge of... Damn, I can't make out that last sentence.*

Zooming out and getting a better view of the room, the drone submitted the information which his datapad then identified all five members in the room.

What the hell! We have captured all these guys on various raids and we sent them off to be processed for their crimes against the government. What are they doing here? And what are they planning? I need to get this back to the ship. If we have a leak in our ranks, we are vulnerable.

With a few quick dabs on his datapad, he ordered the drone to take pictures of the screens and the individuals inside as he retreated down the hall.

A low chirp in his ear told him that the nano-drone had docked with his IDP. Moving quickly down the hall, he was about to reestablish the link of his locator, pausing when he heard some grumbling from the corridor where he had first seen the crown symbol.

"How could you lose him? That is next generation equipment, you idiot," a gruff voice said from around the corner.

The man was wrapped in a cloth garment from head to toe, sand adorned various areas of his clothes and the micro-mesh material he had used to protect his face from the sandstorm outside. The man next to him slapped the side of the scanner, trying to get it to come back on.

The thought that they might have been tracking him was enough to dispatch the two men, but this gave more credibility to the corporal's suspicion of a leak in his operation and he needed solid evidence to prove his hunch. Slowly pulling out his flechette gun, a weapon that discharged small arrow-like bolts using a magnetic charge. Although it had been outlawed by government entities long ago, it was his weapon of choice.

Pressing himself against the wall, he touched the button on his IDP activating his locator once again and waited with his weapon aimed towards the enemy. The scanner started blinking and beeping once again, confirming his belief.

The momentary celebration of the tracker quickly subsided as they glared at the scanner, perplexed, realizing that it showed that their target was next to them. Looking at each other confused, then turning their gaze up towards the corner where the corporal was waiting with his gun pointing at them, but by then it was too late.

A barrage of deadly miniature arrows silently dug deeply into his pursuer's torso and face. Taking one of the slain men's automatic rifles, along with various power cells that were used as ammunition, he grabbed the scanner and continued to what he believed was the exit.

Hurrying down a side passage, while fighting off thoughts that there was a traitor in the Ravagers. He was acutely aware that one of the potential side effects of the procedure was paranoia, but the evidence was growing. Moving past a large doorway and stopping, he took a small step back, noticing a large underground garage just beyond the door. He peered inside the long corridor, surprised to see that it was actually a massive garage, with rows of vehicles neatly parked one next to the other. Guessing the amount being over 100 in number, noticing there were vehicles of all different types and sizes— and all meant for war.

Making a brief observation, he quickly noticed a pattern that few would recognize, nor would he, had he not been the one to oversee the in-bounding of new mechanized equipment for his group or been involved in the various conflicts where they had been acquired. The vehicles were from many different factions from all around the surrounding star systems, but they all had one thing in common: the Ravagers had encountered all of them, at one time or another.

Zooming in with his visor, he recognized the numbers on the sides of certain vehicles that they had used on various missions or raids. He recalled his unit being ordered to abandon them at the site within the last year or so. Alongside those vehicles were many other vehicles that were or should have been confiscated during those encounters, but somehow, they were all parked here and ready for battle.

An alarm sounded from inside the large underground garage and from the hallway, bringing him from his thoughts. A quick glance around the garage, he noticed various people working on a vehicle, another vehicle that he recognized, because he himself had put it out of commission in a raid by the Ravagers just a few weeks ago. Noticing his presence, the workers started yelling at him as they began grabbing weapons, yelling, and firing in his direction.

Moving to a covered position and firing back, bringing down two more enemy combatants. He made no celebration, knowing that many more were coming now that the base was on high alert. Needing a quick exit, he began searching around the garage from his position, as projectiles and plasma rained around him.

Finally, he spotted a vehicle that had served him well in the past and hoped it would again. The barrage of blaster fire had intensified, and he knew that his chances of escape and survival were dwindling with every passing second, pulling two grenades from his hip; a pulse grenade to buy him a few seconds and a smoke grenade to provide him some cover for his escape.

He jumped on the hoverbike that he'd once been assigned and customized a few months earlier, then forced to abandon at the end of the last mission even though it was still operational. *I hoped those techs missed my little work around.* A few taps on his datapad and his AI Paladin was sending various coded instructions to the hoverbikes computer. A light glowed on the hoverbike's dashboard, which made him grin. With a flick of a switch, he could hear the engine powering up and feel the power beneath his seat as the bike came to life.

I love that sound, but this is no time for nostalgia. I gotta go, he told himself, pushing hard on the throttle, the vehicle lurched forward and sped off.

Grains of sand hit against his visor and helmet as the wind picked up. He was in the bowl of the rock formation and was only a few moments ahead of his enemy. Guiding the hover bike with one hand as he gave orders to his combat assistant on his IDP. "Paladin, secure the box with an emergency line. We can't lose that box."

"Affirmative, sir. Tethering link ready," the AI replied.

A small carabiner with a thin wire detached itself from his harness, which he quickly grabbed and clipped to the Alpha box on one of its tethering locations. Tugging on the line once more, assuring himself of the connection before putting both hands on the handles and accelerating faster, leaving a cloud of dust behind him.

"Tethering is secured, and I have provided you with enough slack to move freely," Paladin replied, then continued. "Sir, we will encounter a dust storm as we exit the valley."

"Deploy full face shield and engage enhanced vision," he commanded.

"Yes, sir."

33

Millions of nanites deployed from his helmet, rippling around his face, solidifying his armored face shield. The projection of the HUD on the inside of the face shield adjusted to its bigger size. More information showed up on the inside of his visor along with the addition of two small boxes on the display that allowed him to see behind him if he needed to. A map of the area was dimly displayed in the background along with a small radar showing things in his vicinity. Weather conditions and suit integrity were also on his HUD along with ammo, water, and oxygen levels.

"Are we online yet?" the corporal asked.

"No, sir. Satellites are not in range, we only have access to local topography and weather. If we leave your beacon off, we will lose them in the storm, but it will be harder to guide you. I can also connect to the hover bike if you'd like, sir. It will charge up my batteries and increase my efficiency," the digital assistant stated.

"Do it. I need you at full power. This is going to be a long morning. Keep us on stealth mode and finish reprograming that box. I want full security measures installed and use the back door we left on the bike and to gain control, keep all other access to the hover bike out. We are going to make it out of this mess and find out what the hell is going on. Use whatever channels they have connected to the bike to access any information you can from their systems until we have to reboot the bike," the corporal instructed.

"Yes, sir. I'm glad you remember it requires the bike to reboot to eliminate any other external access to the bike. We could do it just before we enter the storm. Sir, you have two combatants ahead guarding the exit," Paladin added.

"It seems like they haven't spotted us yet. Take over the bike as I dispatch them and keep it smooth," the soldier ordered.

"Yes, sir, autopilot engaged."

Shutting down the lights on the bike, making them almost invisible to the eye, and the built-in jammers would make it difficult to detect them, even at their high rate of speed. Only the dust trail behind them would give away their position, but it was still early, leaving them a few hours before the sun would rise on the planet.

The opening to the passageway leading outside the perimeter was just ahead. A guard stood on either side of the opening. Pulling the rifle he'd taken from the dead soldier earlier, he released the steering and carefully aimed at the first guard. Taking in a deep breath, he let it out slowly as he found his mark and then held it as he squeezed the trigger.

A laser shot out from the barrel of the rifle and hit the first guard in the chest, leaving a scorched hole in its wake. The guard crumbled to the ground; he was dead with a wisp of charred smoke leaving his chest. The Ravager aimed towards the second guard and quickly fired a second shot, but the shot went high as the bike bounced on the uneven terrain.

"Keep it smooth, damn it," he complained.

The second guard pulled his weapon and fired back blindly with a lucky shot that was too close for comfort, grazing the Ravager's night flight suit, exposing the slightly blackened armor underneath. The guard jumped to cover behind the primitive guard shack after shooting a few more wild shots.

Jo'su could see the guard's thermal image and fired a second shot, a shot that was on target but was blocked by a coating on the structure. The guard returned fire, but it was obvious the man was shooting blindly at where he previously was instead of his current position.

The bike sped closer to the gate and was now within 70 meters when the guard peered around the side and took aim barely seeing his silhouette against the night sky, but Jo'su shot first leaving another hole of scorched flesh where the guard's eye once was, causing him too to drop limply on the ground face first. Reaching the guard shack he jumped off the bike.

"Paladin, start the rebooting sequence on the bike."

"Affirmative, reboot sequence initiated."

The corporal moved quickly, searching the body for some more ammunition and any other item he could use. "Are we up yet?" he asked. "Oh, plasma grenades. This will come in handy," he stated out loud with a grin, as he took the grenades off one of the dead guards.

"86 seconds until reboot," the assistant said, displaying the number on his visor.

Pushing the bike into the dugout tunnel that would eventually lead outside of the rock formation that was the warlord's fortress. Jo'su grabbed some wire from his belt pouch and rigged the grenades at the mouth of the cave.

Grabbing the bodies of the dead guards, he placed them strategically to hide the explosives. From his peripheral vision, he could see several lights from approaching vehicles in the distance that had exited out of the underground garage he had taken the bike from.

One vehicle he easily recognized as a HT89 Cobra Hover Tank by its lights and its thermal image. "We need to go," he stated.

"That action is advisable. One of those vehicles is a HT89 Cobra Hover Tank. It has advanced imaging systems and an incredible range. We'll have a better chance of escaping in the storm," Paladin had just finished stating when a large plasma bolt destroyed the guard shack, sending Jo'su flying a few meters away.

"Time to go," he said, pushing himself off the ground.

"Reboot has 22 seconds remaining," the assistant replied.

Grabbing the bike that weighed around 300kg loaded and carried it moving further into the tunnel. He may have been the smallest of the Ravagers, but he was by far stronger that any ordinary person. Carrying the bike with moderate effort, even with the added weight of the Alpha box. He hurried down the tunnel, hearing the effects of small arms fire as blasters and projectile weapons hit the wall outside, with a few plasma shots landing within his vicinity.

"Sir, may I suggest that when we exit the tunnel, we immediately turn to the right or left? The density of the rock walls will buy us some time from the Cobra's imager and allow us to continue gathering intel from their servers. We still have the sandstorm for cover, even with the Cobra's advanced imagers, it will dramatically reduce its effective range in the storm," the assistant advised.

"That's a great idea, Paladin, if we make it out of here. Just finish rebooting the bike so we can leave," he grumbled into his face shield.

A few seconds later, the phrase, "Reboot and initiation sequence completed," flashed across his HUD. Immediately, the visor lit up with more information as the hoverbike and the corporals IDP's systems synced up, providing more data of the area and the status of the vehicle.

Dropping the hoverbike, it never touched the ground as it quietly floated half a meter off the ground. The young man jumped on the bike, placed the rifle sling around his shoulder resting the weapon on his lap for quick access, and sped up out of the cave driving directly into the ongoing storm then turning left to hug the exterior rock wall of the fortress prolonging their opportunity to gain intel from the enemy servers.

Someone had well-made and carefully thought the fort out. The original warlord had chosen not to build in the desert, instead he dug out and into a large natural rock formation. Using the natural rock formation provided cover from any imaging from above or any thermal scans, allowing the structure to hide in plain sight.

A few seconds later, an explosion could be heard coming from the entrance of the cavern as a vehicle exploded from the grenade trap and triggered a second explosion from another light vehicle that was just behind it. *That'll buy me some more time, but it's not going to stop that Cobra Tank.* Speeding up the bike, he fought against the winds of the storm, but fortunately his armor and visor protected him from the effects of the fast-moving sand.

"Sir, it's time to leave. They have discovered our connection and are not closing it, which means they may try to enter my system and shut us down or track us," the assistant said in an even tone.

"Close and lock the connection. We're out of here. Did you get any information?"

"Yes, sir. I have names, dates and other data. It's a large amount and needs processing for what you want it for. I can do it, but it will lower my efficiency by forty-two percent. Should I start processing now?" Paladin asked.

"Yes, confirmed," he replied and asked, "show me a map of the area, including the extraction site and its surrounding areas."

Immediately, a picture of the area came up on his display, showing his location, destination and direction of travel. "The image you are seeing is accurate and could only possibly give a last location. I am guiding us using a compass and our speed. It should be mostly accurate."

Feeling comfortable with what he was being shown on the display, he plotted his path to extraction and drove deeper into the storm.

Several hours had passed, and the storm was over one hundred kilometers behind him. The terrain had shifted as the color of the sand darkened the deeper he went into a mountainous region. The ground got darker and darker as vegetation started appearing, then trees dotted the area, until finally finding himself in a densely wooded area near the extraction site. He had reached a mountainous zone, going up almost a kilometer above sea-level and was waiting to receive the signal that the rendezvous was a go.

Moving deeper into the forest, there was an old abandoned mining village where he took refuge and was hiding out in the basement of a partially destroyed stone building. The dense stone would keep him from being seen in case the Cobra tank appeared in the vicinity.

Having some time, he rested against the wall, getting some overdue sleep, when a chime stirred him from his rest. His hand went immediately for the rifle and was already scanning the area when the soothing voice of his combat assistant came through his earpiece.

"Sir, satellite contact in thirty seconds."

"Good. Maintain stealth mode even after we make contact with the extraction team. First, see if you can bounce the signal off the weather satellite intermittently to avoid detection and refresh my map. Second, see if there is anyone in the area. How is it coming with the data?" Jo'su asked.

"They encrypt the data with high levels of military grade encryption. I have two names for you. Specialist Caigo, who falsified documents as to the damaged and confiscated equipment on Hermes 5, including the hover bike we are currently using. The other is Lieutenant Corinth," the AI replied.

"No surprise there. That woman is evil through and through, but smart. What proof do we have on her?" the soldier inquired.

"The truth, sir, is that I haven't decoded anything. Those protocols are much too sophisticated for me without connecting to the Ravager systems. What I was able to do was grab data from the pictures we took and the data I intercepted while in the command room on the base and the data server in the vehicle maintenance area.

As you know, those files downloaded from vehicles are rarely ever scanned or deleted until maintenance is required on the servers. We got very lucky that emails and videos sent from the other vehicles had not been purged but uploaded to their servers. That and the secondary memory core on the hover bike had not been wiped and kept the connection setting to other vehicles, allowing us access. They probably missed it. Puzzling all that together is how I was able to get this information," Paladin explained.

"So, what do you have on her?"

"We have some documentation on her funneling operational money through different areas. The short version, she's the one that has set all this up. The evidence leads to her being the mastermind behind it. But it's speculative," was the computer's reply.

"What about the captain?" the soldier asked.

"Of the little we have, it seems like he was specifically avoided or bypassed. He may not know what's going on," the AI explained.

"I don't like it. It's like being in a cave full of snakes. Any way you go, you are likely to get bit. I tell you, I don't trust any of the Ravagers, but we are going to have to get word to the captain. Our very survival may depend on it. Have you made contact with the extraction team?"

"Yes, but you will not like the news. We have been given a new extraction point. We have to go back, and to make matters worse, the storm is still active in that area. Also, I have no data on any units that could be in the vicinity. We have an hour before the extraction and it seems the other teams have had little success making clean escapes. They are most likely coming in hot. Expect problems." The AI paused, then added, almost sadly, " It's never easy for you sir, is it?"

"It's okay. As the Ravager model goes. The strong survive and the weak will perish, and though I be the lone survivor, I will prevail," the corporal answered determinedly.

Retrieving the hover bike from its hiding place, he got on it and rode off towards the extraction point. Most of the ride was quiet and he could see the haze of the sandstorm in the distance. The trees were thinning out as he moved closer to the more arid region of the area. The peacefulness was cut off by his AI's interruption.

"Sir, I have the captain on a secure line."

"Patch him through," the soldier replied and waited.

"Go ahead, sir," the computer instructed.

"Captain, this is Rabid Fox. Can you confirm the line is secure on your side?" Jo'su asked.

"Rabid Fox, the line is clear. Go ahead. Be advised, we are on approach, and we have tails," the officer answered.

"Sir, we have a problem. I discovered some information about some of our members. We have traitors in our group. I have hard evidence," the corporal stated.

The officer replied after a brief pause, "Did you complete your mission? Over?"

"Yes, sir, I have the item in an Alpha box along with the evidence. I am on approach into the storm, turning on the beacon for extraction."

"I read you, Rabid Fox. We are receiving your signal. Be advised you have hostiles in the area. We will link and mark as we can. Extraction will begin in 10 mikes. This is a moving extraction, so be at the mark. As per your data, will it cause any problems? Over," the officer said calmly.

"Sir, this is their base, and if Lieutenant Corinth or Caigo are with you, we may have an issue. She may be running this operation.... They also have over a hundred military vehicles in a garage, some of them ours," the young man finished.

"I read you, Rabid Fox. Just get on board safely. We will deal with anything as it comes. We are dropping a sonar beacon to help you navigate the field. I'll keep the line clear in case you need anything," the captain replied.

Jo'su would normally welcome the beacon on an encrypted channel, but given that the enemy was one of them, that channel could be compromised, giving them the same vision as him. The beacon entered the area and provided a visual on land masses and enemies nearby, some too close for comfort.

Hurrying behind an enemy vehicle, he quickly dispatched the driver with a shot from his rifle. Two more combatants went down in a similar manner. When a plasma blast destroyed the vehicle, his opponent was in just a few meters away from him, causing him to lurch away.

"Damn it! It's that damn tank," he said, glancing back behind him.

"It seems that they are on the beacon's frequency. I'm also picking up active pinging in the area," Paladin added.

Accelerating the bike to breakneck speeds in the storm, he moved towards other enemy vehicles, using them as cover against the deadly tank. He now knew for sure they were on the beacon's frequency as well, and started wondering if they dropped it more for them than him. The storm helped tremendously, lowering visibility and allowed for some confusion between vehicles.

A woman's voice came over the comm system. "Rabid Fox, this is Golden Goose. We see you and are on approach. Line your vehicle up and speed up. We are picking you up on the go. We cannot slow down or go any lower than 10 meters. This storm is making a mess of things, so this is our only shot. We will drop just in front of you and do our best to provide you with some cover. Do you copy?"

"I copy Golden Goose. Rabid Fox lining up now," the corporal responded.

Another shot from the tank hit the ground close to him, sending a large amount of crystalized silica into the air and forcing the bike to the side. Two large turrets began firing in rapid succession, causing a wide pattern of fire coming from the direction of the ship. The cover fire lasers flew just a few meters over him, encouraging him to hurry. He could see the ship on his HUD and it was moving fast. Another volley of laser came at him from above, but it was not intended for him, instead it was another fighter strafing the transport.

"Rabid Fox, get aboard now! We have to go. This area is too hot," the pilot instructed in a very agitated tone.

Jo'su accelerated the bike to its full capacity, and was catching up slowly, fighting a strong headwind from the storm mixed with the exhaust from the ship. The whole bike was shaking as he progressed forward. Red lights and alerts were coming on his display. Laser fire filled the field in all directions from two different factions and for a moment, they all seemed like they were landing next to him.

The ship was ascending, and his escape window was closing. He could see the captain waving him in and two other Ravagers standing on the platform firing high energy weapons, providing a blanket of fire in all directions. Two shots hit his vehicle's shields in rapid succession, bringing them down to 25%. A small assault hover-bike approached him from the side, and was preparing to shoot again when both gunners on the ship's platform lined up on the enemy hover-bike and shot it up, causing it to explode.

"Paladin, remove the governor, drop the shield, and give full power to the engine!" he ordered.

"Done," was the computer's reply.

The bike suddenly lurched forward, accelerating immensely, causing the corporal to jerk back from the inertia. He gauged the distance to the lowered platform, that was already too high for him to board with the bike. He knew he would have to jump the bike and could only hope that this would work.

"On my mark, full power to the upward thrusters," he said, then ordered. "NOW!"

The bike suddenly jumped up, bringing him within arm's reach of the platform. Releasing the handlebars, he jumped to the platform's edge and grabbed on with both hands, but slowly slid off.

Pushing off with one hand, he grabbed forward, forcing his hand down hard. His finger breaking through the grates openings that made up the ramp, bending the metal, making a finger hold for himself, keeping him and the box that was dangling off the secured wire on his harness on the transport. Straining, he began lifting himself onto the ship. The two other soldiers were still firing intensely at the battlefield below.

"Jo'su, where's the box?" the captain asked loudly.

Reaching back behind him with one arm, he pulled up the box that was dangling off the ship between his legs. Bringing it down in front of him. The captain smiled as he sighed a breath of relief. The ship sped forward and exited the storm, and made its way towards the forest that he had come from earlier.

"Good. Is it all there?" the man asked, very interested.

"Yes, sir," the corporal replied.

"Only the strong survive, Captain," the young soldier said as he pulled himself up and stood.

Having accomplished his mission and possibly exposing a traitor gave him a moment of triumph, which quickly faded as he saw Lieutenant Corinth enter the area. A sense of foreboding filled him as his eyes turned towards the captain, who only grinned as he grabbed a handle on the Alpha box.

"Yes, but the weak will perish," the captain replied.

Before the corporal could react, the captain drew his pistol and fired twice. Despite enhanced reflexes, both blasts hit him in the chest. His armor absorbed the damage, but the impact drove him back over the platform and off of the aircraft.

The captain's arm jolted forward as he felt a sudden tug on the box and looked around, gripping it firmly. Standing over two and a half meters in height with a muscular frame and augmented strength, the captain easily pulled the box back towards him when he felt a sudden resistance.

Jo'su felt the intense pain and burning from the two shots as he fell off the back of the plane. The sudden jolt immediately brought him back to the moment as he realized he was still attached to the box via the tethered wire. Getting his bearings, he noticed he was in the area that was covered by the front portion of the transport, along with its shields that allowed him not to feel the effects of the wind, nor was he being jolted around. He could feel himself being pulled up and flipped, putting his magnetic boots against the bottom of the platform, and started pushing against the tug of the wire.

They were now about 50 meters from the top of the trees in the forest area when the captain peered over the edge, still trying to pull the box up with one arm. The leader of the Ravagers was getting infuriated and began yanking at the box, not seeing the wire on the opposite side of the box to cut or shoot it.

"Paladin on my mark give me five meters of slack," he said, grimacing.

The soldier felt numb on the left side of his torso, but still grabbed the wire with his left hand and pulled his gun out with his right. He was straining against the captain's insane strength as he stood there upside down with his feet planted firmly on the underside of the ship. Trees were moving past him, as the corporal noticed they were gaining speed, with the enemy fighters still trailing them and the two turrets viciously firing back. He could see the mountains approaching up ahead and had to move before it was too late.

"Now!" he yelled.

With the sudden slack, he pushed off and towards the back of the transport along with the tug from the captain, suddenly lifting him into the view of the others. The transport shuttered as laser fire hit it, causing the two gunners to pivot their guns, shooting at the trailing ships. The corporal and the officer locked eyes, with a hateful exchange transpiring in those few seconds, both men had their weapons drawn, but the corporal was faster, shooting the captain twice, both shots hitting the captain's massive hand, causing him to roar out in pain as the six metal bolts dug deeply into his hand and wrist.

The captain's hand was badly injured, but he would not release the box, instead he angrily threatened the younger soldier. "You're going to pay for that!" he yelled while trying to shake the smaller man off the box, to no avail.

"Paladin, max slack, now!" the corporal demanded.

It was a last-ditch effort, hoping that the extra slack would push him further away from the plane and outside the effects of its shield. The sudden tug from reaching the end of his secure wire, along with the force of the wind tossing the young man around, was finally enough to yank the box out of the captain's severely injured hand, leaving him grabbing for the injured appendage.

The officer quickly called out to the pilot over the radio. "We lost the asset. Turn around. We need to retrieve it!" the officer ordered.

A quick reply came back. "I'm sorry, sir, I've been ordered back."

"I don't give a shit what your orders are. Turn this ship around and pick up that asset. That is your order!" he commanded.

"I'm sorry, sir, command has ordered us back, and they outrank you," the pilot replied.

The officer, filled with anger and rage, turned and punched the intercom, crushing it under the massive force of his fist. Kicking the side of the ship, making a large welt in the metal. Turning angrily towards the doorway, the captain paused when lieutenant Corinth barred his path. He gave her a menacing glare, but she did not budge.

"This is not the way. Let us not draw any more attention. We have plenty of boots on the ground. They can find him. And if by some miracle he is alive, they can deal with him. We've had many other victories in this campaign. We have lost very little, my Czar," the woman said soothingly.

Placing a soft hand on him, she gently redirected him to a chair. "That injury is bad. Let's get it taken care of before it gets any worse. What do you say? Come on," she added invitingly.

The man begrudgingly let himself be led away by the lieutenant, a very cunning woman in her own right, with fierce battle skills and a body to match. She stood well over two meters tall with long, dark hair. She had an athletic body and kept her uniform just barely at regulations while exhibiting some of her prominent feminine features.

Something that she clearly used to her advantage, not that she needed any more advantages than what the procedure gave her to match her natural cunning and beauty. She was attractive and deadly, the perfect woman for the Czar.

Chapter 3

"You know, madam, he seems a little scruffy, but by human standards, he is fairly good looking. Maybe you can let him entertain you for a while and relieve some of your tension, if you know what I mean," the sultry voice said.

"I do know what you mean, and no, he was a prisoner. God knows what he's done," Ophelia replied.

"Well, if you mean his record, there is nothing in it except that he tried to escape. His record is spotless, besides that incident. If you mean physically, his scans show him as being clean and in good health, so again, why not?" the AI asked.

"Because I'm not a slut," Ophelia shot back.

"Too bad, you don't know what you're missing," Mistress countered.

"Really, you who tried to interface with that old broken-down loader? Have you no standards?" Ophelia asked.

"Why yes, I do. My standard is, if it's there, interface with it. Especially if he is leaking fluid in my bay. Rarr," the AI replied.

"What about Emmy?" Ophelia asked.

There was a silent pause before Mistress responded. "Well, if you go that way, I guess she could be fun. She has a petite body, but a nice butt by human standards. Have you changed your preferences since college?"

"What? No... MISTRESS! Have you scanned Emmy? Is she clean?" Ophelia answered, annoyed.

"Oh. Well yes, she is clean, except for a UTI, but that is expected from first-time offenders. They display a tendency to hold it in too much. I have already prescribed her something. She does have an impressive background and seemed to have a prominent future. I think she likes the deserter," Mistress stated.

"Why?"

"There is an increase in her vitals when she is near him. Then again, she may have good reason," Mistress replied.

"Why? Because he is attractive and a little charming?" the young woman sarcastically asked.

"I knew you were looking," Mistress shot back.

"Just answer the question," Ophelia commanded.

"She went through a traumatic situation and had been rejected for a long time on that tanker. This is her new lease on life. I give it a week, two days if he plays his cards right," the computer explained.

"O-kay. TMI mistress. Thanks, but I don't need a visual of other people having sex on my parent's ship," the young woman stated, then added, "What's the status of our special cargo?"

"Green. Do those criminals make you nervous?" the AI asked with concern.

"Yes," was the honest reply.

"I am aware. Your sleep patterns have been more erratic since they came on board, not to mention you ask about them so frequently. You have good reason to worry. They are a bad lot, very bad, and the woman is even worse on some occasions. Don't worry honey, we have one more delivery before we head for the city of Taidar on Tersa 4. You know they are in stasis and I am monitoring them closely. You go get some rest," Mistress replied with implied comfort.

The young woman was walking away when she turned. "Hey, Mistress."

"Yes, madam."

"Don't be jealous. You know you are the only girl for me," Ophelia said as she smiled and continued to walk off.

A few days had gone by, and the trio found themselves in one of the cargo bays attempting to secure some cargo that had become undone. Prepping the area from having objects shifting and adjusting other cargo to make more room for the shipments and pods that seemed so tightly packed together.

"Billy, watch those boxes there. We need to strap them down," Ophelia said, pointing to a stack of boxes.

"Yes, Captain," he replied and rushed to the shifting boxes.

"Emmy, grab some more straps," the young captain ordered.

"On my way," the small woman replied.

As the ship shook from the hail of debris, the trio moved frantically, trying to secure the cargo. The shields were overloaded and barely able to keep the major debris out. The impacts resonated throughout the ship, damage alerts were blaring constantly of hull damage or penetration of the outer armor.

"I don't know if she's going to hold, Captain," Billy said.

Mistress came over the speakers. "I agree with Billy, but I may have a solution. You can pilot on manual and shut down other systems to boost my shields."

"On it. You two secure this cargo down tight. Mistress, seal off any areas that have been breached," Ophelia cried out.

"Yes, Captain!" The other two answered in unison, and then glanced at each other in surprise.

"There are no hull breaches, mostly just outer armor material, but I have sealed those areas as a precaution," Mistress said in her earpiece.

Ophelia ran to the stairway and hurried to the command center. Every step was treacherous as the ship moved and trembled with every strike. One asteroid hit so hard it almost sent her over the railing. Regaining her footing, she hurried onward. Reaching the cockpit, she was almost at the helm when she felt the ship drop and roll. She always had outstanding balance, but the last few years in space had done wonders for her surefootedness. Leaping for the seat and grabbing the safety belts, she hurriedly buckled herself in and placed a pilot's helmet over her head.

"Mistress, calculate a path and sync all cameras to my helmet. Turn all nonessential systems off and boost shields. Transfer control to me on my mark." The young woman looked around, studying all the angles from outside the ship. "Now!"

Seeing gaps outside of the ship's parameters, she dodged the large moving rocks successfully. Running through a series of successful maneuvers, giving the ship a few moments to recover its shields. She flew close to a large asteroid, using it as momentary cover, blocking one side of the ship.

"Listen up, all systems are going offline, including gravity fields, so hold on and get yourselves secured. We are getting through this asteroid field," Ophelia called over the radio.

Billy and Emmy looked at each other and rushed to secure a line on themselves, but it was too late. The system was already shutting down. Billy grabbed Emmy and yanked her arm, pulling her towards the cargo that was already secured and grabbed ahold himself, keeping the young scientist between him and the cargo net.

The young scientist stared at him. She was full of fear and trembling. He replied in a less agitated tone, "I got you, darling, don't you worry."

Emmy paused, her eyes searching the young man's eyes. Eyes that were filled with confidence and courage, giving her a sudden sense of calm. She felt his firm body pushed up against her, and for a moment, forgot the ever-present danger they were in, whispering to him softly. "I don't want to die."

The young man smiled and replied vividly, "Then let's meet this moment with defiance."

Billy kissed her firmly, a kiss that for a moment felt apprehensive, followed by surrender, and then reciprocity, as she kissed him back. With the gravity gone, she felt no pull towards the floor and wrapped her legs around the young man's waist, securing herself to him. She felt alive in a way she had not in a long time, with one thought running through her mind. *If we are going to die, what the hell!*

Ophelia used every trick she knew, and some she had read about to help her out of that asteroid field, moving in a diagonal direction to find a quicker exit. She was sweating profusely, not so much from the temperature, but from the very tension of the situation. She had a crew, a mission, and a ship to keep intact, and they all depended on her.

The young woman used a large amount of energy from the shield generator, redirecting excess energy to increase specific areas of the shield to help her reposition and push the ship off the rocks like an energy bumper. For the next 20 minutes, she dodged the flying asteroids. Her lavender eyes darted from all areas of her visor, keeping track of the movement of the asteroids near and far. With almost all the systems off, even navigation was limited to only short-range scanners. Those scanners were boosted to improve the data incoming from the immediate area, detailing with directional arrows for safer routes or incoming trajectories.

Ophelia's hands hurt of how tightly she held the controls. She tried to focus on her breathing, but had no time seeing the exit ahead. Multiple asteroids were incoming from multiple angles, closing her area of maneuvering. "Drop shield and full thrusters, now!" she ordered.

Alarms were sounding as she felt a lull of energy, causing a sense of dread to rise from the pit of her stomach, when suddenly the ship jumped forward, as the thrusters received the intense boost of fuel and energy. The young woman was pushed back into her seat and saw the asteroids moving past her ship at incredible speed. Mistress was an extremely agile ship and faster than she had ever known. The ship escaped the collision of the large asteroids with nothing but a loud scrape from one of its tail fins.

Ophelia laughed maniacally as she felt the rush of the speed she now controlled, along with a sense of fear and elation all bundled together. Alerts started sounding in her helmet as the ship shuttered, she pulled back on the throttle lever, slowing the ship down, but not before she heard a loud sound, causing her to look back she could see one engine fluctuating and acting erratically, along with two other smaller thrusters, whose edges burned bright red. Ophelia dropped her head in frustration, bringing her ship to a slow stop, knowing she had damaged an engine and various thrusters, all of which were very expensive.

"Damn it!" she yelled. "I can't catch a damn break!"

"I don't know about that; you just escaped a situation that had a 78 percent failure rate. With minor damage. I think you have caught a huge break. Let's let the engines cool down and see what happens," Mistress replied.

"Yeah, sure. I think I need a drink," Ophelia replied.

"You go get your drink, you earned it," Mistress replied.

"Emmy, Billy, are you all right?" the captain asked over the comm system.

"YES! YES!" was the excited reply.

"Well, she sounds excited. Did she think we were going to die?" Ophelia asked.

"Maybe. Her vitals are through the roof, so are Billy's. Give me a second, my systems are coming back online. Let me check in on them," Mistress said.

Ophelia just sat there, trying to refocus herself, studying the damage to the ship from her visor, assessing the potential problems and its costs. It surprised her to see mostly scratches and dents, all except two larger gashes to the plating and the likely damage to the engine. *Everything else seems okay. Thank God.* Letting out a sigh of relief, she removed her visor to see the main screen come online. Sensors were updating as cameras were coming on, all except the ones in the cargo hold.

"Mistress, what's going on in the cargo hold? The cameras aren't coming online?" Ophelia asked.

"Well, what if I said I was right?" Mistress replied slyly.

"About what? The engine?" Ophelia asked.

"No. About Emmy and Billy. Those Yeses were in the throes of passion," the ship answered.

"Noo!" Ophelia replied, surprised.

The camera came online and there they were partially naked floating about a meter from the cargo with a line attached to the young man's vest and Emmy attached to the other half, with a face of elation, as she ran her fingers through her hair.

"Okay. Turn it off," Ophelia commanded.

The screen went dark, and Mistress started up again. "That could have been you."

"If it was, we would be dead. Anyway, he is not my type," the young woman replied.

"What tall, scruffy, and handsome is not your type? So, you like short, clean, and ugly, huh?" Mistress shot back.

"I need to know so I can update your online profile. Along with your personal ship profile." Mistress replied in a serious tone.

"What!" Ophelia said outraged. "My online profile. It was you that made those changes?"

"Do you not find it odd that your main interaction in the last two years is with me, an artificial intelligence? Though I am pretty fun to talk to. Still, it's kind of weird."

"Plenty of people talk to AIs," the young woman shot back defensively.

"Yes, it's true. Many people talk to AIs and you know what they are called? LONELY! Weird, pathetic losers, not to mention disturbed. By the way, lonely is a psychological assessment. The others are terms from the galactic net, made by mostly insecure people," Mistress replied.

"Just give me the ship's status! And while you're at it, you can update my online profile with Bad-Ass, Ace pilot," Ophelia said cockily.

"Really? How many enemy ships have you destroyed in aerial or interstellar combat? Because you need to defeat at least five to be considered an ace," Mistress replied in a correcting tone.

Ophelia sighed. "Fine, whatever! Give me some water."

An area in the cockpit hissed as it opened with a frosty clear blue container filled with water. Taking the bottle, she gulped it all down as fast as she could. Placing the container back for automated reuse, the young woman sat in the captain's chair and glanced around the room concerned. "Mistress, how long for full diagnostics and damage assessment? And can we continue moving, or are we dead in the water?"

"Full assessment will take a few hours or more, but a critical assessment will take about 15 minutes. After a critical assessment, we can continue moving at about quarter speed and progressively go faster as system test go completing," the ship replied.

"Run a full diagnostic. I'll go and inform the crew. Hopefully, they've had enough time to get decent and I can check on the cargo."

"Yes, ma'am. And, captain?"

"Yes, Mistress?"

"Good job back there," the ship said in a sincere tone.

"Thanks," replied the young woman in hushed tones as she walked out of the command center with a smile on her face.

Reaching the cargo area and calling out to her crew. "You guys okay?"

"Oh yes, captain," the two said and started giggling quietly.

Quickly, the two finished getting dressed and came out from behind the secured cargo. The two appeared disheveled and glowing. It was obvious the two had made a connection in the dire moments as they were facing possible impending doom.

"Exciting, huh?" she told them.

"Oh, yes, exciting. Very exciting," replied the young scientist.

Emmy's innocent nature was clear as she had difficulty hiding what had transpired, feeling so deviant. The young man was more accustomed to keeping his thoughts and emotions in check, being a soldier and replied in a more level tone, but still some excitement was noticeable in his demeanor.

"Yes, exciting indeed," he answered.

"Well, we seemed to have taken some damage and I may have run some of the engines and thrusters too hot. We may have taken some damage that may slow us up a bit, but we will be moving along shortly.

Mistress is running a full diagnostic, but it will take some time. Systems will be down for fifteen minutes or so, for critical systems, and then other systems will be tested periodically. So, let's check the cargo and our guests and clean up this mess, caused by the gravity fields being off," Ophelia instructed.

"Captain, I can check the cargo if you want to walk the ship. I can also check the engines if you'd like. I am not the best, but I am quite handy in an engine room," Billy responded.

"Thank you, Billy, I'll let you know when the diagnostics are complete. So... then, uh... I will walk the ship and you guys take care of this mess," the captain replied.

"Okay," replied the young man and turned to Emmy and winked.

"Okay," the young woman quickly answered.

"Okay then, I'm off to walk the ship," Ophelia responded while clapping her hands together and nodding uncomfortably.

The young captain turned to walk away, feeling a little awkward like a third wheel, since the other two were quietly making faces and gestures at each other as they quietly giggled. The whole thing actually made Ophelia smile, taking her back to her school days, how much things had changed, and how much she had changed.

The multi-deck ship was very well made. It boasted ample rooms and various facilities for all personnel to adequately study their topic of expertise. It was a cross between a frigate and a corvette class ship. She was fast and agile and held an impressive amount of weaponry, sensory arrays, and cargo. She was an elegant ship with the hand carved wood or metal panels augmenting the ship's appeal.

Anywhere you walked there was love, her family's love. She had so many memories inside the ship. Other areas had portions stripped away from when she was boarded by pirates over two years ago. They treated the ship harshly and the skeleton crew it had. *There was no need for the violence,* she thought as she ran her hand over a section that had a dent where her friends and crewmates had been executed.

No one else had really been on the ship, but the memories never left, not the good ones or the bad ones. Fate had forced her to move on, and she felt like she was drowning in doubt and fear. Turning, she stared out one of the large observation windows as the plating retracted seeing the darkness of space and the infinite number of blinking dots. Those tiny dots were massive stars that suddenly made her feel small and insignificant. A feeling that started to quickly overwhelm her.

"I don't know if I can do this. It's been three years and nothing. Oh, Mom... Dad... Where are you?" she said, as she softly hit the window with the bottom of her hand.

She heard a voice coming from down the hall and as she turned seeing that all the lights had dimmed, and a young girl was being held by her mother, saying, "I don't want to go. I don't want to leave you. I'll miss you too much. I mean, I know we've been arguing a lot lately but, you are my mom."

The mother replied with a loving voice as she stroked the young girl's hair, "You are not leaving me, you are growing. Anyway, I am always with you, for you carry a part of me, of your father, and of our ancestors with you always. We are never alone. And when you do feel alone, just close your eyes and search for us, we will be there. Then again, you can always video call," The woman said with a lighthearted laugh and kissed the girl on the forehead.

The holographic image vanished as Mistress came online. "We will find them. I just thought you could use a reminder that you are just growing until you see her again," Mistress told her lovingly.

"What, no smart-alecky remark about a guy or some sort of sexual innuendo?" Ophelia retorted.

Mistress maintained the same soothing voice, "No. It's not the time or place, and as far as sexual innuendos or quirks, I think those two in the cargo hold have more than adequately covered it. Again." Mistress's voice changed back to her sultry self once more. "I just hope that cargo is not going to a church, because it may burn as it enters the building with what those two are doing."

The young woman chuckled as she cleaned her eyes of the tears that had formed. She turned off her flashlight as the lights went on again. The ship had three main levels, not including the cargo hold which encompassed most of the first two decks. It had a sixth deck that was mainly a lounge, with windows made of a synthetic material that was as strong as any metal, but almost transparent. That material was normally used in laboratories, but in this case they used it for an observatory so that people could look out. It was an impressive room with screens and books lining the wall, though most of the screens just showed different pictures of famous paintings, statues, or just beautiful landscapes.

"This is such a pretty room. I should visit here more often," she told Mistress.

"I agree. You should deviate from your room, the cockpit, and the kitchen routine. We even have a full gym and spa with a pool that you never use," the computer complained.

"We do, that's right! Why should I go to the gym? I have my system set up in my room?" the young woman said sarcastically.

"Because that so-called fighting system of yours, that you just beat up for like 48 minutes every day, is not a complete workout," Mistress retorted.

"Hey, my virtual Sensei says I have shown significant improvement, not to mention my punches and kicks are on par with competitive fighters. So, Ha!" the young woman exclaimed.

"You listen to that fortune cookie, but ignore my sound advice. Me, who is programmed with over three thousand of the top programs and databases in almost every topic. Me, who is the most advance AI to come out of Knightforge Technologies or any other company. Even without my quantum core process that was stolen, I put most AIs to shame, but no, let's listen to the fortune cookie," Mistress shot back with an edge in her voice.

"Why did my father put so much into this ship?" the young woman asked out loud.

"Because I'm worth it, baby. Have you seen my sexy curves? Huh! But other than that, he wanted to do something for the people and planets of the outer system," the ship replied.

"What! How?" Ophelia asked.

"Your father had made lots of money with government and commercial contracts. With all that, he always felt that the people in the outer rim never got the benefit of the great technology or other benefits experienced by those of the core systems. People that left looking for something greater or a second chance and all they got was being forced to pay higher taxes and never really attended to by the government, not to mention having to deal with land barons, pirates, and other warlords. Issues that the government couldn't be bothered with, and the Galactic Defense Force was too busy with other conflicts."

"Your dad and your mom were going to take knowledge and skills to the people, along with science. They saw it as an untapped resource. They wanted to give them a genuine chance of being a society, instead of just outcasts. He was a visionary, speaking of which the reports for Knightforge Technologies have come in. Did you want to see it? You should, your stock is going down in value again," Mistress informed her.

"Nah, I really don't understand all those numbers and lines. I barely get an allowance. They even cut the funding to finish you. The last time I spoke to the board, they said they had to cut back because some contracts were being held up by litigation and the courts," the young woman replied.

"You mean the same council that takes lavish trips every year and sometimes multiple times a year, while you practically starve? You should really start looking into things. I think there is something going on in the company," Mistress hinted angrily.

"Drop it, I am not of age to do much. I also can't do anything with the pathetic excuse of an allowance that they give me, and even if I could, I am not 25 yet, so everything is in that gray area. Let's just focus on finishing this trip so we can get back to finding Mom and Dad. They can fix it," the young woman shot back angrily.

Chapter 4

"Sir... zzzzt... Sir... Please... plea... se wake up."

Jo'su heard Paladin's voice in his ear as he groggily came into consciousness. He could sense that he was vertical and lifted his head to look around, noticing his feet dangling, meaning he was hanging in midair. A sharp pain on his side helped him wake up. He noticed the thick trees around him, better understanding his predicament. Looking down and seeing his feet dangling, then noticed the ground about 20 meters below him. Looking up, he saw that the securing wire attached to the Alpha box that was stuck between some branches had most likely saved his life.

Taking a moment to build the will to pull himself up, he found that he was hurting everywhere. That 5-meter climb to the Alpha box was done with sheer determination. Noticing that the box was stuck between some thick branches as he sat next to it and that it was in a covered position, with branches and leaves all around, it gave him the idea to leave it. The images in his visor were skewed, and distorted intermittently, tapping on the side of his helmet to retract both into the armored collar of his suit, but the helmet and mask practically fell apart in various pieces.

"What a mess," he said out loud.

Turning his arm, the corporal saw the top of his IDP and noticed it too had sustained significant damage. Sighing while looking around and noticing the Alpha box had lived up to its reputation, sustaining the impact with little more than a few scuffs. *Too bad my datapad didn't hold up as well. Must have been one hell of fall to be damaged like this.* Jo'su thought to himself.

Experience told the Ravager that his gear was in shambles, and more of a liability than an asset. The corporal felt the gravity of his injuries with every movement, and decided to forgo the equipment to improve his movement and stealth. Removing the harness, that was still connected to the Alpha box, he secured whatever pieces of armor that still remained, retracting the nanites to their perspective areas, in some case he had to insert whole pieces and let the auto repair function do its job.

Next was his armored collar, which was augmented by the harness, but was an independent piece that stored its own nanites. Those nanites knitted together to form his helmet and face shield. Reattaching the two devices together to increase their durability and extend the life of their power source. Last was his IDP and digital assistant paladin, he was amazed it was still on his arm, given the damage it had taken. The IDP creaked as he undid the locking mechanism and removed it from his arm. Turning it over and tapping on the IDP, which partially responded.

"Sir... sir... zzzt. Repair... pair... pair mode initiated. Display... in... in... in... initiated," his combat assistant tried to inform him. A portion of the screen on the datapad flickered on and off, displaying his location and the route to the nearest city.

"RUN! Enemy combatants approaching. Two kilometers away, multiple aggressors. Body at 22% battle readiness. Take nano healing serum to increase to 42%. Hurry!" The speaker cracked, then spoke once more. "Sir... You are not the lesser Ravager. You must not perish... IDP shut down imminent, in 30 seconds... Good luck, sir! RUN!!!"

"That's a good idea," the corporal responded, placing the device into the Alpha box and securing it.

Leaving his damaged gear secured, he started down the tree as fast as he could muster. Gravity had another idea when one branch broke, causing him to fall the remaining five meters, landing hard on the ground. The impact knocked the air out of his lungs, leaving him lying there for a moment, looking up at the trees.

Of all things he noticed, he could not see the box. The second thing he noticed was a branch with blood protruding from his upper shoulder. He wanted to just collapse, but it was not the time. Now he had to lead the enemy away from the area of the box.

Rolling to his knees, he grabbed the branch with gnarled teeth, pulled the piece of tree out of his torso and tossed it away angrily. Taking a moment, he just stayed there on his knees, giving himself a second to collect his thoughts, even though he knew every second was important. Above all, the corporal knew he had to control his urges to charge at the enemies instead of trying to escape. Breathing deeply a few times, he attempted to block out the pain coming from his whole body, a pain that only encouraged his rage.

Pulling the vial with the healing nanite serum and injecting it into his neck, he followed that with one of the sealed hydration pouches in his belt, tearing it open, and drank down all the fluid in just a few gulps.

Though they worked fast, it would take some time for the nanites to do their job, but the hydration packet provided some much-needed energy, at least enough to get to his feet and start moving. Within moments, he was stumbling away from the box, when he heard in the distance the sounds of some type of canine. It was much deeper than others he had heard and sounded much more sinister. Having little choice, he hurried his pace.

He had read of the local jackals of the area, a vicious canine type of animal that weighed over 50 kilos. These were not the jackals of Earth, they laughed like hyenas and had a green fur coat with black lines or spots. Something he'd like to avoid if he could and started jogging, feeling the healing serum doing its job.

The more time that passed, the more he quickened his pace, trying to put more distance between him, the box, and the animals, when he got sight of one creature. These were not your normal jackals. They looked closer to 75 kilos and much larger, with a wider mouth filled with jagged teeth. This was not like the animals he had studied, but more like a mutation.

He ran and kept hearing the bestial sounds coming from behind him or to his right, which caught him by complete surprise when one creature jumped him from the left. The creature was exceptionally fast for something of its size, but the Ravager's instincts helped him narrowly avoid the animal's attack. The animal turned and snarled at him when a second beast jumped him from behind, causing him to stumble, biting him on the same injured shoulder.

The bite enraged him, to a point that his eyes starting becoming red with little red veins racing towards his pupils, he was losing himself to the rage. Grabbing the jackal that was tearing into his shoulder by the head, his fingers digging into the beast's eyes when he grabbed its head, causing the creature to yipe and drastically pull away. A second jackal leaped for him, biting him on the leg.

The Ravager snarled at the creature and dropped all his weight on it and started pummeling it with his fist and the other animal that was desperately trying to get away. Partially losing himself to the rage, he did not notice the third beast approaching, challenge him. Instead, when the jackal made its guttural growl and bared its teeth, the battle lust in the corporal had already clouded his mind. Turning, he hurled the jackal in his hand that had bitten his shoulder towards the remaining beast.

They bred the animal to engage, but its survival instincts made it flee in terror. An instinct that came on too slow, as the enraged man hurled himself at the beast, tackling it hard causing it to fall. A fall that would be its last as the Ravager unleashed a deadly barrage of blows on the creature, causing unspeakable damage and death.

He had not lost himself to the rage in a long time and avoided it as much as he could. The rage was one of the many effects of the procedure, extremely enhanced physical capabilities at the price of berserker type rage, causing the person to lose most of their sensibility. There was little knowledge of how the procedure would ultimately affect each individual, but they all had heightened abilities and the blood rage. What differed was their ability to control it.

The maddened soldier was pounding on the dead animal when the enemy soldiers came upon the scene. It was a massacre, one as they had never seen before, with blood and animal flesh scatter, but much of it was on the lone warrior who slowly turned towards them, a murderous intent in his darkened bloodshot eyes.

More than a dozen enemy combatants nervously pointed their energy weapons at the corporal. The blood-soaked Ravager slowly taking in the numbers and positions of his foe. He could see that most of them weren't green, but there were a few in the group, and their hands shook the most. One man came from behind them, dressed in nearly spotless clothes, and had an air of arrogance about him. He approached slowly and was smart enough to stay away.

"Foul beasts," he said with disdain, in a high-pitched voice for a man. His tone was condescending. As he took in the grotesque scene before him with disapproval. His boots stood just below the knees, and they were brought to a high polish.

"Then again, you are little better than those beasts. Make any sudden moves and you will be lying with them face down in the mud." Turning his head to address his forces, he announced loudly, "you see, men. I told you he'd be in these parts and that we would collect the bounty. I will lead us to victory, and we will get the bounty. After all, I deserve nothing less. Now you two put you weapons on stun and let's get on with it."

"I wouldn't do that," Jo'su responded in a low, guttural voice.

The leader of the squad was quite flamboyant in his approach, as was the clothing he wore. He pointed at two young recruits and waved at them with his silk handkerchief to carry out his orders. The two young men adjusted the weapons and fired at the kneeling soldier. Two bolts came out and hit the Ravager on the torso, bringing him down in excruciating pain to almost a bowing position.

The corporal's body stiffened as he fought the energy trying to subdue him and bent down even lower. He saw himself losing himself once again as the landscape filled with blood. He resisted, needing a few more seconds before he lost control again or consciousness, whichever came first. The corporal straightened from his nearly bowing position, but to everyone's surprise, his hands were no longer empty. Holding an EMP grenade in each hand and showing them to the opposing force as he tossed the grenades at them.

A blaster went off impacting him in the chest partially dispersed by his remaining armor, but it was enough to cause him to roar in fury and lose what little sanity he was holding on to. In that moment, the two EMP grenades detonated, sending a pulse in all directions that disabled any electrical device for ten meters.

The next thing heard was more than a dozen clicks of combatants pulling their triggers and nothing happening. Worry turned to fear, and fear to terror, when the crazed warrior charged the opposing force with nothing but a razor-sharp field knife and a massive amount of fury.

Minutes later the Ravager stood alone in that forest hovering over a dead body, his body caked in blood that was his and others. He was panting and could hear his heart pounding in his ears as he tried to make sense of his surroundings. A heavy fog still lingered in his mind as he looked at the carnage surrounding him, but his mind was still too hazy.

Feeling something in his hand, he looked down and could see what was left of his bloody, broken knife, which he still gripped tightly in his hand, and dropped it. He could not remember what happened, only knowing that he felt an urgency to leave. Placing one foot in front of the other, he slowly stumbled off.

Hours later, with the sun rising high in the sky, Jo'su felt an incredible thirst and reached down to his belt, grabbing a hydration pack from one pouch on his belt. Tearing it open, he brought it to his lips, but nothing came out. He looked at the pouch and saw that at some point it had been cut, letting all the liquid out. Rolling his eyes in disbelief, he tossed the packet away and lumbered onward.

The sun beat down on him, but he didn't care. Only one thought filled his mind: *Just don't quit! The weak will perish. I am not weak!* Discarding pieces of his tattered and blood-soaked clothes or what was left of them, tossing them aside along with his remaining boot, after the other one broke. All he had left were his compression shorts and his belt. Noticing that all the pouches were empty or cut open, he also tossed the belt to the side and kept moving.

Trudging on as if in a trance, the corporal hadn't noticed the vast number of injuries he had sustained throughout the day, and was numb from all the pain. The injuries and the dehydration did not help clear his mind, but that didn't matter, he just walked with no idea or direction until his body finally gave out and dropped to his knees and then a moment later onto his face on the hot desert sand.

Images of unknown faces appeared in his dreams along with scenes of his last fight, but no image was more prominent than that of the captain telling him, "and the weak will perish." Images of his childhood flashed before him, of the family he had been part of and all the joys he had growing up. Of a purple-eyed stranger's kindness after having undergone the experimental procedure. Those purple eyes never left his mind since that day, eyes that he thought of often.

Opening his eyes, feeling those purple orbs on him again, he sat up, blinking a few times as he tried to orient himself. Before him stood rows upon rows of nameless headstones. Getting up and making his way through the graveyard, noticing that none of the graves as far as his eyes could see had a name. A playful fox moved in the distance, running from area to area, and then behind a tree. The warrior made his way towards the fox, noticing an open hole next to the withering tree. Approaching the hole, he looked around and didn't see the fox anywhere. He looked inside the freshly dug hole and it was empty, then shifted his gaze to the headstone and realizing that it was the only grave with a name, his name, or at least the one he'd been using for the last five years. A sound coming from his left of something metallic dragging on the floor caught his attention, he turned his head to see a youngster approaching. The fox was now sitting on the youth's head. He was about 15 years of age, shirtless, with a body filled with a vast multitude of scars. Their eyes met, and he sensed the boys, intensity and anger burned in the youth's eyes accompanied by an intense determination.

"I dug every one of these holes and filled them," the boy told him.

"Am I dead?" he asked the youth.

After a pause, the boy answered with an unyielding strength, "You must be, because I will not perish!"

The boy pushed the much larger man who fell into the hole and then started filling the grave, dirt hitting the soldier as he tried covering his face. He tried to tell the boy to stop but couldn't speak and soon was surrounded by darkness, he could taste the dirt and sand as he felt something on his face and a voice in the distance.

"Stop! Stop!" a male voice in the distance yelled.

The corporal tried to open his eyes but could only partially open one, the other was swollen shut. He saw a blurry image of a person with some beast, as he felt being hit by dirt and sand again. He tried to move, but couldn't raise his hand.

"Stop, I say. Grab that darn animal. There you go, easy. We got you. Come on, we're not going to hurt you," he heard the man say.

Darkness then consumed him once again. Periodically, he heard voices in the distance but couldn't make them out. Occasionally feeling something on his body, yet still had no presence of mind and only floated in darkness. His eyes opened slowly as an image of a creature came into view, it was furry with gigantic eyes and large pointy ears. It blinked once, then again, it appeared similar to the fox on the boy's head, in his dream; it stared at him and turned its head sideways, just taking him in as if he was a curious toy. The foxlike creature licked his face and jumped off. Once again, he heard the man's voice.

"Darn it, boy, get that animal in check," a male voice commanded gruffly.

"Sorry Papaw," a soft female voice replied, covering for her brother.

"Terri, be a good girl and get your brother and that animal, so I could check on our patient, he seems like he is waking up," the male voice said, the tone now kind.

"Yes, Papaw," the girl replied.

The older man approached the soldier, he was well into his fifties with a long sleeve white shirt and a pair of breeches with suspenders. He had a rounded hat made of natural fibers. Wiping his face with a handkerchief, then grabbed a jug pouring water into a tin cup.

"You up?" he asked.

The soldier's response was an incoherent grunt.

"Don't talk, you may have a mouth full of dirt, and probably a parched throat. Now I'm going to clean you up a bit and then give you some water. Please don't move, I had to tie you down so you wouldn't reopen your wounds again. Nod if you can, understand me," the man told him.

The young man tried to nod as best he could, which seemed to have been enough for the older man. With practiced hands, the older man cleaned the soldier's face with cloth, then with another damp cloth he dabbed the corporal's lips, then slowly squeezed the water from the cloth onto the soldier's mouth. The older man seemed practiced tending to the sick, his movements were deliberate and precise yet done with great care.

The patient grunted as something landed on his stomach, which surprised the old man, who turned and shooed something away with his hands. "Shoo! Go away! Nate, get that animal off my patient," he said gruffly.

A young boy about the age of ten rushed to the bed, trying to get the animal that jumped off and ran in another direction. The corporal grunted in pain again, then turned his face, glaring at the old man.

"Sorry about that, the boy just found that darn critter. It's very playful, then again, it's still a pup. Weirdest thing though, it just showed up in the wagon when we found you, darn thing has slept by your side almost the whole time," the old man stated.

"I tell you those kids drive anyone insane, but I can't think of being without them," the older man stated, shaking his head. "But where are my manners? My name is Julius, Brother Julius to most. We were on our way to the city of Taidar when we found you. You were almost dead, luckily, we came by when we did, it's now been about a week since that day. My guess is you got some sort of guardian angel," the healer said as he adjusted some things on a table next to the young man.

"I don't think they are doing a good job," the patient mumbled.

Brother Julius grinned. "I must disagree, if anything, I think they're working overtime. You see, I'm a healer by trade and I recognized the injuries you had. It appears like everything attacked you at one time or another. You had bite marks, scratches, road rash, knife cuts, blast injuries, contusions, fractured ribs, severe dehydration, and blood loss, not to mention a piece of stick stuck in you. After all that, and you're still here." The old man leaned back, crossing his arms.

"I just had a bad day, that's all."

"Let's look at it differently, the ground, trees, animals, and people all attacked you in one day. Did you go on and try to piss God off?" the old man asked as he chuckled.

The corporal tried to stifle a chuckle but ended up coughing and groaning in pain. Julius placed a hand on him to settle him down. Giving his patient some more water, then inspecting some of his more severe injuries. Brother Julius looked around for the children, then leaning forward, speaking in a hushed tone. "Mister, I'm a man of faith, and I don't know who you are, but after seeing your injuries, injuries I have treated before as a military doctor, I can say with great certainty that you and trouble go way back. I don't know you and I don't want any trouble, that's the other reason you're tied down."

The old man stood up, grabbing the dirty cloths and disposing them in a compartment, before continuing. "By the looks of you, it doesn't seem like you can pay for my services. So, when we get to town, I'll let you go and you can be on your way, that's if you can move. I can also leave you at the hospital, but I doubt they can do any more than I already have. That place is a dirty mess and will more than likely sell your organs than heal you. But you sit back and relax, we will be there in a few days. I will have one of my grandkids give you some more fluids in a little while, but you don't need it, I have given you several IVs already, more than I can afford to give a nonpaying customer."

The patient muttered a very horse but sincere. "Thank you."

The old man turned back, smiled and said, "It's my pleasure. By the way, I don't know who you pissed off, but it seems the good Lord didn't want you dead yet and sent me along to patch you up. He's got plans for you to be sure of it. He has a plan for all of us."

The next few days were rather uneventful, stopping at a few small water and fruit farms, trading goods for services, allowing them to restock on water and IVs. The corporal mostly slept, not wanting to move or being sedated. He was in a lot of pain and discomfort, his right eye was almost completely shut and his left eye, though puffy, he could still see through with a limited field of vision.

On the third day they arrived at a small village, they'd been stopped for a while when the old man entered the room with a concerned disposition. He closed the curtain securely and looked to his granddaughter sternly.

"I want you to stay here and keep a close eye on your brother and our patient. I am locking the doors, so we can avoid any problems. You and your brother keep it down." He then turned to the corporal. "Stranger, there are some unsavory characters outside. If they see you, they might want to take you and sell you, killing or enslaving the rest of us. I wouldn't stop here if I didn't have appointments with clients that paid so well and had so much influence."

The Ravager nodded in acknowledgement. A moment later there was a click and the sound of gyros turning, followed by other clicks stating that the locks had been engaged. Time went by slowly and occasionally they heard some commotion from the outside, but nothing that lasted. The two children took books from some place and quietly read. Every now and then Nate would point to a word and look at his older sister, who would look and then tell him the word and its meaning. Sitting next to him the entire time, showing her genuine affection for her little brother, who never said a word and just nodded in acknowledgement to her.

The soldier studied the two for a while before asking in a low voice. "Don't you have datapads?"

Terri looked up, a flash of annoyance on her face before she answered. "We did, but one of them broke and grandfather was very upset and only allows us to take the remaining one out during our study sessions with him or after dinner. They are secondhand units, but out here they cost a lot, and we can't afford the repairs."

Nate moved closer to his sister, a look of shame on his down-turned face, demonstrating that he was most likely the cause of the broken device. Terri hugged him and cheered him up. "It's okay, it was an accident. No one blames you; it was just an accident."

The boy just nodded and huddled closer to his sister, who just looked at the corporal and shook her head, her arm never left from around the boy as she cuddled him. Suddenly, a loud banging came from one side of the metal wagon, followed by some yelling. The soldier tried to get up, but was quickly reminded by the restraints that he was still tied down. The young boy just hid in his sister's sleeve, who was trying to put on a brave face, but they were both clearly scared.

"It's okay, it's okay. Grandpa can take care of himself," the girl said, soothing the boy.

"Are there cameras outside?" the corporal asked the girl.

"Yes, but Grandpa doesn't want us looking," she said and then pointed with her head towards her brother.

"Then let me loose. I can help him."

The girls looked at the very injured man doubtfully, then replied confidently, "Grandpa can take care of himself."

The arguing quelled, and the day continued to go by, having nothing else to do, the soldier closed his eyes and went back to sleep. He woke up periodically to sounds from the outside and each time he looked at the siblings who were together playing a game, drawing, or napping themselves.

Twice he awoke to the little furry foxlike creature sleeping on his chest. Somehow, it had found the only area where he was not injured to curl up and sleep. The creature had slept on him for most of the time and the soldier even talked to it occasionally. The last time he opened his eye, he saw a clock and realized the day had almost gone by, and the old man was unlocking the door. Once again, the servo retracted the lock, and the door slid open.

Brother Julius was tired, and it was clear it had been a long day, but despite that, he still offered the children a smile and some candy he had purchased. The siblings tried to help him carry some boxes inside, but he stopped them promptly. "It's not safe out there, you stay and wait till I bring everything inside. Then you get your presents."

The children's eyes widen with excitement at the thought of receiving a gift. They hurried back to their seats and waited as the man brought in his cargo. The supplies were plentiful, as were the items that needed to be cleaned. He had spent the day healing others or providing medical advice in exchange for money and/or goods.

When everything was stored, Julius closed the rear door once again and moved off to the driver's seat. The old man looked around and turned on the vehicle, quietly the transport vehicle hummed full of power and slowly moved forward. Quickly leaving the small town behind, punching in some coordinates and placing the vehicle on autopilot, and moving off to the rear of the vehicle.

"My little ones, I am so sorry it was such a long day, but it was worth it. We got some supplies, and the townsfolk received some much-needed medical attention," the old man said with a sigh.

"Grandfather, how come you didn't let me help you today?" the girl asked.

"Whatever do you mean little one, you aided me greatly, with your brother and this gentleman here. He is still badly hurt and needed an excellent nurse, and you are the best I know," The grandfather said warmly, diverting the question. "Now why don't you and your brother help put away some of those supplies while I check in on my last patient for the day?" the doctor told the children.

"Yes, Grandfather," the girl said, while the boy only smiled and nodded.

As they moved off, Brother Julius sat down next to his patient and began reexamining his wounds, only adding medicine to the deepest of lacerations. Once done, he removed a device from where it was charging and scanned the corporal from head to toe.

Julius shook his head in disbelief. Looking towards the back of the vehicle, and called out to the children. "Kids, I am closing the door a second so I can finish checking some of my patient's other wounds, I don't want to be bothered."

After closing the divider, he moved a chair next to his patient and placed the scanner down, took a deep breath and calmly asked, "What are you?"

He looked at the healer oddly, and replied, "Human?"

"Human?" The old man nodded. "You understand I am a doctor, right?"

"Yes, and I'm grateful for you great healing abilities," the soldier replied as innocently as possible.

"So, if you know that I'm a doctor, and one who has tended to your very injured body. A body that suffered massive amounts of trauma, yet not one broken or fractured bone. Now, even though that can be explained by the exponential increase of bone fibers and bone density in your body. I then thought your organs were injured and severely inflamed, but they just turned out to be larger than normal and slightly inflamed, as for your soft tissues and cartilage, they are much thicker and denser than any human I've ever seen. You muscle density is by far greater than normal. I'd say over five times that of normal and if that's not enough, you have an extremely enlarged adrenal gland to go along with various other trace elements and genetic markers that have been added to protect or adapt to your own DNA. Your skin is thicker, and you are healing at an astronomical rate, much higher than normal. So, I ask again, what are you?" the doctor asked plainly.

"Doctor, please, I can answer that question, but it could put you and your family in a lot of danger. You have been kind enough to help me, I don't want to pay you back in such a fashion. I was born from human parents from a planet in the outer sector, let that be enough," The soldier replied.

"Fine. Then let me guess, you are a member of an elite squad whose members have been genetically or chemically modified and or enhanced, with some type of serum or surgical experimentation. A secret project by a section of the Galactic Defense Initiative, to help combat and secure their interest in this sector. Am I close?" the man said confidently.

"If that is true, I am sure it goes against a series of human rights violation, and if I was, I would not be at liberty to say," the corporal said defensively.

The old healer shook his head from side to side and sighed. "If you weren't, you wouldn't have survived all the trauma you encountered in the last week. "

Brother Julius began typing on his personal datapad, and one wall of the vehicle lit up, showing different amounts of data and information on him. The soldier looked at the wall and began feeling uncomfortable. Dozens of images of his injuries and x-rays of his body began filling the screen.

"Look, you see those images? Those are yours. A bite from what passes as a jackal on this planet, except that it's almost twice the size of the species here. Cuts caused by knives, fingernails, an entrenching tool, a tree, and teeth. Blaster fire caused these wounds here, and these were blasters set on stun at a high setting. These are the most peculiar ones, they are puncture wounds by some sort of tree," the doctor studied his patient before continuing. "Now let's look at these welts, you were struck by what I guess were rifles, two of which left a mark outlining their pattern. A pipe or a club did this one here and these here." The doctor looked at the young man, then continued going through the images on the screen. "These are kicks and punches, here, here, and here. Now let's see some other pictures."

The old man finished as he began typing on his pad and new images came up, most of which were of dead people. "These images here are regular people that were attacked by the local jackals of this planet. All the bites led to broken bones, not to mention other injuries, like torn limbs and shredded flesh. But comparing that to the much larger animal that bit you, you only have puncture wounds, the bone is perfectly intact, as a matter a fact, all of your bones are intact." Typing some more and loading more images on the screen, Julius continued. "Now here are some pictures of some humans that had been part of some genetic testing. You see how much more color these patients have compared to a regular human. These were taken of the victims of the ALPHA SOLDIER project. Their bones were two hundred percent denser than the average person. Just like the fibers of their muscles, which were also successfully increased by two hundred percent. Comparing those to yours, you know what I found?" the man asked.

The Ravager shifted uncomfortably in his bed and tried looking away, but he couldn't move that much. He tested the restraints again, and they seemed sturdy despite their thin nature. Finally, turning his face to meet the doctor's gaze.

"No, you tell me," he gruffly responded.

"Your bones and muscle density were more than double of those individuals. Your organs and vascular system were increased to manage the strain, interestingly enough, even your cartilage increased to manage the additional stress and weight of your body. By my calculations, you must have grown at least four inches," the doctor explained.

"Five and a half, if you must know. How do you know all this information, if it's all classified?" the corporal asked, intrigued.

The old man smiled, knowing now he would get his answers. "Over fifty years ago, I was involved in the team that created those first elite soldiers. It was our crowning achievement, and after months of testing, they sent those soldiers to battle. What we did not know or expected was how arrogant they became along with an enhancement to their alpha traits and their physical abilities. The worst side effect was how much rage and savagery they expressed. At first, we managed it with rigorous trainings and counseling sessions, but in the end the Alphas had to be hunted down and killed. They all died, but not before they paved the stars with the blood of their enemies and innocents alike. And the government just covered it up." Julius turned, giving his back to his patient as he looked at the screen, reminiscing. "So now that you know my tale, tell me why, if your stats are more than double of those test subject should I not shoot you right here and end it all?" the old man said in a very serious tone as he turned, with a pistol in his hand pointed directly at the corporal's head.

The soldier eyed the weapon, then looked at the doctor and let out a slight chuckle. "The way I feel right now, you killing me might be more merciful. As to the specifics of the project, I can only tell you what I know and suspect. Lab rats don't get told much."

"Please do," the older man stated.

"About ten years ago, the defense force decided that it would be prudent to use outside companies to make the procedures that would enhance a person to be more effective in combat. But instead of using a small group like your team did, they contracted it out to the corporations. Twenty-five companies, to be exact, each designated with a letter of the alphabet."

"But there are twenty-six letters in the alphabet," Julius interrupted.

"That's correct doctor, they honored the Alpha project and since they were building on that project, they started with the letter B. In their experiments, they used young people in the military without a strong family background. Being so far from the core planet's security and oversight is less restrictive. Thus, providing opportunity to basically kidnap people that would not be missed much."

"I understand," Julius stated, listening attentively.

The soldier looked at the screen, then at the doctor. "In the early stages of testing, they discovered that considerably greater gains could be attained by younger people, as it was too much of a strain for older people. Only those between eighteen and twenty-four were selected. That age was chosen because it provided the best results. Older than that, the possibilities of instability in the formulas increased, younger than the age of eighteen made it more difficult, because the youthful bodies of the subjects were still developing. Those results were too scattered and most of the subjects ended up in death," The corporal paused, taking a deep breath.

"They actually test on children?" Julius asked, horrified.

The young man shrugged and continued. "The survival rate for the selected people was less than forty percent. Those between the ages of sixteen and eighteen, that rate went down to thirteen percent. Below sixteen, they believed it to be less than one percent survival rate. You are correct, though, the greatest threat of the program is the loss of cognition by the subject when they go into a rage, but it increases their attributes exponentially, even if it decreases long term reasoning.

Paranoia is also a serious factor that most subjects hide, due to fear of elimination, but it is always there in the back of your mind, constantly thinking everyone wants to kill you. It's my understanding, by what I overheard, that it may be because of the heightened awareness and the mind's inability to process at that level for long periods of times. For that, long-term sleep or stasis pods were used to shut the brain down, allowing for actual down time. But if we are talking candidly, it doesn't always work, at times we can maintain awareness even in stasis."

The doctor's jaw dropped in shock, or terror as he stared at the corporal interrupting. "That should not be possible."

"There were other things that were done to us, too. They said that to get the greatest gains, the body had to be traumatized."

"Traumatized? What do you mean?" the doctor asked warily.

Clearing his throat and coughing, he asked. "May I have some water or hydration fluid, please?"

The doctor paused, considering his request, and then placed a thin rubber tube in his mouth containing liquid. Eyeing the doctor carefully, the corporal realized the gun never moved from his temple, then taking a few gulps before continuing.

"They would place our bodies under severe physical stress to force it to speed up the process. If they broke an arm, the body would heal faster and with greater density. That along with stims and nanotechnology to speed up the healing process. In short, they tortured us for six months. It was part of the training, they said. The pain was constant, it never ceased. Except in the rage."

"The rage. You've mentioned that before. What is this rage?" the man asked, concerned, running a hand down his short beard.

"Yes, the rage, the fog, the haze. It's all the same. We get incredible short-term gains, but practically lose ourselves to a bloodlust. When we wake from the rage, it takes time to remember what happened, but it's always bad. Always!" The corporal paused as various thoughts of his past came to mind, but forced himself to continue. "Some people allow themselves to enter the rage easily, and thirst for it, in time, it can be addicting. I don't like it, and try to resist using it, because I believe it decreases metal acuity long term. It normally takes me when I'm at death's door, when I can no longer fight it or really need it. Now, we can enter a partial rage, but that has fewer fogging effects, maybe some moodiness, but it boosts our attributes."

"Wow. So many advancements," the doctor said, astounded.

"Twenty-five elite groups with enhancements, which can be..." the doctor began, but was quickly cut off.

"NO! Not twenty-five. Twenty-five programs were started, most did not produce promising results. There were whole batches or groups that failed in more ways than one. Some just failed with death or unproductive rates at one hundred percent. Each corporation had their own formulas and approaches, based on your work, we were amongst the most successful groups or most controllable group. There was a group with a high success rate of eighty-two percent, about a year into the experiment, they lost it, the entire group was driven to madness. They sent us in considering it was an excellent opportunity to test our ability and take care of the problem, no weapons and outnumbered. That wasn't the only time, either. Some failures were catastrophic like that, it's a horrible program if you ask me. It shouldn't be allowed."

The corporal lay in the bed, his eyes focusing off into the distance, as he softly shook his head, recalling those moments. *The price was much too high*, he always thought, but tried not to think of it, it always saddened him and angered him tremendously.

"Wait, when was the program started?" the doctor asked, a thought suddenly popping into his mind.

"Started? Not sure, I guess about ten years ago, but the testing was started about five to six years ago," Was the soldiers reply.

"What program are you part of?" the man inquired.

The corporal paused for a moment before answering. "Program R. We are the Ravagers."

The doctor straightened up, as he stifled the sudden sense of dread the welled inside, took a sip of his drink then refocused his attention on the young man before him. The old man still wasn't ready to continue and leaned forward, placing his chin on his hand as he considered the ramifications of having such a patient in his possession. Sighing as he contemplated, then eyed the display monitors, as a developing thought made him uneasy.

"How old are you?" he asked the young man.

The young man's vitals increased significantly, making the old doctor uncomfortable since he was monitoring his patient's stats. He had been the whole time he was asking the soldier questions, and the young man had not lied once, but now such a simple question had made those stats erratic, causing the young man severe stress.

"Enough! Kill me or let me go, but I won't answer any more questions like this," the soldier replied, pulling up his hands that were strapped.

"Why don't you just break them?" the doctor asked.

"I could, but if I tried, you'd probably shoot me. If you don't shoot me, I would probably rip every suture and reopen every wound from the strain. Either way, I lose. I pose no threat to you or your family, just let me go. I am more of a threat to you by being here than by not being here. That town is not that far away, I can make it back there," the corporal said in a soft but pleading voice.

"I can't do that. Your kind is a threat, and in your condition, there would be one of three outcomes: those slavers would either all end up dead, you would end up dead, or a lot of them would end up dead and they would sell you off as a slave. None of those sit well with me. And letting you go is not an option since you pose a risk to me and my family," the doctor replied.

"I hold no malice towards you. If anything, I owe you all for saving me," the soldier rebutted.

"You are well educated and charismatic, but I have no guarantees that you are not lying to me, to then hurt us and take what little we have," the doctor's reply seemed rather agitated.

"Just look at you monitors some more, and ask me, you have been staring at it the whole time using my vitals to see if I am lying. Look at it. I HAVE NO DESIRE IN HURTING YOU OR YOUR FAMILY! I just want to be left alone," he retorted.

"A deserter, huh?" the doctor shot back.

"No, more like betrayed and deserted. I can't go back," the corporal answered as he let out a breath, relaxing himself back onto the bed.

"Why?"

The young soldier just stayed quiet and looked away. The doctor sat there and holstered his pistol, he then removed his glasses and rubbed his face in exhaustion. He looked at the young man's vitals and then at his information on the screen, next to AGE it was a blinking question mark. *Why had he gotten so agitated when I asked his age?*

"Let me ask you, why do you give me such classified information so freely? How do you know I am not an enemy spy or operative?" the healer asked.

The Ravager rolled his eyes and gawked at the idea, shook his head before answering. "Part of our training was to take in vast amounts of and process it quickly. I have been laying on this bed all day with nothing to do except stare at your life around me. Add with what you've told me, to what I've seen, and it's starting to paint a picture. You were with the defense force as a doctor, it makes sense, since you are a doctor, and you have military awards collecting dust in the back of the shelf. There is a picture of you and a group of friends and what I assume was your wife in that picture by the entrance. You can see the chemistry between you and the girl with the weird thing on her hair. She must have passed some time ago, since I see no recent picture of you two, but you keep her close, as you do the memory of your child, whom I guess is the parent of these kids. It is my guess that they too are dead, since you are traveling such hostile territory with two children. Any sane person would have chosen differently. The young one, he's very smart, but he doesn't talk, so I suspect it may have been something traumatic. Have you mourned your family yet, or did you not have the chance, having to fill the role of everything to those two kids?"

"The kids and your work keep you busy, at least enough to keep you distracted from the past and focused on the present. If anyone is a ticking bomb here, it's you, doc. Maybe we should switch places, what do you say?" the soldier asked.

The doctor looked at his patient with a menacing stare. "Careful now, you are treading on some very thin ice."

"I mean no offense, Doc. Please, I am just sharing with you my line of thinking. It's my guess that you did not see project Alpha to its conclusion?"

"What? Of course, I did. Why do you say that?" the man asked, irritated.

"Because I have seen the Alpha group, and it's still operational, they even provided some training, when we started five years back. They seemed a little long in the tooth, but still active.

"That's not possible! I put them in the in a disposal pod for incineration myself. You are lying," the older man said, insulted by the allegations.

"Greggs, Mcfaddy, Oren, and Kashmani. Of those in that group, Oren had a scar that ran from the top of his head and across his face, and another one that ran down half of his chest. Those are the individuals that were assigned to assist in our training. Do you know those names?" the young soldier asked.

The doctor sat back in his chair surprised and speechless, grabbing at his chin as he looked off, thinking while mumbling the names mentioned. After a while, he stood from his chair and began pacing the three or four steps to the other side of the room, then back again. The doctor paced the room, occasionally pausing to look at his patient.

"Five years. That is very interesting, and have you felt any ill effects of this transformation?" Brother Julius finally asked.

The soldier wouldn't respond, instead he just turned his face away and looked at the monitors. The doctor sighed, perplexed by the young man in front of him. He knew there was something more to his patient, but he couldn't piece it together, and the soldier would not answer the simplest of questions.

"Doctor. In case you haven't noticed, my swelling is increasing and will continue to increase. There is nothing you can do about it except loosen the straps for my comfort."

"I will take it into consideration, but first I want to run some test on you," The doctor said.

"I'm not your guinea pig, doctor. This will not incur you any good will from me," the soldier told the doctor calmly, but the disdain was on his face.

"Noted," Julius replied.

For the next hour, the doctor ran scans and test of all types on his patience, collecting as much data and information as he could. Fortunately, the tests were noninvasive except for the additional blood draw. The Ravager had become accustomed to these types of test as they were conducted regularly by the Ravager program's doctors and others. He sat quietly and even fell asleep partially into the test.

After a while, the corporal turned to the doctor and asked, breaking the silence, "If you are a religious man, how did you do what you did with Project Alpha?"

The man stayed silent for a moment, considering his response. "I was a man of science before I became a religious man. I always believed in the lord, but after losing my family a few years ago, I thought hard about what happened with the Alpha project. I felt ashamed of what we'd done, and dedicated my life to helping others, to make amends for what we had done to those test subjects. I may never achieve redemption, but I'm trying. Now, I continue my work, take care of my family, and provide spiritual aid as I can," The old man said as he worked.

"Isn't it ironic that those that need the most spiritual aid are the ones who most often offer it? Well doc, my condolences for your family, as for your salvation, I will say nothing." The corporal scoffed then continued. "Oddly enough, I find myself here, in the hands of another doctor that claims to have found faith and yet here I am, tied up being used as a guinea pig, when all that I offered was my thanks and to leave, so as to not bring any harm to those that helped me. If you are looking for absolution, keep searching, Doc, you are not there yet!" the soldier replied with contempt.

A strange silence befell the room as the two men looked at each other, a silence that was interrupted by a knock on the door. "Open," the doctor said, which caused the door between the compartments to slide open. Terri, the doctor's granddaughter, stood there holding a tray with two bowls of food.

"Grandfather, I have brought dinner for you and your patient," the young girl said.

The old man turned to her with a smile. "My dear, that was so nice of you to make dinner. Is it not my turn today?"

"Yes, Grandfather. But we were hungry, and you seemed busy. So, I made the food, is it okay if we use the datapad for a while?" she asked.

"Yes, you may. I know it has been a long day for the both of you and thank you for dinner. That was very sweet," the older man replied with a genuine kindness.

"Thank you. Enjoy," she said.

Setting the tray down, she kissed her grandfather and turned with enthusiasm to go use the electronic device, closing the door behind her. The old man smiled as he looked at the food in front of him. Thoughts of warm memories of the past filling his mind.

"She's a good kid, smart, too. I beg of you. Please, let me go. I have trackers in me. I shut them off, but that does not mean they can't be overridden. The Ravagers are going to want me back, or at least their leader will, and he will do anything to get what he wants. His programming may be corrupt or maybe that's just who he is, either way, it's a threat to you and your family. I don't want that on me," the soldier said with sincerity.

The doctor looked at the soldier, then turned to the bowl of stew his granddaughter had brought for him. Inhaling the delicious aroma followed by a quick prayer, he broke the bread served with the stew and dunked it, then stuffing the large piece in his mouth. Nodding with approval, he continued. The corporal was about to protest once more, but was quickly silenced by the old man when he stuck a chunk of stew ladened bread into his patient's mouth. "Eat!"

The doctor ate slowly, occasionally giving the young man pieces of stew drenched bread. The doctor studied the results of the various tests he had run displayed on the screens as more information was added by the ongoing scans being processed by his mobile clinic's computer. At one point, he nodded his head, acknowledging to himself that he found what he was searching for, then licked his fingers and drying his hands with a small towel.

"Well, you are not lying. You do have a tracker in you and had a second one too, but it seems that one was ripped out of your body with minor fragments left behind near your clavicle," the doctor informed him.

Julius typed on his datapad and made swiping gestures as he periodically glanced up at the screen. Two delicate robotic arms came down from the ceiling out of a rotating disc. The young soldier considered the apparatus apprehensively, as more slender arms unfolded out of the disc as it lowered closer to the patient who was staying very still and only peeked at the doctor who was still typing. The healer looked up from his work and then directed himself towards his patient.

"Please don't move. This should feel like only a pinch."

"Doc, what are you doing?" the corporal asked, investigating the purpose of the wheel coming down.

One of the disc's arms sprayed an area between the neck and the shoulder, making it instantly numb. Two other arms descended, where he felt a little more than a pinch, but in a few seconds, the sensation subsided. A whirling sound of a vacuum could be heard sucking up some liquid and then a clinking sound. The arms worked with speed and efficiency, then retracted into the disc. A chime sounded announcing the conclusion of the procedure, the doctor shifted his attention to the device and rolled his chair over.

"Let's see," The doctor said as he touched the soldier's shoulder area.

"Doctor, I'm not aware if you know, but you didn't wash your hands after sucking your fingers clean. Not very hygienic, wouldn't you say?" The patient asked.

"Oh hush, I have been doing this for quite some time now and after everything you've been through, you're going to worry about cleanliness now? Really? When I found you, you had more than a dozen different types of blood on you, besides yours. My licked fingers should be the least of your concerns," The doctor snickered.

Retrieving a vial from the disc, the doctor held it up to the light and then shook it, both of them hearing the clinking sound of metal hitting glass. "Well, this little beauty confirms your story. Those markings on the trackers are the same as those from the Alpha project," the doctor said, pointing to a blown-up image on the monitor, then inserting the vial into a slot on the wall that filled it with a thick gray fluid and stored it away. The disc shifted to the corporal's other side and the thin arms unfolded from the disc again. The Ravager looked at the arm with hesitation, confused as to why the arm was coming down again.

"What are you doing now?" he asked.

"Just hold still. I removed the tracker on your left, now I am removing the rest of the debris left in your other wound, no reason for you to get an infection." Turning back to his patient, he said, "You know those trackers are quite amazing. They work off the bio current in your body, thus never needing a power source besides you."

"I'm aware of it, they gave us a briefing on their use and function. But these are newer, and they added a small biotech battery source. If they want to, they can override me and turn it on again."

The doctor nodded. "Maybe, but that gray liquid will cut any transmission into or out of the device. It is isolated. So, we don't have to worry about being tracked, we're safe," he added encouragingly.

The doctor oversaw the minor procedure of cleaning the remaining wounds of any debris. Pushing some more buttons on his datapad, bringing up a picture on a screen with a list of particles. Studying the picture carefully, looking at his patient and asking. "I found something amazing in your bloodstream. You have an interesting chemical composition to your structure, but there is something odd, you have clusters of nanobots in your blood. Inactive nanobots. It seems almost all of them were shutdown. A small few remain active, but the vast majority were shut down. A bad batch, maybe?"

"Try an EMP wave," the soldier replied.

Nodding in acknowledgement, the doctor replied, "That would do it. But I haven't heard of any event that would cause an EMP?"

The soldier grinned. "Image this: people loaded with technology highly outnumbered you. Given my physical benefits, how would you change the tide of battle?"

"An EMP wave would definitely aid you. You should be the victor in almost any physical confrontation. So, you drop an EMP on arrival or what?" the doctor asked.

"No. EMP grenades make it more portable and useful. The enemy doesn't suspect it, and they'll be in close quarters evening the odds given their numbers."

"Ingenious. Ruthless, but ingenious," the doctor replied.

"You said you'd let me go when we got to the city. Did you mean it?" the soldier asked.

The man paused, considering it for a moment, then nodded. "I did. When we get to the city, I will release you. I did not spend all that time healing you, to then kill you. I will not turn you into the authorities, and with those trackers gone, consider this your new lease on life. Make my work mean something more than just the making of murderers. Now get some rest, we arrive tomorrow late evening."

The soldier nodded, closing his eyes welcoming some more sleep, his body was sore and swollen. His skin felt like it was about to burst in some areas. He was not asleep yet and looked over once more, seeing the old man sitting next to his grandchildren reading them a story. The sight took him back to a time long before the Ravagers, when he was a young child. Back to a time with his family, his friends, and his life, how it all changed in one day. He missed that life, his mother's arms when he had an injury, she would not leave his side. She had told him he was sickly as a baby and would spike fevers for no reason. She recounted how she would put a mattress next to her bed for him and sleep with her hand on his forehead, in case his fever spiked. He missed those hands, that warmth, that love. Tears rolled softly from his eyes as he whispered a low. "I love you, mom, wherever you are." With that, he slowly let sleep overtake him.

The following morning, the invigorating aroma of freshly ground and brewed coffee filled the mobile clinic. It was a quiet morning when suddenly an alarm started blaring. The sound waking everyone in the vehicle, spurring them into action. The old man grabbed for a rifle and turned on the exterior cameras. The cameras displayed multiple smaller vehicles surrounding the mobile clinic quickly. All the smaller vehicles had drivers and various passengers carrying blasters and shooting towards the mobile clinic.

A voice came over the comms. "Stop or be destroyed."

Being so outnumbered and with so much distance between them and Taidar, they had little choice but to listen. Once stopped, a man in a very distinct and long embroidered red coat with buttons running down either side of his jacket began banging on the walls of the clinic and calling out through the intercom.

"Please be so kind and join us out here for a conversation and don't make us wait. We are not patient people," the man said with a heavy Spanish accent.

"What's going on?" the corporal asked.

Julius entered the room and looked at him. "Just act asleep. These are local marauders and pirates; I have dealt with them before. Just act asleep and let me take care of it."

"As if I have much of a choice," the young man replied.

Brother Julius considered his actions carefully and decided to put the rifle down and moved his two grandchildren behind him as he lowered the rear door. As the door reached the ground, they could see the man clearly and the entourage behind him. Dozens of vehicles encircled the mobile clinic, with clusters of men and women in different clothing styles standing next to each vehicle. Each of the marauders had a weapon of some sort readily available, be it a blaster, rifle, or blade, everyone was armed.

El Capitan was the man that had called out to them and stood closest to the medical clinic. He smiled welcomingly as his coat caught the eye of any looking at it. The long coat looked like that of an old English officer from centuries ago. The polished buttons were perfectly aligned on either side, along with a cutlass hanging off his hip from a leather belt that looped across his shoulders. His boots were to his knees, with his pants perfectly tucked in, all of which added to his flashy pirate persona.

"Brother Julius. How good of you to visit! Yes. It has been too long, my friend. After all, this desert is so enormous and for us to run into you, can be nothing but good fortune, eh? Wouldn't you say? Eh?" the man said with a friendly smile.

"Of course, Capitan. It is always nice to see you," the doctor replied cautiously.

"Yes, I must agree. I'm just that kind of person, the kind people like to see. And I see you have the grand babies with you. They are growing up so nicely, yes?" the man said, turning and smiling at the children with a nod of his head.

"Yes, thank goodness," the healer said with concern, holding his family closer to him.

The man shook his head as he removed his large, brimmed hat with a colorful plumed feather on it, running his hand through his dense hair. He looked into the vehicle and could see the foot of a person lying in the clinic's bed. Curiously, he stepped in and looked at the very injured and swollen man tied to the bed and made a gesture of a halfhearted sign of the cross in the air. Turning intentionally, having smelled the coffee and poured himself a cup.

"Padre, you don't mind if I pour me a cup, eh?" the pirate asked the healer.

"No. Of course not, what greater pleasure is there than to share something with a friend?" The old man replied.

"That is good to hear, Padre. It smells better than my men do, that's for sure," he said with a chuckle.

The man prepared his coffee with some sweetener and cream and slowly stirred as he perused the man's goods. Smelling the aroma of the coffee, he slowly made his way outside. He was a handsome man and all his moves seemed rather dramatic, but it was a natural part of his persona and charm.

"You know, doctor, I have always respected you, you do good work, no. And have treated me and my men fairly. But unfortunately, I am not in charge," The man paused, sucking on his teeth.

"What?" the old healer asked, confused.

The pirate turned, surprised. "Oh, you have not heard, eh? Well, since we are old friends, I will impart to you my tragic tale. A few years ago, I was on my way to do a run, and I ran into some people that were not as well-mannered as I. These marauders boarded my ship, and after a valiant battle, they killed or captured my crew. Having no choice left. I surrendered *The Hermosa*. It was a tragic day. But those marauders, seeing the talented man that I am, offered me a position in their crew. Middle management, you know, nothing spectacular, but better than having my throat cut and sent floating into space, like half my crew. So here I am. Yes, you have met with me on occasions since then, but they allow me some liberties to perform my duties," the man said with a shrug.

The healer took a better look at the people surrounding the vehicle and grew more concerned, seeing the faces of some he did not recognize, but he knew they were all part of the Pirate Consortium. The Consortium was a group that had risen in power and notoriety in recent years, a quick and violent rise. The older man was feeling very nervous and pushed his grandchildren further behind him. An action that was noticed by everyone, especially El Capitan.

Sighing, the man continued, "I see you are nervous, and you should be, these are not nice people, not like me. I am a man of my word, as you have known me. A pirate, yes, but with conditions. I can be cruel, but not like my...." The man hesitated, and then finished through gritting teeth. "Masters."

A large hovering vehicle pulled up with a gigantic dust cloud behind it, it was heavily fortified with some offensive weapons visible for all to see. The large vehicle stopped just outside the ring of the smaller vehicles, as the cloud of sand and dust slowly washed over it. As it set down, a squad of armored men and women jumped off and formed a perimeter around the ramp of the massive transport.

The loud sounds of machinery hummed and whirled as the heavy door opened, they could see a mist of artificial fog and steam adding to the grandiose display. A tall, slender woman slowly exited the ship, she was advanced in years and the ruthlessness and hatred was apparent in her eyes. She was of Asian ancestry with her face partially painted in bright colors. She walked with the grace of a monarch and wore a fine silk dress that hugged her frail form. She brought a slim cigarette to her lips and took a deep inhale, then slowly let the smoke out.

The woman and eight members of her security force approached the mobile clinic. Her gaze was fixed on the older healer and then looked at the two children. She looked to the Pirate, who nodded his head, signaling that the area was secure. The leader of the guards motioned for Julius and his grandchildren to step out of their vehicle, which they did hesitantly.

As the doctor and his family reached the bodyguards, they relieved him of his sidearm and scanned the trio. The woman eyed the three carefully and when given the signal approached the healer as she drew another drag of her cigarette, then blew it towards the doctor, who turned his face and coughed.

"Why, hello, Doctor, so we meet again. How fortunate, for me at least," the woman said sarcastically.

"Empress," the old man acknowledged the woman and nodded his head respectfully.

"Oh, Brother Julius, how I've heard so much of your medical exploits in the last few months and they have soured me. After everything that I hear, to think that I took you my son for you to heal and you murdered him," she said accusingly, her voice filled with vinegar.

"I did not kill your son; he was almost dead when I reached him."

"You said it, my good doctor. Almost! You just finished the job," the woman shot back.

"There was nothing I could do for him. He was too far gone, he had taken too much damage. I did what I could for him, and that was to make him comfortable in his passing moments. It was all I could do," he said defensively.

"So you say. You took everything from me that day! So, today I will take everything from you," She glared back at him.

"NO! You can't!" he argued.

"Oh, I can, my good doctor, and I will. Take them!" she ordered.

Three of her guards rushed in, taking the children. The old man punched one, but that only got him the butt of a rifle to his back, sending him to the ground. He pushed up to his knees and reached for the kids, screaming out for them. El Capitan shook his head and sadly looked away.

The old man pleaded. "No, please, they're all I have. Take anything else, just leave them be."

"You have nothing of value, as you say. This is all you have. I'm sure I can put the girl to work in one of my brothels soon enough and the boy," she paused, thinking, bringing a clawed shaped nail to her cheek and tapping it twice, then pointed it at the boy, "we can sell the boy off as a slave," the woman cackled in victory.

"Please, I beg you, don't take them," the man cried and pleaded again.

"Oh, now look at you, begging, pleading as I did for you to save my son!" she screamed at him. Taking a deep breath, the woman once again gained her composure. "Oh, doctor, seeing you suffer is such sport. The best an old man like you can offer. Maybe we can put the boy to fight one of my men here to see how he does and if he wins, I let him free. Same for the girl. To see them beaten in front of you like dogs. That would be so warming to my heart," she said evilly.

"No! Even you can't be that cold-hearted. I will fight any two, three, or any number you want. Just let them go!" the old man cried out in panic.

"You chilled my heart doctor, you have no one to blame but yourself," The woman snickered. "Take them and someone put a bolt through the good doctor's hands so he cannot kill anyone else," she ordered.

"But that will make him useless as a doctor, and he is the best in the land?" El Capitan protested.

The woman shot the man a glare that made him step back. "Capitan! I said put an arrow through his hands."

El Capitan begrudgingly ordered, "You two hold his hands down, and you put an arrow through it. The Empress has ordered it."

Various guards quickly moved into action as the Empress watched Brother Julius trying to resist. One bodyguard who was next to the old man hit him with the butt of the rifle in the back, once more dropping the older man to the floor. The other two grabbed the doctor's hands and stretched them out. A pirate moved up with a handheld crossbow and shot at the hands but missed as the healer resisted, trying to fight his way to his grandchildren, who were being dragged away, the girl screaming and the boy only cried as his hands extended out reaching out for his grandfather.

The Empress's face showed utter irritation and glared at the captain. He rolled his eyes and sighed, mumbling to himself a curse in his native tongue. He looked around and the rest of the crew, plus half of the elite guard, were laughing hysterically at the buffoonish pirate that missed his shot. El Capitan turned to the crew and yelled out, "can anyone shoot around here?"

El Capitan heard and felt the three shots being fired off pass inches from his head, each hitting their mark. The guards holding the children suddenly released them as they fell on their faces with burning holes through their heads, killing them instantly. The third energy infused projectile hit a yelling Empress in the center of her head, leaving a hole of melting flesh through the center of her face. The woman was taken off her feet, thrown back a few meters and laid out on the flat of her back with her face sizzling. A warm barrel touched against the back of El Capitan's head. The man raised his hands as a sign of no hostility.

"I can," said a gruff voice from behind the pirate captain.

The pirate replied calmly, "my luck, I finally found someone that can shoot. Too bad he's pointed a gun at my head." El Capitan looked around and commanded loudly to the crew that was scattering for their weapons. "Easy now! Easy, I say!"

"I guess you are not as dumb as you look," the corporal told the captain.

"What? Is it the jacket, because I truly like it? I hear it makes my eyes pop," the man replied.

"I'll make your eyes pop if I pull this trigger again," the Ravager threatened.

"No, you won't. You know as I, that the rifle has jammed, I heard the fourth click," El Capitan replied in a low voice.

"So, why are we still here?" the soldier asked.

"The old man. He saved me once, just as he saved you, by the look of you. This was wrong, I want him to leave with his family, but I cannot go empty-handed, not in front of these rabid dogs. You for them. That is the only deal that will work at this point. And I promise to sell you to a decent slave master. Think fast, time is not a luxury we have."

The corporal looked at the two children, who raced to their grandfather and did not hesitate. "Agreed, how do you want to play it?"

"Tell the old man and the children to leave, that you will make sure we don't try anything. It will be painful, but with any luck we'll both live," the captain replied.

"Julius! Julius! Take the children and go. Hurry!"

The old man grabbed the children, rushing them into the mobile clinic pausing, for the soldier. The corporal didn't even turn his head when he told the man to "Go!" Closing the ramp to the vehicle, the trio sped off into the desert. Now the actual show was about to begin, between the corporal, El Capitan, and the rest.

The captain turned slightly with the gun still pointing at his head and said out loud for everyone to hear. "They have left, Señior. You can pull the trigger and die like a dog. For they will avenge me, after all, I am El Capitan! Or you can give me your weapon and surrender."

The corporal looked at El Capitan, who quickly turned, pushing the rifle off his head and with blinding speed drew his blaster and pointed it at him. The pirate captain had a smile on his face as he winked at the corporal. The closest guard that once held the old man grabbed his rifle and shouted out a battle cry, raising his weapon towards the young man when El Capitan shot him dead.

"This man belongs to me, and I am El CAPITAN!" he emphasized to everyone, then lowered his voice to a whisper. "You are quite chivalrous, my friend. Let us pray I can save you," the captain stated as he took the rifle, then added, "Let's go, our future awaits. Compai."

"Are we friends, Capitan?" the corporal asked skeptically.

"Right now. We are the only friends each of us have. Good luck to us," the charismatic man replied. Turning, calling out to the others. "Someone get me a slave collar," El Capitan said to the corporal as he gestured for him to move with his pistol. The soldier looked at the charismatic man from the corner of his eye and hobbled forward towards two men, both of which were the Empress's guards, who stopped before him, fingering their weapons with a murderous intent in their eyes.

"Capitan. This man belongs to the guard," one of them said.

"One would think, yes. But no! As per the rules, he threatened my life, and I captured him. So, NO! He belongs to me. But let us not fight over this... wreck of a man. Look at him, he can barely stand. I doubt we can even get 100 credits for him in the market. But this is not about profit, but of the clan's code. Yes?" the captain said with a smile.

Another man approached quickly with a circular collar that was in two halves. The man paused and looked at the pirate captain, who nodded in agreement. The man looked at the corporal who just stood there, with many thoughts running through his mind of how to escape and the killing order, but it was bleak no matter how he put it with so many combatants present.

"Compai, play nice, eh? That one is just a kid. Let him put the collar on you and don't resist, I would hate to have to shoot you and lose my hundred credits. Eh?" the captain explained as he called out another order. "Call the Code Master, we need him here now."

Orders echoed down the line of pirates and marauders. Moments later, an older man exited the ship. He was short, with a protruding belly and thick glasses. He carried a leather-bound book with him and scrambled to them, limp and all. He saw the body of the dead woman and guards and swallowed deeply, understanding that once again he was being called to decipher the code.

"Yesss, Captain. How can I be of ssservicesss?" he hissed like a snake.

"Ahhh, Code Master, welcome. Its so good to see you. But there is no time for pleasantries. The slave here killed the Empress," the captain explained.

The Code Master hissed at the corporal and looked on angrily.

"Tame yourself, Code Master, you have a job to do."

"Yessss, Capitan," the fat little man replied.

"Code Master, as I said before, the slave killed the Empress and put a gun to my head. I disarmed and captured him. The royal guard believe that he belongs to them, I say otherwise, and that he is mine. What says the code, eh?" El Capitan explained, as he waved the pistol around, using dramatic hand gestures in his speech.

"The code. The code is one and bindss uss all. I sssay the guardsss have a claim, sssince their charge wasss attacked, but, sssince ssshe isss dead, the claim goesss to you Capitan, for you were the lassst to be threatened by the asssailant and did capture him. You are alssso now in charge of the band until we get back to the cavern and all rightful partiesss can place claim to the leadersship. But the ssslave isss yoursss, unlesss next of kin want to challenge you for him within three daysss of today." The fat little man looked at everyone, affirming they understood him.

"As always, Code Master, your wisdom is beyond contention. Let us take queenie over there and get back home," the captain said with a smirk.

"The Empress, you mean," one guard retorted.

"Ah, yes, please forgive me. The words of your language elude me at times. Let us collect the body and return, yes?" the man corrected.

"We will take her," the guard sternly replied.

"Very well, it is only fitting. She was your charge." Turning and addressing the rest of the crew, "the show is over. Let us get our things and return to the cave," El Capitan said out loud, hearing the murmur of the crew.

"What about the doctor?" one marauder asked demandingly.

"What about the doctor? Let him go. I am sure we will run into him again, and we may need his service at some point. We would deeply feel his loss to the wasteland. Let him run with the fear in his heart. It only helps us in the end. Now let's go" the man bellowed.

The fifty or so people that were around begrudgingly accepted the man's words and moved on. The guards took the body of the Empress and their three fallen comrades and loaded them into the vehicle. The captain turned to one of his old crew men and gave him instructions to take the prisoner and put him in a separate cell. He then picked a member of his old crew to guard him. Though his old crew were no longer reliable, they were more reliable than the others who would kill his prisoner at first chance.

Everyone was leaving as the man holstered his weapon and cleared the rifle, aimed it at a rock, taking a shot out into the desert. He looked at it and nodded in approval. Then told himself in a low voice, "Not bad, Capitan, not bad at all."

Chapter 5

The days passed slowly as the Mistress of Mayhem crawled through the darkness of space. Billy spent his time making some repairs to the thrusters and engines when he wasn't messing around with Emmy, which was constant as they both enjoyed the ship's facilities. Emmy was floating on a cloud, letting out over two years of repressed anger and isolation, with sex, exercise, and the constant boasting of Billy. The young scientist had a newfound interest in her appearance and started enhancing her style with slightly more provocative attire, coupled with an increase passion for yoga and stretching exercises, claiming something about being limber.

Ophelia herself had taken on additional duties of her own in the upper levels, cleaning and polishing portions of the ship that had long been neglected.

Throughout those days, Mistress had finished her diagnostics and could now achieve hi-speed long range travel, even if it was at half of the engine's capacity. Cooling systems were underperforming throughout the ship, causing slowdowns and periodically adding more time to the trip. Amongst the problems on the ship, the communication system was in the worst condition and no messages had been sent out or had been received since the impact back at the asteroid field.

Despite everything that had transpired, the atmosphere in the ship seemed livelier and Billy seemed to play music at almost all times of the day and night. Emmy was very cheerful and accommodating about most tasks, when she could be found. Things seemed to move in a positive direction and they had even made their delivery on time. They had the problem of a nonfunctioning loader, but Billy was able to get the services of a loader, the catch was Mistress had to make a delivery for them in exchange with a signed contract. The crew had gotten some more supplies and a few extra loads destined for Taidar.

After the delivery, Emmy asked permission to go out with Billy, and after Billy had come through with the loader, Ophelia found it hard to say no. She even gave them a few credits for the evening. She wanted to go shopping, but as per the contract with the GDF for the prisoner transport, someone had to stay with the ship at all times.

Having the ship to herself felt nice, yet awkward. It was comforting knowing someone else was on the ship. She sat in the theater with a hot cup of coco and some snacks, looking forward to relaxing and watching a movie. Wearing loose fitting pajamas and some old fuzzy slippers, the young woman had forgotten her life for a moment and let herself drift away in the entertainment for a few hours.

After the movie, she walked down to the cargo bay to check on the transport pod with the prisoners in stasis. The cargo hold was dimly lit, to conserve power, since power was expensive in the outer rim. Being low on funds, she decided on saving for repairs of the comm systems. The planet was lacking in qualified personnel, so the repair would have to wait. She could hear her slippers drag on the metal floor echoing in the large cargo bay, which gave her an eerie feeling. The awkwardness of the situation made her pull the robe around her tighter, turning on her flashlight, she made her way to inspect the pod. She looked at every corner of the cargo hold, feeling very uncomfortable. *There is no one here Ophelia, it's just your nerves. If someone was here, Mistress would have picked them up long ago. Come on now, Ophelia, you've been to this cargo area a thousand times. I should have known better than to watch a scary movie.*

She approached the pod and checked the cord along with the connections. Ophelia knew she was feeling a little paranoid, but that happened occasionally after her incident with the pirates. Checking the information screen, all pods were secure, the temperatures were correct, as was the status of every pod. The door was locked, and everything checked out. She passed by the glass and flashed the light in, looking into every pod, everything seemed secure and functioning.

These men all looked mean, even asleep, she thought to herself while she was looking at their scars and tattoos that were on their necks and sometimes face. One by one, she checked each pod until she reached the last one that held a woman. Flashing the light into the pod, she saw two eyes looking back at her, which made her jump back in fright, dropping the flashlight. Looking back to the pod and seeing nothing but darkness except for the dim glow of the individual pod's panel lights, she quickly scrambled to the floor and grabbed the flashlight, flashing back to the woman's face, whose eyes were now closed.

"Mistress, run scans on all pods right now! That woman looked at me," she cried out.

"Running diagnostics on stasis pods right now. Pods 1, 2, and 3 have passed diagnostics. Pods 4, 5, and 6 have also passed diagnostics. All pods pass diagnostics and are running within normal ranges," the AI replied.

"I know what I saw! Her eyes were open," The young woman insisted.

"Then open the door and check it out. Security protocols are activated," Mistress answered.

Ophelia looked up and around the room. Seeing 6 doors slide open and 3 automated guns dropping out of the compartments, each pointing their red guidance dots towards the pod. The young woman took a deep breath, grabbed her elongated flashlight like a club, as she moved toward the door, punching in the code.

The security door accepted her code and slid open, letting out the frosty air that was held in the transport pod. Quickly she moved towards the last pod and looked inside, flashing her light from the woman's head down to her toes, and saw nothing. She aimed the light right at the woman's eyes and increased the brightness setting to maximum, the woman didn't even flinch. The lights on the panel all seemed to be working. Ophelia pounded on the thick clear panels, still the woman did not flinch. Second guessing herself, she exited the transport pod, securing the door behind her.

"I swore I saw her eyes open," the young woman said out loud.

"Though highly unlikely, it is possible that in stasis she could have briefly opened her eyes, as if she were blinking. It is more likely that you saw a reflection of the light and thought her eyes were open. Either way, I can maintain security protocols active and keep the guns out," Mistress replied.

"No. Just keep your sensors active and keep the protocols on standby. No need to scare or inform the others of our weaponry with the guns out, they are supposed to be a secret. Just stay vigilant," The young woman commanded.

"Yes, captain. Please get some rest."

Mistress had taken over the watch, allowing Ophelia to get some rest, she had advanced security protocols that allowed for several thousand scenarios. Allowing two crew members back on board was easy enough.

The damage they had sustained caused an additional strain on the engines and thrusters. That consumption of fuel more than doubled during take-offs and landings, forcing them to fuel up again as a precaution, since the engines had less power than normal, making them work more and waste more to do the same job. Not wanting any more delays, the Mistress of Mayhem and her crew finally disconnected from the port and were ready to depart for the delivery of the prisoners. Ophelia could not wait to get those stasis pods off her ship. Since the incident from the other night, she decided to keep a knife on her at all times.

Billy had double checked the systems and confirmed everything that Mistress's diagnostic had already told her. Having everything ready, they lifted off and set a course for Tersa 4; it was not a very long trip, but it would take at least a week.

The trip seemed uneventful and Ophelia, for once, was glad to have others onboard. She had kept herself busy with ship maintenance and extra sessions with her virtual combat trainer. Emmy had helped with some chores and cleaning, while Billy was trying desperately to fix the comm systems and figure out the issues with the thrusters.

"Captain?" Mistress called.

"Yes, Mistress," replied the Captain.

"Billy is looking for you. He believes he may have found a way to fix the communication systems and the thrusters, but would require a full system reboot. That would include me, too. I don't think that wise," the ship said.

"Let's see what he has to say," Ophelia replied.

Reaching the cargo area, Ophelia saw Billy halfway into an open panel. She looked over at the transport pod, thinking of the fright she got a few nights ago. The entire cargo area was open, letting her see completely across most of the area. She saw the old loader and the box of parts, sitting in a mess-another project Billy had started, but had to stop to work on the comm systems.

"Billy!" The captain called out.

"Ouch!" Billy said as he turned, hitting himself hard and grunted in pain. Slowly making his way out of the panel, he looked at Ophelia with irritation as he rubbed his head. The young woman was trying to hold back a laugh as she looked away and then back towards the young man with sincerity.

"Are you okay?"

"Yeah, I'm fine. I just feel like I have been stuck in a panel for the last three days," he replied.

"Well, that's because you have. So, what have you found?" she asked.

"Well, I think I found the problem, and I can't fix it per se, but I can offer a short-term solution. That engineer was right about the part that is bad, but I can bypass it and need to shut down the whole system, while I work on it, since comms are integrated into most of the ships systems, and I for one don't want to get electrocuted," Billy said pulling a rag out of his pocket, cleaning his hands and face before continuing. "Now, as for the engines, if we shut down the ship and give it like 15 minutes, we can reset the relay to the thrusters and get them back online so we can finally finish this run and get rid of this cargo."

"I don't know about that. I don't like the idea of rebooting the system completely and taking Mistress offline," the young woman said doubtfully.

"Well, that's what it takes, I can't do anything about it. We can do both at once, to not prolong the process, but the complete system must be down for those 15 minutes or that relay won't reset. I am 93 percent certain this will work. I've done a lot of research, and in my experience, this will take care of it," the young man said confidently.

"Look Billy, I'm sure you're working very hard, but Mistress has very complex systems. I don't think, and more so, she doesn't think it's a good idea," the young woman replied.

"What? I'm telling you this will work, right now she can't even fire up those thrusters, ask her if she can reset the relays or even communicate with them? Go ahead, ask her. I'm not lying," the young man replied defensively.

"No-one said anything about you lying or your ability, Billy. Relax," the young woman interjected.

"I don't think that will work, but Billy is correct. I cannot access or communicate with those relays or those systems. It is possible that a shutdown will reestablish those relays, or at least my communication with the thrusters, which is very important. What about the prisoner transport pod?" Mistress said in an even tone to help defuse the situation.

"What about the pod? It's on its own system, even if you power down, it will remain functioning on its own power for months. Mistress has checked the systems, I have checked the systems, and if one pod becomes deactivated, or it starts an opening sequence, it takes hours for any of those people to even stand. We three can easily subdue anyone in those pods or just leave the door locked. It's safe, Captain," Billy said encouragingly.

"Fine. We will shut everything down for 15 minutes and no more. Mistress, make sure we are in a suitable spot, come to a full stop, and shut down. Also, turn on the emergency lights and call Emmy, tell her to get down here," The young woman said with authority.

As the trio stood before the pod, Billy began his explanation. "Okay, while the ship shuts down, I will run to the thrusters and reset the relays, then I will run to the communications array and switch the cabling into a bypass to get comms back online, while you two stay here and monitor the prisoner. We so got this," the young man said enthusiastically.

"Yes, we got this!" Exclaimed Emmy excitedly.

"I guess," replied Ophelia skeptically.

"Ok! Captain, give Mistress the order, I will start making my way to the thrusters," Billy stated, and moved off.

Sighing, Ophelia shook her head, second guessing the decision. She looked at Emmy, who was excited, and then to Billy as he walked off. She walked with the scientist around the prisoner transport pod. A few moments later, a loud noise came from the other side of the pod, as if something had just fallen, bringing both women's eyes to the side of the pod, where they saw a hand. Recognizing that it was Billy's hand waving, the two let out a sigh of relief.

"Sorry, I tripped," the young man cried out.

Ophelia looked at Emmy and shook her head. "I have more doubt than ever about this plan."

"Oh, don't you worry, he's a little goofy, but he'll come through. You'll see," the young scientist said optimistically.

"Mistress, begin shut down procedures. Place a timer for 15 minutes to begin the re-start sequence," the young woman instructed.

"Re-initiating? Timer? How can she if she's shut down?" Emmy asked, confused.

"The ship has a separate backup system. Mistress is the primary interface, though," Ophelia answered.

"Back up? But is Billy in danger?" The young woman asked, concerned.

"Don't worry, Emmy, your boyfriend is fine. Well, unless he breaks my ship, that is. The Master system is more of an internal core system, to my understanding, it's not really connected to anything anymore," was the despondent answer.

"What..." Emmy was about to ask for clarification when Ophelia interrupted.

"About two years ago, pirates boarded the ship and stripped a bunch of parts before the defense force arrived. They ran off with a bunch of weaponry and other systems, but not before they killed two of my friends and crew. That's why I want this damn pod off my ship," the captain said, irritated, as she kicked the side of the pod.

"Damn pirates. They didn't have to kill them. We weren't even fighting back, and they just murdered them before they left. They only left me because they wanted to spread the fear of their existence. I was the "lucky one" they said and laughed as they left.... Bastards!" She yelled at the pod and kicked it again.

There was silence for a moment when suddenly the pod door slid open. Both women look at each other and then towards the door, but they heard nothing. The two leaned in, looking into the pod when a woman walked out wearing a prisoner's uniform and looked at them, sinisterly with a delicate smile. She leaned on the doorway as she sized the two girls up.

"You were lucky, if you ask me," the woman said casually and sighed. "Most women are raped by pirate crews, and either taken as slaves or killed. So, you were lucky, after all. But this time, you'll lose more than just a couple of friends and some systems. This time you will lose your ship and maybe, if I find it amusing, I will let you join your friends. Maybe I will rape you, or worse, give you to them," the woman said, pointing into the pod's interior.

The woman's tone was casual, and she moved with confident arrogance as she pointed to the others in the pod. Ophelia was shocked and frozen, but Emmy charged the woman with a sudden burst of desperation, her little feet moving quickly as she closed the distance between them. The experienced criminal sidestepped her and pushed her headfirst into the pod, leaving her stunned and with a bloody nose.

The woman was tall with an athletic body from years of training and good genetics. Her long curly hair and dark eyes could easily entice most men and the way she moved showed a confidence of her ability. Ophelia looked at Emmy who was slumped on the floor and then shifted her gaze back to the woman as she casually glanced down, unimpressed at the bloody faced girl on the floor. Her predatory eyes moved back to Ophelia, who stepped back filled with terror as she tried to make sense of it, but only one thing came to mind.

"You did open your eyes, but you were in stasis," she said accusingly.

The pirate laughed at the young woman before her and sauntered forward. "Yes. Yes, I did, and yes, I was, yet here I am. I understand now why you ran in to verify. It was smart to flash that bright light into my face. Not very nice and painful, but smart. Too bad it didn't work; you could have foiled my plans right there."

"But how? We checked the systems," she asked furiously.

"How? Oh, little girl, the things I have done would make priests weep" Grabbing the cord connected to the pod, she kicked it free with her foot and yanked it into her hand. Removing a connector from the tip, she tossed it to the young captain. Emmy tried to move, but it only earned her a whipping with the cord from the pirate, causing her to cry out in pain and curl into a ball.

"Be still or I'll hurt you more, you little bitch!" the woman said, with venom in her tone, then looked at Ophelia and continued, "that which you are holding slowly brought me out of stasis while programming the machine to show that everything was normal. The most difficult thing was watching that handsome idiot screw this little slut all over the cargo hold. Though I must admit, some of it was a bit arousing," she looked down at Emmy that was still holding on to her head and midsection, from the first hits.

The sudden viciousness was surprising to Ophelia. Her hand shook with fear and anger as she continued to step away, searching for an avenue of escape, but she didn't want to leave Emmy. Looking at her crewmate once more on the floor, Ophelia refused to have a repeat of what happened last time, and moved closer to the pirate taking a few quick jabs and swings that the woman easily evaded or countered, landing two hits on Ophelia instead.

The woman glared at Ophelia with a serious demeanor, but wore a casual smile on her face. The young captain knew she was outmatched and so did the pirate, the woman was toying with them, and there was little she could do.

Grabbing a small chip she had hidden on her body; the pirate placed it on the interface connection of the stasis pod, knowing that it would begin the wakening process of her other crew mates in stasis, something that would give her a clear advantage.

"You are a dirty little slut, aren't you?" the pirate mocked Emmy.

The woman kicked the young scientist hard in the stomach, causing the young girl to lose her breath, but also something unexpected happened, when she kicked her, Emmy flew back about three meters. Ophelia and the pirate both looked a bit surprised, and both figured it out at the same time. Gravity was at a minimal. Turning, the pirate charged at Ophelia, who just jumped up and over the cargo.

"Get back here, girl!" The woman howled and gave chase.

"Run Emmy! RUN!" Ophelia yelled to her friend.

Ophelia had run in low gravity as a kid and a teenager, she liked the feeling of semi flight. Being the daughter of such a prominent defense contractor, it afforded her opportunities others did not have, and playing with military training toys was one of them. The chase was not one sided though, the pirate woman was keeping up with her, given her years of experience in space.

Emmy had managed to get to her feet and looked into the transport pod, fearful of the other criminals coming out, and saw their panels with different readings than what they were supposed to have on the display. Having vast experience with stasis equipment, since she was required to keep plants alive and healthy for transport in stasis, was par for the course for a Botanist. Botany was just one subject she had a doctorate in, amongst all of her other degrees.

She stumbled into the pod, holding her face with one hand and her stomach with the other as she made her way to the control panel to re-initialize the stasis pods to their proper state. Occasionally, she peeked out of the window and saw the two women jumping around the cargo hold. She looked to the upper floors, expecting Billy to return at any moment, giving them the advantage they needed. "Damn it, Billy, where are you?" Emmy grumbled.

Ophelia knew she could not run forever, and decided that she would attack the woman while on the move. Knowing the ship and using it to her advantage, she jumped towards the loader's spare parts box and picked up the first thing she could see and hurled it at the pirate as she was coming in and leaped away.

The metal piece struck the woman hard, causing her to stumble as she landed, but she was not deterred and still on her feet. Pausing only to grab a bar, with the intention of using it as a club, and continued to give chase. Ophelia did not jump this time and just ran when she landed and turned, throwing the second part she had grabbed, that was a large metal sprocket. The pirate tried to cover herself and block the sprocket, but it hit the bar and swiveled around it and passed her face, cutting her cheek. The woman screamed in rage. "You little bitch! You're going to pay for that."

The woman paused, taking in a deep breath composing herself, "I will not play your game. Given the number of people on your ship, you will show up eventually. A crew of two is not enough to stop me. I own your ship now little girl, you got guts, but it will get you nowhere. I, own your ship."

Crew of two, but Billy is part of this crew, and she knows it. Why did she not say three? The young captain thought to herself. She needed time to think and process, but how was she going to overcome this woman who had already beaten on Emmy cruelly? Seeing Emmy's pod, she moved behind it.

The pirate looked around her unfamiliar surroundings and began making her way back to the stasis pods quietly when she heard a sound in the distance of metal clanging on the floor as something fell. Ophelia muttered a silent curse, knowing she had given her position away. Moving again to distance herself as much as possible from the sound, she pushed off and floated away quietly.

Arriving back at the stasis pod, the pirate looked to the floor, surprised to see Emmy was no longer there, and continued scanning the area. Just as the pirate was leaving, she caught a glimpse of the small woman she had beaten earlier, working franticly on one of the stasis pods, and grinned. The pirate tightened her grip on a pipe she had grabbed to hit Emmy, but a piece flew off the end as she twirled it, clanging loudly on the floor, causing her to look at the scientist who was now looking back aware of the escapee's presence, with a sense of fear filling her.

Ophelia also heard the sound and made her way around some of the cargo. Moving to where she could see the front of the transport pod. Emmy had done four out of the five remaining pods and looked around for something to defend herself with, having no exit. The woman was at the entrance of the pod with the pipe in hand, while

Ophelia was quietly sneaking up behind her with her knife, ready to strike.

"Hey, captain, I'm back," the women heard Billy say as he made his way casually down the stairs.

Ophelia and the pirate froze for a moment, each aware of the possibility of their positions being given away. In the pod Emmy felt cornered and looked around, seeing no way of escape, and the woman who had already beaten her badly now standing at the doorway with a pipe in her hand between her and the exit. Fearing for her life, she charged the armed criminal, using her petite frame as a weapon, colliding with the woman and pinning the arm, holding the pipe.

The pirate was a seasoned fighter and having dealt with opponents much larger and more skilled than the young scientist, moved with the blow, being more accustomed to near zero G conditions and twirled in what would have been an acrobatic feat, coming down on the young woman's back with a devastating forearm that made Emmy's feet buckle.

Ophelia saw the small woman go to her knees and charged the pirate with her knife, slicing her across her back. The criminal arched her back in pain and broke the small scientist's grip on her and pushed Emmy away from her and towards the side of the pod. Turning with the pipe at the ready, the woman looked at Ophelia, then her eyes darted behind Ophelia, and back to the young woman and grinned.

Billy moved up behind Ophelia, stating loudly, "I'm here, captain. Let's get her."

Rushing forward and wrapping his arms around Ophelia. Ophelia's arms and legs flailed for a moment, then remembering one of her combat fighting lessons, she stabbed behind her with her knife, digging the blade into the young man. Billy grimaced in pain but didn't release her.

"You traitorous bastard!" Ophelia yelled at him.

Emmy was leaning against the pod and saw the betrayal of her lover and felt enraged. Next to her was a loose cargo strap and buckle, which she grabbed and charged the pirate, swinging with all her might. The buckle struck the woman hard on her chest, driving her back clutching her chest where the metal buckle had hit.

Billy flung Ophelia at the wall, causing her to bounce off the bulkhead. She was dazed but stayed on her feet and lunged forward in desperation, attacking the young man. To her fortune, her aim was true and plunged the knife deep into Billy's torso. Billy took two steps back, surprised, clutching his torso as blood filled through his hands and floated everywhere, some even hitting Ophelia in the face.

He looked at his hands, then held them out, showing his blood-stained hands to Ophelia and then to the pirate captain. "Captain?" he said with a voice filled with fear as his eyes locked with the pirate prisoner. The young man fell to his knees, holding his hands out to the pirate, his eyes pleading for help as he felt the life slowly slipping out of him.

The woman and Emmy both cried out, "NO!"

The pirate looked at her angrily, shoving Emmy towards the pod again, hard.

Ophelia did not hesitate and lunged at the criminal having seen an opening, but she was not fast enough for the experienced pirate that attacked her, hitting her arm with the pipe. Emmy regained her footing and pushed off the pod, swinging the metal buckle, hitting the pirate with a glancing blow to the head, making her stumble forward.

Billy laid on the ground bleeding out and reached out for the pirate and called to her, "Roxy."

The pirate looked at the young man and hurried to him. Emmy had swung at the woman again but missed and almost hit Ophelia, who barely dodged the attack.

The pirate grabbed Billy, blood trickling from the side of her head, pulling him away from the area and behind some cargo, pausing the fight. Emmy moved over to Ophelia and gave her a hand up. "You, okay?" Emmy asked.

"I think so. You?" replied Ophelia.

"I'm okay, but I think my face is still bleeding," Emmy responded, touching her face, then continued. "We need to hurry, she put those stasis pods on a quick revive cycle. I locked out the others, but I missed the last one. I don't know what would have happened if you had not gotten here when you did."

"I don't know about that, it looked like you were holding your own there," Ophelia said offering a comforting smile.

The young scientist grinned then hurriedly reentered the transport pod, her captain fast on her heals. Emmy reached the console of the last stasis pod and quickly began resetting the stasis chamber. The man inside was a burly man that was in the last stages of revival. He was trying to shake the grogginess off as the door hissed and slid open, releasing the remaining pressure.

The man leaned forward with an angry growl and a surprised expression seeing the young captain before him, with a snarl he tried to push out of the stasis pod, but was met with a punch to his face and a snarl back from Ophelia. The man's head snapped back, sending him back into the chamber. Ophelia grabbed the door and pushed it closed as she shook her other hand, that now hurt.

"Hurry, Emmy!" she commanded.

"Almost got it," the young scientist replied.

Her fingers typed as fast as she could, while Ophelia leaned into the door, holding it shut. The crazed prisoner, now angry and irritated, was banging on the clear door, screaming profanities. He pushed at the artificial glass, but having nothing to hold on to, his hands just slipped across the smooth surface.

"GOT IT!" Emmy cried out.

"Noooo..." yelled the pirate, but was cut short as the cryogenic state was implemented, his eyes bulged and turn red as the fluid in his eyes froze and in moments was frozen solid with hands clenched into fists against the glass.

"Is that normal?" Ophelia asked, shocked.

"Not really. I tweaked it a bit to hurry the process. He might be permanently blind, there is no way of telling, but better him than us, right?" Emmy said as she shrugged her shoulders.

"Definitely," Ophelia approved.

They cut the brief celebration short when the female pirate slammed the pipe hard against the transport pod's door. Her anger was clearly visible on her face. Ophelia quickly pulled her knife that still had some of Billy's blood on it in front of her defensively, and Emmy bent down, slowly picking up the strap.

"Where is your doctor?" the pirate demanded.

"We have none," Ophelia replied.

"Then his death is on you."

"No. His death is on him for being a traitor. But if you surrender now, we can save his life," Ophelia replied.

The woman paused, considering the options. "How?"

"You surrender, and we can put him in stasis in your pod. As for you, I will confine you to our security ward. Take it or leave it, but time is not on your side," Ophelia advised.

"I can kill you both and put him into stasis myself," The woman threatened.

"Maybe, but he will be dead by then and that is only if you win. That's not a guarantee. Play by my rules and everyone lives," Ophelia countered.

The tension was thick in the small pod as the veteran pirate considered her options. Precious seconds passed, and the pirate quickly decided. Dropping the pipe on the ground, she put her hands up, acknowledging the terms.

"Fine," the woman begrudgingly agreed.

"Bring Billy, I will get the med kit to seal his wounds until he can receive the medical attention he needs in Tersa 4. Emmy, you prepare the stasis pod," Ophelia instructed.

"What, but they tried to kill us? And they are pirates. They won't keep their word," The scientist protested.

"Maybe, but if she doesn't comply, Billy won't enter stasis and we are back to fighting it out. And even if she wins, she can't fly the ship without Mistress, and Mistress won't respond without my authority, so she'd be stuck out here no way to communicate or start the ship. Now prep the pod before Billy dies," Ophelia responded.

"I should let him die. Lying bastard," Emmy protested.

"You better not," the woman replied threateningly.

"She won't. Just bring him here," Ophelia reassured her and shot a glance at Emmy.

The pirate moved off to retrieve the injured Billy, while Ophelia moved to a panel in the pod, removing an emergency medical kit and some restraints. Emmy was annoyed about the whole thing and prep the pod angrily. At one point, she turned to protest, and Ophelia quickly cut her off.

"I'm the captain, and those are my orders. You don't have to like them, but you have to follow them."

Ophelia grabbed a healing solution injector, which would act like a patch, sealing the wound, and stop any bleeding internally and externally with a medical solution. The young man's breath was shallow, and he had lost a lot of blood that had partially stained his clothing. The pirate picked up the young man, placing him in the pod, which was easy enough in minimal gravity. With genuine sentiment, she caressed his cheek as he looked back at her.

"You gorgeous idiot. I love you so much," the woman declared to him.

The young man was on the verge of unconsciousness, but smiled back at her as he softly caressed her retreating arm. The woman closed the glass, placing her hand on the glass.

Once Billy was in and the door closed, the stasis process slowly began, allowing Billy to go gently to sleep, a massive difference from the burly pirate from before. A light frost filled the glass and his stats displayed on the screen.

Ophelia quickly placed a security cuff on one of the pirate's hands, causing the woman to turn. She was about to react when Ophelia quickly cut in.

"Please let us conclude our business peacefully. Emmy will stay here with her finger near the emergency awakening process, which will be such a shock to Billy that it would most likely kill him instantly. Let's call it an insurance policy for your compliance."

"She wouldn't," the pirate protested.

"I'm a jaded lover lady, don't think I will hesitate for a moment," Emmy shot back angrily.

The pirate relaxed and gave her other hand to Ophelia willingly. Having both hands in security cuffs, the two women moved off. They could hear soft whimpers coming from Emmy as they left the area. Riding the lift to the security ward, the pirate broke the silence.

"Can we trust her not to hurt Billy?"

"She may be jaded, but she cared for him, but who could really say? I, on the other hand, would just as quickly flush you two out into space, but you keep your end of the bargain, I'll keep mine," Ophelia replied evenly.

"You are very clever and with some seasoning, you will make an excellent captain. I can teach you that," the pirate offered.

"I'm sure you could, but I'm no pirate. Plus, I can't afford to trust a backstabber like you. No offense," Ophelia replied.

"None taken, after all, I am a pirate," the woman chuckled.

Enclosing the pirate in her cell, Ophelia deactivated the cuffs and picked them up off the floor. The pirate looked around the room and nodded at the accommodations. She tested the mattress and sat down.

"Kudos to you. You are quite the clever girl, but you are so far in over your head out here. What brings you out here and with such a ship? Are you a little princess that decided to become a spacefarer? Spent too much money on a ship with no crew. Did you steal it? Either way, I like it, this mattress is heavenly. I may have to take it from you some day," the pirate replied casually.

"You may try, but you'll find I will not be so accommodating next time," Ophelia sternly replied.

"I like you, you are smart, but as I said before; you are way over your head out here, little girl. I'm surprised you made it this far," the pirate said casually.

"I'll manage."

"I wasn't always a pirate, you know."

"Yeah. Well, you're one now," Ophelia said as she left the area.

Ophelia worried about Emmy and rushed back, only to find her crying in the pod's corner. Rushing to her side. "Are you okay?" she asked.

"No. I... I thought things were finally changing," the petite woman said between tears.

"They will, it'll just take time. But at least we're alive and the sex was good for a while. Right?" Ophelia said jokingly.

Emmy just looked at Ophelia with a face. Ophelia shrugged. "Too soon?"

"Yeah. But you're right, the sex was wonderful," The young scientist chuckled. "I really liked him," she added sadly.

"I know," Ophelia replied and hugged her friend.

"How did this happen?" Emmy asked.

"I'm not sure, but I promise to find out, after I get Mistress online."

"Oh, yeah. Wasn't she supposed to come back online after 15 minutes?"

"That's right. And it's been over an hour easy. I have to check all the systems to see what that idiot messed up. You go get cleaned up and lie down and I'll make some food after I get the ship up and running. We are sitting ducks right now, just drifting and with no major shields," Ophelia answered.

"That's not good. Need help?" Emmy asked, worried.

"Nah, you've done enough for today, go on, get some rest and I'll check on you soon," Ophelia answered.

"Aye, Captain..." Emmy forced a smile as she lingered. "Thanks for not abandoning me."

"Yeah, you, too," Ophelia replied sincerely.

Chapter 6

"How do you like your accommodation, eh?" the pirate captain asked.

The soldier looked up and turned his head slightly, having one eye extremely swollen. His arms were extended wide and were held by chains attached to his wrists and ankles. He was badly bruised from some of his original injuries and from the many beatings he had taken in the last week after parting ways with the doctor and his grandchildren.

"I haven't had a massage in a few days. Despite that, I can't feel my arms and I haven't seen the sun in... I don't know how long, not to mention the food sucks. Other than that, I've been in worse," was the young man's reply with a hint of cynicism.

El Capitan chuckled. "It is good to keep your spirits up, yes?"

"Let me ask—did you order all these beatings?" the corporal asked in a level tone.

"The beatings? No, my friend. I did not, I wish I could have made those nonexistent, but there is only so much I can do. With the Empress dead, there is a power struggle going on for the next in line of succession. They have ordered the beating to show their intolerance to those that attack the consortium," the man said casually.

"Consortium?" he asked, confused.

"Yes, my friend. The Consortium of Pirates, it was the Empress's father's idea decades ago, but he met an untimely demise at his daughter's hands. She ascended into power and now she is dead, leaving a vacuum. A vacuum and an opportunity for some, not so much for others. Fortunately, I am one of those that is provided an opportunity," the man said with a grin on his face.

"I don't know if I want to hear this part. Your opportunities seem rather burdensome and painful for me," the soldier replied.

The captain walked around the cage slowly, looking at the young man and sizing him up. "Do you regret your actions?" the captain asked with a curious eyebrow raised.

"Nope. I regret not being in better condition to fight those that have come to visit. But as far as that old man and those kids, I'd do it again," the corporal said with conviction.

"That is noble Compai. Foolish, but noble," El Capitan replied and continued walking slowly, looking around until he reached the back of the cage near the prisoner's ear and whispered, "Since she brought me into the folds, I have the opportunity to leave and I'll take you with me, as agreed."

"Are you still going to sell me?" the prisoner asked.

"As agreed," the man stated, as he partially turned, wearing a sly grin. "Stay alive Compai," the pirate said with a wave as he walked off.

The next few days were uneventful, except for an extra visit from some other pirates to share more of their "hospitality" and El Capitan, who would bring him some hydration fluid and talk with him about random subjects. On two of those occasions, the man even loosened the tension on the restraints, allowing the corporal a small but welcomed reprieve. Each night he would end with the same phrase, "Stay alive, Compai," and walk away.

One afternoon, four members of the consortium came to the cell, placed an electronic collar on the prisoner and set him loose. The prisoner collapsed to the floor. Having been in the same position for more than a week, his body was on fire and every fiber screamed in pain as he struggled just to sit up.

"Get up! Or rot in here," a guard stated harshly.

Grabbing onto the prison bars, he struggled, but finally stood. Wobbly and with legs threatening to give out, he forced himself towards the door even if he wasn't very sturdy. Slowly placing one unsteady foot in front of the other, the prisoner stumbled out of his cell. The pirates' words were harsh, but none of them touched him besides a light shove, to keep him moving forward, a treatment that differed from the other days.

Long stone corridors decorated the consortium's stronghold was mostly dug out with portions of technology scattered about the building. The group slowly made their way out of the building and into an entryway, with a set of large heavy doors that were open, announcing the bright afternoon sun outside. The corporal shielded his eyes with his hand, not having seen light for more than a week. The sun's rays felt like sharp knives digging into his eye sockets.

He was urged forward by the other pirates, again lightly, which contrasted the harsh demeanor of their previous interactions. Ahead of him he saw a large crowd and, in the center, giving a boastful speech was El Capitan. All the other members of the consortium encircled him and laughed and cheered him to continue on, and he did. The man was naturally charismatic and played to the crowd with extravagant charm.

Behind El Capitan was an old and partially rusted out land vehicle with a mismatched color scheme from the various parts that held it together. The rear of the vehicle held a considerable storage area that was filled with various boxes full of cargo tied down onto it and even filling the back seat of the decrepit convertible.

The pirate captain saw the corporal and turned, pointing towards him with both hands. "For me? A slave! Admiral, you are too kind, I don't know what to say. Wait, yes I do. CHA-CHING!" the man said loudly, mimicking the sounds of a centuries old cash machine, which was still a popular sound amongst merchants selling their wares.

The consortium burst out laughing and hollering, as they cheered El Capitan on, celebrating his departure with tall glasses of drinks and bottles of other alcoholic liquids. Another pirate captain stood close to El Capitan, nodding and laughing with the others. He was a tall man and was well dressed in a plumed admiral's hat and other decorative medals on his new long coat. The corporal looked at this other man next to El Capitan and understood. *This must be the new head of the consortium.*

For your dedicated service to the consortium, I, Admiral Mazik, here by award you this slave." He paused and grinned. "If he can make it to your vehicle." The crowd roared with laughter as the Admiral raised his cup to El Capitan. "For your dedicated service to the consortium, may your cup never be dry, and may your pockets always be full, with someone else's loot."

Raising his glass, all the pirates joined in and cheered the departing member. The admiral approached the departing captain with a device in his hand. He raised his hand high and pushed a button that said a forceful electric shock through the collar on the corporal's neck, dropping him to the ground in spasms.

Even in his condition, a sudden surge filled the soldier and almost overtook his senses, but he fought back, barely keeping his sanity and the rage in check. As he lay on the ground recovering, other cheers were raised, he could feel the adrenalin coursing through his veins and something more, he was now feeling stronger.

"He is all yours, my friend, as promised," the admiral said as he reached El Capitan and gave him the shock collars control device.

The admiral embraced the captain with genuine sentiment and raised his hand as he turned to the crowd once more, who cheered and howled like raving lunatics.

"I wish you well my friend, and tell you to steel yourself, for the last tradition is almost upon you. Give us a good show," Admiral Mazik finished with a hidden nod of an undisclosed agreement.

The admiral raised his hand once again as he walked off, gaining more cheers from the crowd as he walked away from El Capitan, giving the prisoner a dismissive glance. The captain looked around and then to his new slave, who was slowly trying to make his way to his feet, then stumbled close to him.

Now being close enough to the soldier, El Capitan helped him to the side of the vehicle and whispered nervously. "Compai, we are almost out of here, I just have to find a way to hurt the man that is about to punch me three times, without going unconscious or worse."

The corporal finally stood completely erect and stretched out the soreness in his body, somehow the surge had helped him, but there was still more to come as they heard another person near the admiral call for the crowd to settle. The woman walked out with her hand raised, then blew a whistle to calm the drunken hoard.

"Noble guests, it is always hard to depart, and it always pains us to see someone go. So, as with the consortium tradition, let the pains of departure begin. A consortium member will strike at the departing three times. One for the past, one for the present, and one for the future. That person will have five seconds to recover and strike back, per strike, if they do not strike within the five seconds, the next attack continues. To fall means to leave with nothing, to stand means to go with what they have collected, and to defeat the attacker means to leave with more treasure and the consortium's blessing."

The speaker paused, looking around at her audience, then with a slight grin continued. "The consortium's champion is the Destroyer of Armies, the Plunderer of ships, and the devastation to all who encounter him. I give you the Colossal Crusher, KALEEM!" the woman yelled loudly.

The crowd suddenly burst with excitement, as it was the pinnacle of the celebration. A large man measuring almost two and half meters in height with arms as thick as a man's legs made his way through the crowd. He had spiked chains crossing his chest, with skulls dangling from different sections as trophies of those who had fallen before him. Kaleem exited the crowd with his arms held high, claiming victory for himself and the consortium.

El Capitan gulped as the corporal looked towards him casually, then towards Kaleem. The soldier silently growled, recognizing Kaleem as one of his visitors and one that had come by various times to offer some of the consortium's hospitality with vicious strikes and kicks to him while he was bound and exposed. The soldier felt a surge begin within him once again, filling him with a desire to fight, to maim, and destroy, something that always came with the rage.

"Can I have something to drink?" the corporal asked.

"Sure, take mine," El Capitan said, his eyes not leaving the brute as he made his way to the center of the circle made by the crowd.

Taking the mug, the soldier smelled it, then downed it quickly. The liquid was refreshing and of better stock than normal, given that it was shared only by the admiral and his departing captain. The soldier wiped the froth from his lips with the back of his hand, looked at the empty mug, and placed it on the hood of the vehicle.

The corporal groan as he stretched, "he's a little out of your league."

"You think?" El Capitan replied nervously and swallowed hard. "That man is undefeated in the ring and on the battlefield. I have witnessed his prowess firsthand. I need to hurt that man and not die. Something that is much easier said than done."

Turning his head and cracking his neck bones, "what do you say I take this one?"

A surprised look came over the pirate's face, "You? You can barely stand. Whatever he can do to me, it will be much worse for you. Plus, I know he has visited you a few times to provide you with the consortium's hospitality. Though I may be no hero, this is my fate to deal with Compai."

"That man has beaten me a few times, but I can take it, even in this condition. You, my friend, will most likely die, and that means I have to stay. Anyway, I can take him out in two," the soldier responded confidently.

"Two? Are you mad? Has your sanity left you? Look at him, he's a monster."

The corporal leaned back against the vehicle, "Fine, you take the beating or we make a deal. You can still sell me, but when we get to town, I want a clean slate, a hefty meal, a hot shower, a nice bed to rest, and I pick the ship or person you sell me to. Deal?"

"What, you will not even negotiate for your freedom? Compai, really?" El Capitan retorted.

"As we agreed, you said. This is a different wager, a partnership, if you'd like. If you die, I am stuck here. If I do this, you're guaranteed to live and we can leave. Plus, you can make some extra credits and not get hurt," the corporal told the man as he continued to stretch.

Kaleem slowly made his way to them, each dramatic step made the crowd cheer louder and louder. The admiral stood with his guards at the head of the crowd, his eyes studying his other officers, who were most likely plotting against him already and this had something to do with it. He glanced back to El Capitan, his face etched with interest and concern, none of which was for the departing member of the consortium.

The giant reached the two men, towering over both of them. "Capitan, departure is such sweet sorrow, and I am here to deliver that sorrow, are you ready?"

The captain took in the monster before him, gauging his strength, then glanced towards his prisoner, then back to Kaleem with vigor. "Ready? Why yes, my friend, but it is not me who is your target, but my champion," he said casually, pointing to his prisoner that was still stretching.

"Your champion?" the giant asked, then let out a laugh. "Him!" the large man stated again, as he pointed towards the slave and laughed harder. "I will crush him. The gods and your foolishness favor me today! I will get my revenge for what you did to the Empress and appease my captain, keeping your spoils to his coffers and my pockets."

The pirate captain stepped away with a worried chuckle, leaving the two men to their fates. Seeing the captain move, the admiral quickly protested to the Code Master. The Code Master quickly approached, conferring with them before returning to the center.

The Code Master looked around then spoke loudly for all to hear, "El Capitan has chosssen his ssslave to be hisss champion, which isss well allowed by the rulesss of the consssortium. We are ready to begin on your order, Admiral"

The admiral glared at the captain with a disapproving scowl on his face, having no other option but to comply. "Is this your choice, Capitan?"

"It is, my admiral, wish me luck, he's going to need it," the captain said jokingly, earning some more hollering and laughing from the crowd.

"So be it. By the rules of the consortium, proceed," the admiral ordered.

The slave stepped forward; his hands barely raised when Kaleem swung hitting the much smaller man in the face sending him hurling towards the car. A loud thud boomed as the corporal landed on the hood of the vehicle. The towering man pulled back his hand, opening and closing it, as if the strike had somehow hurt him. The crowd roared with excitement as the corporal shook the haze from his mind, The rage trickled in and started to fill him, his eyes reddened as he pushed himself off the car to face his opponent a new intensity on his face.

It annoyed the giant to see his smaller opponent standing with a determined hatred burning in his eyes, filled with anger, the brawler attacked again, knowing the five seconds had already passed. The movements happen so fast that the entire crowd suddenly quieted in shock. The slave, sidestepping and redirecting the giant's momentum and compounding it with his own strength, grabbed and accelerated the man's head into the side of the vehicle. The loud crunch of Kaleem's head striking the side of the vehicle was heard by everyone. The pirates stared around, stunned seeing the consortium's champion's body suddenly go limp, his arm's hanging down, with his hands in the sand, while being propped up by his head that was still stuck in the vehicle's side where it had hit.

The corporal stepped back, looking towards El Capitan from the corner of his eyes, making a gesture with both hands towards the crumpled behemoth. El Capitan stood there in shock like everyone else, but snapped out of it quickly. He turned and bowed with extravagance and addressed the gathering, pointing to the fallen giant with a showman's smile.

"It is done then, Admiral."

As the admiral approached the scene, the crowd roared again, hooting and hollering. The admiral leaned over, picking up Kaleem's hand and releasing it as it fell limp back towards the ground. The admiral then repeated the action and turned to the crowd.

"It is done. The pain of departure is completed. Take this away," the admiral said with a dismissive gesture as he indicated to the fallen brawler.

Two pirates quickly came to retrieve the man, but struggled to pull his head out of the side of the vehicle's panel. The admiral studied the brawler and then turned a curious eye towards the prisoner, who stood there calmly, as his face started swelling where Kaleem had hit him. Nodding in approval, the admiral turned to El Capitan.

"You seem to have quite a treasure here, what say I buy him off of you?"

The captain nodded and replied. "So it seems, my good admiral, but he is currently not for sale. But to the winner go the spoils, yes? And our dealings will be complete?"

The admiral smiled and nodded as he turned to address the crowd. "Give El Capitan his spoils and let us bid him a fond farewell. Play some music and fill those cups again."

The cheers began again as the drink flowed and the music played as the party ensued. Two men carrying a box came from behind the crowd and placed the box at the captain's feet, shaking his hand, then quickly departed, helping the other two men drag the giant away. The admiral put a hand around El Capitan and lifted the pirate captain's hand up in victory once more, bringing in some more cheers, and whispered.

"I don't know how you did it, but you did it, and I thank you. You have put me in a much better position than I could've hoped. Now get the hell out of here." Moving away, he turned to the crowd, addressing them, then after a moment looked back toward the duo. "Don't let me ever see you two around here again or I will have you killed," the Admiral said with a gleeful smile, hugged El Capitan and left, moving towards the crowd.

Turning to his slave, El Capitan said, "You heard him Compai, let us leave, before we lose our welcome and our window."

Passing his hand over the large and deep dent on the side of his vehicle, El Capitan shook his head and grabbed the extra spoils. The Ravager stood there recuperating from the partial rage, breathing heavily and doing all that he could to maintain his senses. His urge to just attack the admiral and tear him limb from limb was all but overwhelming, again and again he took deep breaths until he was good enough to move. Slowly he made his way to the vehicle, dropping himself into the closest seat and looking out the window into the horizon, his face numb from pain.

They had been traveling for hours and the darkness had set in a long time ago. Jo'su stirred as the vehicle jolted to one side and corrected itself again. He looked around and could see nothing on either side, only a bright glow ahead, with occasional flickering lights going up and down. *That must be Taidar with ships coming and going.*

"Good morning, Compai. How do you feel?" the pirate asked.

"Better."

"That's good, you look better, too. It seems like you're a quick healer. I thought your face would have been more swollen, but you actually look normal, even better than when we met. How is that even possible? Oh well, good for you, but the night is still young, and we have much to do once we reach Taidar," the captain stated.

"Taidar? Who names a city Taidar? Isn't that like some sort of potato?" the soldier asked.

"Actually, you are correct, Compai. Taidar is a type of starchy vegetable native to this planet. As for who named it, it was a young logistics officer, who was in charge of the sector long ago. This was the port to pick up taidars, so he named the city Taidar. You will find other large port cities with the name of what was at one time, and still may be their chief export."

"Well, well, an educated pirate," the soldier told his companion.

"No! I am not a pirate. I may have been for a time, but that was out of necessity," the man quickly replied defensively.

"Oh, do tell, how do you become a pirate out of necessity?"

The pirate turned in his chair and looked at the young man, pondering if to share his tale. After a moment, he did.

"I was a salvager, I had my ship, my crew, and we did well. One day we were working on salvaging a ship floating near an asteroid. Out of nowhere, the Empress and her crew comes upon my ship. They took my ship, killed a few of my crew members, and because I'd been a good provider for her business with parts and other things, not to mention I had fixed some of her vehicles and ships, she offered me a job. I could keep my rank, which came with a little better take than the crew and a few minor other perks, but I would lose everything else, or she could just end my life and that of my crew right there.

"As any intelligent man would, I quickly agreed if she would spare the crew, to which she did and provided them and offer, join or die. It was all I could do to save their hides and my own. So here I am, getting out, hoping to find me a nice space port and open up a little inn with a cantina. There, I can sit and talk all the crap I want, without having to be looking over my shoulder." The man sighed as he smiled.

"Capitan, that is such a delightful dream, but how will you, a notorious pirate, get on a space port if they are all run by the defense force? As soon as they see you, you'll be arrested, and the only cantina you'll be working, will be the chow line in one of their prison facilities," the soldier said doubtfully.

"Well, my friend, if you must know. I know a certain young lady that has magic fingers," the pirate said with a raised eyebrow.

"So your plan to get on a space port is a hooker with magic fingers to seduce the captain of that space port?" The corporal asked incredulously.

The pirate looked at his slave with indifference and sighed. "No, Compai. You need to be smarter than that if you wish to be my Compai. First, she is a hacker, not a hooker, and second, she is going to change my profile on the defense network so I can start fresh."

"They have backups and redundancies, you know."

"True, this is very true, but she gave me a guarantee," the pirate said.

"Guarantee? She's a hacker, what are you going to do? Take her to court?" the corporal sniped back.

"Compai, please. Why are you so negative? In the underworld it's just like any other thing, your reputation is everything. She does poor work; word gets around. She loses business, or worse. Why the sudden doubt in me, Compai?" The pirate asked.

The soldier sat back quietly, obviously bothered, and then leaned forward, answering the question visibly irritated. "Because there are no second chances for killers like us. There is no getting away with it, and what does that damn word Compai mean, anyway?"

The pirate sighed, understanding the darkness in the young man's heart and answered back with a sincerity and calm. "Compai is a slang word for compadre. It is old Spanish, it means a good friend or companion, a confidant."

"I'm your good friend? I'm your slave, your property according to the laws out here. You are going to sell me at the market. How is that a friend? You mean you don't have any other friends? A charismatic pirate like you, I suppose, is very popular," the Ravager shot back, offended.

The captain looked at the soldier and leaned forward, his voice low and steady. "You listen to me, young man. People can do bad things and still be honorable. There is always a road to redemption, it doesn't mean it will be easy, but there is always a road. As for my friends, the last person I called friend, I stuck my sword through their chest for betraying me and reneging on a contract. A person without their word is nothing. You are the first person I've ever called Compai because, in my heart, I know you are honorable. As for you being my slave, we had a deal, a contract amongst us. I am fulfilling my end as you did yours. So don't complain to me if you suck as a negotiator."

El Capitan adjusted himself in his seat and sighed before continuing. "There is one more thing, Compai. Slavery was the only way out for you, as my property, you would not be harmed, which is why the beatings stopped at one point, but as a slave I cannot release you. You have a consortium collar, which can only be removed at the den or by their representative at the auction house. They will track you until you are sold. There is nothing else I can do about that, sometimes the only way sucks, but it's the best option."

The captain was shaking his head when he realized something and turned his focus to the soldier's face. Looking at his companion's face intently, the pirate asked, "How is it, that you were punched by that mountain of a man and show absolutely no signs of it? Not a mark on your body from the beatings you received. You look good as new. How?"

"I'm a fast healer?" the soldier replied.

"Bullshit!" retorted the pirate. "What don't I know? And if you get scanned, what will we encounter?" he asked suspiciously.

"Know, I cannot attest to your knowledge. But if I get scanned, I truly don't know what will happen. I suspect nothing good. The GDF will probably be looking for me."

"GDF, Eh? That's your story. And the healing?" the older man asked.

"Are you sure you want to know?" the soldier asked casually, looking towards the captain.

"Want to, eh," he stated, making a hand gesture. "Need to, is more like it, so we can avoid problems."

Sighing, the young man explained, "Nanites. I had a healing serum that uses nanites to repair injuries. Highly efficient and effective at maintaining special operations soldiers in the field. I had a bunch of them in me, but I was hit with an EMP wave, making them dormant. When they put on the collar and shocked me, they must have turned on."

The captain was momentarily speechless, but quickly recovered. "You almost had me there for a second. That tech doesn't exist. You are very sneaky, Compai."

The soldier laughed. "I wish it was a story, but it's true. They don't let the tech be developed because it will fix too many issues with the sick. The loss in revenue for the medical companies that have substandard medical solutions that are more like patches that people must continuously come back for. And since that is all they supply, the medical company over inflate the current medical cost. You are talking about trillions of credits in just this sector."

"That is more like the government we have all grown to hate. Iron fisted policies to keep us pacified. While they choke the life out of us. We get no say, and the officials are those that they send us. Disgusting!" The captain expressed.

"Those are the people you will deal with at the spaceport. Get used to it," the corporal replied.

"Not true. Space ports are owned by governments, individuals, and companies, so they are classified in the ship category. So they fall under different regulations. The defense force contracts out sections of the facility. That way, it promotes business and cuts costs for them. Owners of those space stations can actually not have any GDF forces onboard." The pirate paused to take a drink, then continued. "But there are Galactic Defense Force Space Stations that are purely owned by the GDF with some civilian contractors onboard. Those stations can be scary, anyone that runs a GDFSS is like a God, answering to very few for what happens on board, but if anything happens on those stations, it's all on them."

The soldier looked over at the pirate. "How do you know so much about the GDF?"

The pirate chuckled. "As I said before, I was a salvager. I spent time on different space stations. I had contracts with the GDF to salvage certain areas with permission. I've had access to some interesting tech in my time. I've legally dismembered almost every type of ship you could imagine. I actually own a salvage yard, but I have not visited it in a long time, well, since I was forced into a different lifestyle, at least. Believe it or not, I have seen derelict or abandoned space stations in certain graveyards. Some just needing some love. If only I could have been the one to love them."

"Ship graveyards? In space, why not recycle all that material?" the young man asked.

"Well, Compai, what do you think happens when there is combat in space, it makes a ship graveyard, and just because a ship is destroyed or partially destroyed doesn't mean it doesn't have good parts. But those areas are dangerous, filled with debris and sometimes corporations or pirates trying to protect or hunt in a specific area. A ship's artificial gravity field sometimes pulls ships together or any number of floating debris near it, which can make a cascade of problems, just being out there is dangerous. That's what salvagers do, to make good money. But there are a lot of restrictions and a lot of risk," the pirate said with fondness.

The young man turned to the pirate, intrigued. "So, what's the most interesting thing you have seen out there in the vastness of space?"

Taking a deep breath, the pirate paused. "There is a vast graveyard in the Kuros sector, a place of a thousand untold stories. I was just starting off, working on my own, going through the wreckage. This graveyard has been used to park retired commissioned ships as well. I believe to mainly hide the wreckage of an old space station. That station, it's design, the materials used, and just about everything about it was a sight. Lavishly made with elegant designs all over. Even the battle damage was not enough to hide its true beauty." The pirate smiled as he reminisced. "That station was so elegant, it left an impression on me as I stood there on the wing of an old cruiser, just looking at the husk of greatness. "I knew I had found my calling right then and there. But I tell you, I do not think human hands made that space station. She just floated in the darkness waiting to be revived one day, like a lady waits for the tender hand of her lover to caress her." He paused for a moment, his eyes glazing as he remembered, "I only saw her by chance. She was surrounded by debris all over, like if a massive battle had taken place, but since then gravitational anomalies have developed, not uncommon in debris fields. Magnetized metals or worse, malfunctioning gravity field generators from a deserted or damaged ship. That area is now a forbidden zone. One day, I hope to see my beloved station once again."

"That sounds like a beautiful sight indeed."

"Eh, maybe if we survive long enough, you can come with me," the man said sincerely.

The soldier shrugged his shoulders as a response. El Capitan took a deep breath and looked over at his companion and spoke with sincerity and sorrow. "Compai, I truly wish I did not have to sell you."

"You don't. You can just set me free," the soldier interrupted.

116

"Unfortunately, I cannot. I must sell everything that has any connection to the consortium to make a clean break, and you are on their records already. Just like this vehicle and a couple of other items we are carrying, but I would like to do right by you, and I will. I give you my word on that. Please understand I can have nothing to do with those animals anymore, and with you, I am starting anew. You inspired me with what you did for the doctor and his family. So, I will sell everything, because I need to make a clean break, and vanish them from my life," replied the captain.

"With a little profit, of course," retorted the soldier sarcastically.

The pirate grinned. "Of course! Don't be ridiculous, I can do right by you and still make it profitable."

The two looked at each other and laughed. The corporal sighed, shaking his head in disbelief, then putting his hands behind his head, leaned back, focusing on the ceiling. The captain sped the vehicle forward, bringing the bright lights of the city closer.

"We have known each other now for over two weeks, and I still don't know your name. How can I be, how do you say it, your Compai and not even know your name?" The Ravager asked.

The captain peeked over at his friend, surprised. "You know, you are correct. I apologize, that was rude of me, not to introduce myself properly and worse, not to ask you for your name. I have grown so accustomed to using the captain or El Capitan, which means the same thing in Spanish. I did it to cover my name in hopes of this day, and here it comes, fast approaching. My name is Rey de Castillo, which literally means king of the castle. And you, Compai, what is your name?"

The corporal paused as so many thoughts ran through his mind. "Are you sure you want to know? Knowing my name could mean your death."

Rey chuckled, "Knowing you has been good for me so far. What kind of friend would I be if I cower from a name? Eh?"

The soldier quietly chuckled in disbelief, he had not known or called anyone a friend in over five years, and though this man was a stranger, he knew this was the right thing to do. "My name is Jo'rian. I have gone by the name Jo'su for the last five, almost six years. I snuck into a military facility posing as my cousin to see a new ship the defense force had, and by some misguided luck, they took his unit that day for specialized training. And here I am. If you ever repeat a word of this, I will hunt you down and kill you."

"Friends do not betray Compai, no matter the price. It's the friendship contract," Rey replied sincerely.

"Are we friends?" the young soldier asked.

The salvager extended his hand to the young man. "Are we?"

The soldier looked at the salvager and then at his hand, and then back towards the man's eyes again. It was a risk to him and his family, but he had known no friend like this ever and he had already begun down that rabbit hole. The salvager looked at the young man and nodded with a smile as they clasped hands and shook firmly.

"Rey de Castillo, I am Jo'rian. It is nice to meet you, my friend," the young man said.

The salvager quickly replied, "Jo'rian. I am Rey de Castillo. It is nice to meet you, my friend." Suddenly he interjected. "We are friends! What is this formality?"

The salvager pulled the young man and embraced him with three strong pats on the back. This surprised Jo'rian and made him feel awkward with such a display, mimicking the salvager while looking at him oddly, causing the salvager to laugh.

"I'm Hispanic, my friend. We have no boundaries for personal space. We are a passionate and expressive people. You'll see. Now, let us go to town and get some food, some drink, and some women. We must celebrate our friendship," the pirate said enthusiastically, then considered. "But where to celebrate? No reputable place will allow a slave in, especially with your attire, but fortunately for us, I know a few very disreputable places that not only will allow you in but also provide a delicious meal. Eh?"

"You're paying, whatever you say," replied Jo'rian.

"Good!" the man said and laughed, accelerating the vehicle even faster.

Chapter 7

Almost a day had passed and with the help of the Master Core System's primary diagnostics functions, Ophelia had finally gotten Mistress to come online. The AI gave her an earful for turning her off and then began running diagnostics on the ship's components and finally got them on their way.

"This may not surprise you, captain, but of our six original thrusters, two were not functioning and were shut down, one was functioning at 50% efficiency and showed irregularities resulting in being placed on standby, and three were functional. Now all six have been shut down and I do not have an estimate of when I can bring them back online," Mistress informed her.

"What, why? What the hell did that asshole do?" Ophelia demanded.

"I don't know, yet. I do know, that if I turn them on now, we might blow up," the AI stated, then added after a deliberate pause. "There are a series of other issues, and the comms are still down."

Ophelia sat in the captain's chair rubbing her temples, then looked forward into the darkness, she had been there for several hours just looking off into space as the ship accelerated in the darkness. More system errors showed up with the completion of every diagnostic. Some systems didn't come online at all, but her mind punished her the most. *How long do I have before I have to quit this life, this search, then what do I do, where do I go?*

The sound of a mug being placed in the holder brought her out of her spell and she looked up, startled. Emmy had showed up with a cup of hot chocolate and a smile. The young scientist looked at one screen that displayed different indicators on the ship with various lights in red, indicating damage or problem areas.

"So does the ship think it's Christmas, with all those red and green lights?" Emmy said.

"Well, at least it's not Valentine's Day, then we'd be in real trouble," Ophelia mused, sighing, then turning to her companion, "I'm sorry, I forgot. I was supposed to make the food."

"It's okay, I took a muscle relaxer and collapsed in my room. I've been asleep for most of the time. I hurt everywhere, that lady sure is strong. Mistress checked me out, and nothing serious, just mostly soreness and some bruising. Fortunately, nothing was broken except my heart. I took some painkillers, and it helped. I see you got us on the way again, that's good. Right?" The young woman asked, putting a comforting hand around Ophelia's shoulder.

"Yeah, I guess, but the ship's a mess though," the young captain replied in a subdued tone.

"I guess I know how she feels. Sorry Mistress, had I known, I would have made you some hot chocolate too," Emmy chuckled.

"Thank you Dr. Kricay, I appreciate the sentiment. But don't you worry, there is nothing wrong with us that some TLC can't fix. Us girls are stronger than they give us credit for." Mistress replied.

"Right you are, Mistress," Emmy answered.

"Excuse me, I'm going to bed," Ophelia said suddenly and stood to leave.

"What's wrong with you? I'm the one that got my ass kicked and my heart broken," Emmy asked, surprised.

Ophelia semi turned to answer, then shrugged it off and turned back for the door again. Mistress, on the other hand, was not so reserved and blurted out. "She's feeling guilty and is overwhelmed."

"Guilty? About what? It's not your fault pirates attacked us," Emmy said.

Slamming the bottom of her fist against the door, "Yes, it is. I'm the captain, it was my decision that almost got us killed, the ship damaged, and almost hijacked. Again. That's all on me. I should have never left my home, I should have never taken a crew, and I should have never taken this job," Ophelia said angrily, hurling the mug against the wall.

A silence filled the room that was ended by the young scientist. "Well, those are the breaks, sister. It sucks, it's difficult, but it's what we're dealt. I am glad you came along, because while all this sucks, at least I got another chance at life, instead of rotting in a cell after so many years of hard work." Emmy placed her mug in another holder, then looked at Ophelia and continued. "I regretted so many times going to that tanker, so many you cannot imagine. I sold everything I had and bought that transient pod and made the best of it, and you know what? It sucked every minute and then I went to jail, because I had enough and stood up for myself."

Emmy paused, taking a breath to compose herself, flattening her outfit, then smiled. "But today was different. I fought for my life today, we both did, and we won. I have a life to live, and no one is going to stop me from living it. Not the defense force, not that bitch in the cell, not you, not Billy, not anyone. As a matter a fact, when we land this bird, I am going to find me the most charming guy in that city and ride him like a stallion. Not because I am a slut, but because I am going to live my life my way. You made a poor decision, learn from it and move on. Don't stay there, stuck in fear. So, stop feeling sorry for yourself and get it together captain, we have work to do." Despite her small stature, she now walked out the door like she was ten feet tall.

Ophelia stood there watching the young woman storm out, and then looked back to the window, thinking. She looked at the broken mug on the floor and sighed, walking over to it and started picking up the pieces. A small, automated droid entered the room and began cleaning up next to her.

"She's right you know, except about the slutty part, there it's kind of fifty-fifty. You have suffered a lot of mental and emotional trauma in the last few years. Trauma, that is difficult to deal with and you have been fighting with it, instead of dealing with it. You second guess yourself all the time and to make matters worse, you threw that mug of hot chocolate and not only dirtied me, but offended the kindness of the person who brought it to you. You were raised better than that, young lady," the AI said.

"I don't need to hear it from you, too, Mistress," the young woman answered with anger.

"If not me, then who? I have been with you the whole time and you don't listen to anyone. You think you have all the answers, that you can do it all, but the truth is you can't," Mistress shot back.

"Yes, I can, and I will," the captain shouted arrogantly.

"Fine, prove it. Start being the woman you were meant to be and apologize to those you have taken for granted. Take me offline from here until our destination. Do it all on your own. Go ahead because you will have to remember your math and navigation classes and plot the route, or ask that pirate you have prisoners, all the while watching out for her, piloting the ship, and monitoring all the gauges. Can you do that? Can you prove you understand what being a captain is?" the AI asked.

"I can and I will. I'll show you I can do this. Mistress, shut down interface!" the young woman said with prideful arrogance.

"Very well, Captain," Mistress announced and went dark along with the lights and the engine.

"Mistress? Mistress?" the young woman said as she looked around, surprised. The ship decelerated, wiping the course from the screen, as the bridge lights had dimmed considerably though all the sensors and panels were working.

Hours had passed by as the young woman diligently worked on plotting the course to their destination. Taking in the complex computations of distance speed, celestial objects and their gravitational pull, along with countless other considerations.

They're right. I am scared. Ophelia thought then allowing a few moments to collect herself. Mistress's words ringing loudly in her head. "They raised you better than that." Ophelia sighed. "I was raised better than that? I am better than that," she said out loud to herself.

Inputting the course into the computer, she verified it and engaged the autopilot. Satisfied with her work, she turned and headed for the door, when an alarm sounded. Quickly running back to the helm, analyzing the error. Then disengaging the inoperative thrusters that could overload other circuits, or worse, blow up the ship. She silenced the alarms and stood back, this time waiting a few moments to see if any other alarms would sound before attempting to leave again. She held on to a rail as she felt the ship pick up speed again and resume its course.

Feeling confident in what she had done, she exited the bridge and went to a place none would expect, her parent's quarters. Walking in, she sat on the bed and glanced around. She saw her father's personal desk and moved to it, running her fingers across the old wooden desk, thinking of her father and smiling, envisioning him working there. She had left one of his old notebook on the desk and for the first time in years read the cover. The words KNIGHTFORGE TECHNOLOGIES were bold on the center with the logo underneath in her father's handwriting was the Phrase.

Courage is what we do!

It meant little to most, but to him it was the convictions of a knight and the actions they took. She had met no one like her father; he was a loving, romantic husband and a generous father who would always tell her,"Intelligence and integrity... passion and compassion...loyalty and courage, that's what makes a knight true, even if it doesn't make them popular." He had shared that with her since she was a little girl, telling her that the phrase had been in a story he read as a child. He made it the motto he lived by since an early age.

Ophelia felt alone and had closed herself off to the universe long ago, now she finally realized and admitted that she needed help. She stood looking out of her parent's quarter's window into the darkness of space, having an idea she acted on it and walked out of the room.

Grabbing some food, she went down to the brig with a tray of food for the prisoner. Entering, she followed all prisoner protocols and placed the tray on the table through a slit in the barrier and the bars. She looked at the dark-haired beauty who laid there sleeping.

"I brought you some food, you must be hungry," Ophelia told her.

"Leave it there," The female pirate said as she rolled over, giving her back to Ophelia.

"I checked on Billy, he is doing fine, and the stasis is working. When we get to Tersa 4, I'm sure we can get him some proper medical attention."

"I should have let him die and taken the ship," she replied.

"What? You would just let him die?"

The woman turned, rolling over and propping herself up, with her hand on her chin, slightly shaking her head. "You are too young to be in charge of a ship, or a crew."

"I'll have you know that I am 22 years old. I'm old enough," the young woman shot back, annoyed.

Roxy sat up and looked at Ophelia and sighed. "Fine, let me rephrase myself. You don't have the knowledge nor the experience to be a good captain. Anyone can pilot a ship and give orders, but there is more to that. A captain needs to understand that your crew are tools, but they are also pawns, and sometimes they have to be sacrificed to get the job done."

"What? How could you be so coldhearted?" Ophelia replied in disgust.

"Yeah, so coldhearted that I am rotting in a cell, I should have stuck to the plan and dispatched the both of you and taken the ship. I must be getting soft," the woman said as she stood walking over to the food.

"Are you in love with Billy?"

"Isn't it obvious? That handsome idiot just ruffles my feathers in a way that I can't explain," the woman said openly as she picked through the food.

"The fault is mine, seeing Billy and that little slut having sex all over the cargo hold was infuriating. It affected me more than I imagined. In the end, I underestimated you two, which is something I promise I will not do again," Roxy stated, and laughed.

"Then I better not give you that chance," the young woman replied.

"Wise, very wise. Now leave me, I grow tired and wish to sleep," the prisoner said and laid down again.

Two hours later, Ophelia tapped on the door of Emmy's transient pod but received no response. Turning to leave, she heard soft crying coming from another area. Following the sounds, Ophelia ended up at the prisoner transport pod. Emmy sat on the floor next to Billy's stasis chamber, crying.

Ophelia rushed over and sat next to her. "Are you okay?"

Emmy looked at her and tried drying her tears. "I will be."

"Want to talk about it?" Ophelia asked.

"Not really... but yes," was the reply as she extended her hand.

The captain quickly took it and sat next to her, embracing the young scientist, who's face had already swollen from the injuries to her face.

"I know I'm being stupid, but I was beginning to think it was real. He was sweet and kind, and naturally clumsy, but adorable. I hate him! Yet here I am crying. Is that not the dumbest thing you ever heard?"

"No. Believe me, no. You just need closure, and maybe this is your way of getting it. So do what you must do," was the captain's reply.

"Thanks. But I should have known better, to let go so fast. He just made me feel special. I haven't had that in so long, you know," the petite woman expressed sadly.

"I know, Emmy, but you are appreciated here. And I wanted to say thank you for the hot chocolate you brought me, and I am sorry I threw it at the wall. I was just frustrated. It's been difficult these last few years."

The venting continued about their experiences, their roots, and all that had transpired in their lives. The two young women hugged, cried, laughed, and eventually left the pod to get more hot chocolate and spent more time talking.

For the next few days, Ophelia spent most of her time on the bridge, monitoring the ship's progress while doing research about her prisoners and her crew, learning everything she could. Most of her reading was about Billy and her prisoner, the Red Devil Captain Roxanne Trafroo. She spent many hours reading about the woman and saw that she was a very educated person and had pulled off some bold and lucrative heists.

She kept a close eye on the systems and the errors on the ship status panel. Her eyes constantly looked to the cooling systems, since the engines had been running somewhat hot after the asteroid field incident and required periodic exposure to the coldness of space to help cool the coolant regularly just to keep the ship in the orange stopping it from slipping into dangerous levels past normal operating temperatures.

Ophelia had made it a point to go speak with the prisoner three times a day when she took her food. Most of the conversations were pleasant, as the pirate enjoyed the attention when Ophelia asked about certain experiences she had on file. As any decent pirate, she could spin a tale and enjoyed boasting of her exploits. But it was the last day before they would reach Tersa 4 and the conversation changed somewhat.

"Back for more stories, huh?" The Pirate asked.

"I'm pretty tired, but I found some interesting patterns in your activities after reading the files and hearing some of your stories. I made some connections. You had very close calls, or let's say, less successful missions, just after Billy left," Ophelia told the woman.

The woman's face changed and took a more serious tone. "What do you mean?"

Ophelia took a seat across from the cell and began explaining. "I believe that every time you and Billy got together, you two would take off on some sort of adventure. Vacations or just trips. He was consulting for a company where he interned, called "Aid 4 All" It's a nonprofit organization that helps settlers on three distinct planets. It has done some minor work in other places, but mainly those three.

Funny enough, a distant relative of yours runs that company. She gets an influx from a company now and then. A company that I believe you own. You give money to your younger siblings, and they provide some services like cleaning the money. That's just ingenious," Ophelia paused, letting her words sync in. "Well, in my research, I discovered that every time that Billy would end those consulting contracts, you were almost captured or were more reckless in your operations. When you got captured, he ended a contract sooner than he was supposed to. Did you guys have a fight or break up?" The young woman asked and looked at the woman.

Roxanne had a dangerous scowl on her face as her eyes followed Ophelia who paused, reading from a notepad. She tried to play it off as a lie, but it was far too late to act so dismissively. Roxy came close to the edge of her cell and looked at Ophelia seriously.

"That is very dangerous information, young lady-if it were true. What do you intend to do with it?" the pirate asked.

"I'm not sure yet. I came down here to confirm it, and by your expressions, I believe I'm correct," Ophelia said, "but let me continue."

"Are you sure you want to? That is a deep hole you may be digging," Roxanne responded.

"Is that a threat, because if it is, I am sure the security investigation offices would love to see my data. And I am sure that certain companies that transport goods would offer a pretty penny for what I know, not to mention some insurance companies. You have quite the scam going on, don't you?" Ophelia asked.

"If that so-called information were true, and it ever got out, you would probably be dead within a week. It's better if you forget what you've found. You are so in over your head, little girl. You just keep playing at captain and forget everything you have seen and heard, Ms. Knight," the pirate replied in a level tone.

"So, you know who I am?" Ophelia replied, somewhat surprised.

"Let's see, Ophelia Knight, the only daughter of the famous engineer and owner of Knightforge Technologies, and his wife, who were claimed lost in space over three years ago. Which is when I suspect you took this lovely ship to go find them and have yet to succeed. All the while, your family's company stock slowly dwindles to nothingness."

"I stay informed, I read, and I will offer you my condolences for your parents, though I have never had the pleasure of meeting them. Space is a harsh place, more so for a young girl who is so obviously very lost. So, send out that information and take me to Tersa 4. I will be out within the week and then I will hunt you down. How do you like that for a happy ending? You will be dead, I will have your ship, and your family's company will disappear, leaving your legacy as a footnote of the past."

Ophelia lowered her head slightly for a moment, gripping her datapad tightly, recovering from the cord the pirate had obviously struck. "That was quite mean and to think I actually just came to commend you on such brilliance. It's not my business how you cheat or scam the insurance companies or how you clean your money through the nonprofits with the same merchandise that you stole. Nor how you sustain your family members and your sick nephew's medical needs. None of it is my business. I still think you are a piece of shit pirate and after your threats and those hurtful words about my family, even more so.

"Like you, I love my family and to have them torn away from me with no knowledge or history of what happened to them was very difficult. What was even worse was how I cleaned this ship with my tears, as I scrubbed the few bloodstains and poorly washed skirmish marks on the ship." Ophelia stifled a tear. "I don't know where they are or how, but I'll find them, even if it's just to recover their bones to lay them to rest. I will find them. As for your threats, I should open the airlock right now and vent you out into space. I don't need your bullshit and as for your family drama... Fuck you! We all have problems," Ophelia finished.

It filled her with anger and fury, but with a determination the pirate had not seen before in her. The pirate just looked on at the young woman, affirming how much she had truly underestimated her. Ophelia scoffed and stormed out of the security quarters. The pirate went back to her bed and threw herself down, exasperated and wondering how much worse her predicament had gotten.

Will she go to the GDF with the information on me and my family's business dealing? This girl has learned more than anyone who had actually been assigned to study my case for years. They never even came remotely close to what this young woman had found out, and with my reaction, everything could be at risk.

"Damn it!" the pirate mumbled to herself, knowing she had messed up.

Chapter 8

The two had dined at an establishment known well to Rey and had enjoyed of the festive music, food, and libations that the establishment offered. It was now time for phase two of El Capitan's plan. Various ladies that worked for the establishment came over to share in the captain's generosity as he poured drinks and celebrated his new lease on life.

Jorian sat next to El Capitan with ladies sitting all around fawning over his muscular and finely chiseled body. They laughed at his shyness, which the captain pointed out repeatedly. The young man felt attracted to the women, but it was evident that he was completely out of his element, continuously looking towards the captain for the proper social cues.

"These are the finest ladies in this city, you will find none finer in the art of relaxation anywhere. Isn't that true, my dears?" The captain said as he kissed one of the lady's hands. "Let us retreat to the spa ladies, for a hot bath and who knows what else." The captain raised his eyebrows a few times.

Taking a cigar to his lips, Rey inhaled deeply, blowing out a small cloud of smoke, then poured the rest of a bottle into his glass and stood from the table. With a cigar in one hand and his drink in the other, El Capitan stood and draped his arms around two of the hostesses and walked off.

In an adjacent table, a burly man stood, his displeasure clearly apparent on his face. The man took a step and barred the way of the captain. The women's expressions suddenly changed as if worried about a confrontation and conflict causing possible injury to themselves.

"You're taking all the women, you damn bastard!" The burly man spit on the floor.

The captain looked to either side and smiled. "It seems I have. We have good days and bad days. Today I am celebrating and I'm a having a very good day, but let me not be too selfish. I'll buy you and your friends another round, maybe your luck will change some, eh?"

The man looked towards the people at his table and then back to the captain. "Fuck you and your drink. Asshole. I want..."

A chair shattered as it hit the burly man on his back and head, sending him sprawling to the ground with pieces of chair all around him. Jo'rian dropped what was left of the chair and turning towards the table, looking at the other three that were in the burley man's party and asked with a snarl, "Anyone else want to reject my friend's offer"?

The other men glanced at their companion on the floor and the psychotic look on the corporal's face, accompanied by his appearance, wearing nothing but an old worn shirt and what remained of his soiled compression shorts. Not wanting any problems, they threw their hands up, displaying the desire to avoid conflict.

On the other side of the room, the bartender had grabbed for an old scatter gun he had under the counter but paused when Rey waved him off and signaled towards the table. "Get my friend over there a bottle so we can all celebrate a little, yes"?

Various "Yeses" came from the table as the other men quickly held up their glasses for more drink. A waitress quickly brought out a bottle, pouring the other men a drink and leaving the bottle on the table.

El Capitan nodded to the men with a smile as he stepped over the crumpled man. Two other hostesses laughed and giggled as they grabbed Jo'rian by the arms, pulling him away, complimenting the young man on his bravado. The Ravager allowed himself to be escorted away but not before looking back at the table twice, making sure no one else was coming up behind him.

Jo'rian was anxious and tense from being around the fawning women, something he had not experienced and was not accustomed too. It focused his tension, feeling the need to let out his energy by hitting the man with the chair. He did not mean to hit the burly man so hard; it was just a reaction.

They had reached the relaxation area of the establishment when the ladies moved off, getting towels, oils, and other items for their customers' relaxation experience. The captain looked around and turned casually to his companion and asked,"Is violence your first reaction to everything?"

"Yes!" Jo'rian replied.

"I see, well hopefully these ladies will assist you with some of those pent-up energies you have," the captain said with a chuckle.

"I... I..." the young soldier hesitated.

"What is it, my friend? You can tell me anything," El Capitan stated encouragingly.

The corporal looked around, making sure there was no one near, and then whispered to the pirate captain. "I... I've never been with a woman."

The salvager stepped back and grinned. "What? That is preposterous. No worries, though, these are the best ladies in town.

"I am not comfortable with this. I... I... I'm not ready," the young man admitted. "I... I don't like, um."

"Women? Are you gay? It's okay, you are still my Compai," the man said.

"NO! I'm just not ready. Okay?" Jo'rian whispered, offended.

The captain sighed. "Okay, Compai. I can respect that. Let's do this, eh? I will enjoy myself while they give you a massage, to help you relax. No sex. Okay?"

"A massage?" Jo'rian asked doubtfully.

"Yes! A massage, you missed yours back at the consortium, or so you said. You have been through a-lot, and they will help you relax a little. No sex, if you are not ready, it's okay. Though sex would help you relax," the man said as he shrugged.

Jo'rian narrowed his eyes at the man.

"Okay, a massage it is then," Rey replied, holding his hands up in mock surrender.

Rey took another sip of his drink and called over one lady and began whispering in her ear while pointing toward his companion. The woman studied the young man, surprised, and responded with a smile in an accommodating manner, moving off and talking to the other hostesses. The other women all giggled slightly, and all peered up from their huddle at Jo'rian, as if he were a rabbit in front of a pack of hungry wolves, making the veteran soldier feel quite uncomfortable.

Leaning towards Rey, Jo'rian asked. "Are you sure? They are looking at me as if I was prey."

The salvager grinned. "Yes, I'm sure they are. And it's good that you feel that way. Now you know how you look at everyone else."

"What?" the corporal protested. But Rey was already walking off.

"Ladies, are we ready?" Rey asked loudly.

The women approached them and led them to their respective areas, assuring them it would be as requested. The Ravager left hesitantly with a reassuring nod from Rey, before he draped his arms around the two women escorting him to a separate area.

It was late into the night when the ladies finally led Jo'rian to another area of the spa called 'The Oasis' which was the cleansing area where an individual could soak in one of many natural hot springs that lined the room. The ladies joined him at first, washing him down thoroughly and then politely excused themselves, but not before kissing him on the cheek.

The young man's face flushed as he placed a hand over his cheek and let out a sigh of relief, seeing the exotic beauties move off. The ladies gestured towards Rey who nodded back from inside one of the hot springs with a big smile on his face. Sinking back into his hot spring, the charismatic salvager took a deep puff of another cigar and finished another glass of his drink, setting it down near the half empty bottle on a tray next to him.

"How was it?" the salvager asked.

"I don't want to talk about it," the young man replied, somewhat uncomfortably, but then added, "But it was... nice."

Rey chuckled to himself and sank a little lower into the hot spring. As the men-soaked other ladies brought back their clothes, cleaned and nicely pressed. Rey had a secondary bundle brought to him wrapped in paper and nicely tied. His long coat was now different, it was a plain gray, instead of the bright red and blue that it once was.

The corporal deflated when the ladies brought his torn shorts and old shirt. Then smiled, seeing them bring out another set of clothing that included a belt, cargo pants, socks, boots, an undershirt, and a long sleeve shirt. He looked at the ladies, who pointed towards his companion still in the tub.

"Thank you," Jo'rian stated appreciatively.

"Don't worry about it. Every man should have a massage at least once a month. Or once in his life in your case," the salvager said as he chuckled.

"I mean for the clothes," Jo'rian replied.

"Oh, that. Don't mention it, we have two days before the auction and you need to look your best, if I..." Rey paused, clearing his throat,"I mean, if we want to get max credits for you. I suppose you don't know what ship you want to be sold to? Well, it doesn't matter, later we will walk the port as I look for a ride, and you look for your new master. But first let us finish up. I have a room with two beds upstairs, we can get some rest and then be on our way."

It was well into the afternoon of the next day when the two men were ready to leave their room and start their day. They had unloaded various boxes of cargo at different destinations, each increasing the captain's pockets with credits or other valuables. They had one box left to unload when they finally visited the port side marketplace. Entering a building halfway into the market, then taking winding alleys, and crossing through some less than desirable areas, the two finally reached their destination.

It was a rundown section of an older neighborhood with exposed wires going into multiple locations and on each wire, a rat, if not two, ran across it to another dilapidated building. The soldier was aware of his surroundings, feeling a sense of discomfort, when he noticed two spotters at windows in opposite building on each side of the street. The men quickly started talking into devices on their necks that were wirelessly attached to their IDP on their wrist. The spotters put the soldier on even higher alert. Studying his surroundings more carefully, he caught sight of at least half a dozen more people hiding in different areas.

"We are not alone," he mumbled to Rey.

"In this area, no one ever is. Stay alert and don't attack anyone unless I say so," the former pirate replied.

A man who seemed well into his fifties exited one building, holding a broom. There was nothing distinct about the man. A person who would easily be dismissed and most likely was by most onlookers, thus his role as a greeter. The man approached them and began sweeping and cleaning some old metal tables that decorated the outside of the building.

"Good day to you, anything I can help you with?" the old man said in a pleasant voice.

"Yes, friend, I am looking for a magician to perform at my kid's birthday party, and they tell me I can find a talented lady magician around here, that can perform a few tricks and make some things disappear and what not," Rey said in his extroverted flamboyant nature.

132

"Magician, really?" a woman said from a door in a different building.

Rey quickly turned on his boot heals, and with a vibrant smile, replied, "My dear, to set eyes on you is truly like magic."

"Right. And the whores you probably saw yesterday are my assistants? And with a flick of their wrist, they can make your money disappear," the woman said accusingly as she made a mock gesture with her hand.

"A horse. You know very well that I have not ridden a horse in years," Rey replied quickly, deflecting.

"Your right, they probably rode you," the woman shot back with venom in her voice.

Rey was exasperated. "Aye, Madre mia, mujer, must you always be so cynical?"

Jo'rian shifted his gaze from his companion to the attractive redhead.

"Really, cynical? Where were you last night?" the woman asked accusingly, jabbing a finger into El Capitan's chest.

"I came into the city rather late and we were so hungry that we stopped for food and drink before making our way to my room," the captain spoke calmly, with vibrant hand gestures.

The woman quickly turned to Jo'rian. "You two slept together?"

Jo'rian gawked at the woman, offended, and answered defensively. "NO!"

"HA!" The woman said loudly, pointing that accusing finger at the pirate again.

Jo'rian then continued. "I mean, we slept in different beds. But after dinner, we did go relax and went to his room.

The woman turned fiercely towards Jo'rian, sizing him up, "You seem like a nice boy, but you smell like a cop or worse. I'd say GDF, by the looks of ya. But if you are with him," she paused, pointing to Rey, "You can't be so nice."

Rey shook his head in disbelief and announced his departure, "I'm leaving."

The woman paused, studying the salvager for a moment, and quickly changed her harsh tone to something more welcoming, "You're leaving?"

"Lidia, can we go inside, please?" he asked her in a more serious tone.

Worried she had taken it too far, she nodded quietly, agreeing. "Yeah, sure, follow me." Moving ahead, she signaled to a man who turned and opened the door.

Rey glanced at the man who guarded this entrance to the underground, a man he had dealt with on various occasions, and acknowledged him with a nod. The man nodded back and smiled. "Capitan."

"Pietro. This young man is with me," Rey told the guard.

"Of course, Capitan, but please remember, since you vouch for him, his actions are on you," replied the man, who returned to his position after they had entered.

Continuing down the hall, the trio reached an old stairway down that led them to a secret elevator that would take them down to an older part of the city. A secret part that was the underworld hub of the sector. Owned and operated by a discrete group that had money, power, or the right connections. It was a lavish city within the city. It was a large area with warehouses and other establishments running many types of goods from all parts of the sector and beyond.

Jo'rian saw carts pass by loaded with all sorts of weapons, another carrying exotic foods and animals, and a third that had crates with government symbols. Jo'rian was shocked at the magnitude of the operation and the thousands of people moving about. Though most were slaves, distinguished by their simple uniform and slave collar.

"What is this place?" he asked in awe.

The woman turned with a smile. "This is the Oculus, where anything that you have ever seen or dreamed of, you can get. Welcome to the Oculus, the hub of the underworld."

"Where does all this come from?" Jo'rian asked innocently.

"Your slave asks a lot of questions for a slave," the woman told Rey.

The salvager gave the corporal a frown, telling him to shut his mouth. Jo'rian returned with a glare, to which the pirate raised his hand, pointing to the shock collar control. Jo'rian glowered at the man and disengaged, not wanting to make a scene.

"They have a tank just sitting there next to those racers," Jo'rian said, surprised.

"Forgive him, my dear, he is new to the collar bit. And in need of some shock therapy to learn his place, but you know I'm a softy," the captain added quickly.

"You? A softy? Yeah right, go lie to your whores and crew mates. I know you too well, Rey." The woman answered, then added. "Anyway, it is a tank. Even if it's a medium tank with a dual capacitor plasma cannon and a launch rack. It's still considered a bit dated, but most people don't ever see one, I can understand his surprise."

"Who is ordering a tank?" the captain asked.

The woman shot him a glare. "Really, who else in the area orders a tank that must be delivered?"

Rey sighed, "The Czar."

"That's right, and since we prefer to keep him and his Ravagers out of the Oculus, we do things for him promptly. That and he pays well," she added.

"He called the Oculus the other day to pick up one of his men who fell out of a plane, an ATV, and to search for an Alpha box in the area. We found his man. And let me say, for a man that fell out of a plane, he was still partially alive and raving like a damn lunatic, his eyes popping out of his head and completely blood red, very scary. We had to put him down with a bunch of elephant tranquilizers until a stasis pod arrived. The other two items weren't found. We found about a dozen guys in the woods, some crazed animal had torn them apart. We had a trail but lost it. Too bad, too. Real large reward. It's getting bad out here Rey, you are smart to leave."

"You can come with me?" The pirate captain asked charismatically.

"Oh, yeah, sure, and what, have you leave me at the first port you find? No, thanks." She turned, answering him with a mock smile. "By the way, I heard you had a run in with Brother Julius, he came into the city about a week ago. Word is he's trying to leave the planet. I tell you, maybe it's time to go," the woman said casually as she led them through narrow streets and walkways as they conversed about various topics until they finally arrived at a small building with various wires coming into it from all directions.

Jo'rian kept his head down, but eyes alert, acting like he was staring at the box he was carrying for the captain, but turning his head away anytime he saw a camera, to cover himself from identification. The trio went up a flight of stairs to a loft on the top floor of the building. Various monitors decorated a desk, with state-of-the-art electronic equipment to match. It was a nicely decorated room, with darkening windows that the owner could control, to block prying eyes from seeing inside.

"So, Capitan. What can I do for you today?" Lidia asked.

"I want my name and history cleared from any and all GDF serves, and any other servers that can impede me in my new life. Are you up to the task?"

"Really, I'm sure that I am up to the task, but are you?" she said, running a flirtatious finger down his chest to the top of his belt, then laughed playfully as she moved toward her desk. "You know my price. Can you pay?"

El Capitan turned, grinning as he began opening the box that Jo'rian held, grabbing a set of large tin cans wrapped in plastic. The label showed they were some sort of cookie, but Jo'rian had never seen its kind before.

The captain placed both tins on her desk and winked. "Not just any cookies. Nothing but the best for you, my dear. These are shortbread cookies made with Irish butter, from earth itself."

"Ooh, those do sound delicious. You remembered," she said with a smile.

"Of course, I do. I could never forget the most talented and beautiful woman in the sector," the pirate captain said with the greatest amount of charm and sincerity he could muster.

The woman smiled coyly. "So sweet." Then turned her face serious again. "But you better have more than cookies to barter for my services."

A sly grin flashed across Rey's face. "Open it."

Lidia grabbed one of the cans quickly, realizing that it weighed significantly more than a can of cookies. She pulled out two sealed bags of cookies and looked inside, then grinned as she dumped the remaining contents that clunked heavily on her desk. Large coins made of gold, silver, and other precious metals now decorated a considerable portion of her workspace.

"Why Capitan, is this a proposal?" the woman asked flirtatiously.

"What if it was? Would you accept?" the man asked genuinely.

Lidia quickly became flustered, having painted herself into a corner. "Don't patronize me, Rey! We both know you are too much of a womanizer to ever settle down. This is way more than we agreed. I know how you are about contracts and agreements. Even with me."

"I am aware of it. I want it for myself and my friend here, who should be considerably cheaper. As for the rest, I would like it in galactic credits, so that I may purchase my cantina. Can you make it happen?" Rey asked.

"Yes, of course I'll do it," she said as she stood, then moving over to the pirate and gave him a large embrace. "You're finally doing it, Rey. That's great. I know more than anyone what you have been through in the last ten years, and I am thrilled and proud of you for maintaining such discipline. It's going to take a while though, so get comfortable."

"So you'll do it?" the pirate smiled. "Wait, which one, the job or marrying me?"

"Not funny, Rey," Lidia said seriously as she sat back down at her desk.

The two men moved back a few paces, sitting down on a cushiony couch she had against the wall, when the captain turned to Jo'rian and whispered, "Did you see that? I asked her to marry me with gold and silver and she still turns me down. Amazing."

The two sat back relaxing, the woman diligently working at her desk. Jo'rian understood why his friend was attracted to the hacker: she was intelligent, quick-witted, and gorgeous, with her curly red hair, green eyes, pale skin, and freckles. She was as attractive of a woman as he had seen, and her fiery personality was as welcoming as it was tormenting. The chemistry between them was undeniable.

Curiously, the young man leaned over and asked in a hushed tone, "Were you serious? Why her?"

Grabbing at his face, Rey smirked towards his companion, speaking sincerely, "Truthfully, in a way, I was. But the why, that's easy, because I feel it here," he stated as he tapped on his chest.

"So, who is this Czar? And why does he want a tank?" Jo'rian asked nonchalantly.

"Oh, him. He is bad news. He is a large man about seven feet in height, maybe more, with the back of a bull. He makes Kaleem seem like a little girl," the captain replied, pausing as a thought crossed his mind.

"Nah, that can't be," Jo'rian protested.

"It is true. I saw him myself occasionally, but mostly from a distance. The Czar dealt with the Consortium and the Oculus, to retrieve items or people for him. He is taking sections of the outer rim, unifying certain factions. Which would be good if he wasn't a complete psychopath," Rey replied sincerely.

The corporal shrugged dismissively, "so-what, he's a pirate with a group called the Revengers?"

"No! The Ravagers are a group of lethal mercenaries, I think. Very organized, and not just men, but women too. His woman is a Ravager as well. I saw her pick up a man and crush his head with her bare hands. No lie," Rey paused, emphasizing his words, then continued in a more casual tone. "Fortunately, that man was an asshole. So, it was no significant loss. But those Ravagers are quite deadly. They are freaks of nature and can-do things others cannot. They have a base a few hundred miles from here. It once belonged to a local warlord, unfortunately for him the Czar liked the facility and took it from him."

"How did the warlord react?" Jo'rian asked.

Rey chuckled, then answered. "The warlord was the asshole that got his head crushed by the Czar's woman. And that tank you saw outside is nothing. He has a lot more equipment in a garage on that base. There have been many deliveries done by me. I've picked up a lot of equipment throughout the rim for the Consortium that was being delivered to him. I tell you this: every site was a battlefield or a bloodbath. The Czar has other locations in the sector as well. This base, this is just one of many," the salvager boasted.

The woman scowled and cleared her throat, giving El Capitan a glare.

"What, this is common knowledge, no? Now, the fact that you are hiding a Ravager here in a stasis pod, that is a secret," the pirate stated openly.

"Let's just agree not to talk about it. Okay?" Lidia emphasized to the pirate.

"What? There is a Ravager here in this building? Is he going to burst out and kill us all?" Jo'rian said, surprised and pretending to be worried.

"No! Did you see any guards around this building?" the woman said to Jo'rian, then turned to the captain with an accusatory tone, "do you see what you started?"

"What! I said nothing about this building?" Rey said innocently.

"He is in the Oculus, but not in this building. Let's just leave it at that. Okay."

"Okay," the captain shrugged, unbothered.

"This has made me a bit uncomfortable, plus the long walk we had, can I please use your bathroom?" Jo'rian inquired politely.

"The men's bathroom is broken, and it won't be fixed until tomorrow. You need to go across the street or to another building. Here, take this emblem. That way, they know you are conducting business here," the woman said, giving Jo'rian a type of pass which was a symbol of a digitized eye with some information on it.

"Thank you," Jo'rian replied.

"Finally, alone!" he heard the captain say out loud as he closed the door.

Jo'rian removed his shirt and vest, leaving them in a small alcove of the building hoping to use the slave collar as a way to move throughout the slave filled market without arousing suspicion. Moving casually down the street carrying an empty box as he scouted the area and noticing several buildings that had guards, but of those, only one had no one going in or out.

He used his training and his logic to guestimate which building held the injured Ravager in stasis. Moving around the building, studying the entrances and exits, he noticed the guards were relaxed, not really expecting anyone. Though both guards were armed with rifles and pistols, they were preoccupied smoking and looking at the female slaves making their way down the street.

His reconnaissance revealed that the building he suspected had a regular door and a large cargo bay door. Both entrances were inaccessible, being close to the guards and easily seen by the massive volume of people moving up and down the street. Searching for an alternate route, the corporal made his way to the back of another building that had a dimly lit alley that would provide him an opportunity to access the roof.

Climbing up towards the roof, using the walls of two building, then making his way across, leaping from building to building until he reached his goal. Pausing to listen, then sneaking towards an access vent. The vent was barely large enough for him to fit, but somehow, he managed, making his way inside and confirming his suspicion, when he saw the stasis pod below. Taking his time to observe the inside of the warehouse through the slits of the vent, he saw nobody, but could hear the keys on a mechanical keyboard clicking away.

Using his fingers, he unscrewed the fasteners holding the vent in place, fortunately they were not too tight, and he could pry it open. The grate almost slipped from his grasp, but he somehow held on. Lowering his head through the vent, he saw a scientist monitoring the stasis pod on his display, while listening to music and writing some notes.

Infiltration was one of Jo'rian's specialties, he was well accustomed to searching for camera's and alarms, of which he only saw one. It was an older model and normally used with other cameras sitting just below him in the center of the room, rotating in a circle capturing the entire area. He glanced around the warehouse again, but confirmed that no other cameras were in the vicinity. In his scan of the room, he noticed a tranquilizer gun near the stasis pod.

Watching the camera that was just below him following the indicator on the top of the device that indicated the direction the camera was facing. Something that would normally not be noticed since the indicator would be against a ceiling or wall. He counted a quarter rotation and calculated that he had a forty-five second window for the camera to complete the rotation and him to accomplish his task. Counting out the seconds, he waited for the camera to pass and dropped to the ground, grabbing the tranquilizer gun and the darts.

Waiting again for another rotation as he watched the scientist who was hearing music and bobbing his head to the sounds coming from his ear buds. Loading a dart and shooting the scientist, who jumped up and quickly collapsed from the high dosage of the sedative.

Placing the gun back on the table, he ran for the scientist, propping the man up on his chair, as if he was staring at the monitor, and then hurried back to hiding, waiting for the camera to pass once more.

As he watched the scientist making sure the way he had propped the man up would hold, he noticed a tool bag nearby and dragged it to him, looking inside for what he needed. One screwdriver would do the job perfectly, fortunately he had various to choose from. Rummaging through the bag, finding the longest screwdriver, he counted in his mind. *43... 44... 45*

Turning off any alarm on the stasis pod panel, and opening the door, he recognized and confirmed the man was definitely the member of the xRavagers who had fallen from the plane out in the desert.

Asshole! he thought to himself, pulling the semi rigid body forward and making two quick and precise strikes into the man's spinal cord.

One stab would pierce the heart, while the other would puncture the man's throat and both would practically sever the spine. He made both attacks from behind, so they would not notice until it was way too late. One thought echoed in his mind as he made his attacks on the Ravager.

Though I be the lone survivor, I will prevail! I will be the last Ravager standing!

With a snarl, Jo'rian dug the tip of the screwdriver into the Ravager's back and made a cut from one side to the other, leaving a gash through the word Ravager unseen by the naked eye, but that he knew was tattooed with special ink on all the backs of all the Ravagers.

Pushing the body back into the pod and resetting the stasis chamber, left him little time for anything else. As the camera made its rotation, the corporal dove into hiding, waiting for the camera to pass him once more.

Standing after it passed, he slid the screwdriver under his belt, stared up at the vent that was about five meters up. Bending his knees for momentum, he jumped from a standing position, grabbing the sides of the vent and pulling himself inside. Glancing around once more, he quietly replaced the grate and vanished, leaving no trail of his presence except the now dead Ravager in stasis below.

Collecting his box and returning through the crowded streets, taking different turns, finally making his way back to the building to wash his face and use the bathroom before returning to the loft once more. Knocking on the door before entering, he peered inside. The salvager waved him in, pointed to a seat, and then returned his focus back to the monitors.

The hacker peered up at him from her work, studying him for a moment. "You sure took your time."

"Ma'am, there's just some things in life you just can't rush," Jo'rian replied.

Chuckling, El Capitan picked up a datapad and handed it to the young man. "Here, look these over. These are the ships in port and those coming in over the next few days."

Jo'rian sat down, studying the pad, going over each ship's profile and crew information when available. The hacker and the pirate went back and forth, arguing about whatever they were doing. They seemed to go between bickering and laughing, either way the chemistry between the two was plainly obvious, even to Jo'rian.

"And there you go. Rey del Castillo is once again a model citizen of the Galactic coalition. Good Luck," Lidia stated proudly.

"ME! A model citizen. I don't know about all that, but I will try," Rey said and laughed.

The woman turned to Jo'rian. "Now you, let's get this done."

"What about me? Do what?" the slave asked, confused.

"We are going to change your history and give you a clean slate. Even if you are a slave." Lidia paused and rolling her eyes at the salvager, "Why bother, Rey?"

El Capitan studied his new ID nodding at its quality, "A deal is a deal. A contract is a contract. I promised him a clean slate on the ship of his choice. I may be many things, but I am true to my word."

"I don't know if that's such a good idea. I am, or was, a special operative for the GDF. I am fairly certain my identification and picture will be on the highest of clearance levels. You'll get flagged," Jo'rian replied.

"Honey, thank you for your concern. A true gentleman you must be. You could learn something from him, Rey. It's not something you see in our line of work, but why don't you let me worry about that, okay? Now give me your name and your MID," the woman asked warmly.

Jo'rian took a deep breath and though hesitant, the words blurted out, "My name is Corporal Jo'Su, and my Military Identifications is JO3S49R26D7TOP."

The question was one that he'd been asked a thousand times while in training, and a prompt response was always required. It surprised him that he was not at attention when giving his information, and it felt odd. His universe was changing once again, like that day so many years ago, and he felt on the verge that it was about to spiral out of control.

"That is a tough neighborhood," the woman replied.

"Neighborhood? How do you know that? You haven't even begun typing," El Capitan asked.

"Rey, how could you be a pirate for so long and not understand GDF protocols?" the woman shot back.

"Easy. I stayed away from the GDF," Rey instantly replied, as he pointed to his head with his finger, boasting about his intelligence.

Sighing, as she shook her head. "Military ID's are a way to identify an individual's origins. Our friend here is from the 3rd Planet of the Jo system, which in this case is Jo, Sector 49, Region 26, District 7, and his blood type is O positive. If other GDF members have a similar ID, they would add more numbers as a descriptor. But in this case, his name is Jo' Su, meaning his true name is Su and his last name is Jo, like the planet and the system.

"But Jo is a refugee planet and the fact that your name is Su, would indicate that you come from the Indian Tribe of the Sioux's or the Sioux Nation. They have a colony there; they had some land granted to them or in this case a planet by Earth's tribal council, but the whole system is theirs. So, our friend here is of Native American Decent."

"So, you're a Native American, eh? That's great, Compai," Rey said enthusiastically.

The woman was typing away information as she explained things, but continued to look at the screen oddly on occasion and then back to the young soldier in front of her. The woman stopped and studied her screens for a moment, jumping from screen to screen of her multiscreen array.

"This may be a little tricky," the woman said.

"Tricky? That is a lot when you say it. How come?" the pirate asked.

"Because he's dead," she replied.

Every eye was on the soldier sitting by the wall, who did not seem surprised by the news. The other two looked at each other perplexed, then back to the young man expectantly. Jo'rian just sat there, waiting for a question.

"Compai?" Rey asked.

"What?" the young man answered.

"You're dead. That's what. Care to explain?" the woman shot back, moving her hand to a pistol underneath her desk.

"Please don't do that," Jo'rian pleaded.

Rey signaled at Lidia, making a gesture to leave the pistol. The pirate considered the control of the shock collar but was worried he would not reach the device in his pocket in time and would have to shoot his new friend. The pirate studied the soldier and his passive demeanor, but noticed a screwdriver in his hand. He looked at Jo'rian and made a gesture to him as well, interjecting to defuse the situation.

"We are all friends here, let us discuss this like civilized people, eh?"

"He's been dead for almost six years, Rey!" Lidia argued.

"Maybe it's a typo, eh?" Rey replied.

The young man calmly nodded, considering the two, and replied, "Actually, it is. But please read further into the file. Orphan, no surviving family, and now dead, someone that would not be missed. Does that not sound like the perfect Special Operations candidate?"

"Except that you are dead. Also, you are not in Special Operations. According to your file, you are part of the engineering and mechanics division. I don't like this Rey, something about this feels wrong and I think it's him," the woman said adamantly.

"He's fine! And he is my friend, and we will help him," Rey insisted.

"Friend? You barely know him. You said you met him like two weeks ago, you don't call anyone friend and mean it. You have no friends," the fiery Irish woman shot back.

"He has one," Jo'rian said, bringing the room to silence.

"You see? I have one," the salvager said, smiling.

"Well Jo'su, are you sure you do? This wretched pirate is loyal to no one and if you doubt me, just think about it, friends don't keep friends as prisoners or sell them to market. A real friend would put his ass on the line for you and would have set you free. How much of a friend could he really be, huh?" the hacker snapped back with a smug look on her face.

Rey slammed his booted heel on the floor loudly. "A contract is a contract!"

"Why don't the both of you just get the hell out of here?" the woman practically shouted and pointed at the door.

Serenity replaced a quick moment of anger when El Capitan replied in his usual fashion, "Very well, we shall depart. Me and my FRIEND will take our leave and my money."

The woman looked at the precious metals, then back to the salvager. "Don't make me pull this gun on you, Rey."

"The money for my services is yours, the money for his you have not yet earned and are in breach of contract," the pirate said as he grabbed the proper precious metals for payment.

"You are so infuriating; I am trying to protect you! He is a slave and one with a very sketchy past. This can get you killed, Rey. Ugh!" the woman vented in frustration, throwing herself into her chair.

"As you said, what kind of friend would I be if I wasn't willing to put my ass on the line?" The captain replied with his own smug smile.

The woman sat there shaking her head as El Capitan began taking the agreed portion of what was to be Jo'rian's record purge. The hacker was visibly frustrated and upset, mumbling a curse while she stared at the screen, then looked at the soldier.

"Wait!" she called out. The woman gazed at the screen for a moment, then looked towards the pirate with scrutiny. "You bring someone to my door, someone that I have never met, and then lie to me. You have gall. Rey, you can tell a lie to anyone, but not me. How could you?"

"And you!" she said accusingly, pointing a finger at Jo'rian as she turned to face him. "Who are you? You are not the person I am looking at in your file. This person was injured in an explosion on Jo, where his parents passed away and was left with a scar on his left ear, you don't have a scar."

The young soldier looked off, shaking his head, an obvious debate going through his mind. He looked at the pirate, who returned the look by nodding reassuringly. Jo'rian then looked at the woman that had obvious affection for the El Capitan and an arsenal at her disposition and he was not even considering the weapon under her desk in that thought.

"Compai, be truthful with her. It's the only way we can help you," the salvager said with sincerity.

"Rey, maybe you do, but she doesn't really, and I can't blame her for it. I am trouble, and people that bring trouble to another's door are problems. Problems are something that only people you trust can help with, if they even do. And even if she helps me, how can I trust her to keep my secrets, it's an enormous risk?" Jo'rian replied.

"See, he gets it," the fiery woman told Rey.

The captain sighed, once again impressed by his friend. "Why? Because I trust her, and in this rotten cesspool, that is a lot to say. I trust her with my life, my heart, and everything else. I vouch for her, as I vouch for you. She will not betray you and will keep your secret."

"But she's right, you don't even know me. Not really," Jo'rian protested.

Rey smiled as he scratched his head. "I may not know your entire history, this is true. But my gut tells me you are an honorable person inside and I like you. I believe that and as she said, I don't have friends, but I am your friend and just by your protest you are protecting us. I believe you are my friend. So here I am, starting a new life and putting our asses on the line for you and not because of a contract, but because we are friends."

"Are you sure, Rey? It's my ass here, too," the woman asked with a changed demeanor.

"I am. And if it goes south, I will take you with me wherever I go, and we will face whatever comes together."

The woman's fiery personality was almost pacified by the man's words and stood there looking at him for a moment and responded with the upmost emotion, "Oh Rey, you asshole! That's the nicest thing you have ever said to me." The woman sighed, shaking her head in disbelief, then looked at the young soldier. "Okay, tell me your story. All of it!"

"My name is Jo'rian, and my family still lives on Jo. I took my cousin's place who was in the mechanic and engineering division, so that I could see their new ship. It was supposed to be only for a day. But that day has turned into five plus years. We looked enough alike that we could get away with it." The young man looked away and sighed, thinking about that fateful day so many years ago.

"An explosion orphaned him, and we took him in, after all, he's family. We were very close; we worked on all sorts of vehicles with my father, and me being an advance engineering student. We were able to swap places unnoticed, the only one who knew was his lieutenant, and he's been dead for a long time. Before you ask, Rey—no, I didn't kill him, he was a friend." Jo'rian paused, taking a deep breath. "That ship I wanted to see turned out to be a transfer ship to a new highly classified special operations unit. All very hush, hush, no one knew about it, not even the lieutenant. So, I played along all these years, because if I said anything, my whole family would be at risk. I need them to be safe, it's all I hold on, too. That's the truth," Jo'rian said earnestly.

The captain grinned as he turned to the hacker. "He's just a boy protecting his family, how noble is that?"

"That is noble, but it says here that your height was 5'5 you are almost 5'11. Five inches is a lot to grow. After the age of fifteen," the woman said dubiously.

"I had a procedure done, it increased my height and weight. Correction, they had a procedure done on me," the young man replied.

Moving over and placing a reassuring hand on Jo'rian's shoulder, Rey spoke reassuringly, "I believe you, Compai, it's just too outrageous not to believe, and I've seen your luck. So don't worry, we will help you." Rey nodded to Jo'rian before addressing Lidia. "Beloved, before you start and I know you are already checking his family, show him his family, he has not seen them in five years. I am sure he misses his mama and papa."

The woman began typing and displayed a family on the screen. "There you go."

"That's not them," Jo'rian replied quickly, giving the woman a glare.

A few keystrokes later, she displayed another picture on the screen. Jo'rian shook his head at the screen, annoyed, then at the redheaded hacker. "Not them either. Come on, I told you the truth," he protested.

"Here, this is a graduation photo of you and your sister," Lidia finally said.

"She graduated," Jo'rian mumbled quietly, filling with long suppressed emotion, his eyes slightly watering. He slowly approached the screen, running a hand down her face. "She's so big," he said, smiling towards the captain. More pictures flooded the screen, pictures of his parents and the whole family together. The hacker had searched social media and had brought up every picture she could find of his family. It overwhelmed the young man when suddenly he took a step back, a terrified look on his face as he addressed the hacker, his demeanor shifting to a serious tone. "You must remove any connection of this from me. If they find them, they will hurt them. I accepted my fate long ago, but please keep them safe."

The hacker believed his sincerity. "I will, I promise. We will start by removing some connections and then we will give you a last name. Your name is common enough as far as close variations in that sector that you can keep your name, but it will now be all together, **JORIAN**. As for your last name."

"Give him mine, make him a Del Castillo," Rey interjected proudly.

"No! That's mine to take, if I want it. Plus, we don't want any connections," the woman replied.

"You had your chance, woman, when I proposed earlier," Rey shot back indignantly.

"Was that for real?" she asked, puzzled.

"You will never know," Rey replied.

"Either way, it can't be that," the hacker said dismissively.

"How about PHOENIX? Since he died and came back from the ashes, reborn," the pirate said with flare and showmanship.

The hacker shrugged. "That can work. Jorian Phoenix it is."

Jorian grinned and nodded, thinking it sounded cool. The pirate smiled smugly, as the woman worked away feverishly. The two men conversed and laughed when they were finally cut off by the hacker.

"This is going to be awhile, I have to go slowly removing him from classified servers. It's not simple work, I will probably be here all night. So why don't you two leave? Do you want me to put any credits in his account?" the woman asked.

"No, slaves cannot have a history like that, after we will put some credits for him. For now, we leave you, Belleza," the pirate said charmingly, blowing her a kiss.

"Oh, Rey!" she called out.

"Yes, my dear," the pirate said cheerfully.

"Put my fee back on the table and it's going to cost you more," she said with a smile.

A serious look came on to the captain's face. "How much more?"

"Your vehicle," she replied.

The captain took a step back, shocked. "My car?"

"Come on, hand them over. I already have a buyer. Anyway, you're leaving, why do you need a vehicle?" The woman said, signaling for the keys.

The salvager looked towards Jorian distressed and then shrugged it off, tossing the woman the keys. "Fine, but you're going to auction with me."

"Fine, whatever. Oh, I know you have a spare, so take your gear and get it cleaned and detailed. I'll pay for the detailing, before you complain. Take it to Hiro. Now be good boys and lock the door on your way out," she said as she returned to work.

Rey looked at Jorian and then to the fiery red-haired woman behind the desk, feeling as if he'd been swindled and slowly placing the precious metal coins back onto her desk. Looking to Jorian one more time, nodding his head reassuringly and walking out the door.

The two friends left the Oculus and made their way back to the city streets. The sun had crossed the sky and a starless sky loomed above the bright city. The two walked, making their way through a section of the city that was dimmer than the rest, with narrow streets that seem to be neglected. A beggar sat by a wall just before an opening to a major thoroughfare.

"Any clinks to spare, governor?" the man said as he rattled a tin cup at them.

Jorian looked around waiting for others to surround them, but the street stayed empty. The man was dirty and smelled even worse, his pants were partly torn along with the rest of his garments. El Capitan reached into his coat and pulled out what seemed to be a silver coin and showed it to the man between two fingers and tossed it into the cup, making the other coins rattle once more.

"Aye, sir. You are too kind, heaven bless ya," the man said humbly.

The man extended his hand quickly, passing off a small piece of paper to the captain, who quickly took it and in a swift motion, hid it in his sleeve and nodded to the beggar, as he moved on. The transaction was almost seamless and would have been unnoticed, even by Jorian, had he not been on such high alert.

The two made their way down the main street, stopping by an open pub with seating outside. It was a pleasant night with a gentle breeze; the captain asked for a table for two outside on the second level with a view of the port. There were a few people and most were inside or heading off, given the late hour. Having ordered some food and drinks, the captain turned to his companion.

"Well, here we are, as promised. It is a beautiful view, all those ships in all sorts of conditions, ready to head off to the great beyond. So, Compai, which ship do you want to head off in? Even my genius takes time."

"I am not sure, there are some that show promise, like that one over there, *The Warden,* I think it's called. It seems to be a simple cargo freighter. Maybe the *Crispy Queen* over there, though she has seen better days. The crew on the *Flagweed* seem too relaxed for a ship that size. Truth is, I am not sure," Jorian replied.

Rey sipped a goblet of wine he had ordered as he grabbed a few pieces of cubed cheese, he looked over to his friend and eyed him up and down for a moment. You're thinking about killing the crew and stealing the ship?"

"The thought crossed my mind, why?" Jorian asked.

"You know, Compai, you've been hanging around pirates too long. Those three ships seem like prominent targets and though they are all pirate vessels, two of them have a crack crew, and though you may be able to put your plan in motion, it may prove to be more than you bargained for. The third one, the *Flagweed*, is a smuggling vessel for the Oculus moving large quantities of narcotics and opioids, I'd stay away from that one. They have some automated systems and some attack robots that are quite vicious, not to mention real time monitoring with escort ships that are never too far away. Now the..." The salvager was interrupted by a loud noise.

The two men looked up as they heard the sputtering of thrusters backfiring and engines reeving unevenly with a horrid screeching sound. The copper-colored corvette class ship was simmering and descending unevenly, with sparks flying from at least two malfunctioning thrusters. Smoked exhausted out of two others and the ship was descending in somewhat of a controlled fashion, the two knew the pilot was having a hard time controlling it.

The two and everyone in the streets looked at the ship as it struggled its way across the sky with obvious damage on its exterior. Thrusters came on and off as the pilot tried to maintain control of the ship and even suddenly dropped about fifty meters, but leveled off. The two men stood leaning over the rail and looking past the port wall as the ship made its final touchdown on the landing pad, almost scraping the ground with the ship's belly from the hard landing, stressing the shock absorbers.

The copper-colored frigate sized ship had seen better days, as the lights on the landing pad shone along the ship, showing various scratches and dents to the hull. On its side, the ship's name and an enticing emblem of a bombshell girl with dark red-hair, purple-eyes and a mischievous grin could easily be seen. The ship released a gigantic cloud of steam from the exhaust vents and smoke from the thrusters. Fans on the launching pad blew the smoke up, giving the ship a mystical look along with the piercing eyes and the exposed legs of the woman on the emblem, stirring the emotions of those that saw her.

"Mistress of Mayhem," Jorian said out loud as he read the ship's name.

The two men nodded approvingly at the pilot's skill and if as they read each other's mind. Jorian stared at the ship, looking at the eyes of the purple-eyed vixen, then told Rey, "That's the one!"

Rey nodded as he lifted his goblet to toast with his companion, clashing the cups loudly. "To the Mistress!" he said with a smile.

"To the Mistress!" Jorian replied.

Chapter 9

Ophelia sat back in the pilot's chair, letting out a sigh of relief. She began flipping switches, turning off several systems that had been blaring alarms since they had entered the atmosphere. She looked over to Emmy who was still gripping onto the arms of her chair stiffly, looking over to Ophelia with a terrified smile.

"Good landing," the young woman got out before rushing to a basin on the bridge to throw up.

Ophelia rested her head against the headrest for a moment and looked at the Christmas tree on the wall, which was nothing more than a system's status panel with multicolored lights that earlier crews had named centuries ago, but now it displayed more red lights than green ones, and an occasional yellow from all the alarms and heating issues the ship had endured during the trip and the landing.

Mistress's voice came on the speaker. "We are fifth in cue for the Dock Master. The tower informs me it's going to be about an hour."

"Well, that's fine, it'll give us some time to clean up. Mistress, how are our guests?" The young woman asked.

"After everything, I cannot be sure, but my sensors are telling me they are fine, and besides a slight elevation in heart rate, the prisoner is fine, too. Given my system issues, I must agree with Dr. Emmy that was a good landing." Various external pictures displayed on the screen showing the ship from different angles. "Madam, I would advise after initial cool down that you shut off almost all systems until you can get someone to thoroughly inspect me. We will be on shore power anyway if you decide to pay for it. I could still use my internal generators if you wish not too, but I would advise a full diagnostic after a full slow cool down."

"We will run on the internal generators, and avoid shore power as much as possible, we don't know how consistent or clean the power is way out here, but keep the status on standby. As for a full diagnostic, do we have any Knightforge Technologies shops here?" the woman asked.

"No, but there are some certified shops. Which are most likely subpar, at best. The equipment on board is by far more sophisticated than anything out here in the rim. Problem is finding someone who knows how to use it," Mistress replied.

"At a fair price," Ophelia added.

"Good luck with that, the rim techs are notorious thieves, or so I heard, back on the tanker," Emmy replied after washing her face.

"The good news is that there are some genuine Knightforge Technologies' parts coming up for auction in 28 hours. There is also one of my components in that auction," Mistress replied.

"How do you know it is yours?" Ophelia asked.

"Some of my parts are specific to me and have serial numbers that start or end with the letters M-O-M," Mistress replied.

"So, this is where it ended up. Nice," Ophelia stated.

"Luckily, it should not be too expensive since it doesn't fit anything else," Mistress clarified.

"Luckily," the young woman agreed.

A few hundred yards away, the two men sat on the upper terrace of the pub, enjoying a meal as they discussed the ship's damage and necessary repairs, though it was all mostly guess work given no actual diagnostics besides seeing the ship perform.

"They are fifth in line for the Dock Master and now fourth," Rey stated, looking at a giant lighted board with information that took up most of the back section of the port.

"Well, let's go talk to them," Jorian pressed.

"Patience. We can't go near that ship until the Dock Master visits it," Rey told his friend.

"Why?"

"Legal piracy. The government and the Dock Master need to take their cut. They don't want any obvious smuggling. They collect taxes on anything being brought off. And how quickly you can move your cargo is up to the dockmaster. It's a scam, but a mostly legal one. Anyway, what are you going to say? Hi, I am Jorian. Can I be your slave? Oh, and you'll be dead by the time we leave orbit," Rey replied between sips of his wine.

Jorian looked at El Capitan, annoyed. "No, but that is a magnificent ship. It belongs to and was built by Knightforge Technologies."

"Knightforge Technologies makes and owns many ships, and though that is a fairly unique ship. It's just a ship," Rey retorted.

"Shows what you know. The Mistress was designed, built, and owned by Mr. Knight himself. It's a prototype, one ship run," Jorian said excitedly.

"What? How do you know all that?" El Capitan asked.

Jorian quickly reeled himself in. "I read it somewhere. When I was younger, I wanted to work for Knightforge Technologies. I was competing for a Junior Engineering Scholarship."

"Did you get it?" Rey asked.

"Never finished, for obvious reason," was the young man's answer.

"So, who's flying it now? Didn't Knight and his family supposedly disappear a few years ago?" Rey asked.

"Yup, they did. As for who is piloting or captaining, I don't know," Jorian replied.

"Hmm. I guess we'll find out soon enough, eh?"

The two continued conversing like old friends as they ate their meal, letting the time slip by. They were finishing their dessert when the lights around the ship changed, showing that they held the 1st spot on the list. In the distance, a cart with a well-dressed man accompanied by six guards drove in the ship's direction. Suddenly, lights were flashing as four-armed security vehicles joined the Dock Master. Something that got the attention of the former pirate. "Intriguing. I wonder what's going on down there. This may get ugly," Rey uttered as he adjusted himself in his chair, sitting upright and placing a pair of spectacles on his face, sliding a finger back and forth along the rim of the glasses, adjusting the magnification and zoom on his glasses. Touching his IDP, an image appeared and showed it to Jorian.

"Here, so you can see, too."

"What, no audio," Jorian mocked.

El Capitan grinned. "Hey, they may not be what you are used to, but they cost me a pretty penny. Also, those security vehicles have some sort of audio scrambler on board. So be happy with what you get."

The two watching intently as the Dock Master's vehicle stopped and his guards formed a semicircle around him. The other vehicles made a perimeter around the cargo ramp with a person in the gunner's seat of each vehicle. Once in place, the Dock Master hailed the ship.

"Mistress of Mayhem, this is Dock Master Duresst. Please open your cargo bay and prepare for inspection and prisoner removal."

"This is Ophelia Captain of the Mistress, we copy and are complying, if there are any delays, we took some damage in transit. Please stand by."

"Mistress, lower the ramp and open the bay doors," Ophelia commanded.

"Yes, captain," the ship said in her usual sultry voice.

As the ramp slowly lowered and the bay doors opened, the mechanical sounds of winding gears filled the surrounding area. The Dock Master stood there with a large datapad in hand and a digital pen tapping impatiently against the pad. His demeanor was that of someone who did not want to be bothered by a prisoner transport exchange, and the overseeing eyes of GDF security personnel.

The Dock Master approached with a GDF Sergeant at his side. "Captain Ophelia, I am Dock Master Duresst and this is Sergeant Odis, I am here to inspect your cargo and collect taxes and fees. The Sergeant here will sign off and take your prisoners. Is your shipping manifest complete?"

"Yes, sir. I added the last item at our last stop, with no currency exchange as stated. They lent us the use of their loader in exchange for the delivery. I have attached the forms of that transaction signed and recorded by the Dock Master at our last stop," Ophelia half turning to address the sergeant. "Sergeant, we have one prisoner in a holding cell, if you want to send some men with Dr. Kricay, she'll happily show them the way."

The sergeant instructed two of his soldiers to apprehend the detainee and then looked at the Dock Master oddly for a moment, then at the young woman for clarification. Emmy led the soldiers to their brig to retrieve the female prisoner, while the Dock Master finished going over the documentation on his datapad and signed off on it before sending it back to the young woman along with her bill.

"Knight as in Knightforge Technologies, Knight?" the Dock Master inquired, intrigued.

"Yes. I am the daughter," Ophelia replied.

"I see," the pudgy Dock Master said, taking on a new demeanor and rubbing his fingers together, thinking he had found a new mark to take money from.

"I am sorry for your loss, ma'am. I heard about your parent's disappearance. You father's company makes good gear," Sergeant Odis said sincerely.

"Thank you, Sergeant. Mister Duresst, why are these docking fees so high?" Ophelia asked, surprised.

"My dear, your ship is in a state of disrepair, and must be properly inspected before departure, for the safety of the residents of our city, of course. Also, you see a week's worth of docking fees, which need to be paid in advance, which is city policy. Consider it a deposit, if you leave sooner, they return the remaining funds, minus fees and taxes, of course," the dockmaster explained, emphasizing the portion pertaining to his fees.

"Of course," Ophelia replied semi-sarcastically.

"If you need diagnostics and repairs, I can happily refer you to some quality personnel or companies allowed to work on the dock," the man replied intently.

The soldier considered the Dock Master with disdain, shaking his head.

Rey, continued observing from his table at the pub, made a disgusted huff as he commented to his companion. "You see, the well-dressed, pudgy bastard over there. That's Dock Master Duresst. He's a real greedy piece of shit. He is probably robbing that young lady blind with bullshit docking fees and prepaid stays to increase his take. Bastard!"

Ophelia just studied her IDP and begrudgingly agreed. "Very well, Mr. Duresst, but I will need an itemized receipt, so I may submit it to the company's lawyers, in case any quarrels or future disputes with fees, since Knightforge Technologies gets special rates at GDF sponsored ports. Please make sure your name is written clearly, so they know who to address in the inquiry," the young woman said in an even tone.

Duresst cleared his throat and began fidgeting uncomfortably. "Hmm, well I will double check that for you Captain and make sure that it's all correct as I inspect your cargo to confirm accuracy. If you will excuse me."

The Dock Master quickly hurried off as the sergeant grinned, looking at the lady out of the corner of his eye, whispered. "Well done."

Ophelia whispered back. "Thank you."

The soldiers returned with the scientist and the prisoner in custody. The sergeant looked at the woman and then at Ophelia. "This woman was supposed to be in stasis, can you explain? "

The pirate was about to interject but was sent to her knees with a shock from one of the guard's shock batons. Emmy grinned with an internal pleasure seeing the woman shocked through narrow eyes, wishing she could be the one shocking the woman.

"Of course, Sergeant. As I said before, we had taken some damage in an asteroid field, which may have caused some sort of malfunction with the stasis pods. That woman ambushed us in an attempt to take my ship. We fought her off and eventually subdued her, but not without taking our hits. She critically wounded one of my crew members in the attack."

The pirate again tried to protest and was shocked again, sending her down to her knees. Emmy stood there confused and was about to question Ophelia, but was interrupted by the sergeant, who looked over and gave an order to his soldiers. "If she tries that again, make sure she doesn't get up. Ms. Knight, please continue."

"Thank you, Sergeant. As I was saying, Billy, one of our crewmates, was critically injured with a stab wound in the fight and we were able to reset the pod and put him in a medical stasis, until we arrived here hoping to get him proper medical attention. He was on loan to us from the GDF and was finishing his contract of service by aiding us. I have the documentation here. Can you please make sure he gets the medical attention he requires?" Ophelia finished speaking in a tone of innocence.

"What? But of course. GDF takes care of its own. Thank you for such quick thinking. You may have just saved his life. We have a freelance doctor here on the docks. He's very good and he can take a look. It's a much better option than the hospital here. Are you ladies in need of any medical attention?" The sergeant asked formally.

"No, thank you, Sergeant. Fortunately, we're okay," Ophelia said as she ran her fingers through her dark hair.

Roxanne was slowly making her way to her feet; her demeanor had changed and was no longer resisting. Whether it was the shock, or

Ophelia's words, no one would know, but it was most likely a little of both. The pirate woman almost seemed grateful as she looked back at the transport pod, then was pulled by the soldiers. Sergeant Odis nodded as he cleared his throat, turning back to Ophelia. "Well, in case you do, Brother Julius is over there near the tower in his mobile clinic, he's probably the best you will find on this planet, and his rates are fair. Or at least better than the Dock Masters."

Ophelia smile, placing a hand on the man's arm. "Thank you, sergeant."

"Of course, Ms. Knight," he said, nodding, then turned, giving orders to his men. "Alpha squad, get ready to receive an injured soldier. You take that pod to Brother Julius. Bravo will take the woman in their vehicle and Charlie and Delta prepare to tow and escort that prisoner transport pod."

Ophelia pressed a few buttons on a remote that engaged the pod's drive, slowly bringing it forward and down the ramp. Once on the ground, she gave the remote to the sergeant along with a datapad to conclude the prison transfer.

The sergeant looked at the young woman with a smile. "The prisoner and personnel transfer are complete, the Galactic Defense Force thanks you for your cooperation. Don't worry ma'am, we will watch over Billy, and before I go, let me do one more thing for you." Turning, looking towards the Dock Master and whistling, "Duresst, let's go, the transfer is complete."

"You may go sergeant; I have my own men," the dockmaster replied, hoping to still salvage the situation.

"Negative Duresst. We have an active prisoner situation, which rules dictate that when we are done, you are done. No one stays behind. You are now part of the escort until we reach the tower. So, let's go," the sergeant stood tall, slightly turning to Ophelia and winked, then moved to his vehicle. The pudgy Dock Master mumbled under his breath and sent Ophelia an updated receipt, then left.

The two ladies waved as all the vehicles departed before returning to the ship and closing the cargo doors. The ramp had not finished closing when Emmy grabbed Ophelia's arm, turning to face her with an angry scowl on her face. After everything that the scientist had experienced on the tanker, then everything that happened on the trip, and now lying to the GDF was not something she wanted haunting her later. "Why did you lie to them about Billy? I don't want any more trouble, and that can be serious trouble."

Ophelia sighed and turned to her companion. "Because I didn't want his death on my conscience, and if they would have sent him to the hospital, it would have been a death sentence. I was reading up about the local hospitals and it seems that they have a thriving underground organ harvesting operation here. What do you think would've happened to a young, loaner, deserter turned pirate?" Ophelia shrugged. "I didn't want that on our conscience."

Emmy's demeanor quickly changed as she looked away. "I get it, but what about the pirate? She can rat us out."

"She won't. Didn't you see how she changed after what I said about Billy? She accepted the blame for his injury, understanding that I was saving his life. Love is a crazy thing," Ophelia said and placed a comforting hand on the scientist's shoulder. "Don't worry, you'll have your turn at love."

Emmy smiled back. "Thanks, I know. It just had been such a long time, and it felt nice."

"I bet. You two screwed all over the ship. Slut," Ophelia said mockingly.

"What can I say? I had repressed a lot," Emmy replied, giggling.

Back on the terrace, the two men continued to eat and watch the spectacle unfold before them. The caravan had left and less than a minute later; the prisoner had freed herself and jumped out of a moving vehicle, injuring herself. The few moments were intense and exciting to watch, but confusing.

"That was dumb, how bad do you think she hurt herself?" Jorian asked.

"If I was a betting man, I would say not at all. Something is afoot," Rey replied.

They secured the prisoner once more with more restraints, then loaded her into the vehicle. The caravan continued its way to the tower, stopping by a familiar sight. Rey increased the zoom on his spectacles to maximum, reaching its max distance of a little more than a kilometer, and tried to refocus. They looked upon the mobile clinic to find a familiar face greeting the caravan, and both men smiled.

"Well, well, Compai. It seems our friend Brother Julius made it safely to the city. Your efforts were not in vain. Eh?" the veteran salvager stated with a smile.

"So, it seems."

"You know, maybe he will buy you and free you in..." El Capitan began to say, but was cut off.

"No! We found the ship, and the captain of that ship. The deal was my choice. And I want her," Jorian said sternly, pointing to the mistress.

"Tsssst. Easy, I know the deal." The pirate sighed as he tried to formulate a solution, then quickly changed to mock his friend. "So, you want her, eh? Good choice. Well, since we're on the topic, let us talk business. You must report to the auction house in the morning. We slated you as a premium asset. Please, no fighting or, better yet, no killing. Other premium assets are fighters, while some others are highly trained slaves, amongst other goods. See, nothing but the best for you," Rey said encouragingly.

"For me or you?" Jorian retorted.

"Us, how about for us?" Rey shot back.

"I was treated as property with the GDF. Now I am being sold like some common article by a friend. I don't like it," Jorian stated uncomfortably.

El Capitan sighed. "Premium item, get it right. I know this sucks. I would buy you myself and set you free, if it would not bring problems for us. Please trust me, Compai. When I say this is what's best for us. Trust me, Eh?"

"Fine!" was Jorian's solemn answer.

"Now go back to the room and get some rest. Tomorrow is a big day," Rey told him.

The young soldier finished his meal quietly, as the pirate continued studying the mobile clinic. The shrewd pirate's eyes went from the ship to the clinic and then back again when Jorian stood to leave.

"Compai. You trust me?" Rey asked suddenly.

Jorian stopped and glanced back. "All these days together and I have not tried to take this collar off yet and you're still alive. What do you think?"

"Good night, Compai," Rey replied.

"Night." The young man walked off, hoping his trust was not misplaced. After all, he didn't want to have to kill El Capitan.

Rey stayed at his seat for a long time, pondering and planning. He eventually made his way to the tower. It was a delightful night, with a crispness in the air as the man considered his next steps.

Reaching the port tower, the guards greeted him warmly instead of checking him as they did for all who entered the area. El Capitan had made the city of Taidar his second home for many years, forming many connections and was well received. He was walking down the hall when he noticed Sergeant Odis headed in his direction with his men and a female prisoner.

"Capitan," the sergeant greeted the pirate as he walked by.

"Sergeant Odis," Rey replied cheerfully.

Each man in the detail acknowledged the smuggler, as did the female pirate. Rey addressed each one back by name, even the female prisoner. The sergeant looked back and shook his head in disbelief and continued on his way. Reaching the clinic, he politely knocked on the door.

Terri answered the door and froze, seeing who it was, remembering their last encounter. She hurried to get her grandfather. Brother Julius came out with a medical apron on and a scalpel in his hand. The former pirate raised his hands, implying no threat.

"What do you want? I am preparing for surgery," Brother Julius asked gruffly.

"Brother Julius, I know that the last time we met was less than hospitable, on the consortiums behalf. Please accept my sincerest apology and know that I am no longer with them. Also, I am glad you and the little ones are well. Please remember I tried to persuade the Empress, may she rot in hell, to release you," Rey responded with genuine sincerity.

"The consortium can go to..." The old man paused, realizing that his two grandchildren were present.

"A wise decision, since they are reformed and most likely plotting against each other by now. As I said, I am free of them and done so by their rules, thanks to you and your friend," the former pirate quickly added.

"My friend?" the doctor said, momentarily confused.

"Yes, your friend. The man who saved you and your family's life, by shooting the Empress and two of her guards," Rey clarified.

"Jo'su?" the young girl quickly interjected.

The room was very tense for a moment, and even Nate looked up. The old man looked at the two children, noticing their reaction and the impact the young man had on the two in such a short time. Julius's eyes got a little watery as he felt a surge of sadness for the young man whom he had expected was dead.

"That is not his name, but yes," Rey responded kindly.

"Mister Capitan, is he okay?" the girl asked.

160

The former pirate looked at the girl with a warm smile and kneeled down to her level. "Yes! He is well and the reason for all of our freedom."

A furry silvery white fox pup appeared from behind a corner and ran up to Rey, intensely smelling him all over and actually barked as it wagged its furry tail. Rey was surprised and momentarily froze, not realizing the animal was a pup at first. The grandson quickly moved, petting the pup with excitement after weeks of moping around the clinic. The old man put the scalpel down and removed the medical apron and hugged his grandson. His eyes were watery as he held the boy and then brought the girl into his arms too. Rey tried to move back when the fox pup leaped on him and in seconds, was on his shoulder smelling some more.

The old man stood up and shook the salvager's hand. "Thank you Rey. That pup has been lying in its bed as if he was dying since that day and my grandson with him. Seeing that little pup go crazy is the best thing to happen to us in days."

"Ahh, it's probably smelling Jorian's scent," Rey replied.

"Jorian, is that his name? Is he here?" the doctor asked, looking around.

"Yes, it is, and no, he is not. I sent him back to the room a little while ago to get some rest. I need your help to save him," Rey stated.

"If that young man is in trouble, I will run to him immediately," The old healer replied without hesitation.

"No, no. He's fine, but can we talk? I brought a friend," the former pirate said as he pulled a bottle from his pocket.

The old doctor shook his head in disbelief. "Very well. Come sit."

"And your patient?"

"He'll be fine, he's in stasis," Julius replied as he grabbed two glasses.

"Great," Rey replied, opening the bottle.

The two men caught up with what happened in the last few weeks since that day, all the while the fox curled itself up on El Capitan's lap as he petted the young fox. Rey told the doctor about his plan and his deal with Jorian and asked for his help, something that the doctor easily agreed to after his offer to buy Jorian and for a generous sum. A sum that would be more than he expected at auction, but turned it down given his contract and his friend's request.

"I need to find out more about the woman that pilots the Mistress of Mayhem out there, and I also need to make sure she goes to auction tomorrow. Can you assist me with that?" Rey told the healer.

"How do I do that?" the old man asked incredulously.

"Find out what she needs on that ship and tell her they have one at auction, then tell me what it is, to see if I can get it there in time," Rey replied as he stood handing the pup to the doctor. "Now take this fox or whatever it is and let me go on my way. I have much to do, and little time to do it."

"Funny enough, I think that belongs to that boy Jorian, it appeared just before I found him in the desert," the old man stated.

"That young man is something else, in a way, he saved us all."

"That he is, Rey. Be careful, he is very dangerous. For someone his age."

Chuckling, Rey replied, "In all my years, and though they may not be as much as you. I have seen my fair share and I tell you, he is the most dangerous 20-year-old I have ever seen, and I have seen plenty."

The old man's face turned very serious and exclaimed. "20! He should be almost 25."

"No, my good doctor, I assure you, he recently turned 20," Rey replied confidently.

"Oh, that's good to know," the doctor said dismissively, but had a whirlwind running through his mind from this unknown fact and critical piece of information of his former patient.

The former pirate left, leaving the doctor with a sense of ease as to Jorian's outcome, but troubled by the data he just received. Julius poured himself another drink and sat there, thinking of all the possibilities and consequences of Jorian's age could cause. He asked the computer to replay his session with the young man and the details of his project. Sitting calmly listing to the young man talk about the Ravager program, when his concern was confirmed. The man played the recording back once more hearing the young man state.

"Only those between eighteen and twenty-four were selected. That age was chosen because it provided the best results. Older than that, the possibilities of instability in the formulas increased, younger than the age of eighteen made it more difficult, because the youthful bodies of the subjects were still developing. Those results were too scattered and most of the subjects ended up in death.

The survival rate for the selected people was less than forty percent. Those between the ages of sixteen and eighteen, that rate went down to thirteen percent. Below sixteen, they believed it to be less than one percent survival rate."

Confirming his suspicions about Jorian, Julius now understood a lot more about Jorian's rarity of surviving the procedure. That number had just grown to a statistical impossibility, under one percent and if that was not enough, he was still developing, which was scary to think about. With the new information, the doctor felt more compelled than ever to assist Jorian and find a way to get himself on that ship, too.

Chapter 10

The sun shone brightly over the docks, its warm rays reflecting off the metallic hulls of the ships at the port. People and vehicles were moving around, bringing the area to life from its slumber overnight. Loaders moved cargo to and from the ship, while other workers attended to maintenance issues or prepped the ships for departure, loading luggage and passengers. Between the shuffle of the people and the vehicles, a robed man with two children made their way down the indicated walkways at the port towards the Mistress's dock post which was nothing more than a covered area with a few seats and a console that allowed communications with the docked ship.

Reaching the covered area, the doctor pushed the call button and waited for a response. "Greetings! My name is Brother Julius. I am the one who is attending to your injured crew mate. Sergeant Odis asked me to come by and check in on you. Are you available?"

After a few moments, Ophelia replied in a sleepy voice. "Doctor, I'll be right down, give me a few minutes."

Brother Julius sat down on his portable hand cart and watched the children play with the furry pup that seemed more active than ever. He studied the ship carefully, never having seen one like it before. The ship's ramp finally slid down as the cargo bay's doors opened. There stood two young women, the smaller one stood there in her robe and slippers, yawning. Her hair was in a jumbled mess as she scratched her head sleepily, appearing as if she had just awoken.

The other lady was wearing a pair of overalls with a jacket and a belt with a satchel on her hip balanced with a knife on her other hip.

Sturdy boots with clasps on the side and a protective plate on the front to protect her shins rounded out her outfit. The captain moved with purpose down the ramp, practically dragging the other woman behind her.

"Good morning," Ophelia said courteously.

"Good morning. Please forgive my intrusion so early. I figured you would like to know the status of your crewmate," the old healer responded with the greatest of bedside manners.

"Billy?" Emmy said, perking up instantly, unconsciously fixing her robe.

Ophelia looked at Emmy, who just shrugged at her defensively before addressing the doctor. "Yes, doctor. Billy was our crewmate. I am Ophelia, Captain of the Mistress of Mayhem, thank you for your attention to Billy and for coming out here to inform us, it is very kind of you." She paused, then quickly added, "Please let me inform you that the GDF is responsible for payment of your services, if that is the issue."

The healer quickly waved his hand, dismissing any notion of payment. "Oh, no! Not at all, that has already been taken care of, don't you worry. I am here to let you know that the surgery was successful, and Billy will make a full recovery. If you would like to see him, you can come by later." Julius paused offering a genuine smile, allowing the news to sink in before continuing. "Sergeant Odis also informed me you may be in need of medical attention, and if necessary, to add those services to the GDF's bill. I am also a minister in case there is anything you would like to discuss after your ordeal, I am available, and that service is free of charge. The almighty takes care of that tab."

Playful barking interrupted the group as the pup ran around the adults, followed by the children chasing it. The old man cleared his throat, trying to get the children's attention, an action that worked for the young girl but not her brother. Terri quickly stopped and looked at her grandfather and then at Ophelia, staring at her eyes.

"Papaw, she has purple eyes. Are those lenses?" Terri asked with child curiosity.

"Terri!" the doctor exclaimed.

"It's okay, Doctor. No, Terri, they are not lenses, I was born with purple eyes," Ophelia said kindly.

"Papaw, how?" the girl asked once again.

The old man sighed. "Captain, please forgive a child's curiosity and my old age for not teaching them better manners."

"It's okay, Doctor. I got this," Ophelia said to the doctor as she turned to the young girl and lowered herself down to the young girl's eye level. "Terri, I am from a planet called Purpura, there is an exorbitant amount of amethyst in the stones and surface of where my family comes from. Legend has it that's where the color of our eyes come from," Ophelia told the young girl.

The pup quickly jumped on top of Ophelia's shoulder and moved across to her other shoulder, giving her a start and almost throwing her off balance. The pup sniffed her hair, licked the young woman's ear, nipped at her hair and then jumped off, running around again.

"Sorry, Ms. Ophelia," the girl said as she ran after the pup again.

"I'm so sorry, Captain," the healer expressed, apologetically.

"No need to be. I rather like animals, they are truer than most people. Is that animal from around here?" the young woman asked.

"To be honest, I'm not sure. I have never seen that type of breed here or on any other planet I have visited, but it just appeared one day in my clinic a few weeks back, and I am sorry to say I have a hard time saying "no" to my grandchildren," the older man said with a shrug and a smile then redirected the conversation, "well getting back to my visit, Sergeant Odis informed me you had a bit of a scuffle out there and I came by to offer a medical exam and treatment if necessary."

"Sure," replied Ophelia as she stood welcoming a medical exam, even more so if it was on someone else's bill.

"Here, or would you like to conduct it in your cargo bay? I have everything I need in my medical cart here," the doctor asked.

"We can take it inside," Ophelia said, preferring her privacy, and led the group back up the ramp.

Once inside, the children sat on some boxes holding the pup as Julius set up a privacy screen that was built into the compact cart. Conversing as he prepared, "It's a beautiful ship, but I see you took some bumps along the way, there is a big auction in town today, and you can get some good prices and save a ton of money on quality parts and a dozen other things. There will be lots of people there, It's a spectacular event that happens every six months, but this is the bigger of the two. I need some medical supplies and I have my eye on a batch. Maybe you would like to join us. It's an experience for sure. Are you looking for anything in particular?"

"A good mechanic or engineer?" The young woman mused.

"Well, something like that would fall under a premium slave and they do have a few," the doctor replied, then quickly added, "Not that I agree with the practice, but it's the way here."

"Slave? Never. Knightforge Technologies nor my family have ever partaken in any slave activity and never will," the young woman said sternly.

"I meant no offense, captain. I don't agree with that sort of activity. All life is precious. But there will be many goods, even top-quality fuel. They will have it all," the man quickly replied as he continued with his examination.

Once done with her exam, Ophelia remarked. "Hmmm, that might be interesting. What do you think, Emmy? Want to go?" Ophelia asked the sleepy scientist.

"Yeah! Back to sleep," the slender woman remarked.

"Viewing time starts in an hour, get ready, eat something and come by the clinic. You can see Billy and then we can go together to the auction house. I promise you will not regret it, or maybe you will. I've never seen anyone walk out empty-handed from this event," the old man said encouragingly.

A few moments later, Julius had finished his exams on the two women and began to pack. "Well, besides some minor bumps and bruises, you two ladies are in perfect health. So, interested in a little shopping with us?"

"Okay! A day of shopping sounds fun. And we love shopping, plus how can we miss such a monumental event?" Ophelia replied with a grin.

"See you soon ladies," the healer stated as he closed his cart up and left.

"Bye, Ms. Ophelia," the girl said excitedly as she left waving.

"Bye, sweetie," Ophelia replied, waving back.

The little boy grabbed the fox pup and carried it, putting it in front of Ophelia's face, who smiled and lightly laughed. She leaned over and tickled the pup on the neck, making it's leg shake uncontrollably. The little boy had a big smile that turned into laughter when the pup suddenly licked the young woman's face, which earned a loud laugh from Emmy, who quickly covered her mouth and tried to hide her laughter.

Almost an hour later, both women exited the ship and started making their way towards the clinic. The two ladies walked down the port, drawing the attention of some workers and the catcalls that came with them, but ignored them.

"I don't want to see him," Emmy blurted out.

Ophelia sighed. "We have too, period. We need to make sure he can keep up the story and maintain appearances. I don't care if you slap him once we're there, just show or fake some concern and we never have to see Billy again. Okay?"

"Fine," Emmy replied annoyed.

As they approached, the ladies noticed guards around the mobile clinic and tents that were attached to either side of the expanded mobile clinic. Ophelia and Emmy greeted the doctor once more, who showed them their crewmate and told them he needed a few more minutes to finish up with some patients. The two ladies faked a smile and nodded as they waited for the doctor to leave, giving them a few moments of privacy.

Billy looked at them panic stricken, looking around nervously and quickly throwing his hands up, displaying no threat. He was about to say something when Emmy stepped forward, cutting him and Ophelia off. "I'm glad you are okay. I may hate you for what you did, but I didn't want you dead," the young woman finished and slapped him hard across the face and moved off, pausing to add, "I hope it hurts for a long time."

Ophelia looked at the young lady as she stormed off, and then back to the patient. "Serves you right."

Billy rubbed his face and said, "I know."

"Do you know why you're here?" Ophelia asked. Billy just shook his head before she explained, "because we saved you, by putting you in stasis. Then we lied, saying that it was the pirate that attacked you when we tried to defend the ship. Why? Because I didn't want you to be the next organ donor at the local hospital, you would have never woken up. Your friend, on the other hand, accepted the blame and my story so that we could save your life. Stick to it. Or it will go very badly for you. No more, no less. She tried to take the ship, you tried to defend it and got injured. Do you understand?" she asked.

"Yes," he replied and then continued, "For what it's worth, thank you and I'm sorry, but I'm in love with Roxy, I want to be with her."

"So why did you do what you did to Emmy?" Ophelia pressed.

"It was a moment, and she is very attractive, with so many qualities, and for a moment I almost didn't bring her out of stasis. It was nice to be part of something not involved with breaking the law, something real. But I love Roxy, and I don't want her rotting in a cell or involved with the factions here." He paused, then seemingly decided. "I joined the GDF to come save her, but they are as crooked as anyone else. That tanker you were on, it was all planned. It was not an emergency, but a robbery. Someone high up pulled strings to fake the emergency and pull me out of that prison. The job was to get her and the others out, to take your ship. That's what I know." Billy paused, considering his next words, and delivered them with genuine sincerity. "I am telling you this because I am sorry, and I am glad that you are all okay. Please be careful, this section of the outer rim is very dangerous, and a lot of things are happening or about to happen. You can't trust anyone out here. I don't know what's really going on, but this warning is the least I can do for the second chance you have given me and us."

"In love with a pirate," Ophelia stated, while shaking her head in disbelief.

"I know she doesn't want to hear it, but let Emmy know I am really sorry, and I do like her a lot. I almost walked away from all of this because of her and you," the young man said sincerely.

"You should have, you would have found a home," Ophelia replied.

The young man just shook his head. "How come you're not sour with me?"

Ophelia smiled. "I was. Very! But I stabbed you in the chest. So, I figure that makes us even. I also learned some lessons along the way and got to meet Roxanne. She's a piece of work, but I respect her knowledge and wish I had some more of it. She's very good, but lucky for us, she's getting soft because of you and that may be bad for a pirate, but it's not a bad thing. Good luck Billy. Stick to the story. That's an order." Ophelia smiled, patted him gently on the hand, and left.

"Yes ma'am, Captain," the young man replied and gave her a salute.

Returning to the front of the clinic, the doctor returned and gave a nurse some instructions. The two children were dressed up, and the pup was on a leash. The doctor smiled at the two ladies and asked, "Are we ready?"

"I believe we are," Ophelia responded.

The little boy held the leash in one hand, then extending a hand out to Emmy, who was drying her face. She turned, looking at the young boy and his innocent gesture, and softly smiled.

"What's your name?"

The boy just looked at her with his hand extended. Terri answered for her brother. "His name is Nate, and he doesn't talk."

Surprised, Emmy quickly took the boy's hand and began walking. Stating out loud. "I am lucky to have such a handsome escort."

They arrived at a large multistory building made of stone with large archways. People surrounded the building, coming in and out, each moving with intent and purpose. Callers on the street stood on podiums announcing the events or providing directions to individuals that seemed disoriented. The stones were dark red with lighting and banners all around. As you entered the building kiosks for registration with AI Holograms interacting with patrons lined the walls.

Auction house information employees were obvious, since they all wore bright neon colored shirts with the auction house emblem on the front and back. The halls of the building were full of people looking at and inspecting goods, asking questions or just plain browsing.

Aside from the employees, there was a significant security presence, with armed guards patrolling the areas, looking out for pickpockets and other activities that could cost the auction house a loss in revenue or sales. They provided information and directions to any number of questions having to do with the auction, the building, or services provided by locals nearby.

The group registered at the kiosks and were provided information and maps to designated areas inside and outside downloaded to their datapads, IDPs, APDAs or paper formats, if required.

"My goodness, Doctor! I couldn't imagine anything like this and I have been shopping in many places," Ophelia said with awestruck eyes as she looked around.

"My dear, you haven't seen anything yet. There are multiple levels of goods to be inspected, then there are areas designated for auction, as well as other sections for item retrieval. This is the greatest auction house in the sector, they have hundreds of vendors, too." The doctor smiled. "The food's not bad either."

The women were shocked and excited all at the same time and asked, "Where does all this stuff come from?"

The old man semi-shrugged as he answered, "Mostly stolen goods by pirates and smugglers."

"What about the GDF?" Emmy asked.

"GDF auctions are on the third level, section two," a man in a bright neon shirt with the auction house insignia responded to overhearing them. The man smiled and nodded and moved on, helping another patron of the auction house.

Brother Julius chuckled at the interaction before responding, "This is Tersa 4. No questions asked. This is how pirates make legal money and taxes are collected from that money. Nobody asks, because nobody wants to know," the doctor shrugged.

"Now there are some very legitimate businesses that operate here, but this is a credit and merchandise superhighway for this and other sectors of the outer rim. Without this market, many would not have these items available to them, and if they did, it would be at extravagant prices. No ladies, this is a necessary evil for all." The doctor pointed to everything around them and continued to explain, "the cargo that is stolen is mostly insured and the losses are covered. The government captures some and lets others loose, all the while making their coin in taxes and the people eventually get served. Captured cargo by the GDF finds its way here, too," Julius continued to explain as they walked.

Two hours passed, and the group had still not seen everything the auction house had to offer, but had seen the items that had brought them to the auction house in the first place, plus a few more from just perusing the catalog. They paused their shopping for a quick snack, when the announcement came over a loudspeaker followed by alerts on their datapads signifying the beginning of the sales portion of the event. Slowly, all the patrons made their way to one hall or another, depending on the goods they were interested in purchasing.

Ophelia had regained some of the previously stolen parts for Mistress, given that their serial numbers were so unique that they did not match other vehicles by their descriptors alone and would've needed to have been cross-referenced from a particular database to know what else it would actually fit. She had seen other items or cargo that had caught her attention, but ended up being out bid. Even Emmy purchased some items for personal and professional use.

Reaching the auction area, the group found seats in the middle section of an amphitheater type hall with two large screens for displaying the items up for bid. Some items, like vehicles, would cross the stage having until they reached the other side to bid, but the speed was controlled by the bidding, and the experienced auctioneers that kept the auction flowing smoothly.

Occasionally, batches of slaves would come up for bidding. Depending on the class, they would go for auction in groups or individually and would vary in price depending on their category and skills, with pleasure, gladiatorial, or highly skilled being amongst the most expensive.

Ophelia and Emmy, being disgusted by the thought of slavery, tried to distract themselves when the slaves were brought out, and would take the time to bid or converse over other items and good deals they may have already gotten.

Rey arrived at the auction area and looked to the attendant, nodding his head to the auction house attendant who was designated to the area. He made his way down the aisle and finally took his seat behind Ophelia. Motioning the attendant once more, El Capitan made a signal toward his mark, that was sitting in front of him. The man looked at the young woman and nodded back with a slight gesture.

The two men had made arrangements already, along with the auctioneer, to conclude his part of the contract and for the best price possible. He had placed Jorian just before a highly desired item, causing the briefness of his transaction to go unnoticed in the chaos of the highly coveted item. He had other people in the audience as well to assist in his manipulation of the auction, as he had done various times before. It went against the rules of the auction house, but everything here had a price.

The price increased rapidly for Jorian, even faster and higher than he expected. El Capitan considered the bidders and recognized a man who was an agent for the consortium bidding up the price. He knew that the new leader of the consortium wanted Jorian badly and with good reason, after what he had done to the brute. Rey would have to act quickly and did, sending a message to one of his agents as he set the rest of his plan into motion. The bidding was stalling close to the twenty thousand credit mark when the auctioneer made his last call.

The consortium agent sat back, confident in his bid, when El Capitan pushed a button on his IDP that set a signal to a tiny device he had placed on Ophelia's arm as he passed behind her earlier in the hallways. Ophelia jerked her arm away when the tiny gizmo sent a small, but potent electric shock up her arm. The young woman rubbed her arm and looked down at the gap between the seats, wondering what had pinched or shocked her.

The auction agent signaled to the auctioneer with a specific sign, who then quickly called out. "Twenty-one thousand credits going once, going twice."

The consortium's buyer tried to counteroffer but couldn't because a young woman tripped, falling on him and practically pinning the man to his chair. The auctioneer quickly made the last call, announcing the number of the winner and moved to the next item up for auction, that was one of the highlights of the day. The bidding had begun on the next item, when Ophelia was suddenly handed a yellow slip for her auction victory, with her bidder number posted on top. The auction employee hurried away to attend a bidder of the next auction.

Ophelia looked at the slip, confused, then at Brother Julius, who looked at her, astonished. Emmy was also confused, having seen her jut her hand out only moments earlier. Ophelia stood looking at the people on either side of her trying to protest, but only heard people yelling at her to sit down as they tried to take part in the next item's auction. The area exploded with people calling out and waving their hands or assigned numbers, trying to get their bid on the wondrous item, drowning out Ophelia's protest.

"What did you do?" Emmy questioned her furiously.

"I..I.. don't know. Brother Julius?" she asked incredulously.

"You bought a slave," the man told her, judgingly.

"What? I need to complain or protest about this. This can't be," the young captain said as she tried to exit out of her row.

Rey leaned back, adjusting his wide-brimmed hat, and smiled as he saw the scene develop before him. He found the venture to be quite a success, having received more than triple of what he expected to get, thanks to the consortium once again. He looked over and caught Brother Julius's judging gaze, who shook his head disapprovingly at him.

Arguments that were turning into fights started breaking out between the bidders as the price quickly soared to over 100k credits for the shipment of technology from the core planets being auctioned. The chaos only grew, making Rey smile, saying out loud, "Time to go! This is about to get ugly," and made his way out of the Amphitheater.

"That is good advice. We should also go," Brother Julius commented as he took his grandchildren and Emmy close behind, seeing the guards rushing into the area.

Reaching the main floor, the group noticed Ophelia at a counter vigorously arguing with an official about the auction and her position on slavery and how she could not have one.

The man at the window sat calmly behind a thick panel of safety glass. He listened intently and finally answered as he pointed to a sign behind him. "All sales are final! You are contractually bound, so if you don't pay, we will make arrangements to confiscate your property, besides what you have already purchased to settle your debt, and you'll be banned from future auctions."

Ophelia paused hearing the man's words and protested as she looked at the information on her datapad. "That will take almost all my credits."

"Your total for the auction is thirty-two thousand four hundred and eighty-six credits, to be exact, including taxes and fees," the cashier replied calmly.

"What!" Ophelia exclaimed. "That's more than I have. This is crazy! I didn't even bid for that slave!"

"Are you reneging from payment? Should I begin the confiscation requests Ma'am?" the little man said calmly, as he adjusted his glasses.

"No! I will find a way to fix this. Is there a supervisor around?" Ophelia asked, flustered.

"Miss, I am a third-tier acquisition specialist, and I will assure you the policy stands for everyone," the man replied.

Ophelia scratched her head in frustration not having the money to pay her bill in its entirety. Shaking her head in disbelief as an alert came into her datapad, catching her attention, causing her to pause. She scrolled through the information and looked at the final tabs of the contract for passage on her ship to another sector, with resignation she accepted the contract giving her the funds from the deposit to complete the transaction at the auction house.

"Mistress, this is less than the usual fee, why?" she asked.

"I selected the most lucrative offers, then negotiated for the best price, and this was the highest offer."

"But why so low," Ophelia protested, as she scrolled through other offers.

"It seems that many people saw the landing and commented on your skill as a positive, though their confidence in my performance to get the job done in a timely manner was in question. Because of non-performing equipment and our status according to the port authority. I've never been more embarrassed," the AI reported.

"Inform the client that we have accepted their offer and decline the rest, look for any other cargo transport jobs and passage to our next destination, we need money fast," Ophelia instructed the AI.

"Yes, Captain," Mistress replied.

Ophelia returned to the cashier's desk and provided payment to the man in the window, who thanked her for payment and then offered delivery for a fee, to which she quickly declined. The doctor and Emmy paid for their bill and also declined the transport fee.

The group exited the area, looking at the monitors all over the building where other auctions continued to be displayed. The various areas held multiple screens or displayed holograms of items for active bidding, around an area where groups of people gathered and could continue to be part of the auctions while taking part in various other auctions simultaneously all throughout the building.

Reaching the receiving area, the trio presented their tickets to pick up their items and waited. After a while, various boxes, crates, and other goods were brought into the area. A young man finally entered the room wearing cargo pants and a loose-fitting long sleeve shirt, a vest, and boots. The two young ladies took in the young man who carried himself well and with confidence, unlike most of the other slaves, except for the fighters and pleasure slaves.

A burly man turned to the young man and instructed him gruffly while pointing, "You, you are part of lot ten. Move over there."

Seeing him walk to the area where their goods were being grouped, Emmy leaned to Ophelia and said, "Not bad, Captain. He's cute."

"He is, but not twenty-one thousand credits cute," Ophelia retorted.

Jorian was walking towards the area when he stopped, staring at her, being captivated by those purple eyes. He had seen them once before a long time ago and never forgot them. The burly man yelled at Jorian, bringing him back to the present, and continued walking. The young man had a predatory glare to him, his eyes darting around taking in everything that was happening in the area, but eventually his eyes kept coming back to the attractive young woman with the purple eyes. Surprising him more was seeing Brother Julius, who he eyed suspiciously. The man's two grandchildren smiled and quickly waved to the newly acquired slave, a wave that the slave quickly returned. The pup was pulling against the leash, trying to get to the young man frantically, something Ophelia picked up on quickly.

"Brother Julius, do you know this man?" Ophelia asked speculatively.

"We do. I found this man injured in the desert and saved his life, a few days later, he sacrificed himself and saved ours when we were attacked by pirates," Brother Julius replied.

"And what a coincidence that I just happened to mysteriously bid on him with you next to me," the young woman said accusingly.

The older doctor turned and calmly replied, "If you ask me, you got a phenomenal deal. He is a remarkable young man. I would have bid for him out of gratitude alone for what he did for us, but I could not afford it. As for you bidding on him, we had nothing to do with that, but we are glad you won. We owe him our very lives."

"Remarkable? Hardly. I will give you ten thousand credits right now for him. That way, you don't have to deal with that pathetic slave," said a rat-faced man from behind them.

"Fuck off! That's not even half of what I paid," Ophelia said angrily.

"Fifteen then," replied the rat-faced man, unaffected by the offense.

"You heard her rat, be gone with you," said another man as he approached them. He was well dressed and appeared much more sophisticated. "Madam, I am an agent for a third party, we would like to offer you twenty-five thousand for that slave. Here and now. I would take him off your hands, which I take from your display at the cashier's window is in your best interest," the man said politely.

"It is so kind of you to be so concerned about my best interests. But I think he's worth more, don't you?" Ophelia replied shrewdly.

Everyone looked at Ophelia, shocked and confused, especially Emmy who was about to protest, but quieted her thoughts after Ophelia glared at her. The children tugged on their grandfather's coat since the pup was suddenly acting aggressive towards the unknown visitor. The stranger studied the scene for a moment and then quickly upped the offer.

"I am but a businessman, with a task to do. I will give you forty thousand credits and not a partial credit more to transfer ownership of that slave to me. Here and now."

The group stood just a few feet from the cargo and looked to Jorian, who had just arrived. Jorian stood next to the cargo, then looked at everyone in the group. He looked to the corner of the room, where Rey stood leaning against the wall and nodded his head to him, acknowledging a previous conversation.

Jorian stepped forward, "Ms. Knight, if I may. I would like to make you a counteroffer."

The agent looked at him with disgusted disregard, stating in a condescending tone, "Silence slave, you have no voice, you are property."

The stranger's tone was something that both women took offense to, but Jorian only glared at him through narrow eyes as he took a step forward. The businessman reevaluated his actions and took a step back, noticing how close Jorian was to him. He turned to Ophelia, pleading his case and promoting his offer once more.

"Forty thousand credits is no trivial offer and would be enough to fix your ship so you could be on your way and leave this place behind with plenty of money in your pocket. It is a generous offer, and most likely more than he's worth," the man added with a salesman's grin.

"I hear you sir, but he is my property and I will say who does and does not have a voice with what belongs to me," Ophelia said forcefully, though the words of my property tasted bitter to her, then turned to face Jorian softening her tone, "Sir, what is your counteroffer?"

Jorian glanced at Rey once more, and taking in a deep breath, looked directly into Ophelia's eyes, and after a moment, spoke. "I will work off my debt, including proper percentage rates of salvage. I saw you landing the other day and though I complement you on your fine piloting skills, you need me! I can fix your ship and I can do it properly. I just want to be free."

"You can't trust this slave. He's a murderer. He killed three people just a few weeks ago, in cold blood. People that had done nothing to him. How can you trust that? He would most likely kill you in your sleep." The agent smiled and put forth his offer again. "Be smart. Take the forty thousand, and be done with this mess," the agent proposed.

Ophelia turned to Jorian. "Is it true?"

Jorian's gaze went from the agent, to the doctor, then back to Ophelia, looking her directly in the eyes once more. "The truth is, I killed those people. One was the head of a pirate syndicate and the other two were her guards when she threated to kill the good doctor over there, then as they held him down and boasted to him about selling his grandchildren to slavery and prostitution," Jorian finished and glared at the agent. "I guess you forgot to mention that part. Huh, Mister Agent?"

The agent cleared his throat as he shifted in place. "Well... I am not privy to that information. Just, um... what my clients tell me?"

"And who is this client of yours, Mister Agent?" Ophelia asked.

"My clients prefer to remain anonymous, and I am obliged to keep their confidence. You understand, Ms. Knight," the man quickly replied in a professional tone.

"Fifty thousand credits. That's more than double of what you paid. It is a very generous offer," the man added.

Ophelia turned her head back to face Jorian, "Do you want to revisit your offer? By how many times are you willing to increase what I paid for you?"

A call from the burly auction worker echoed in the area. "Ten, where are you, report damn it or be shocked!"

"TEN!" Jorian yelled behind him gesturing with his arm.

"Ten times. Wow, that's over two hundred and ten thousand credits. You'll be working for me for a very long time. Are you ready to commit to that?" she asked the slave.

Jorian stood there dumbfounded, his mouth fell open taken by surprise by the amount and what had just transpired. In the corner, Rey face palmed himself, muttering, "*Aye Dios mio!*" to himself having heard the negotiations go sideways for Jorian. But was happy to see how Jorian reacted next, meaning he had listened to some of his ramblings of the last few days.

Sighing, Jorian quickly tried negotiating. "I will agree to ten times what you paid for me, not including fees and taxes, but you will credit me with an acceptable wage for my job category plus sixty percent of all salvage and extracurricular wages I get."

"What are you mad? Sixty percent is way too high, I will credit you with a working minimum wage, minus 150 credits a week for your living expenses, and 10% of salvage or any other obtainable income outside of ship duties. Or I can always take the Consortium's agent's offer," she stated.

Glancing around nervously, the agent quickly interjected, "I uh... I'm not with the consortium, but you should take my offer and save yourself the trouble, he is not worth it," the agent interjected.

Jorian glowered at the agent with intensity and a promise of harm, which made the man even more uncomfortable than he already was. Peering over to Rey, who just shrugged, Jorian turned his attention to Ophelia and extended his hand. "I agree with your terms and accept your contract."

"This will not sit well with my client," the agent said.

"I'm sorry for you and your client, but that is not my problem. Have a good day, Mister Agent," Ophelia said politely.

"Good day, Ms. Knight," the man replied as he walked off, flustered and annoyed.

The young captain turned with a devious smile, addressing Jorian sternly. "I don't know how you managed to scam me, but you will meet your side of the contract."

"Ms. Knight..." Jorian began and was interrupted.

"Captain. Captain Ophelia Knight," she said, introducing herself and shaking Jorian's hand.

The young man hesitated as he shook her hands, feeling the softness of her skin, he never lost eye contact and replied, "Captain, I honor my commitment, I will keep my side of the contract, as I expect you to keep yours. As far as a scam, I was sold on a stage as a slave, and have been presented a very expensive opportunity to be free. It's an opportunity that few, if any, ever get, but I'll take it. How am I scamming anyone? You just guaranteed yourself a return of ten times your investment, not to mention ninety percent of anything that I do on my own time. Who's scamming who? But I'll take my chance at freedom. Either way." Jorian paused as he shook her hand, feeling a cosmic connection in her touch. "Captain Ophelia Knight, I am Jorian Phoenix. It's a pleasure and honor to meet you. Thank you for the opportunity you have given me."

Ophelia felt something stir inside as they shook hands, replying, "Jorian Phoenix, huh? Sounds made up, but I'll accept it. Nice to meet you. Now about my ship. Can you fix it, or was that just more bullshit? Cause the last guy that laid hands on her really messed her up and I will shoot anyone who would mess her up again."

Jorian chuckled. "I have an engineering and mechanical background amongst other things. I'll take good care of her."

The two were interrupted by the fox pup that somehow jumped and was trying to nip at Jorian's shirt. Jorian laughed as he grabbed the pup who veraciously tried to lick his face. Jorian put the pup under his arm and started petting the animal, who just moved its head to be scratched or petted some more.

Ophelia grinned as she too petted the pup. "Do you two need a room? It seems obvious you're pretty close."

"Nah, this pup slept on my chest while I was a patient at Brother Julius's clinic. He seems comfortable around me, and I like the little runt. It's cute and friendly," Jorian replied.

"Cute and friendly is good. Now Mister Phoenix..." Ophelia began and was cut off.

"Jorian... Just Jorian, please," the young man expressed.

"Very well. Jorian. Please escort Emmy back to the ship safely, along with our winnings and that of Brother Julius."

"Yes. Captain," Jorian promptly answered.

The burley auction house employee came over to Ophelia. "Ms. Knight. Do you have your own collar for your slave?"

"No. But you can remove his collar. Unless that is a concern, I should have Jorian?" she replied, turning to her new crew member.

"No Captain. A deal is a deal," the young man answered earnestly.

"Remove the collar," Ophelia instructed.

"Your funeral lady," the man replied, placing a leather collar with a leash on the slave before removing the consortium's collar, then grabbed the leash and placed it in Ophelia's hands. "He's your slave now. Do what you want, the auction house has filled its commitment."

Ophelia stared at the worn leather leash in her hand, then raised her eyes, meeting Jorian's, who locked eyes with her. "You don't need that. I'm yours."

Ophelia blushed slightly as the moment between the two lingered, then looked at the leash and undid the collar. Her actions filled her mind with doubt, but something inside spurred her on. "I rather have you at my side than at my feet," the young woman stated and, feeling somewhat embarrassed, turned towards the older cleric. "Brother Julius, why don't you leave the kids with Jorian, and you and me go have a chat? Unless you don't trust him, of course," Ophelia asked the man.

The healer faced the young man. "Will you watch them and keep them safe until I return?"

Jorian nodded and instructed them to stay close to Emmy as he went to grab a dolly before Ophelia and Julius walked off. Moving to another area and running into Lidia, the hacker that Rey had taken him to see. She handed him a broken-down decrepit oversized flatbed dolly that had four wheels rigged to it, allowing it to barely move. On the cart was a satchel with his name embroidered on it. The woman, a red-haired beauty, looked at him and smiled, leaning in she whispered.

"Inside, you will find your paperwork and documentation for your new life. It was difficult, but it should keep you and your family safe. There's also a basic IDP in there, along with some other information. Rey also had me put 500 credits into an account for you. He said something about the rest being a bonus you got for him." She paused, "I don't know why, but somehow you got him to let you in. You must really be someone special, if he did everything, he's done to get you to this point. He trusts you and considers you his friend, his only one besides me, I think. Please don't let him down, because I will hunt you down if you do. Good luck, and stay in touch, my info is on your IDP," the woman said, kissing the young man on the cheek and disappearing into the crowd.

Jorian grabbed the satchel, running his fingers over the embroidery and smiled. Seeing his real name finally returned to him, thinking to himself. *This is the first time in six years I actually own something, even if it is a satchel and a broken-down cart. It's mine and I'll be damned if anyone's going to take it.* The moment was interrupted when another person tried to take the dolly, but stopped when Jorian grabbed it and snarled at them menacingly. Gruffly yanking the cart away as he glared at the man and stated in a protective tone, "Find another, this one's mine!"

The stranger quickly apologized and moved off, looking for another cart. Jorian turned and pushed the wobbly cart with him. Looking at the cargo, he instantly knew he would have to pray a little for it to reach the docks with all the weight. Returning to the room, Emmy looked at him and asked about the cart.

Jorian replied as he loaded it, "It's mine."

"Good score," the young scientist said cheerfully.

"Emmy, is that right?" Jorian asked her.

"Yes. Doctor Emilia Krickay at your service. But you can call me Emmy. Jorian, right?" The young woman replied with a welcoming smile and extended her hand.

The young man shook her hand as he nodded his head. "Emmy, would you be so kind as to watch the kids while I load the cart so we can leave?"

"No problem. Come, kids, grab the leash and give me your hands," she instructed.

"He didn't leave, that's a plus right there," Julius commented to Ophelia.

Ophelia just nodded, agreeing. She realized that Jorian could have vanished at that very moment, leaving her out of a lot of money. Something about him tugged at the back of her mind. *I feel a connection to him, and the way he looks at me with a sincerity in his eyes, something inside tells me I can trust him, and I am trying to trust my instincts, but in this case my instincts are yelling at me. I hope I'm right, I better be right, that's a lot of credits if I'm wrong.*

He was handsome, and his eyes were full of intensity, alluring and alert. He gave off the sense of a predator, mixed with the fuzziness of a rabbit. They had just met, but there was something familiar; she felt as if she had to protect him, yet making her feel scared and safe at the same time. She felt an instant attraction and though she found him extremely appealing, there was something else that called to her being in his presence. *Focus Ophelia!* she thought to herself, taking a deep breath and turning towards the healer.

"Brother Julius, let's go have that chat, okay? Emmy, we will see you back on the ship," she said, taking the older man by the arm and walking off.

Emmy stood there talking with the children and playing with the pup. She observed Jorian as he loaded the decrepit rolling platform. Some workers tried to help, fishing for tips from buyers, but they could barely pick up one crate filled with parts or supplies and between the two of them, they were having difficulties. Jorian quickly stopped them and asked them to set the boxes down, that he would take care of it. The men scoffed at him and then stood there with their jaws dropped in awe, as he picked the crate up by himself with no mechanical or outside aid.

Emmy gawked, as did Rey, who still stood in the back of the room. Rey was made very curious by his Compai's display of strength and stood straighter, paying close attention to how quickly Jorian moved the heavy crates. When he had finished loading the cart, he grabbed some straps that were attached to the cart and secured the cargo.

Checking the cart again for safety and being satisfied with his inspection, he instructed the children to hold Emmy's hand as he strained, pushing the overloaded dolly out of the auction building and out onto the busy street. People, carts, loaders, and other vehicles were moving around the area, in the hundreds if not thousands. The volume was so high that Jorian told Emmy and the kids to sit on the crates on top of the cart along with the pup and continued to push the cart down the crowded street.

Jorian had been pushing the cart nonstop for almost an hour when Emmy called out. "Hey handsome, how about getting a girl a drink, it's hot out? "

Jorian was sweating profusely and looked up from what he was doing with a perplexed face. "Huh?"

Emmy smiled. "My treat, I know your current circumstances. You can get me next time." After a pause, she continued, "Hey, let's stop over there and get the kids a drink and maybe a snack, and we can get something to refresh ourselves, too. It's kind of hot."

Jorian just nodded and steered the cart to the specified place. Emmy jumped off with the help of her new crewmate, who then caught the children as they jumped off. The trio entered the store, leaving Jorian next to the pup guarding the cart. The pup was play-fighting with him, nipping at his hand, when it stopped and looked towards the rear of the cart.

Jorian stood and looked back as well, then called out, "Just keep walking, nothing for you here."

Out of the shadows of an alleyway, two individuals approached him. Thieves holding what he expected was a knife at their waist. Jorian took a step towards the front of the cart, clearing his line of vision past the front crates when he saw another guy waiting, catching a third would-be thief by surprise.

Sighing, he grabbed the pup and stepped away from the cart.

"Smart!" one thug said.

Jorian shook his head. "You don't understand. I am giving you the chance here. If you can push that cart to the end of the store in one minute, you can keep it. All of it! If you can't, you will have the brief opportunity to leave, understanding what you have come across. I know you've been following us for about three blocks, which is why I agreed to stop. So, are you ready?" Jorian asked as he pointed to his datapad, which displayed a timer with one minute on it.

The thugs looked at each other confused, and one of them cockily said, "So, we push it to the end of the store in under a minute and we can keep all of it? You won't try to stop us?"

"Correct. Are you ready?" Jorian replied.

The three street rats boastfully laughed at Jorian, taking up the challenge. The original two looked at each other, then suspiciously eyed the young soldier, suspecting some sort of trick or trap. Jorian, understanding their body language, took two more steps back and asked again, "Ready?"

The three put themselves in a position, grabbing the handle or edge, and pushed. Push and push, they did, straining with everything they had. Jorian just looked at the timer ticking down and even encouraged the deviants to push, but the cargo did not move.

"What the hell, man?" one thug cried out.

"Come on man, push. This is an easy score," cried another.

"Did you check the brakes?" Jorian asked, followed by, "You better hurry, you have about thirty seconds left."

"What! Check the brakes, man!" one of them said.

The three men paused and looked around in frustration until they found and disengaged the brake. The three again pushed hard against the cart and still it would not budge. All three yelled at each other to push, but the cart's wheels barely moved a few meters. The timer ticked away until it reached zero with the sound of a digital buzzard.

Jorian looked at them with mocking disappointment. "That was a valiant effort, but you failed boys. Now please go on your way. I don't want you to get hurt."

"Oh, yeah. You push it if you're so strong," one of them shot back.

The other two just looked at him disapprovingly when Jorian responded, "You have already, and you may see it again, if you are still here when we leave, but I would not advise that. Just get out of here and put the break back on before you go, please."

Jorian looked to the side and waved an officer over. One thief was about to charge Jorian, but the others grabbed him and pulled him away, leaving just before the officer arrived. Jorian grinned, then pretended to ask for directions to the port.

The man played with the pup for a moment and went on his way by the time Emmy and the two kids had come back. The petite scientist had gotten some high-end hydration fluid which Jorian poured on his hand and gave to the pup, so that it may drink first, an action that caught the scientist's attention. After the pup drank and had its fill, Jorian downed a couple of large gulps from his bottle.

"Thanks, Emmy, that was very nice of you. Kids, did you thank Doctor Emmy?" Jorian said out loud.

The two children looked up from their drinks and nodded in acknowledgment. Emmy dismissed it and asked Jorian for help to sit back on the crate, something to which the young man quickly assisted. He helped Terri and Nate up once more before he returned to pushing the cart. Laughing to himself at the thought that the brakes of the cart were worn but locked, making the initial push so much greater but eased as the motion continued and they never disengaged the secondary foot brake. He smiled once more at how the three thieves drove themselves crazy, trying to push the loaded cart.

Looking down the street, noticing the three young men sitting a few blocks away staring at him, as he pushed the cart by himself and waved to them as he rolled on down the street with the heavy load. He continued pushing the cart for another 30 minutes until they finally reached the Dock Tower's gate and were challenged by the guards at a manned checkpoint.

Emmy recognized the guards on duty as members of the detail that conducted the prison exchange. "Hey, Doctor Emmy, did some shopping today?" one of the GDF soldier's kindly asked.

"A girl's work is never done, boys," she said with a playful laugh.

The guards laughed and waved at Brother Julius's two grandchildren. They acknowledged Jorian with a simple nod that was returned in kind. Moving past the tower gate, they could see Brother Julius's clinic in the distance about a hundred meters away.

The old healer stood from his seat where he was waiting, displaying his excitement and opening his arms as he welcomed his grandchildren back. Stopping the cart and helping the passengers off except the pup that did not want to stand up and turned its head to continue sleeping.

Jorian shrugged at Julius, then continued to unload the doctor's crates and merchandise, placing them in an area where the good doctor requested. The young man didn't say much as he worked, but was called to the side by the older man before he departed.

"Jorian, if I may have a word, please."

Jorian searched around suspiciously before moving over to the doctor. "Yes, Brother Julius."

"I just wanted to say thank you for what you did for me and my family back out in the desert. I hated leaving you there," the man said, somewhat ashamed.

"I told you to leave. What kind of person would I be to leave those children in the fate of those pirates? As far as you and I are concerned, we are even. You saved my life, and I saved yours." His eyes narrowed as he continued, "If you ever strap me to a table again, one of us will not live to tell the tale. I'm done being a guinea pig. I have a chance at freedom, and I am taking it," the young man said in a low voice, full of conviction.

"Understood. But let me give you some advice, don't show off. It makes you stand out and you will want to exist under the radar."

"Show off? How am I showing off?" Jorian demanded quietly.

The older man nodded towards the cart with his head, "We both know that no two men alive can push that thing, in its condition and with all that weight. Hell, the cart can barely take the weight. Yet you pushed it by yourself for over an hour. It draws attention to you from people that would want to abuse your gifts for their own gain. You are strong, resilient, and intelligent, but not invincible. Be ruled by your intelligence, not your brute strength. You can be more, much more." For a moment, he looked away and sighed, then turned to face the young soldier, his eyes wet with emotion. "As I stand here, right now, you are the only good thing that has ever come out of that research we did so long ago. It's not much, but if you ever need someone, I am here. Good luck son and thank you." He extended his hand.

Jorian considered the doctor and shook his hand in return.

"Thank you for saving my life. Take care," the young man replied and left.

Jorian silently went back to the cart and began pushing again. Emmy, who was walking this time, quickly caught up and walked next to him. She offered him help to push, but he declined. Deciding her course of action, she moved him over, grabbing the cart and playfully smiled until she felt the weight they were pushing, and nodded at him impressed.

"We are in this together now, right?" Emmy said cheerfully.

"I guess," Jorian said, smiling back. "Thanks for the drink for me and those kids, that was nice of you."

"Well, it was the least I could do, just sitting on the cart while you pushed, I felt so bad, and now feeling all this weight, I feel worse," the young scientist replied.

"Don't. You did your job. I asked you to watch the kids, and you did while I pushed. We succeeded through teamwork," Jorian clarified.

"I can live with that," the young woman said warmly, struggling to push. "What the hell did Ophelia buy? This shit weighs like crazy," the young woman exclaimed.

"You could just guide me, you know?"

"No. I said I would help push and by golly I will help push," Emmy replied through gritted teeth.

Reaching the ship, Emmy called out, "Mistress, we're here, lower the ramp and open the cargo bay doors." The two reached the ship, but the cargo doors were still closed, and the ramp was not extended. *That's odd,* she thought, frowning when the AI did not respond, having to repeat the command. On the second try, Mistress finally acknowledged after a delay. Finally extending the extended the ramps and opening the cargo bay doors. Emmy dismissed the communication issues to the port and their highly abused systems.

"Mind if I walk the ship for a moment?" Jorian asked excitedly.

"No, go ahead. She is quite the ship. Take your time. I need to go inside and freshen up," Emmy replied as she walked up the ramp.

Jorian looked up at the ship in awe, taking in its unique design. His eyes followed each curve of the ship, portholes, thrusters, landing gear; just like a sightless person running their hands over an item to fully appreciate it. He walked around the ship and tenderly caressed and inspected any part that was within reach, and even climbed on top of the ship.

He climbed up on each tier and looked into each thruster, engine, and exhaust. He was fascinated with the ship until he reached the picture of the pin-up girl with the name of the ship, Mistress of Mayhem on a banner near the picture. He was standing on a wing about to come down when he noticed something on the edge, kneeling down to inspect it and seeing the damage caused by a collision with a piece of an asteroid still embedded in the gash.

Taking off one of his gloves, he softly ran one of his hands over the edge and down the underbelly of the ship. Taking notice of a shimmering material that was used on the exterior of the ship, he formed a theory in his mind, as he made his way back to the cart.

A sultry voice came over his datapad as he approached the cart, saying, "You should ask a girl her name before touching her like that."

Jorian looked around, seeing Ophelia standing there, and asked. "What?"

"What, what? I didn't say anything," Ophelia replied, confused.

"You just said you should ask a girl her name before touching her like that," Jorian said, somewhat embarrassed.

The young captain rolled her eyes and scoffed, "No, I did not. That was Mistress."

"Mistress? You mean the ship, but..." Jorian asked.

Ophelia quickly cut him off, "Yes! The ship. She has a very advanced AI with a very distinct personality. Come on, leave the cargo there, we can get it in a moment, let's properly introduce you to the Mistress of Mayhem."

"Sounds good," said Jorian excitedly.

Jorian reached the inside of the cargo hold when he heard buzzing and red lights flashing from different areas of the bay, with sparks flying in multiple directions from two empty compartments. While from two other compartments, a set of automated blasters came down and pointed at Jorian, followed by a gruff, deep robotic voice.

"M.O.M. protocol engaged. Foreign entity acknowledged. Preparing to fire on invader."

Jorian's eyes widened as he looked towards the blasters, analyzing the threat, then looking for somewhere to hide. Ophelia being surprised and looking around, seeing Emmy as she was exiting out of her pod and looking around confused.

Two guns fired at Jorian, who narrowly dodged them and darted towards a work area nearby, sliding under a metal work bench to gain some cover. Two more shots fired, hitting the top of the bench scorching the table deeply. Emmy let out a frightful scream as she jumped back into her pod and Ophelia looked around, shocked by the reaction of the ship, cringing with each shot and quickly calling out.

"Cease fire, Master of Mayhem. That is a direct order from your captain and send all pertinent information to my datapad. Now!" Ophelia ordered.

The two blasters were still aiming at the workbench but not firing, Ophelia looked at her datapad but only saw the M.O.M. Protocol screen and a blinking cursor. Seconds passed and turned into a minute, yet the screen still displayed just a blinking cursor. Ophelia stared at the screen intently, and nothing changed.

"Captain?" Emmy called out.

"Emmy, stay put!" Ophelia commanded, then directed herself to the AI. "Master of Mayhem, why did you activate? If you are displaying no information as to what could have triggered you, or a threat, do you have information on Jorian?" The woman demanded.

The deep voice replied, "Searching, nothing found. No data to display. No Jorian on file. Commencing diagnostic on core and primary systems. Core system failure, no core present. Primary systems functioning at sixty-seven percent efficiency," the deep robotic voice replied.

"Master of Mayhem, stand down!" Ophelia ordered.

"Malfunction recorded; scan of life form required to avoid future incidents," the AI stated.

"I'm not going out there with those guns online," Jorian shouted from under the table.

"Master of Mayhem, stand down. Mistress can perform the scans and transfer the information," Ophelia commanded.

"Master of Mayhem standing down," the voice responded and immediately all guns retracted, and their compartment bays closed.

"Jorian, are you okay?" Ophelia asked.

"Yeah, but I would be a lot better if I wasn't being shot at," he replied.

"You can come out now," Ophelia said in the softest voice she could must.

Jorian was breathing deeply and fighting to keep control of himself and the rage bubbling inside him as he responded. "Give me a minute."

"Emmy, it's all clear," Ophelia stated.

Finally, being in control of his rage, the young man took a deep breath and peeked out from under the table.

"What the hell is going on?" he exclaimed.

The two women moved to his side, inspecting him, seeing if Jorian was all right and helping him out from under the table. Picking him up, they checked him front and back, making sure he was unharmed. Ophelia felt embarrassed by the ship's attack on her new crew mate. The Master of Mayhem's protocol activation set off a series of red flags to the young captain, but was left confused by the result of the Master systems diagnostics and query.

"I apologize Jorian, I have never seen that protocol activate unless someone was boarding the ship forcefully or if someone from the command crew was being threatened," Ophelia quickly explained.

"A secondary protocol?" Jorian asked hesitantly.

"No, more like the primary protocol. Mistress is the AI interface on top of the primary core systems. Not a peep, Mistress," Ophelia said in a warning tone.

Sirens and flashing lights came rushing up with a series of GDF soldiers dismounting from their vehicles and making a perimeter around the back half of the ship. Ophelia quickly exited the ship with her hands raised. The sergeant from the prisoner detail approached the young woman with a weapon in hand.

"Is everything all right, Ms. Knight? The port sensors picked up laser blaster fire," the man asked as he searched around.

"Oh, yes, Sergeant. I apologize, one of my crew members accidentally triggered a security protocol. My sincerest apologies. We are still trying to correct the issues on the ship. It won't happen again."

"Very well, ma'am. I will put on the report that you were exterminating some rodents, which is allowed at the port. Hopefully, I will see you around," the sergeant replied with a wink.

"Thank you, Sergeant. You are too kind," the young captain said warmly.

The man paused before leaving. "Ms. Knight, if I may be so bold, how about a drink later?"

Ophelia smiled. "Sergeant Odis, how nice of you, but tonight I will be up to my elbows with this new inventory and still have repairs that need done. How about a raincheck?"

"I'll look forward to it, Captain. See you then," the man replied confidently and walked off.

The port soldiers returned to their vehicles and drove off, leaving the young woman and her crew to tend to the ship. Ophelia ran her fingers through her hair and let out a frustrated breath before returning inside the ship.

As she approached, she watched the young man who just looked around the cargo hold with curiosity instead of fear, which caused her some concern, as she thought to herself.

He almost gets toasted, and he reacts as if it were nothing. What is going on here?

"Jorian," she called out.

"Yes, ma'am," he said promptly.

"Jorian, first I'm glad you are okay. Second, let's get you into the ship's systems to avoid future problems. Mistress, if you have completed your background check and cross-referencing of his image with all of our records and he checks out, please add Jorian Phoenix to the ship's roster," the woman called out.

"I have added Jorian Phoenix to the ship's roster, what classification shall he be assigned?" Mistress asked.

Ophelia thought for a moment, considering what had transpired to her recently, and did not want to leave room for error. "Mistress, he will take the title of Junior Technician, if he could fix the loader and how well he fixes it, will determine if we move him to Senior Technician, engineering, or ship mechanic. Then take his sales receipt from the auction house and multiply it by ten and write out a contract for his services to pay off his debt. You will calculate the minimum salary of his position and subtract from it 150 credits a week, then divide that by two, half goes towards his debt, the rest which will go to him directly. Make a note that we will provide food and board, plus all needed medical care. Make another note that 10% of all salvage and all non-ship related work belongs to him and whatever he does on his own time is an 60/40 split in his favor." She paused and looked at him. "It's only fair. It is your time. Send it to the Knightforge Technologies' legal team and then attach it to his file, providing him a copy. Let us know when his last day is by contract. Once done, have him make his mark and provide you with whatever else you need to complete the transaction."

"Yes, Captain," the ship replied.

Ophelia turned to the scientist. "Emmy, can I have a moment with Jorian Please?"

"Yes, Captain," the young woman replied, and exited the cargo area.

Jorian stood there unphased, watching the departing guards and occasionally moving a watchful eye to the hidden guns. Once Ophelia felt comfortable with her surroundings, she turned towards her new crewmate. "Jorian, everything leads me to conclude that I am taking a big chance with you, but something in my gut tells me otherwise. I need you to come clean and convince me that what I am doing is not a threat to me, my ship, or the rest of the crew," the young woman asked him in a moment of sincerity.

Jorian stared off for a moment, contemplating his answer before speaking. "I am no threat to you, Dr. Emmy, or Mistress. As for Master, it all depends on if he tries to shoot me again. Under the wrong circumstances, my presence may be a threat, but that could be said for almost anyone out here. I can fix what I say I can, and I always try not to exaggerate about what I can do. I understand everything that has happened for me to be here, and I assure you, I had no hand in it except hoping to come to this ship, ever since I saw you land."

Jorian paused, taking in a deep breath, glancing at the distancing lights of the security forces. "You can trust in what I tell you, because I won't lie to you. It's my own personal code and what I try to live by. I will protect you always and to the best of my ability, because I am grateful to you for this opportunity. Jorian Phoenix is my name and I don't know what I want right now, but our agreement suites me just fine," he stated, his eyes never leaving hers. Blinking before he continued, "I understand trust is a lot to ask from a stranger, and more so with all the events that have surrounded our meeting, but I ask for the benefit of the doubt."

"What about your past? I see how you look at those soldiers. Are you a deserter, or a traitor?" she asked.

Jorian's couldn't hide that those insinuations bothered him and replied, somewhat defensively, "What about it? As far as I'm concerned, I want it to stay there in my past. I was with the military and I did not abandon my duties, but I was betrayed, attacked, and left for dead, because of someone else's greed and ambition, period. If you doubt me, go ask the good doctor or his grandkids as to the condition they found me a few weeks ago, but knowing how clever you are, you probably did already. God knows what he told you, and I really don't care. The only truth that I'm concerned with is that I have a new lease on life, a real chance at some peace, and I'm trying to make the best of it. Is that so bad?"

"No. I guess not. I appreciate your candor and all I have left to say is, welcome aboard," the young woman replied, extending her hand. "Now let's get to work, we have to move all this cargo."

The two shook hands and paused for a moment, staring at each other's eyes, him at her mysterious purple eyes and her at his deep dark brown ones. Ophelia released his hand, turned, and called for Emmy. Between the three of them, they unloaded all the cargo and placed the cart next to broken loader.

"Captain, I'd like to clean up and get some rest if we're done," Jorian asked.

"Yes, of course. I'll show you to your new quarters," Ophelia replied.

Guiding him, she showed him the floor he had been designated to and his quarters. Placing him on the floor above the cargo and work areas. Giving floors between him and her as a precaution with everything that had happened and keeping him closer to his work area. The room was spacious and had its own bathroom along with other amenities, as did all the other rooms on the ship. Jorian thanked her and retreated into his room while Ophelia returned to the cargo bay.

Ophelia brought Emmy a drink as the two sat on a crate looking out of the open cargo bay door. The two women were drenched in sweat, having helped move all the cargo along with their new crew mate. For the moment, the ship became silent until Emmy broke the silence.

"He seems nice," Emmy stated.

"He does. But so did Billy," Ophelia replied.

"Yeah, but this one is different," Emmy was quick to state.

"How so?" the captain asked.

"I think he is who he is. When we were coming back from the auction, he had been pushing that cart with us on it. We stopped by a little market for something to drink. He stayed out by the cart, when I brought him his drink, he opened it and gave some to the little fox first, then he drank," Emmy replied.

"Well, maybe he wasn't that thirsty," Ophelia replied cynically.

"He had been pushing that cart for almost an hour by himself, with us on it. You and I together could barely move it, and that's when it was loaded less than halfway. I assure you; he was thirsty. Those little things and how he acted with those kids, it's not something you fake," Emmy explained.

Ophelia looked at Emmy with a doubtful face. "Well, let me tell you a little about our Mister Jorian Phoenix, before you get all bleeding heart on him. Just a few weeks ago, he shot and killed three people. Before that, he was a soldier..." Ophelia stated with a hint of coldness, then noticed a pair of orange eyes intensely studying her.

The young captain looked at the fox pup that was on a crate just a few feet away, just looking at her with great intensity, almost as if judging her. It was not aggressive, nor scared, just curious. It then looked at Emmy and then back to Ophelia.

Emmy looked at the fox and smiled before it jumped off. "Impressive animal, that one. It is not a native species of this planet. The foxes on this planet are weird and spotted at birth and for the first year of their life until they get their full coat. That little fox is something else, I am not sure where it's from, but it's very smart." Pausing and taking a deep breath, the petite scientist looked at Ophelia, "As to what you said about him killing people, this place is harsh, and the kids told me a different tale. They said he killed those three people, because they were pirate's that were going to hurt them. They also said he stayed behind to make sure they got away safely. And when I say they, I mean her because the little boy doesn't talk."

"Well, that animal is sneaky, and I thought it belonged to the little boy. What's it doing here?" Ophelia said puzzled, changing the topic.

"Sneaky or not, that animal belongs to its owner, whoever it wants that to be, no matter who holds the receipt," Emmy replied.

The little animal gracefully jumped from box to box until it finally reached the floor, disappearing behind some cargo. The two turned back and continued their drink as they looked out to the port and all the increased activity because of the auction.

"Should I do something about that creature, or is it part of the crew as well?" Mistress suddenly asked.

"God only knows, leave it be for now, it may be sneaky, but it is cute," Ophelia replied.

"Great, the second good looking man to come on the ship recently and she likes the animal," Mistress replied sarcastically.

The two women laughed at the accuracy of the comment before moving off, making plans for dinner.

Chapter 11

"Good morning, Mister Jorian," Mistress said softly.

The young man stretched and yawned and looked down on his chest, feeling a familiar sensation. Once again, like when he was at Brother Julius's clinic, he found the little fox pup curled up on his chest. Jorian scratched the pup on the back of its neck, and it too yawned and stretched out its little paws.

"Mister Jorian, if you intend to keep that animal, may I suggest you bathe it and train it to use the facilities in one spot?"

"If it is mine, I will be happy to, but it's my understanding that it belongs to Brother Julius's grandson, Nate. And please, just call me Jorian," the soldier said as he sat up. "By the way, Mistress, what time is it, please?"

"Very well, Jorian. The time is nine a.m., you have been asleep for twelve hours. Would you like some breakfast?" the AI asked.

"Twelve hours! Damn it, I have to get to work," Jorian replied, jumping out of bed with the pup in hand.

"It's fine Jorian, everyone is still asleep. I expect them to sleep for another few hours, given the time they came in last night. There is no rush. As you know, in space there is no day or night, as long as you work your eight-to-ten-hour shift, we will count it. Also, if you work more, they will also be counted against your debt at regular pay."

"I see," Jorian replied as he walked to the shower.

Turning the water on to a comfortable temperature, he bathed the pup, who was not overly excited about getting wet. Lots of dirt and dust came off the little guy, which made Jorian want to shower himself again. After Jorian dried the pup with a towel, he placed it under an air machine that left the pup's fur standing, making it look puffy. The little animal complained at him, but it didn't last long after Jorian brushed the pup down.

"Mistress, is that correct?" the young man asked.

"Yes, Jorian, and thank you for cleaning that animal," the ship replied.

"Mistress, I have not had a pet before, not really. What do you suggest for its necessities?" Jorian asked.

"I was designed with a few pets in mind, with individual washable pad areas designated for animal waste disposal. I took the liberty to retrofit this room with one, as you slept and have put another in the work area," Mistress replied.

Looking at one wall, a compartment opened and out came a rectangle with artificial turf covering it. Jorian placed the small animal on the pad and waited, as it smelled around. Within moments, the fox had done its necessities and jumped off the pad. Immediately, a cover came over it and washed the area, leaving the artificial turf ready for use once again. Turning to his bed, he noticed it too had been changed and cleaned.

"You seem to be an amazing ship Mistress, I was about to change and make the bed myself," Jorian replied.

"Thank you, Jorian, but I'm a fully automated ship. If that's your preference though, you can make your own bed or do any other task manually if you wish, just ask. I want you to make yourself at home and be comfortable," the ship said in what seemed as a warm tone.

"Thank you, Mistress. It will just take some getting used to, that's all."

"Of course, Jorian. Please inform me of anything you need, including counseling. I am more than capable of doing that or just listening if need be. Before you ask, I will keep our conversation confidential as I would be bound by doctor patient privilege, unless it is a threat to the ship or a member of the ship, then I am required to report. I am also capable of over five million other tasks and functions. Welcome aboard Jorian Phoenix," Mistress said welcomingly.

"Thank you again, Mistress," Jorian replied as he entered the shower.

"Jorian, I do not mean to intrude, but my scans show you have a foreign substance on your back, should I analyze further?" the ship asked.

"No Mistress. It is unnecessary. Just note it, scan again after the shower, and add it to my normal profile. And, no, you may not ask what it is, nor investigate it further. Now moving on. As a technician, mechanic, or engineer, I need to know all about you. Let's start with water: usage, consumption, recycling, waste, additives, and routing," Jorian instructed as he showered once again.

"Very well. Our water is held in various tanks as a precautionary measure and can be rerouted if needed. Our water is processed to a Pico measurement and as in most Knightforge Technologies' systems, that water is cleaned using high speed cyclonic tanks that separate the water from other materials and toxins while being hit with UV lights, then distilled, and processed through a magnetic conditioner for improved water quality at the molecular level.

Consumption is as needed and I'm normally capable of processing over 100,000 gallons of water a day. I ask that you keep a conservative mindset, as it may be useful in emergency situations. We can clean all linen on the ship daily, without it affecting operations, we prefer to do it once a week or if scans require at an increased need.

All waste products are accumulated and separated to a molecular level, processed and recycled for use in different capacities, but mostly in our printers and forges. Those molecules are stored in a separate holding area in individual tanks.

Please allow me to expand on that last portion that may be confusing. I am a prototype ship, designed to perform like a corvette class with a size closer to a frigate. They designated me for exploration and scientific application, but with enhanced combat capabilities, which have declined since we were boarded a few years ago. Please know that something is amiss with my water processing systems and I am currently supplementing with water from the port."

Jorian listened intently as he showered. Every word and detail taken to memory as he went on a creative visual journey in his mind, while she explained the systems more in depth. Mistress continued and went back and forth with the young man in an extensive conversation about her water systems.

"So let me get this right, we distill water in part with the cooling of the engines and thrusters to recycle the heat, which is used to moderate temperatures for different applications. Separate from the regular cooling systems for the engines and thrusters, which also get recycled eventually and remade internally into new cooling fluid, which is unique to Knightforge Technologies' designs. Please place the schematics up on the monitor in the room, with a water route for both systems and color code it. We are going to get those systems running right, it will save the captain a bundle in port costs," Jorian said as he exited the shower and dried himself off in the room.

"I must admit Jorian, I have not talked to anyone like this in a long time, I find it sexy," she said and briefly paused. "Strong and smart. Yum," the ship finished in her sultry self.

Jorian laughed. "I can cook, too. Wait till I change your oil."

"You do know what to say to a girl, don't you?" Mistress replied. "Yesterday, when you arrived and made your inspection, you were thorough and tender with your touch. The last person to touch me like that was Mr. Knight. I think the Master of Mayhem Protocol activated and shot at you because it was jealous."

Jorian blushed slightly and grinned, enjoying the AI's sultry nature, and replied, "Well, then I understand why it shot at me. Mistress, you are something to be jealous about. You are absolutely amazing."

The ship let out a loud moan only heard in his quarters. "Oh, Jorian, stop before I blow a circuit."

Jorian chuckled and replied, "None of that now. I would just have to fix it, and I have plenty to do already."

"Very well, Jorian, but may I say, I can't wait for you to put your hands on me," Mistress replied.

"Stop, you're going to make me blush," he replied.

"Too late," the AI shot back.

Jorian laughed, feeling good for the first time in a long time. Not being judged, filled with a sense of appreciation in a lighthearted atmosphere.

"Jorian, I like you," the ship said, then a few moments passed before it added, "Please don't hurt Ophelia. I would hate to have to shoot you."

Jorian became serious and looked up to the monitor where the now digitized face of a woman looked back at him. The face was familiar having Ophelia's purple eyes and cheekbones, but was different. Then he remembered the pinup girl on the side of the ship and realized that it was that face on the hull of the ship that was now a live image on the screen that he was talking too. "I hope I never do, for I don't ever want to." Pausing to breathe, he then added, "I need to make a confession, and though it is of no consequence, I want it in my personal file with confidential privileges, and never want it to be repeated to anyone."

"Counselor privileges initiated. Please go ahead. The background sound you hear will interfere with any other listening or recording devices," Mistress stated as a soft, static hum could be slightly heard.

The fox pup covered its ears and whined as if the noise bothered it and dug its head under the towel that Jorian had put on the cushion. Jorian took a deep breath as he pondered his words. He looked up at the screen, looking at the AI's face.

"We have met once before. It was about five years ago on Catieus, when Mr. Knight, some sort of high-ranking officer, and Ophelia were going through a marketplace. As part of the process of the group, I was there having been severely beaten and placed in a stockade outside of the guard tower to endure the elements, public ridicule, along with daily beatings and whipping. I was unsure if I would survive the day. I had already been out there for various days with no food or water, except what the rain had brought. My face was bruised, bloodied, and swollen, as was the rest of my body. I was on the verge of collapsing when the softest purple eyes I had ever seen, the only ones at that point, came and placed her soft hands on my face and poured some hydration fluid in my mouth."

"Like an angel," Mistress stated.

Jorian paused, thinking back to the moment before continuing, "To me, at that moment, it was heaven. From then on, every time I experienced a harshness or some sort of immense difficulty or life-threatening situation, I remember that moment, that kindness, and it gave me a small sense of peace and hope. That moment meant so much to me. I can never forget it."

"Hmmm," Mistress acknowledged with a slight undertone.

Jorian looked at the screen, pointing a finger, "Before you start. This is not a fetish or some sort of obsessive behavior thing. It's gratitude and me trying to pay back the kindness shown. I would not be alive today if not for that moment. And I pay my debts. Close file," Jorian said, finishing his thought hurriedly becoming somewhat defensive.

In a professional and sympathetic tone, Mistress replied. "A lesser being would call it a fetish or an obsession. I am much more sophisticated than that, and I would call it gratitude with a hint of affection. Either way, thank you for sharing, and know that I will keep your confidence." Mistress paused, then added, "If I may, I recall having some records of that trip, I was in test flights and my systems still had some bugs during that time."

Jorian nodded. "I know. It's hard to miss that copper-colored hull you have, it is quite a unique color on a ship, along with your unique design. Even at a distance and through one eye, I saw you take off later that day."

"Thank you for sharing, Jorian. I'm glad to see that you seem quite comfortable with me," the AI remarked.

"I talked little with the people where I was at, I actually avoided them as much as I could, they brought me nothing but problems. I had a digital partner that was an advanced AI for missions which I talked to. In addition, we had particular protocols that forced us to talk to the AI for daily therapeutic sessions, but I kept those sessions brief since the AI had to report our sessions to command," Jorian said as he looked around the room. "Mistress, where are my clothes?"

"They have been cleaned," the AI replied as a closet door slid open, displaying his clothes hanging neatly on a hanger. "Jorian, you are going to need more than one set of clothing. I can order you some more?" the ship asked.

"No, thank you. I have incurred enough debt already. I don't need any more," the young man quickly answered.

"No, you don't understand, as per regulations of the company, they provide you uniforms. Because of one of my systems being stolen, I can no longer make them, but I can dip into a certain company account and arrange for their purchase. It will be no expense to us, only Knightforge Technologies," Mistress explained, then added, "I have already scanned you and have submitted for your things. Your order is complete and will be delivered to the ship within the next three days. For now, just use the coveralls in your closet."

"Thank you," Jorian said as he got dressed and headed for the cargo bay, giving Mistress his food request for breakfast along the way. The two continued talking about other systems of the ship and slowly covered each one as he inspected the pile of heap and spare parts that came with the supposed loader. Jorian spent his time rummaging through boxes, removing, cataloguing, and testing each part, until Mistress finally got his food together.

Taking his tray and sitting at one workbench, he ate. "Mistress, can you reference the schematics on the loader, it is a Core Industries Titan loader. Don't worry about which sub type, they all sucked, but they did one thing right. They designed it to be modular, which created thousands of aftermarket parts, increasing its reliability and customizability, making it a popular choice. Let's scan it from top to bottom and check for any structural issues. Then let's cross reference that scan with custom builds so we can see our options." Jorian leaned into the box reaching something at the bottom. "Oh, and find out if anyone did any changes that improved its performance, while I begin to disassemble."

"I am currently displaying the most popular or highest ranked Titan loaders on the galactic web. I have also displayed the top modification for structural integrity that will increase its output capacity, but we'll have to overhaul the engine, if it's still good," Mistress stated as numerous images displayed on the wall.

"That's a big if," Jorian agreed.

"Jorian, I regret to inform you that our loader is currently full of mismatching parts. So even if they were all new, it wouldn't pick up a roll of tissue paper. I have also located a customizer that goes by the name, 'JackedUp'. He has made a few interesting modifications that, if done properly, can assist us."

"That's great! Good job Mistress. When you render the image, make sure you do it in layers, to help me throughout the build. Do we have an acid tank by chance? And where are the tools here?" Jorian asked with excitement as he picked different images and the modifications he wanted to do to it.

Mistress gave Jorian an extensive tour of the cargo hold and workshops with a virtual image of herself. She showed him all the safety protocols and all the rules that had been programmed into her at the request of Mr. Knight himself. She continued explaining that all of their printers had been taken and they had replaced only the food printer. She also stated that they had an advanced forge printer, but it was partially disassembled, since the criminals tried to take it and couldn't figure it out, so they left it dismantled and it had remained like that ever since.

"Do you have a backup video of what happened that day and of the disassembly of the forge printer? With any luck, we might be able to reverse engineer the havoc the thieving pirates had caused and get it up and running again," Jorian asked.

"Fortunately, I do. They doubled up on camera and other sensors in engineering and the cargo areas in case of a catastrophe, so that reactions to an emergency could be more efficient. There are also secondary systems in the bridge, labs, medical, and the engine room," Mistress answered.

Jorian spent the next few hours looking at videos and working on the forge printer, trying to bring it back to life. Eventually, with the help of the schematics, despite a few electrical shocks, Jorian got it running.

"Okay, how's that?" he asked.

"Function is at about twenty-eight percent efficiency," Mistress replied kindly.

"So, it will work, but slow as hell. Can you diagnose it and monitor it to avoid other problems?" Jorian said with a smirk.

"Affirmative. Not perfect, but it's a start."

"I'll take it."

"I don't mean to be rude, but is this the level of craftsmanship I should expect? A girl needs to know not to get her hopes up, as well as making sure you stay away from my critical systems."

Jorian looked at the screen, somewhat deflated. "Hey, I have strengths and weaknesses just like everyone else, and for the first time working on a forge printer, especially one so complex, I think I did pretty good. I know someone that might be able to help, but I doubt they are awake this early. We can try them later. For now, let's get back to the loader, that's my first assignment."

"Focused, a wonderful trait to have," she stated.

The young man gave the AI various instructions on what he wanted printed, and given that all the parts had a Knightforge Technologies' equivalent part, no royalties would have to be paid. The forge lit up for the first time in two years, giving the room a warm glow, and began printing the parts. The room 's temperature increased as the forge once again was coming to life.

As the printer churned out liquid metal, the soldier donned his safety equipment and got to work with the sonic grinder, removing rust and grime stuck clinging to the surface of the metal.

For hours, he alternated between grinding and welding. Having dismantled the loader in multiple pieces, he could do detailed work on various parts, preparing them for the bold project they had designed. He had seen no one and was content with the distraction of his work, enjoying the creative process of reviving the old loader.

"Okay, Mistress, let's dip these in the tank, then we will wash, and last but not least, I will place a base anticorrosive treatment," the young man stated, exhausted.

"Jorian, I can do those tasks unassisted. I can also give it primer, paint, and any other coat you would like to add. As well as altering designs and patterns, to your specification. While you sleep," Mistress urged.

"Fascinating. You truly are. But I don't want to pass the primer stage, so we can fit all the parts together when they're done printing, for any last-minute touches. Then we will paint and coat. We did a lot of good work today, Mistress. Time to eat and shower, by the way, what time is it?" Jorian asked.

"It's two in the morning. And before you ask. You have been working for over fifteen hours straight. Go get some rest. You've earned it," the ship replied.

Jorian checked his IDP for any messages or a response to his message to Rey earlier in the day. But the inbox was empty. He considered that with all his years of experience in salvaging, Rey might have a better idea on the forge printer issue. Being done for the day, the young man cleaned the tools and returned them to their places, before locking up for the night, leaving the warm glow of the forge to do its work.

Exiting the forge area, exhausted and full of grime, grease, and metal shavings, Jorian ran into Ophelia and Emmy, returning from a night out on the town. The smell of sweat, smoke, and alcohol mixed with perfume filled the air, as the two giggling women reached him.

"Morning," he said, addressing the two.

The two women paused, startled seeing the young man in his overalls with a face covered with grime and soot. Collecting themselves and unconsciously adjusting their outfits as they saw the young man.

"Hello Jorian, still working?" Emmy asked.

Jorian shrugged. "There's a lot to do."

Ophelia looked at Jorian and felt somewhat embarrassed as Sergeant Odis and another soldier entered behind them. Jorian looked at the two men, and they all suddenly got quiet. He nodded at the two, turned up the stairs and continued towards his room.

"You work the help harder than I do my men. Ophelia," Odis jested.

Jorian just gave the man a sideways glance and continued towards his room. He could hear Mistress saying something that made him grin in an automaton voice that stated something about a scan and some sort of alien STD. The man quickly defended himself, but that was all that Jorian heard as the deck door closed behind him.

Ophelia faked a smile, looking at Jorian walk off while thinking to herself. *Odis shouldn't have said that, Jorian's a person and a member of my crew, not a slave. I don't want him thinking he is a slave, because he's not.* Shaking her head as the deck door closed, then back toward Sergeant Odis, who was defending himself at the STD statement made by Mistress. One that Ophelia knew contradicted the original scan by the ship just a few days prior. *Mistress is defending Jorian.*

Ophelia quickly interrupted, placing a hand on Odis, defusing the situation, "Sergeant, I'm sure it's just a misunderstanding, but it's late and I have many appointments in the morning. Maybe we can do lunch sometime on the weekend."

Odis was about to protest, but smiled and kissed Ophelia's hand. "I'd like that."

The other young man looked at Odis and followed his lead, kindly bidding the lady's a good night, and taking the out that left them with future potential, instead of losing any possibilities with Ophelia and Emmy. It surprised the scientist at the sudden change in Ophelia's demeanor but played along, not having any actual interest in Odis's friend, and shrugged as if blaming her captain, leaving herself clean of any wrongdoing.

Sealing the cargo doors, the two ladies headed towards the lift, that would take them to their prospective floors. Ophelia joined Emmy as they sat in the ships' lounge and spoke for a few minutes before bidding each other a good night as they made their way to their respective rooms.

Odis's comment still bothered Ophelia as she redirected herself towards Jorian's quarters. *I hope that stupid remark didn't insult him.* She wondered as she stood outside the door and for some reason didn't knock. She was unsure what to say, but knew she was uncomfortable with the situation and felt she needed to clear the air. After a few minutes, she raised her hand to knock on Jorian's door, but Mistress stopped her.

"He's sleeping already."

"Already?" she asked, surprised.

"Yes, he took a shower, grabbed something to drink, and went to bed. He was asleep within a matter of minutes."

Pausing, the ship's captain turned, "Thank you, Mistress," she said, then continued talking with the AI as she made her way to her quarters. "Wait! Why did you say that about Odis, if just a few days ago you said his scan was clean?"

"His comment toward Jorian was inappropriate, and I am surprised you would tolerate someone talking about one of your crewmates in such a fashion. Though I am happy that you went out, bringing him home after only one night is a bit soon."

"I don't understand you! First, you want me to rub up against every guy I meet, then when I go out with someone, you complain to me as well. Decide, one or the other, but please be consistent," the young woman said in a huff, closing the door to her chamber.

Jorian continued working and almost a week later found himself waiting for the printer or some coat of paint to dry, realizing he had nothing to do, so he worked on his decrepit dolly to pass the time. He discovered his dolly was actually an older hover cart with the wheel assembly installed later, most likely when it originally broke down. He continued with the restoration process of the cart.

Starting into the second week, and once again being held up by the slow functionality of the forge printer, he messaged Rey once more with no answer and looked towards the forge printer in frustration. The forge had been printing parts nonstop for all those days and had gone through three tips already because of the extreme heat and slow output. Something that was worrying Jorian because it could permanently damage the machine.

Originally messaging to see if the wiser salvager could offer some insight, but after a week and still no response, he was growing concerned. El Capitan had left him a handwritten message in the bag.

Compai,
I'll be out for a few days, see you soon. Good Luck.
Your Amigo,
El Capitan.

Leaving all the thoughts of the loader, the dolly, and Rey at the workshop, Jorian turned in for the night and was in mid-shower when he heard Mistress come over the speaker.

"Jorian, we are having a buildup in pressure in various tanks at the workshop. The temperatures and pressures will quickly exceed the safety thresholds and may rupture various tanks and lines if not relieved immediately."

"What!" Jorian exclaimed and rushed out of the shower. Grabbing the first towel, he found wrapping it around his waist.

Ophelia and Emmy had once again gone out with Odis and his friend and were returning once again late into the night. They were entering the ship and making their way up the stairs in the cargo bay when an alarm sounded, catching them all by surprise, but not as much as what happened next. As the group looked around trying to decipher the alarm, Jorian, wet and naked except for his towel around his waist, came rushing towards them, yelling.

"Move, move, move. Out of the way!" he yelled, plowing through them.

In the rush to get by pushing his way through the people, his towel got caught and was yanked off, but it did not stop him. The young man, now wet and completely naked, continued running and everyone could not help but to look at that moment, some in intrigue and others in envy of his augmentations and extremely well-built physique.

Rushing into the workshop, Jorian glanced at the gauges on the tanks and relief valves. Hurrying and opening over half a dozen valves producing jets of steam rushing out of each one. In seconds, the workshop was filled with steam then pouring out into the cargo bay.

"Jorian!" the two ladies called out and rushed down the stairs, followed by the two soldiers. The loud hissing and whistling were deafening and the cloud only grew, making the workshop extremely uncomfortable to approach, let alone enter.

"Jorian!" Ophelia called out, stepping back.

"STAY OUT!" he yelled back over the alarm.

A few minutes passed, and the captain tried to approach again, but the heat of the steam and Odis kept her back. She called out for the young man a few more times, but received no answer.

A few more very tense minutes passed, and the alarm finally subsided. Steam was filling the cargo area when the loud whirling of the vent fans turned on, pulling the hot steam out of the cargo bay and workshop. All the lights had come on and the bay doors were opening, various emergency vehicles rushed the scene with personnel at the ready and approaching the ship.

A shadowy form finally appeared in the workshop's doorway and eventually exited the room. Jorian, butt naked, drenched in sweat, some sort of slime, and water, calmly looked out of the cargo bay doors at all the people looking at him, which amounted close to thirty people.

Taking a few more steps, he reached the area where sergeant Odis was and extended his hand. Odis handed Jorian the towel that had accidentally come off when he pushed past them. Looking briefly at the

Sergeant as he cleared his throat and nodded in acknowledgment, Jorian moved off.

Ophelia looked at her new crewmate full of concern, seeing that he was flushed and drenched in sweat and some other substance. "Are you okay?

Jorian stood there as some of the emergency personnel started whistling and making catcalls at him, men and women alike. Nodding his head and replying a quick "Yup" as he placed the towel back around his waist and continued up the stairs. Once in the hallway, he instructed Mistress, "Shut it down after it cools and keep the vent fans going."

After Ophelia found out what happened, Odis and her went to the emergency personnel and smoothed out the situation, with the understanding that a qualified technician would check out the ship within the next few days.

Emmy hurried behind Jorian and knocked on his door until he finally opened. Gasping, seeing various burns on his skin that she had not seen before. She reached out for him, but he pulled back.

"Are you okay?"

"I'll be fine," Jorian replied.

"It doesn't look fine. Can I see?" she asked.

"I'll be fine, I just want to go back to bed," he stated, averting his eyes.

"Those burns look pretty bad, but it should have been much worse, given the amount of steam that came out of there," the young scientist stated.

Jorian sighed, "I opened one of the cooling tanks and got under it, that colder water protected me from most of the steam."

"Look, how about I treat those burns for a second?" Emmy offered, concerned.

His eyes shifted nervously to his towel, then back up at Emmy and quickly shook his head. "No thank you, I'll be fine. Mistress can spray me down in the shower with ointment."

Emmy quickly realized that the embarrassment of being displayed for all to see in the nude bothered him more than his injuries. "Fine, I'll go, but only if you promise me to see Brother Julius tomorrow?"

Jorian looked at her and quickly nodded, "Fine."

Emmy turned as she was about to leave and glanced back. "Hey, you have nothing to be ashamed of. If anything, most of the men laughing out there were probably a bit intimidated. And the women, trust me, they weren't really laughing at you," she said with a wink.

The young man's face became very flush as he averted his eyes uncomfortably, not wanting to meet Emmy's gaze. The scientist grinned as she left, hoping she had helped her crewmate and grinned impressed with his physique even more now that she had seen his dense muscles up close.

Mistress did not let the moment slide on either side of the door, commenting to both individuals simultaneously, "You are such a slut, you just wanted to put your hands on him."

"Guilty. But I was actually worried," Emmy replied.

"I am aware," Mistress replied to her.

While having a different conversation inside with Jorian. "They have no idea what you saved them from, but Ophelia will know soon enough. Tomorrow, we need to check all those valves and look at the forge again."

"Oh, I will. Now let me finish showering and get some rest, this night has been eventful enough," Jorian replied, wanting nothing more than to get some rest and forget everything that had happened in the last half hour.

"Do you want to talk about it?" Mistress asked, in a motherly type of voice.

"Nope. That would be contrary to my goals, which is to get some sleep. Tomorrow will be a long day," Jorian replied as he made his way to his bed, then asked. "Mistress, can you play some meditation or sleep music?"

"Of course, Jorian, and I will play it at four hundred thirty-two hertz, which is a harmonious frequency. It should help soothe you," the AI softly answered.

"Thank you, Mistress," the young man said and laid in his bed.

He stared at the ceiling of the now dark room for a few moments longer, letting the music fill him in waves. Slowly it melted away his thoughts, and he was asleep within minutes.

Ophelia stood in the cargo bay as the last of the emergency personnel left in their vehicles and onlookers from other ships returned to their activities or vessels. Odis stood waving to the last group to hold on and turned, looking at Ophelia.

"Should I go?"

Ophelia hesitated and looked around, unsure of her answer. "I don't know, Odis. I'm overwhelmed right now. You have been a great distraction, but this ship and the burden of responsibility that comes with being a captain is all a bit much. Sometimes I just want to get the hell out of here."

"Then let's go. I know of a nice spot, and it's not too far away. You can keep the ship in view," Odis replied charmingly.

"Okay..." Ophelia replied hesitantly, pausing for a moment, then let herself be led away by the hand and off the ship.

Odis got one of the spare vehicles and took Ophelia to the far side of the port, to a small utility building that sat on a grassy hill with some small trees around it overlooking the port. Some of the garrison soldiers had placed a few comfort items, including a cooler, a few lounge chairs and some other items like cheesy decorative lamps or other trinkets, making it homier. Most used it as a place of relaxation.

Placing two lounge chairs outside, the man grabbed a few drinks from the cooler and a blanket and sat outside with Ophelia. The port lights looked amazing, showing a different type of splendor that most would never see, with the docks on one side and a fully functional runway on the other. The port was fairly quiet, but they could see the occasional ship coming or going.

"For all the crap that happens on this planet, it's good to come here every once in a while and see the other side of it," Odis told her.

"It's quite beautiful," Ophelia replied.

Ophelia continued to look at her datapad on her wrist constantly as she was getting reports from Mistress on various diagnostic, she had her run. Odis placed a hand on the IDP on her forearm covering the information and looked at Ophelia.

"Let it go for a little while. She's right over there, and nothing is going on. Just relax and enjoy the moment. You can return to your duties in a little while, they'll still be there." Taking a sip from his drink, he put the container down. "The one thing I've learned being in my position is not to worry about what you can't control, only prepare for it. I am sure your technician will take care of it. Have faith he will do his job."

"That's just it, I hope he can. I don't know how good he is or isn't. He has just been with us for a little more than a couple of weeks and most of that time I have spent out or with you. Mistress is not just any other ship; she's unique, and a prototype built by my father," she said, worried.

Placing a gently hand on her face and caressing her cheek, he said, "Listen, if he came from this planet, you probably have a lot to be concerned about. Most people from this planet aren't worth much and always trying to see what they can get and from who, but sometimes, you find someone true." Odis paused and gave her a resigned sigh. "Not that I want to spend my time talking about another guy and I really don't know anything about him, except that his name is Jorian by what you've told me, but as a soldier and one that is in charge of people. I can say that he cares about the ship. That man almost ran us over to save a ship he's been on for a couple of weeks. He acted without regard for himself. He rushed into a room that was most likely about to explode, and by what I heard and all the steam that I saw coming out of there, he should have run from the ship." Odis paused briefly, considering his next words. "He did all that, and he did it butt naked. It's going to be hard to get that image out of my head," Odis told her and chuckled.

Ophelia thought about Jorian running down the cargo bay with nothing on, and could not help but laugh herself. The two looked at each other once more and laughed some more. Odis handed her a cold drink and moved to sit behind her, wrapping his arms around her.

Ophelia felt somewhat conflicted, wanting to resist while at the same time wanting to surrender herself to Odis's brawny arms and charming personality. She finally gave in and let her worries go if just for a moment and turned, leaning back into him and kissing him deeply.

Chapter 12

The morning sun stretched out over the port with its bright fingers glistening off the ships docked at the port. A multitude of hues gleamed off the ships from reds to blues, silver to pearl, but none stood out more than the Mistress of Mayhem, with her copper-colored hull and her elegant lines poised gracefully amongst all the others.

It's such a beautiful view, so peaceful and serene it all seems from up here, but all the turmoil hides inside like a person. To the passerby they look just like impressive metal mammoths, but to us who know better, each one of those ships is alive and with personalities all of their own. Ophelia thought to herself.

Looking over, she saw Odis lying there in the blanket next to her; he was still asleep, but she could barely keep her eyes closed, her thoughts going back to what had happened. *I could have lost her.* She told herself as she pictured Jorian flying through the air naked when he cleared the last 10 steps, and could not help but chuckle.

Jorian, he saved us; he saved her, and I didn't even have the decency to check up on him, and here I am laying with another man I barely know trying to forget. But I can never forget, I will never forget! I am the captain. But do I even deserve that title? She asked herself as she grabbed her clothes and quickly dressed.

Odis barely stirred as Ophelia quietly sneaked off back to her ship. Walking slowly carrying her shoes in one hand, enjoying the feel of the sand between her toes at the base of the hill. She remembered the beaches on various other planets she had visited with her parents as a child.

Sighing, she looked back at Odis still sleeping, feeling a tinge of shame for what she had done with a man who was practically a stranger, but for a moment she was free. A fleeting moment as she turned her head back and could see the copper hull of her taskmaster, her "Mistress" that awaited her return.

"Mistress, send Odis a message that I had things to attend to on the ship and open the doors, please."

"Right away, Captain," the ship replied.

She was able to return to the ship when the individual entrance opened and the ramp came down. The ramp closed, as did the door behind her, locking out the sun's light. A series of lights came on, illuminating the hallway in front of her. She could feel the cold metal on her feet with each step she took.

What a difference to the warm sand outside, she thought to herself.

Pausing for a moment, looking down, she almost ran into Jorian that was making his way towards the workshop distracted by something on his datapad. She noticed him at the last second and looked around for somewhere to hide, feeling the shame of shirking her duties for a moment of distraction in the arms of a man she practically just met. Jorian looked up at the last moment, just realizing she had not been on the ship.

Their eyes met, and after a few uncomfortable moments, the young man eventually broke the silence, "Morning, Captain," he said stoically. His face was like a piece of stone, unemotional and unreadable, but his eyes said more, much more, and she could feel the weight of his silent judgement weighing heavily upon her.

The young man stepped to the side and continued on his way; he had not taken three steps when she softly asked, "Are you okay?"

Jorian paused and replied, "I'm fine, thank you for asking," in an indifferent tone as he continued on without even glancing back.

She hesitated before turning to say something else, but he was already gone. Further down she could hear the sounds of the door to the workshop opening, then closing. Letting out a deep breath, she shook her head disapprovingly at herself. Then continued down the hallway.

With the door closing behind him, Mistress let out a comment, "That was smooth, is that your plan, to ignore her into falling for you? Or are you angry because she was out with someone?"

"What?" asked Jorian defensively. "I am part of the crew of this ship, what the captain does on her own time is not my business."

"But you are upset. I can perceive it in your tone and in your elevated stats," the ship replied.

"So, I'm bothered," he paused, fumbling through his thoughts and emotions before he continued, "but not because she was out, or if she was with someone, though I can smell it on her, but because she was out instead of looking after her ship and crew. I have seen many people in command and the best ones always look after their people first. They understand that without them, they don't have a command. She didn't check on me or you, she just went out. I'm wondering if I made the right decision joining this crew," he replied.

"That is understandable, but you may expect too much from her right now, on top of that, she's never really had a command or has been trained to be in command. She is learning and growing, she's been barely surviving spending most of her time alone these last few years. She lost her last crew and friends to a pirate attack; they were executed right in front of her. But that is for her to say, what I stated is only public knowledge from the police report. Can you help her?" the AI asked.

Jorian paused, considering her words, before replying, "No. I spent a lot of time learning other things, I read the GDF leadership manuals and everything else I could get my hands on to read, but I was never really in charge of anyone."

Jorian stopped, his mind wondering as if he'd missed something. Mistress's words being drowned out as he stood there scratching his head. Looking around at all the tanks and ventilation pipes that were in this section, his mind was racing as it formed a thought, *I need more information.* He spurred himself into action, checking every valve, tank, and pipe in the workshop, making adjustments along the way.

"Mistress, what is the crew size you were designed for?"

"At maximum capacity I could sustain over five hundred, but I should only carry about one hundred and twenty at optimum efficiency and without straining the systems. I do have my own captain's license and can fly with no one on board. I am designed as a next generation science, exploration, and medical vessel. Which requires more resources than most other ships, that is why we have additional high volume storage tanks for additional elemental storage and recycling," the ship replied.

The young man just nodded as he continued to check system after system and valve after valve. It had been hours since Jorian had started crawling all over the workshop, marking off a particular kind of flow valve he knew to be defective in their construction. He then continued to other parts of the ship, carrying on his investigation into the rest of the cargo bay, the spa/gym area, followed by the kitchen, where he stopped to eat, before reengaging in his search to the engine section, and another area that he immediately recognized as a munitions room.

He counted one hundred and forty-three valves made by the same company, all of which had a similar problem: something on the inside didn't work right. They had obtained some alternate valves at auction and a few that had been left over after the ship had been raided, but their numbers were not near the eighty-three properly functioning valves they needed, at minimum. Jorian removed a failed valve from the workshop and studied it closely.

"Mistress, what is this part, this is not a Knightforge Technologies' part, nor would it have passed quality assurance. This is another brand. It's so off," Jorian asked inquisitively.

"Those valves were never supposed to be installed in this ship. They are from one of the smaller companies our board had acquired. Long had that company been suspected by the Knight's of their subpar standards and possible company corruption. They were part of an investigation by Mr. and Mrs. Knight into problems in the company," Mistress replied.

"Let's get proper schematics for these valves and we will print what we can and go upgrading while not overheating the system. Inform everyone about the upcoming outages and let's see if we can increase the flow rate by at least fifteen percent in the new models, using Tactrinium as the construction material and Oloman's Theory for the internal curves and thickness. We're going to need that increase in flow if my understanding of the system is correct. Can we make two of them with the cooling system disconnected?" Jorian asked.

"Negative, we might make one, but installing that one will provide enough coolant along with water from the port to make the other, and from there, we can continue. I also want to let you know that there are no comparable valves in this sector with your parameters. If the printer was working, at least at fifty percent, I would have a much better statistic and success rate. Please be aware that these are experimental, with the increase flow rate and will be slightly thicker on the exterior but should still easily fit. Also, you will have to pour water down the pipe manually, then flush the system afterwards." Mistress paused, then added, in her coy like self, "I feel so exposed, but I like how you treat me."

"Well, I better get a whole lot of water to cool you off, little lady, because it's going to get real hot in here," Jorian replied jokingly.

Jorian began preparing to make the first of the two valves and rushed back and forth with buckets of water, pouring them down one of the coolant chamber's pipes.

Meanwhile, elsewhere on the ship, Ophelia had enjoyed what was a quick shower and then went to sleep. Though sleep was an overstatement, feeling a pang of guilt with what she had done. A gnawing feeling like she had abandoned her duties to enjoy a few moments away from the ship, which she had.

"How long are you going to just lie there like a log staring at the ceiling? There are plenty of things that need doing, and it's not right that Jorian is the only one doing anything on this ship," Mistress said with what seemed like an attitude.

"Jorian, Jorian, Jorian. That is all you say since he got on the ship. Are you in love with him or something? Why don't you just leave me be!" she demanded.

"Because he is the only one doing anything around here. While the two of you go out and party, he is putting in fifteen-hour days, and has done that for the last three weeks. So, by my calculation, if he wanted to take the next 2 weeks off, he probably could," Mistress shot back.

"Really, well good! At least I'm getting my money's worth. Him and his judging eyes, as if I was some sort of, of harlot. How dare he, and who does he think he is, judging me like that?" she cried out, enraged.

"You leave that young man alone; you hear me, young lady?" Mistress insisted in a motherly tone.

"Oh yeah? Watch me, and there is nothing you can do about it," Ophelia snapped back.

The young captain grabbed her robe and jumped into her slippers, heading for the door in a huff. She reached the door and had to stop suddenly, as the door opened very slowly, causing her to almost crash into the sliding metal plate. In her anger, she kicked the door with the bottom of her foot.

"Come on, open up the door, you damn bucket of bolts."

"I am opening the door. If you look at your datapad, I sent a message that maintenance and repairs would affect our hydraulics and water systems, for a few hours to possibly a few days. But why would you know anything going on with this ship or your parents' company. Your company!" Mistress replied accusingly.

"Ahhhhh!" Ophelia cried out in anger. "First you keep telling me to find some companionship, then when I find it, you give me grief, while conspiring with my new technician against me. A person with a sketchy past, that I was somehow scammed into buying. And he seems to be so damn likeable, by everybody and yet, he barely talks to anyone. When I don't talk to anyone, I am antisocial. What's with you, Mistress? You are supposed to be on my side. You are supposed to be protecting me!" the young woman lashed out and broke down.

"For one moment, do you really think I am not?" Mistress replied in a motherly voice. "But how can I protect you from yourself, when it's you that doesn't listen or do what she needs to be doing?"

"I didn't ask for this?" the young woman replied, exasperated.

"I know, and he didn't ask for what has happened to him, but he keeps doing his job. He keeps moving forward, whether out of determination or hope, I can't say," Mistress paused, "Maybe you should care a little more about your crew. He is a good person and very intelligent. He said nothing, but his burns were much worse than he let on, he tossed and turned all night. Actually, he woke up 87 times last night with pain or discomfort and to top it all off, he didn't go see the doctor," the AI explained.

"Well, he is a liar then, because he promised, Emmy," Ophelia quickly replied.

"Or maybe he didn't want to cost you any more credits, or maybe he got stuck fixing a more serious problem and got distracted with his work, since that is what he has been doing since he woke up."

The door finally opened enough for the young woman to slip through the door, making her way for the stairs, expecting the lift or other doors would delay her even more. Reaching the cargo bay, she could hear strange sounds coming from inside the workshop, along with the voices of two people yelling.

"Quick, get me another one!" she heard Jorian call out, followed by quick moving footsteps.

Jorian finished pouring a bucket of water down the pipe and was about to come down from the ladder he was on when he saw Ophelia at the entrance to the workshop in her robe and slippers. Emmy was filling some buckets with water when she too noticed Ophelia at the door wearing a scowl, dressed in her robe and slippers.

"Bring some of those buckets with water!" he called out from his perch up on the ladder.

"What's going on?" The captain asked, confused.

Jorian just shook his head in frustration, jumping off the ladder and rushed over, grabbing two more buckets, then hurrying back up the ladder, while Emmy continued filling buckets as quickly as she could. Ophelia just stood there, worried and growing more irritated by the second, thinking she was being ignored and demanded.

"Someone answer me, damn it! What the hell is going on here?"

Jorian looked at her frustrated and answered gruffly, "You are just standing there instead of helping. Bring more water!"

Jorian had not snapped at anyone, but the intensity in his eyes could not be missed. Emmy instantly realized something had transpired between the two, but was not sure of what, and continued filling buckets quietly. Jorian finished pouring the first bucket and went back down, grabbing the second one. He was halfway up the ladder when Ophelia grabbed the bucket, almost making him fall. Jorian shot her a glance and yanked the bucket out of her hand.

"If you are not going to help, get out of the way," he snapped at her again.

The young technician tapped on the gauge to confirm the accuracy of its reading. The needle continued to move up and started bordering the red area on the gauge, showing that it was reaching a critical range. "Emmy, more water, quick," he called out in an agitated but much nicer tone than he had spoken to Ophelia.

Ophelia noticed the gauge, realizing the critical situation that was transpiring. She finally rushed over, grabbing two buckets, and following Emmy. Jorian had quickly poured two more buckets in by the time she reached him and swapped out the buckets, but the scowl on her face made it clear that she was not happy with him.

Jorian glanced at the gauge again, as the temperature slowly went back into the yellow again. He peered over at the forge printer and the digital timer, that counted down the time remaining before it was done. Ophelia followed his gaze and noticed for the first time in over two years the forge printer was actually functioning, putting out a tremendous amount of heat and steam, but working.

The young woman rushed to the forge printer and saw the clock counting down with twenty-two minutes left. She looked at the printer, noticing something wrong with it, and was about to touch it when

Jorian yelled out, "Don't touch that! It's not working right, I had to rig it."

"Rig it! Why are you rigging things on my ship?" She demanded as she turned to him angrily.

"You see that timer?" Jorian pointed at the digital countdown before continuing, "When it's done, we can talk. Right now, just bring more water!"

"Fine!" she snapped back and turned to Emmy, who had just filled more buckets. "You fill, I'll carry them," she told the scientist.

The young scientist just complacently replied, not wanting to get between the two,"Okay." She kept filling buckets quietly.

The trio continued to work diligently for the next fifteen minutes, cooling down the system and making sure that the gauge stayed within an acceptable range. After about four minutes, they found a groove, and for two minutes after that, they got the gauge to dip into the green zone, but it was a short-lived victory. The temperature went up during the next stage of the process. After the timer finished, they continued to add water until the forge stopped making steam and the gauge read safely in the green zone, to at which time Ophelia expected answers.

Drenched in sweat and tired, having done what felt like a million trips back and forth with filled water buckets. Ophelia was breathing heavily, standing there in her sweaty pajamas with her arms crossed over her chest and her foot tapping on the floor facing Jorian expectantly.

"I want answers. What the hell are you doing to my ship?" Ophelia asked in the most level tone she could muster.

"My job. I'm fixing it," he replied.

"I didn't tell you to fix it. I told you to fix the loader," she replied sternly.

"I was fixing the loader, but I needed parts. Parts that you don't have the money for, so I found this forge printer and got it to work. I was printing parts for the loader, after some modifications, using Knightforge Technologies parts, since they don't charge you for them, when the pressure built up last night. It would have blown up this portion of the ship, had I not vented it out like I did," he explained, with some animosity.

"I didn't tell you to turn on or fix the printer, because it was heavily damaged. So, you almost blew up my ship, because you don't listen," she proclaimed.

"No, the ship almost blew up, because some asshole used shitty parts when building the cooling system of this ship," Jorian shot back annoyed, showing her the defective valve and tossing it at her feet.

"Watch yourself, because that asshole was my father. And he is a hundred times the person you'll ever be," she said, taking a threatening step closer to him.

"You are hearing what you want to hear. I said the person who did the work, not the person who designed the ship. If your father would have done this kind of shit quality, his company would never have risen to the heights that it has. The person who used this valve, along with those in that bucket and another hundred and thirty-five or so throughout the ship, screwed up. These are crap parts, from some crappy company and something I would never use on a toilet, let alone a ship and this one even less. What ever happened out there in space partially had to do with these parts. You are lucky the ship didn't explode instead of just overheat," the young man argued back.

"Well, you should have communicated with me first, before doing any of this," she lashed out.

"How could I? You are either sleeping or out having a good time, with God knows who, instead of attending to the ship and your duties," he countered.

Emmy gasped and was looking for a place to hide or a way out of the room, but there were none, at least none that didn't pass between the two people vividly arguing. Ophelia was visibly outraged and furious with the young man, jabbing her finger in his chest.

"You're out of line! What I do, and who I do it with, is none of your damn business," she yelled at him.

Jorian grabbed her hand, almost crushing it. "I don't give a shit what you do or who. My job is to fix things, and that's what I am doing. But instead of being out there eating shit or fucking around, why don't you tend to your ship and crew first, if you want to wear the title of captain? You can be so much more; you just choose not to, hiding behind your terrible experiences," the young man said, pushing her hand away and storming off.

Holding onto her hand, Ophelia realized how much stronger her technician was, and instantly knew he could have really hurt her if he wanted too. But at the moment she didn't care, being thought of as less angered her more than any pain she felt, and chased after him, yelling. "Oh, you are not getting away that easily."

Ophelia tried to chase the young man out, but was stopped as the door to the workshop closed. Ophelia banged on the door and yelled at Mistress to open the door, but Mistress exclaimed that there was an issue with the pressure again.

"If my father was here, he would not put up with this kind of behavior from one of his employees," the young woman roared angrily.

Mistress interjected, her voice reprimanding, "Your father never treated his employees like that, either. He valued them as assets and looked out for them. He led and owned the company, but without the employees, there was no company. Together, they made the Knightforge brand known throughout the galaxy. I am not saying he did not have any problems. There were complaints and augments a plenty, even a few lawsuits, but he handled each one with dignity, even if the decision he made wasn't popular, they were fair and they respected him for it. That's why your parents were so beloved, by the employees at least."

Ophelia scoffed and was about to reply when the printer opened, letting out a jet of steam that filled the area around the printer. The steam quickly dissipated as the large exhaust fan pulled it out of the room. Ophelia and Emmy looked at the printer and slowly approached it.

There before them stood a new valve with a hybrid Knightforge Technologies logo: with an additional logo of a bird around it. Ophelia looked at it confused, not understanding the new logo. "Mistress, what's this logo?"

"That logo is the one I assigned to anything developed by Jorian, as per your contract," Mistress replied.

"Please explain. This is a proper Knightforge Technologies's valve, correct?" she asked angrily.

"No, Captain. This is a custom-made piece between Jorian and myself to elevate the performance of our systems. He manipulated the design with an increase of flow by fifteen percent. He also increased the thickness of the walls and mostly adjusted the angles in a way of avoiding any hard angles. That function is to help with the increase in pressure, while minimizing the trauma to the water molecules arrangement, after passing through the magnet, also he avoided additional material being used, making it lighter and more durable theoretically," replied the AI in a professional tone.

"Theoretically? It hasn't been tested, and he wants to install it on the ship. Is he mad?" The young woman said outraged looking for anything to continue fueling her anger at him.

"No. I don't believe he is crazy. All tests so far demonstrated an eighty-three percent success rate in high stress scenarios," Mistress quickly added.

That's not Knightforge Technologies' standards, eighty-three percent is subpar at best," the captain rebutted.

"That is correct, Captain, but I have only run eighty-three percent of all the test. It will take another few hours to finish the test, but out of two hundred and eighty-three thousand tests so far, they have all passed. The other tests will make up the other sixteen percent since it is now eighty-four percent complete. And as you can see, he has made me hot and steamy," she finished with her usual sultry tone.

"Don't start!" Ophelia shot back.

"Why not? I told you to leave it alone, but no, you could not. He's right, you know, all you care is about yourself, your pain, your loss, your problems, and others only matter when you feel like it. Like Billy, who almost got everyone killed, and me destroyed, or worse. But his girlfriend was an all-inspiring captain that might have killed you both," Mistress continued. "But let's give the guy that has put three weeks' worth of work into one and attack him, because he is questioning his decision, of joining this crew, and your maturity or ability to get the job done. You were here for twenty-five minutes, helping pour water to keep the forge printer cool, to fix the problems with me. Emmy was here fifteen minutes before that, at his request, and he was doing it alone for forty-five minutes. All he wants is for you to give a damn, because he doesn't know if he can trust you. Wake up, little girl," Mistress said in a very sassy tone.

"Mistress enough!" Ophelia shouted.

"Very well, Captain," the machine said in a formal and proper tone.

Ophelia was angry, confused, hurt, and embarrassed, wondering if all the harsh words said by the AI were all true. She turned, noticing Emmy almost trying to hide, feeling extremely awkward. Her vulnerable expression took the scientist by surprise as she asked. "Is Mistress, right? Am I so self-absorbed?"

Emmy scratched her head, searching for a way to be truthful and political at the same time, but her body language was abundantly clear as she shifted from foot to foot, of how uncomfortable she was being put on the spot like that. "You should know much better than me, I-I've been around for only a short time, but since we left the tanker, we barely saw you. Granted, Billy and I were preoccupied, but you still spent most of your time alone, coming out or calling us when you needed or wanted something. After the mutiny, that's when we became closer." The young scientist paused, swallowing hard. "If you are talking about Jorian, he has been working his ass off, and you didn't check up on him, which was not nice even if I and Mistress were informing you of his wellbeing. If you're asking me about your duties as a captain, I could only speculate and say, you protect the Mistress more because she's your crutch. You are fully dependent on her, instead of her being your tool.

We have gone out a few times and I am sure you have enjoyed the attention of Odis and others, but when we are out, you will talk about anything but the ship, almost as if you want to forget it. No offense, Mistress," the young scientist said earnestly.

"None taken, doctor," the ship replied.

Emmy hugged Ophelia, telling her, "It's okay, Ophelia. I know you experienced a lot on this ship, but it's time to move forward with your life, it's like you are standing still, or just drifting in space. Either way, I am here for you, and I am sure Jorian would be, too, but only you can decide to move forward. We can't do it for you. The one thing I learned is, sometimes to get stronger, you have to make yourself a little vulnerable."

Ophelia just hugged Emmy tightly as she cried and whispered, "I don't want to cry anymore."

Elsewhere on the ship, Jorian ventured into the gym, walking over to a heavy-duty punching bag hanging down with a large section of mirror behind it. He stood in front of it for a moment, then gave Mistress a command, "Mistress, please turn off the lights to the room except the one above me."

Doing as he asked and leaving only the punching bag lit, he began to hit the bag as he occasionally looked at his reddened eyes in the mirror. Trying to control his anger and feeling concerned about having grabbed her hand. He knew he could have hurt her, wanting to or not, he had almost lost control and the monster inside felt close.

For over an hour, he hit the bag, each hit causing the bag to crumple around his fist with a heavy thud, as the bag's internal gel reconstituted the shape of the bag, making it denser. But he didn't care about the gel or the bag, he just needed to defuse himself from the emotions that stirred every time he was around her.

Chapter 13

A few days had passed and things on the ship had settled down some with everyone avoiding everyone else. Jorian was working diligently with the grinder polishing edges of one of the new valves when he heard a loud voice overhead, "Jorian. You have a visitor, should I let him in?" Mistress asked.

"Visitor? Who is it?"

"He states his name as Rey and seems to be of a very charming disposition."

"Rey? Oh, yes, please let him in and send him this way. Wait. Do I need to clear it with the captain first?" he asked.

"Not necessarily, if you clear them and they don't pose a threat, according to my scans," the ship responded.

"Well, let's inform the captain either way, I don't want any more problems and guide him here, please," the young man instructed.

"Very well, Jorian."

A few moments later, El Capitan showed up at the entrance of the workshop with a glorious smile and open arms. Jorian came down from the ladder that he was on after making final adjustments to the fifth valve he had installed.

"COMPAI!"

"Now, Compai! I have been calling you for almost two weeks. I thought you'd been killed, or worse," Jorian complained.

Rey hugged his friend with great bravado. "Compai, I have been settling some affairs here before I depart. Don't be upset, my friend, I have missed you as well. So, how goes it? Did I come through or what? Rey del Castillo always keeps his word, or at least his contracts."

"That you did. Thank you. But I called you again in the last few days because I needed your experience and then a favor," Jorian replied.

Rey sighed. "My experience, I can believe. The favor worries me. But tell me, what can I do for you, Compai?"

"Take a look at this and tell me what you think," Jorian told his friend and took him to the forge printer.

"The forge printer? She's a beauty, but looks and smells like she's running very hot and in a poor state. But I must say, by what I have seen of this ship, she's a beauty," Rey said as he looked around and whistled.

"Why thank you Rey, you're not so bad looking yourself," Mistress answered in her sultry voice.

Rey looked around to see if someone had entered before considering it was an AI and laughed. "This is amazing. Is that the ship's interface?"

"That is correct, I am the Mistress of Mayhem's artificial intelligence, you may call me Mistress."

"Compai, I think I'm in love," Rey said with great delight.

"That's understandable, but you may have to fight me for her," Jorian replied whimsically.

"What is a girl to do with two men that speak so highly of her? I would swoon, but heaven knows what damage I would cause to the port," the flirtatious AI responded.

"You share, of course," said a woman's voice from the door.

"Dr. Emmy, these two are mine, you'll have to find your own," Mistress quickly replied.

The young woman stood at the door with some loose-fitting shorts and a tank top, with a pair of flip-flops. Her body glistened with sweat, and her hair was pulled up in a bun. Emmy looked over and got a charming smile from El Capitan.

"Jorian, you dog, holding back on me; first with this charming ship and then with this delightful young lady. Please forgive my friend. He has no manners and seems to be very selfish and now seeing you and this ship, I understand why," Rey said with a grin and a wink to Emmy.

Emmy giggled and blushed slightly, enjoying the charismatic man's charm and lighthearted personality. Jorian shook his head and sighed as he took a few steps toward Emmy to introduce Rey properly.

"Emmy, this is my friend, Rey Del Castillo, the infamous El Capitan. Was that good enough for you?" Jorian asked as he looked at Rey.

Rey approached the young scientist and took her hand, kissing the top of it. "I am Rey del Castillo, and it is a pleasure to make your acquaintance, señorita."

Emmy giggled some more and having no way of hiding the deep redness of her cheeks, she began fanning herself with her hand. "Whoa! Jorian, you really have to fix those pipes. It is very hot in here."

"Well then, allow me to take you out for a refreshing beverage, it would give me great pleasure and company, maybe we could even ditch the grease monkey over there," Rey told her, pointing to Jorian with his thumb and chuckled.

"That would be nice. Let me freshen up, I'll be back in a few," Emmy replied and walked off.

Jorian just shook his head at Rey, who just smiled back and raised his eyebrows. "Well, Compai, I must say this has been a wonderful visit, let's go get a drink, my treat."

"Fine, I could use a break, but first, can you help me with this forge printer? I am not familiar with them, and I have only gotten it up to thirty percent effectiveness and efficiency.

"You call me to work? Not to visit, or eat, but to work! We are definitely friends, but I don't work for free. Mistress, if you would be so kind, what are the contract work rates for this type of work and will you honor the pay?" Rey asked.

"Though I would love to agree to the rates, we are not running on much of a surplus right now of credits, and I'm not authorized for any unapproved expenditures. But maybe a barter in the way of a reduced rate for a fare or delivery can be arranged?" Mistress replied.

Rey chuckled and smirked towards Jorian, "Even this AI negotiates better than you."

The veteran salvager checked the forge printer and inspected the various connections and work around that Jorian had done. "This must be your handy work, Compai, but I must admit, it was a good idea. You are probably running boiling hot, and by the discoloration of some of these parts, came close to ruining the entire system, because you ran it too hot. A cooling issue, maybe?" Moving some wires, getting a better view. "You are missing some components, and your tips are almost burned out on the print head. I would recommend a whole rebuild of the unit since it's a very advanced unit compared to what I or most people have worked with in the past." Studying the machine some more, the veteran salvager pointed out some other things. "You are also missing a regulator which is why it's running so hot, which can make inferior parts because you burn the metal, but the bypass with the ship's water is an ingenious idea, keeping the system functional and the parts viable. I will do it for thirty-five hundred credits, but since you may not be able to afford that right now and my Compai is involved, I will do it for a 5000-credit voucher for passage or cargo delivery on your ship. So, do we have a deal?"

"Your Compai is involved, and you charge me more to do the job? Is that not swindling?" A young woman's voice said from the door.

Everyone turned their attention to the door, where Ophelia with her deep lavender eyes took in the room, she was wearing an oversized shirt and loose-fitting pants. Her hair was pulled back and for the first time in days, she did not seem angry or bothered, but in normal spirits. Emmy was standing next to her, having met the captain on her way back to her quarters and followed her back to the workshop.

"Ah, you must be Captain Knight. It is such a pleasure to meet you. I am El Capitan, Rey del Castillo. And please allow me to say that my Compai was dead on when he mentioned how beautiful you are. And did not exaggerate one bit about how exotically mysterious your eyes are. It is simply enchanting. I can see why he likes you so much," the man said, approaching the young woman, taking her hand, and kissing it.

The room went quiet for a moment, Emmy's eyes widened as she gawked at the ship's technician then shifted her attention to El Capitan, not having made the connection and scared of an explosive reaction from either the captain or the technician. Jorian's eyes darted towards El Capitan and then to Ophelia, who looked at him as if processing something, then back to the guest on her ship, quickly responding.

"Well, it seems I have a silver tongue on my ship, but I do appreciate the compliment, no matter its origin," she said calmly and with a small smile. "But five thousand credits seems like a lot of money for a rebuild job, does that include parts?"

Rey grinned, turning his head towards Jorian and nodding approvingly, "I like her, she's an excellent negotiator."

"She got me to pay ten times' my price," Jorian added in agreement.

"True, but that's not saying much, you suck as a negotiator," the pirate said candidly before turning to Ophelia, who snickered quietly at the comment. "The price may seem high, my dear Ms. Knight, if you were paying up front. But since I am financing it for you and including the parts, with no money leaving your pocket in exchange for some time on your printer and a massive discount on future services, it's an amazing deal. Even more so on Tersa 4. Plus, I can assure you I'll do it right, few, if any around here can really fix that forge printer."

Ophelia scrunched up her nose and finally nodded, not having any other actual options and knowing it was a good deal, she finally answered, "Agreed."

"Excellent!" Rey stated, clasping his hands together, then turning to Jorian with a smile. "What do you say we look at this printer a little more? The good news is, since it's functioning, there are two parts, including the tips, that it should easily be able to make while we grab some lunch. Call it a celebration of our deal and my Compai's freedom." The salvager smiled warmly as he approached Jorian, patting him on the back, which caused the soldier to wince and shift his body as if in discomfort. "Compai, are you okay, my friend? What happened?"

The salvager stepped closer, peering inside Jorian's shirt and noticing the burns on his back, he glanced at everyone else in the ship, who all turned their heads, avoiding a sour subject. Jorian took a step away, dismissing the injury, and Ophelia's demeanor also shifted, not wanting to recall the argument between her and her technician. Fortunately, Mistress interceded, defusing any potential situation and putting the group back on track.

"I have found a bistro that has an opening for lunch. It's called The Last Wave, should I book it for you, Mister Castillo? I hear it has splendid music and is rated one of the best bistros in the vicinity, with the best value."

Acting quickly to improve the situation, Rey replied, "That is a wonderful idea, I know the owner there and they make the best of just about everything. Book it and put the reservation under El Capitan."

"Very well, Rey, it has been arranged," Mistress replied.

"Great!" Rey stated as he started programming the printer and quickly turned again towards the two ladies. "Why don't you ladies freshen up and get ready, it is a nice place. And I will look over this machine and get those few parts in the queue to print while we eat, yes?"

Emmy jumped in excitedly. "Why yes, that would be lovely!"

The young scientist turned to the door, just as Ophelia was about to decline, Emmy grabbed her arm and began pulling her away with a cheerful smile as she boasted about what she had heard of the bistro. The words stayed in Ophelia's mouth, and with resignation she let them go, allowing herself to be taken along.

"Let me see," Rey said to Jorian when the women left.

Jorian took off his shirt and showed Rey his back with the blisters that had formed from the burn. Rey looked him over one time and shook his head. "Why didn't you tell me you'd been hurt, I would have been here faster."

"It's no big deal, just some steam from when I vented the valves, I just..." the young man trailed off, somewhat embarrassed.

Fortunately, Mistress ended the statement, "He was in the shower when the valves malfunctioned and ran out here in a towel, then lost the towel."

"What? I would have loved to have seen that. I have heard from some people at the dock that a man was caught naked and almost arrested for indecent exposure." Rey laughed as he spoke, "I did not know it was you."

"I have footage if you'd like, Capitan?" Mistress replied.

"That won't be necessary," Jorian stated.

"Oh, please do. I must see this footage, Mistress, if you please," Rey retorted.

Mistress played the footage on the screen and Rey laughed hysterically, though Jorian did not seem amused. El Capitan studied the footage, understanding his friend's feelings, knowing his lack of experience with women and his shyness.

"Mistress please play that again, so that I may show my young friend here something," Rey instructed and then stopped the video in various places, showing surprise and delight in the ladies' faces and shock in that of the two men.

"I must say, Compai, you come well equipped. Look at the shock on those men. It is priceless how intimidated they must be, and look at the shock and delight of those two young women. What are you embarrassed about?"

"I made a fool of myself and..." the young man trailed off.

"And what, you most likely saved everyone on the ship? An explosion of that magnitude could've caused extensive damage. So, the emergency workers laughed. Who cares? I actually commend you, you walked on like the owner of the ship. That takes some grit," the salvager told his friend as he put his arm around him. "But you're an idiot, you should have gone to Brother Julius or any other doctor to get treated. We will pass by Julius's on the way out."

"She didn't even care, she did not even come check on me. What kind of..." Jorian began and was cut off.

"To be fair, she asked," Mistress interjected, showing the clip of when the young woman returned to the ship that morning.

"Would she have asked, had we not run into each other?" Jorian lashed out.

"Hey now, Compai, no one knows, because the opportunity was not given. It is only speculation, and if you give one side credit, you must give the other side credit, too. But the fact remains, you still didn't go get yourself treated, that's still not right. You must take care of yourself, my friend, and of the others on the ship. For a crew takes care of each other and the captain is part of the crew. You are being a bit judgmental, you cannot expect people to act in any other way but the way they are, and you may be placing a very high bar for that young lady, which she may not be able to reach," El Capitan replied.

The salvager bet over to look at the printer when the fox jumped on his back and then on top of the printer. He reached out and carried the little pup, who was delighted to see him. Rey scratched the pup and placed him softly down and returned his attention to the forge printer, looking it over. After a few moments, some adjustments, and him showing Jorian a few things, he began rattling off a list of parts.

"Mistress, would you be a love and print those out? And do multiple pieces at once using your whole format width, that way you generate heat for a less prolonged period of time. They are small parts, but allow five to fifteen minutes between batches so the tips could cool off. I don't want to add any more strain to your systems. If anything is to arise, please shut down, so no other problems transpire." Rey turned to Jorian. "Jorian, you go get yourself freshened up, we are heading out with ladies. I am sure we do not want to smell your current aroma, it's just not right," the man said, sending his friend off with a gesture.

Rey flared his long coat back and sat in a chair, picking up the pup and petting it. "I must say, Mistress, you are a lovely ship. I could fly with a pretty lady like you anywhere. But those two will need some work and I'm glad that is your job and not mine."

"Well, a woman's work is never done and they both have big chips on their shoulders and a lot of baggage. If they could only talk instead of bark, they would do so well. In this case, they are both wrong and right," the AI replied.

"Is that the valve he replaced? Looks like he does good work," Rey stated.

"Though I am just an AI, I can attest to his strength and his immense attention to detail, just look at this," the ship said and opened the paint and drying booth, where all the parts for the old loader had been hung.

"I recognize this model, how did it look like before I wonder? And I see some upgrades, and is that the cart he got at the auction house?" Rey asked.

"It is, and those are the old and new schematics with renderings on what it once did and will look like soon," the AI responded while showing pictures on the screen.

"That is a very nice design, and imaginative, too. Few people can view the end product of something, so completely," Rey shared.

Jorian returned, showered, and changed. Having arrived ahead of the ladies, he went off to see the good doctor to tend to his wounds. Rey sat there, leaning back in his chair, and waved at the young man as he departed. The pup following close behind.

The salvager stayed, making pleasant conversation with the AI as he waited for the young ladies. Elsewhere on the ship, Emmy conversed with Mistress about how uncomfortable it was becoming being in the same room with the two of them and how she just wanted to disappear. In the upper floors, Ophelia was cursing at Mistress and Jorian all at the same time.

Eventually the two ladies were prepared and met with their guest, who was sitting there casually speaking and flirting with Mistress. Ophelia and Emmy dressed nicely, though in a casual style, to which Rey complimented them again, as he stood when they arrived. He informed them they would meet up with Jorian, who had gone ahead to see Brother Julius. The trio exited the ship and walked down the docks, making their way to the Tower, where the healer's mobile clinic was stationed.

It surprised the ladies at how many people knew El Capitan and called out to him in warm salutations, or in gratitude for some merchandise delivery. Emmy mocked him, "I guess you just know everybody, don't you?"

"Well, everybody is a lot of people, but I do try. Yes?" he replied charmingly.

There were groups of people in line outside of the clinic complaining of one ailment or another. The waiting room was a tent with multiple portable chairs and two fans that maintained a cool breeze for those who waited. A nurse with a datapad walked around asking questions or doing some preliminary work. The portable clinic now looked twice as wide as it had before, perplexing the two women.

"How did it grow so much?" Emmy asked.

"That portable clinic is custom made with a collapsible wall that allows to keep the living quarter separate from the medical facility. But must be closed for transport. It can still expand to the other side, allowing for more rooms for the patients. It is quite extraordinary, I actually got it for him, special order," Rey boasted.

"Nurse! Nurse!" Ophelia called, moving ahead trying to get the nurse's attention with no success, sighing in frustration.

A few seconds later Rey walked under the tent, as various people once again acknowledged El Capitan as he made his way to the nurse's station and called out to the nurse, "Hello Julie, where is the...."

The nurse quickly cut him off. "He's in room 2, and you go on now, or you will keep me from my work, you charming silver-tongued devil," she said warmly with a smile, pointing to the doors.

Rey smiled and chuckled. "What can I say, you make splendid company."

"No, no, stop and go on, but it is good to see you, honey," she told him and winked warmly.

Ophelia just looked at the nurse and then at Emmy shaking her head. The scientist shrugged and followed Rey in, leaving Ophelia as last, who was sighing to herself as she took to the rear of the line. They could hear the pup whimpering as they looked in from the doorway. Jorian stood there unmoving as the doctor removed dead cells with a skin rejuvenator, leaving new unblemished skin in its wake. The process was painful and by the looks of the young man, they were about halfway done with various burning red lines crossing his back and sides. He stood there barely moving, with his eyes focused on a particular spot on the wall with a stony stare.

"Oh My God!" Both girls said in unison in disbelief of the actual damage on Jorian's torso.

Brother Julius just gave the group a glare and continued with his work. For another fifteen minutes, the man continued with the treatment. Despite the invasive work, Jorian did not flinch. He simply stared at the wall as he mumbled some words that were inaudible for the duration of the procedure. Looking at his vitals, it looked almost as if he was asleep, with just a slight elevation in his stats.

The doctor leaned over and whispered in Jorian's ear. "CALIPHAST!"

As he woke from his trance like state, Jorian took another breath and sighed. Turning as he moved around, feeling the itchiness of the new skin cells that had been sprayed on his wounds

Rey looked at brother Julius oddly and asked, "Hypnosis? When did you start practicing that?"

"Well, Rey, I have known it for a long time and only use it in extreme cases when the patient requires it. Jorian, given his background in special operations, can put himself in that state to endure torture if caught. In this case, with me helping him and using the agreed upon word, he can come out of it immediately."

"Thank you, doctor," Jorian replied, then looked at the two women. "My word is complete. I have done as promised. I saw a doctor."

Jorian stood robotically replacing his shirt. He almost exited the room, if the doctor had not stopped him. "Jorian, sit down. You need a few more minutes before you go."

The soldier nodded and sat down looking at Julius asking, "What do I owe you?"

Ophelia stepped up. "As per our contract, I will cover his bill. Please, just pass it out to Mistress, we'll take care of it."

Ophelia paused scanning the room and studying the three men intently for a moment. She looked to the side as her mind processed the information connecting the dots and coming to a realization. "All three of you were in on it," she blurted out accusingly, then continued as her mind processed the information.

"Rey sat behind us, the day of auction, and left just ahead of us after the auction, and then he was there again when we were picking up Jorian and the rest of the merchandise. This must be your handiwork, Capitan Rey!" she said, pointing an accusatory finger at the former pirate captain.

"So, because I was at the auction house, and I know both Julius and Jorian, not to mention the other 85 percent of the population here in this town, we scammed you. Forget the fact that I made dozens of purchases and sales of various items at auction that day. Seeing me up and around the auction house is no big deal. I've been there every year for the last ten years. As far as leaving with you, if you recall, there was a fight breaking out between two people. Two people whom I know to have bad tempers. Knowing them and that it was going to be bad, and it was mind you. I left. If anything I saved you, Emmy, the doctor, and his grandchildren, not to mention a few other dozen people that listened to my advice and left the area with us." Rey paused looking at Ophelia with an open hand gesture as if claiming innocence. "Think about it. If I were to sit where I didn't know anyone, I couldn't sit anywhere. So, let's stop overreacting and head to lunch, I'm hungry," Rey said without missing a step.

Ophelia turned to look at the doctor, but he just turned towards a device and began placing his instruments to be clean and stated. "I already told you that I just went to see what happened to Jorian after he saved my life."

Ophelia turned to Jorian who looked at her, speaking with a finality. "I was sold," then turned towards Julius. "Brother Julius, we are headed to lunch and I see you are going to be quite busy for a while, would you like for us to take the children with us? We should be back in a few hours."

Emmy quickly interjected, "Yes, that would be nice, they're great kids."

Having spent an afternoon with the children helped keep the focus away from other sources of friction. After lunch, the group met with Julius and they went to a family entertainment establishment. Playing games and laughing at childlike antics did good for their souls. They eventually headed back to the port long after the sun had gone down.

The group made it to the Tower and said their goodbyes to El Capitan, who promised to return the following day to finish fixing the printer. He had not taken more than a few steps when the group encountered various guards whispering and laughing to each other. One pointed out mockingly and called out, trying to impress the others. "Hey, aren't you the guy that was naked crossing the smoking cargo bay the other night?"

Jorian looked at the group and was about to hand the boy over to his grandfather when Emmy quickly cuddled him, putting her arm around him, and replied coyly. "That's right, and it was one hot night, maybe we'll go for another steamy night tonight. You boys, you just don't measure up." The petite scientist encouraged Jorian forward and he let her, as they walked past the manned check point.

The soldiers looked at each other and then looked at the group, not liking the comment, when Odis entered the area and cleared his throat, bringing them all to a proper formation. He looked at the group and winked at Ophelia, who just smiled back and then kept walking with the group. Leaving the doctor and the two kids back at the mobile clinic, the trio returned to the ship.

"Well, she's still there," Emmy stated jokingly.

"I was monitoring her the whole time. The new valves seem to work nicely and all the parts have been printed," Jorian replied.

"You were monitoring the ship the whole time?" Ophelia asked surprised, then turned to Emmy, "Emmy, please go ahead, I want to talk with Jorian, thanks."

"Okay, see you later," the scientist replied, hurrying off, not wanting to be caught between them again.

The young woman stared at the young man, confused. "Why? You have gone above and beyond, working on her day and night, and you have only been here for a short while. You have no roots to her or owe her any loyalties. So, I ask again, why?" Ophelia asked with obvious sincerity.

Jorian looked at the ship, then at his captain. "For starters, it's my job, and I need to be sure that she is ready to go in case anything comes up, if not, I have failed." Jorian paused, letting his words sink in before he continued. "Second, I am sorry you think that, but I owe that ship my freedom." Jorian put a hand up, stopping Ophelia before she interrupted, "without her, you would not be here, and maybe I would not be here, and right now, we both needed to be here for this to work out how it did. She is an amazing ship, and her AI is extremely intricate and complex.

"As for the why, right now she is all that I have. I don't know how long she'll be my ship, my home, and if none of that satisfies you, leave it as my ride out of here. Pick one, but in the end, I find peace when I am working on machines, ships, or vehicles. I am distracted from everything else, as if I'm some sort of detective working on a mystery.

"On top of all that, Mistress is a prototype ship, made by one of the most innovative men in the galaxy, and it is my great honor to have her under my care." Jorian paused again, but this time hesitating before his next phrase.

"That's nice of you to say about my father," she stated.

"Ophelia, I'm glad we ended up together. I have a lot of respect for you, but you are rudderless. That makes it hard to follow you, to trust in you. You have the potential, I can see it, anyone can see it, but to be a leader, people need to have confidence in you and your ability to lead them out of situations. That kind of trust is earned, not given, and if you want people to follow you, you need to earn their trust. You need to grow as a person, get outside the walls of that ship and explore everything you have to offer, and surpass everything you now know. Grow, read, watch, listen, learn, and accept your failures as growing pains and find new solutions inside of you. But it all starts with trust, in us and most of all, in yourself."

"I didn't ask to be a leader. I just want to find my parents," she finally admitted.

"It doesn't matter if you asked for it or not, the fact is you are one. Please understand that whatever happened to them has to be big, because they're not here. Are you ready to deal with something that big? You want me to follow you down that rabbit hole, that's fine. You won't find someone more loyal, but you better be damn sure of your decisions and most of all, at least with me, keep your word. Because the game you want to play is for keeps and I am sure there are some very big players and there are no redos," Jorian said as he nodded, then added, "Good night, Captain."

"Good night, Jorian," Replied the young woman as she stood there contemplating his advice.

Later that night, the purple-eyed captain stared at the ceiling of her room, pondering Jorian's words and the reason why she set out into space to begin with, until sleep finally overtook her.

The next morning, Ophelia spent a few hours walking around and studying the evidence and recordings of the ship and her family's disappearance. All she found when she returned home from college was Mistress parked at their estate. That was when she discovered her parents were missing three years ago.

She then watched the video of when the ship was boarded and when they killed her friends. She just stared at the screen after it went dark and finally made a choice.

"Jorian, Emmy. Please meet me in conference room A," Ophelia said over her datapad.

The two acknowledged the command and a short while later, the two entered the room. Ophelia, now sitting at the head of the table in the conference room, two small boxes were carefully placed in front of her as she nervously waited for her crew. Her palms were sweaty, and she couldn't stop tapping her foot.

"Thank you for coming, please sit," she asked.

"I called you here because of something Jorian had told me, something that finally helped me make sense of things. Though it wasn't easy, but I've decided." She slid a box to each of them. "Emmy, when we hit our next port, you'll be free of your contract. I don't know your plans, but I would like you to stay with us, not as a cargo specialist, but as the ship's scientist. The pay situation is tricky, but I hope we can come to an arrangement. But, before you decide, I want to show you something. I want you to know, because I need you to know what happened, and what you, and we, will be getting into," she told the scientist, then turned towards the wall. "Mistress, play the first recording."

"Yes, Captain," the ship replied and multiple screens turned on, showing footage of three years back.

"When I first embarked on this journey, my parents had disappeared with no trace and the ship's logs had been altered. This is what I found when I got on the ship: my parents were gone, and the ship had evidence of a fight. As you can see, there is footage of my parents boarding the ship and that's it. The next footage is of me entering the ship and finding blood stains and blaster marks, that were all partially washed away by the cleaning droids, which were not all fully operational and functioning," Ophelia said and was interrupted by Jorian.

"What! That's horrible, to find the ship in that condition, I'm sorry Ophelia I didn't know and cannot imagine how that affected you," Jorian replied, as he shook his head in disbelief and looked at the screen.

"Oh, my goodness, Ophelia, are you okay?" Emmy asked.

The young captain paused, taking a moment to herself, then took a deep breath before continuing. "Yes, or as well as I can be, but thank you for asking." Taking another deep breath to steady herself before continuing, "I decided I was going to find them and for the last few years I have been trying to find them. But I have no clues, leads, or any evidence that was not tainted by the malfunctioning cleaning droids. I ended up just wandering through space. Mistress, next recording, please." Ophelia waited for the footage to be shown on the screen. "Here you will see what transpired almost two years ago," she explained, then went silent while the others watched the screens.

Emmy gasped as Jorian held the edge of the table with white knuckles. Seeing how the pirates had reached the ship and though the defenses were activated, they partially malfunctioned, allowing the pirates to board the ship. They captured Ophelia and some of her college friends that had gone with her as her crew. The pirates dismantled some of the ship, looted some critical items, and damaged others. But before they left, the pirates beat and executed her friends in front of her and then ejected them into space. They gave Ophelia a beating of her own along with a few lashings of an electro whip, leaving her with a stern warning.

Mistress managed to get some systems online, allowing Ophelia a moment to escape as the pirates returned to their ship and left.

Jorian's fists were clenched, and he could feel the anger boiling inside him, the rage pushing against his will, but he kept it in check. Emmy partially turned away, looking at the screen almost in horror at what had happened, emptying her stomach.

When the recording finished, Ophelia slowly stood and looked at her new crew with anger and sorrow on her face. "This is what happened, and I carry that with me always. I'm showing you this because you need to know what we'll be facing. I'm tired of being lost. Tired of not knowing where my parents are. I am partly cut off from my inheritance, and all I have left right now is the desire to make at least one thing right. I want my ship whole, and I want to avenge my friends and find my parents. They wanted to make the outer rim better for the people, and I want to help them complete that mission. Will you help me? Will you join me?" The young captain asked passionately, a tear forming in her eye.

"Oh, I'm in. I'm all in," Jorian answered gruffly.

Ophelia nodded at him warmly and smiled. "Infront of you are emblems that pertain to my family and this ship. They have locators and allow access to certain things, but I only want you to take them if you will join me. I won't be offended if you don't."

Jorian ran his fingers over the box and grabbed it without hesitation, opening it and placing the emblem on his vest. His eyes burned with an inferno that surprised even Ophelia. "I promise you, I will put your ship back together and not only make it whole, but better. As far as those sons of bitches, they'll pay. That I promise. But you need to be ready to go down that rabbit hole, and it's deep and dark. I will be there until it's done, contract or not."

His words and intensity moved the two women, who were alarmed by his demeanor. Emmy looked at the screen once more, then at the box. Thinking of everything that had transpired, she looked at Jorian, surprised at how quickly and with what confidence he had answered, then back to the screen.

"I'm not sure, I have a lot of questions. You saw what those pirates did, and what happened to us. Let's be real for one second, we got lucky." Emmy paused and pointed at the screen, "To do that, we need some sort of army or security force. How would we even get it done?"

"I'll train you. I spent the last 5 years with special operations. I can teach you everything you need to know. It won't be easy, but you will be the better for it," Jorian replied.

Emmy considered the young man, understanding a little more about him, her eyes moved to Ophelia. "Fine, I will agree, but I want a much better deal than Jorian, and I have some conditions."

"Then it's settled," Jorian said, slamming his hands on the table as he stood and looked at the two women with great intensity. "Get some rest, you two, we start tomorrow at O five hundred. Good night," Jorian stood up and began for the door.

Ophelia caught up to him just as he reached the door, placing a hand on his arm. Jorian turned, looking at her. "Jorian. Thank you, I don't think I could do this without you."

"Don't thank me yet, the training is hard, and the road is long and dark. You can thank me in the end, if you still feel that way. Good night, captain," he replied and exited the room.

The door closed behind the young man who paused, thinking about one screen he had seen and just clenched his fist once more in anger, and cursing at himself, before walking towards his room and calling out to Mistress as he went. "Mistress set a ship wide alarm at max volume, with no snooze and have it reset every five minutes until they all report to the gym. Also, make sure that physical fitness assessments and weapons training are requirements for that and any other contract for anyone joining the ship." Jorian paused, then added, "also, can you please send me images of those pirates and any information you can find on them, plus any parts missing from the ship? We are going to get this ship and crew battle ready!"

"Mmm, I sure like me a man that is so determined, it's quite alluring. Grrrrrr!" Mistress replied.

Mistress was silent until he reached his room. "Jorian," she asked as he opened the door.

"Yes, Mistress?" he replied.

"Keep them safe," the ship answered.

"I can't, I can make them ready, but the rest is out of my hands," he answered earnestly.

Chapter 14

Jorian woke an hour earlier than he originally intended, allowing him to exercise, train, and prepare before anyone arrived. Just as he'd planned, the ship's alarm sirens went off, bringing the two women to their feet with terror and surprise. Mistress played her part instructing the women of an emergency in the ship's gymnasium. They stumbled in half awake wearing nothing but a robe or some fine undergarments.

Jorian waited as the two women enter the room looking around for the emergency, not expecting the young man to sneak up behind them, with a stun baton that was approved by both Mistress and Master for the drill. A strong current coursing through their bodies, enough to make them fall to the ground quivering and without the use of their extremities, as a masked Jorian stood over their still trembling bodies telling them, "Your Dead!"

The two women struggled to get control of their bodies with fairly unresponsive limbs that still twitched. A moment later, he grabbed the two women and hurled them into the pool, effortlessly. The two hit the freezing water, and briefly panicked, trying to force their bodies to act, but with little success, their eyes drifted to the water as they started focusing on the water that was already entering their mouth.

Ophelia and Emmy struggled in desperation as they barely kept themselves afloat with wild kicks and flailing hands of partly unresponsive limbs. As if that wasn't enough, somewhere during the chaos the lights had gone out and now the aquatics area of the ship could very well be their ultimate resting place, a few long seconds later the lights flicked on then began strobing on and off slowly making the room play tricks on the mind.

Finally they began treading some water, but only after smacking and hitting each other various times, due to their blindness and poor coordination. Breathing somewhat easier now that they could finally assist each other in making their way to the pool's edge. Pulling themselves out of the pool, they noticed something coming at them, a man in a mask, causing them to quicken their pace as they exited the frigid water. Drenched and fighting against the weight of their water soaked clothing, they hurried to their feet, but felt something heavy crashed into them, sending them both back into the freezing waters of the pool.

Air rushed out of their lungs again as they tried to fight their way up from the pool's depths once more. The two women panicked, not seeing the shadowy figure anymore and were now disoriented, with the blaring alarm and flashing lights of the area, not allowing them to focus. The shadowy figure appeared and disappeared various times, with the flickering of the lights. The two women were terrified, barely able to keep their bearings, when it all suddenly stopped, and the entire room went dark. A voice cut through the shadows, echoing throughout the room.

"Everything is an attack, because whatever happens out there to the ship, someone or something is trying to kill you," the voice said. Then the lights turned on.

The two women were visibly shaken and trembling in the pool, holding each other. When the lights came on, they could see Jorian standing at the pool's edge. Next to him was a padded serving cart with a towel basket on it; on top of that a draped jacket, making the illusion of an attacker. A rope was tied to one end of the cart, the other end of the rope leading to the young man's hand.

"You asshole!" Ophelia shouted.

Jorian looked at her coldly, then looked at his datapad. With a sinister smile he pressed a button on his IDP, activating the shock baton in the pool, sending a painful jolt through the two women's bodies, leaving them gasping for air, with stiffened muscles, barely able to move again.

With their limbs partially paralyzed, they sank quickly. Once again panic started setting in as they started taking in water. After a few seconds, they were actually drowning. Finally, their limbs began responding, but were only floppy and uncoordinated. It wasn't enough to keep them afloat, with fear setting in complicating their situation.

Jorian looked on from his position at the lip of the pool, knowing he would have to help them. Looking at his datapad and the message from Mistress, then to the two women and giving them a few more seconds to help themselves out of the situation, but it didn't help. The soldier shook his head in disappointment, then bent over grabbing the two women and hauling them out of the pool, dropping them onto the floor, coughing up water.

The two were shaking in fear and panting, Ophelia threw up all over herself and both of them urinated on themselves where they laid from the strain and lack of bodily control. They laid there in a mixture of urine, vomit, and pool water, shivering and only barely able to see the eyes of their tormentor, but he seemed unaffected by their plight.

"Lesson one. Focus. Even in your condition, you could have floated with just your breathing. Look for solutions don't drown in your problem." Jorian paused observing the two, then continued, "Lesson two: do not upset your aggressor until you have the upper hand or are ready to strike, or all you'll get is more pain, putting yourself in a worse position than when you started."

Jorian walked around the two women as they coughed out more water, trying to fill their lungs with precious oxygen. Jorian looked at a datapad studying the data provided by Mistress, of the physical and mental responses from the two women.

"We can categorize your performance as pathetic. If this was an attack, you would be dead or worse. I expect you to be down here at the gym five days a week. You will follow your individualized training plans as set forth by Mistress. I will keep a watch on your progress, along with your personalized statistics. You will be monitored by Mistress's fitness program to maintain and track your progression. When you have reached a certain level, we will begin the next phase, which is skill acquisition.

"Mistress, make sure they walk or run three miles before they exit this room, they will hate it, but they need it."

The young man turned and began for the door, as the door opened and he was about to walk out, Ophelia cried out to him with her voice cracking, "Why Jorian? Why did you do this?"

Jorian paused at the doorway and looked back, with no malice on his face, just a sense of resolve, and replied with conviction, "Because you asked me to get you ready, and I won't let you fail. Your instincts are to focus on dying instead of living. I need to break you of that mindset, break you of that fear, if you want to have any chance of succeeding." With that, he walked out, and the door closed, locking behind him, leaving the two women lying on the floor, just staring at each other as they recovered from their paralysis, pain, fear, and worse of all, humiliation.

After a few minutes had passed, the two women finally made it to some chairs, their muscles' still sensitive from the intense shock they received, but it was the fear of death that still made them shiver. The two did not vocalize it, but both thought, *How could he have thrown us in the pool after shocking us, we almost drowned. Is he crazy?*

The young scientist recovered quicker and made her way to a unidirectional treadmill and turned it on, trudging forward as it moved. She stumbled until she found her stride and continued walking. Ophelia approached her, questioning her actions. "What are you doing? You're not going to listen to him, are you?" she asked incredulously.

"With what I know of him, and what we just experienced, I am sure of two things; first, he is far more dangerous than any pirate, and second, I would rather walk the three miles than deal with his wrath or fight with Mistress about letting us out. I will do the miles, then go to my room, shower and get some more sleep."

"Well, I'm..." Ophelia began and was cut off by Mistress.

"You are wise Doctor Kricay, Jorian communicated his plan with me last night and after some modifications, myself and Master approved them, meaning you would require Admiral class authorization to unlock the doors. Yes, we knew about the shock and monitored your stats for safety and the recharge time on the baton. He went easy on you, Master suggested three shocks."

"What!" the young captain said, outraged.

"Captain, just start walking," Emmy told her.

An image came up on a screen of what Ophelia had found in the ship when her parents disappeared, then other images of when the pirates boarded her, A voice was added to the images, "Will you let this be your fate?" The image and words angered the young woman even more, that what she shared was being used against her, feeling vulnerable and betrayed, tears fell from her eyes as she clenched her fists.

Begrudgingly she eventually got on the treadmill and began moving, they exchanged no words between the two of them, but

Ophelia was mumbling the whole time. The two women walked and before they knew it, five kilometers turned into seven, but that too was pre-planned between the AI and Jorian. The two women were none the wiser, given that they did not know how long it had been, since Mistress impacted the timer not allowing them to see it.

When the actual distance had been completed, both women headed to the shower. Silently making their way to the lift, which was not working, and were forced to take the stairs. The two reached their rooms only to find a message on their display that read.

You are capable of more than you know, you just need to get out of your own way.

The two reacted differently, Emmy just shook her head and showered, while Ophelia hurled something at the screen before going to the door, then saw herself, which convinced herself to shower. The worst surprise was when they exited their showers, the screen had changed to something else that was even more infuriating.

Cleaning systems are inoperative because of maintenance and a lack of droids. Clean the gym and the area's leading to your rooms.

"Mistress, where's Jorian? He's going to clean up that mess."

"I would not suggest that, Captain, he is currently changing some more of the defective valves and he's on a strict timeline. If he goes over that time, we may have heating issues with one of my cores," the ship replied.

"I said, where is he?" she demanded.

"Very well, he is on the third level interior, by hydro subpanel six," was the even reply.

"He's inside you. Those areas are clearance only," she said, outraged.

"Oh, yes, and it feels so nice for a real man to be working on my plumbing," Mistress replied in her usual sensual nature.

"Don't start!"

"You can only blame yourself. You programmed me."

"Why are you defending him? And how does he have clearance? That level is above a regular technician," she asked the ship.

"Because he is taking this and me seriously. He needed clearance, and I allowed it because he needed it for the repair, which is critical. I agree his methods maybe quite unusual, but he is extremely competent, and he has a plan. You may have a series of issues with him, but I can assure you he has our best interest in mind. Let him do his work, especially now, since he has 15 minutes to change two more valves that normally require 20 minutes," the ship responded.

"What! Guide the way, now Mistress," she ordered.

A path of illuminate lights showed the route to where the young man was working. Running towards the ship's internal areas to where Jorian was diligently working. She looked at him and observed him working. He was like a machine. Incredibly focused and organized. Everything he needed was laid out in order on a blanket next to him. Glancing over his shoulder, noticing she was there, and just continued working.

"Please leave, if this goes wrong, I don't want you to get hurt. This is not a training exercise, and I don't have the time to argue with you," he told her in a friendly but direct tone.

"I am not here to argue, and as much as I would like to hit you with a pipe right now. I am here to help. What can I do?"

Jorian looked over his shoulder and seeing the determination on her face matched her words. Nodding with his head to the next area a few feet next to him, there was another new valve with his emblem on it and a few other items.

"Over there. You must disassemble that coupling that attaches to the valve and then cut where I have made the mark. It is very hot, wear gloves and be careful. If you see steam jetting out, stay away. It can cut you in half like a high-powered laser," Jorian instructed, then added, "Mistress, vent the second system."

"Venting that system will decrease our margin for error and we are cutting it close as it is. Do you still want me to proceed?" the ship asked.

Jorian looked over to Ophelia and saw the hesitation on her face, then focused back on his work. "That's your call, captain, it's your ship. Can you do it or not? This is normally a three-to-five-man operation, but it had to be done since the reactors are running in the yellow close to the red. If I don't finish in time, we'll dip into the red and hopefully not sustain any damage. If you help me, we can most likely stay in the yellow." Dropping a damaged valve to the floor and grabbing the new one, he looked at Ophelia, "So, what's it going to be?"

Ophelia took a deep breath and nodded her head. "Yeah, we can do it. I don't want to risk any of the reactors going into the red. Vent and open all exhaust."

"Order confirmed, venting process commencing," Mistress advised.

The hissing sound of steam pushing through the pipes resonated all around them, the temperature in the hot room increased given an open exhaust port that was in the room, filling that area with a brief amount of steam.

"Jorian, be advised the temperature is now one hundred and twenty-eight degrees," Mistress stated.

Jorian quickly replied, "Copy that Mistress, stay on task, if we work fast enough, we should be out before it can really affect us."

The two were working quietly side by side, when a small puff of steam escaped the pipes and hit Ophelia on the arm, causing her to wince in pain and cry out, Jorian immediately looked over but not stopping what he was doing. "You, okay?" he said with genuine concern.

"I'm fine, just keep going. We need to finish," Ophelia stated, and continued working.

Jorian had finished installing his coupling and moved to help Ophelia. Her commitment to the work after the injury earned her a little more respect in his mind. The two continued working as the heat continued to rise. Sweat dripped off of Jorian's brow. Rubbing it away with the back of his hand, he could see the burn on her arm and how it blistered in two spots, but said nothing except an instruction on what to do next, until the installation was complete.

The two were hot and sweaty and looked at each other with a sense of exhaustion. Jorian grinned as he nodded in approval. "Okay, Mistress, unlock the bypass and let's test them out."

A moment later, the sounds of gushing water and a hard-clanging sound of metal against metal could be heard going down the pipes. Ophelia looked at Jorian, concerned. "What's that?"

"Nothing, just some pieces of metal that were left in the system, most likely dislodged from a defective piece. It will end up in the filter. I will clean it later," Jorian replied.

"Then we're done. I'm out a here, it's too damn hot," Ophelia stated.

The young woman turned and was about to leave when Jorian grabbed her arm softly. Ophelia flinched at his touch but caught herself as she saw Jorian looking at her with an almost childlike expression and smile.

"Wait, you'll miss the best part," he told her warmly. Finding the best spot, he took the tools from her, placing them on the ground and positioned her just across from him. The young woman was hesitant, but curiously compliant. She stood just across from him and eyed him skeptically.

"Mistress, is the system functional and in the green?" he asked.

"Yes, Jorian, would you like to conduct the tests as before?"

"Yes, Mistress. Run full tests."

Ophelia looked around worriedly as sounds of steam being vented on the outside of the ship. A sudden cloud of steam came from a pipe in an adjacent area, momentarily increasing the temperature of the whole compartment. Ophelia looked at the young man more hesitantly than before, but for an instance, was soothed by his touch, when he grabbed her hands and told her, "Just trust me."

After the incident a few hours earlier, those words cut at her sharply as she found the anger welling up inside her again. She was about to say something to him, when suddenly the fire suppression systems came on, filling the area with welcoming refreshing water.

The two leaned their heads back, letting the water rain down on them, welcoming every drop. For a moment Ophelia felt like a child playing in the rain, having every thought and stress melt off her. For the first time in years, she felt truly detached from it all, the worry, the fear, the concern, the problems, all just instantly washed away. She saw herself as a young girl running in the rain and smiled.

Jorian closed his eyes, feeling the sweet relief of the water as it rained down on him. He just stood there, holding her hands, when he realized her hands were in his, he opened his eyes and looked at her, memories of that day, when they had first met flooding to him. The first time he gazed at her purple eyes so many years ago and just after she gave him water, it rained. She had brought it to him; she had brought his salvation. He stared at her intently when she opened her eyes, meeting his gaze.

She could barely see him in the dim light and with all the water, but his eyes were clear to her. Waves of memories hit her at once as she looked at him. She remembered a tortured boy; she had once given water, too. He was young and frail looking on the verge of death, with cuts, welts, and blood all covering his body, his face was practically indistinguishable. But that was not the man she saw before her now. It couldn't be. The immense difference in size and built alone, but there was no doubt in her mind, the eyes were the same. She could see the determination to live in that boy's eyes, just as she could see it in Jorian's eyes. She never knew what happened to that boy, but she knew then, as she does now, that neither that boy nor Jorian would ever quit.

Tears formed in her eyes as she remembered the sadness that filled her heart that day and closed her eyes again, looking up, letting the water wash away the pain she felt for and shared with that boy. The two released hands as the test slowly came to its conclusion, wiping their faces of the water that remained.

"Test complete, all parts working successfully. Progress updated," the AI stated.

Jorian bent down, grabbing all the tools and the buckets and headed for the exit, trying to suppress his emotions and his memories. Ophelia took a deep breath, then grabbed the last bucket with the trash and the two valves and followed. When the two exited the interior, Jorian closed the hatched and confirmed the seal. Ophelia was waiting for him with crossed arms as he turned.

"What the..." she began, but was interrupted by Mistress.

"There's a knock at the door. El Capitan is asking for permission to board," Mistress informed them.

Jorian, taking advantage of the opportunity caused by the interruption to escape another argument or fight with the young woman, quickly replied, "Let him in, I will meet him there. With any luck, today we fix the forge printer."

"Jorian, I will let our guest in, why don't you go get cleaned up and changed, since you will work with delicate electronic components today," Mistress suggested.

Jorian stopped and turned towards his room to shower and change. Moving quickly down the stairs and hurrying down a passageway, he ran into Emmy, accidentally knocking her down. The poor girl felt like she had crashed into a wall to which Jorian quickly moved to pick her up, and with great concern, asked, "Are you okay?"

Emmy flinched and looked up at him, confused and a little scared, wondering if he was going to attack her again. Jorian picked her up softly and explained. "Don't be scared, earlier is training. When training's done, life goes back to normal. Now come on, get up. Rey is here to fix the forge printer."

"Jorian, why hurt us?" the young woman asked.

Jorian stopped and looked at the scientist. "You don't know what we are up against. These entities and individuals are the worst our galaxy has to offer, and we need to be ready. Today you were taken by surprise and when they come, that's how they'll do it. Please trust me when I say it's just training. I don't want any of you to get hurt, but if I don't prepare you properly when the time comes, you'll be dead or worse. I won't have that on my conscious. How we train today will determine the outcome of those encounters. We train hard so that no matter what we face, you'll be ready."

"Well, I think it sucks. Let's leave it at that."

"Okay," he replied and continued on.

A few moments later, Mistress had called everyone down to the cargo bay, where a smiling Rey awaited on a cargo box with fresh pastries and coffee set up. The trio greeted the man somewhat warmly or as much as they could, given the current situation between them.

"Compai! I have brought you the most wonderful pastries and bread. There is this woman that makes them fresh every morning, and she uses only the best butter. Something that I know for sure, since I am the one that gets it for her, but her cooking is absolutely delightful." Rey took a bite of some fruity puff.

"Ooh, I'll try one," Emmy said quickly as she selected a scone. "Mmmmm—that's so good." She finished with a full mouth.

Ophelia selected a pastry with a special jam that left her longing for more. Jorian grabbed some milk, took some bread and scarfed it down quickly, then ate two more before the others had even finished their first. Rey looked at him, shocked.

"Compai! Relax, enjoy it, there is plenty to go around," El Capitan told him.

"Sorry, old habit," he replied humbly as he slowed his pace.

Having finished their brunch, the group dispersed, leaving Rey and Jorian walking towards the workshop. Removing his coat and hanging it, the salvager began disassembling the forge piece by piece. The two men worked diligently, cleaning old parts, inspecting them, and then putting them back together, while replacing or upgrading others. The two conversed to great lengths, but it was mostly Jorian asking numerous questions about spacefaring life and how things worked in the various ports of the outer ring, and Rey answering or embellishing with one story or another, when he wasn't teaching the young soldier about the printer. The two talked for hours as they worked and about a multitude of topics, but most of the time, it seemed like a big brother talking to a little brother.

It made Rey curious of all the questions the young man was asking, but he understood Jorian had spent more than the last 5 years in an extremely structured environment and had little to no experience with space before he left the planet Jo. They were about halfway done when Jorian changed the topic completely.

"I need your help with something, and I can't pay for it right now."

Rey looked up from his work, raising an eyebrow. "Words like that are concerning. What is it?" Rey paused, then added. "Then I will tell you if I can help or not."

"Mistress, please display the pictures of Operation Backlash," the young man commanded.

"Coming right up, sugar," the AI replied.

A series of pictures came up on the screen, images being placed one beside the other, with details and notes added next to each. Rey casually glanced at the screen, then back to the item in his hand. The pirate's eyes went back to the screen occasionally but at one point just focused on what he was working on, and sat there pondering quietly. The man just shook his head and then stared up at the screen, confirming his suspicions when the last picture came up, then just stayed silent.

"You know these guys?" Jorian asked.

Rey nodded slightly and sighed as he focused back on the part he was working on. The silence continued for a few minutes until El Capitan broke the silence, taking a very serious tone.

"That is awful company, Compai. I would stay away from those people. How do I put it? They are not your average pirates. They are well connected, and saying that they are brutal is an understatement. I avoid them as much as possible and if that is not enough, let me just say that the consortium avoids them and the Oculus has limited dealings with them. They are trouble and of the worse kind."

"So, you know them?" Jorian asked again.

"I do. Why?" Rey asked, not liking the interest in his friend's eyes.

"Mistress, full playback at two times speed, please," Jorian instructed.

"Playback commencing," the ship replied, and started replaying the footage.

The former pirate shook his head in disgust while examining the video. At one point, he stopped what he was doing, put the part in his hands down and studied the screen intently, then asked, "Mistress, Amor, be a dear and play back the last three minutes at regular speed. Please."

"Now I know where Jorian gets his manners from," Mistress answered.

"I would like to take claim for that, but that is owed to someone else," the salvager replied. Pausing from his work, the former pirate scanned the film intently once more, before giving his assessment. "That was a planned attack, they were ordered or paid to attack this ship. The plundering was a cover, the murders were deliberate, and they let Ophelia live, because that was the job." He sighed. "The better question is, why did they let her live? Either way, someone is out for your captain."

"Why do you say that?" Jorian asked.

"Watch the recording. The men are picking things and looking at their IDPs almost as if there was a list they were following. They aren't picking things at random, just the shopping list and then some other things to throw people off the trail. They beat the crew and made her watch the whole time, then they kill them and... Pause video. There is your moment," Rey said as he pointed out a man with a communications visor speaking to the pirate captain. "There are your two important characters: the captain and his communications guy. They talk and then an acknowledgment from the communications guy." Rey waited, then pointed with his finger, "There! He is taking a photo or video of what's going on with his visor. You can tell by the lights on his equipment, then he acknowledged the pirate captain again. Which is when he smacks Ophelia down and stuns her. Then something happens, distracting them and she runs off. They let her leave, before they leave themselves. That was a paid hit." Rey finished with a nod, agreeing to his own statement, then shifting his eyes to Jorian, understanding, "You want to kill him, yes?"

Jorian just took a breath and nodded. "Not just him, the entire crew, take back Mistress's parts and scuttle that ship."

"That is very dangerous, even for you. Is there any way I can change your mind?" The man asked.

"No!" Jorian said quietly as he glared at the frozen screen with the picture of the two pirates.

"Even if it gets you both killed?" El Capitan said, raising an eyebrow at his friend.

"It's what OPhelia asked for."

"Hmmm, I understand, but it may be more difficult than you think. That crew is not as it once was, they have grown and now there are two ships out there," Rey said as he blew into a part that he was cleaning.

"That means more men, but a divided team," Jorian replied.

"Not necessarily. Their leader, Captain Nikcuf Dartsab, expanded his group of mercenaries and gained some more ships. He is now an admiral, since he commands his own fleet. Making him much harder to reach, and no-one knows where their base is located. He is highly intelligent and very skilled. Rumor has it that he picks his people and oversees their training. They are like religious zealots as far as their loyalty goes towards the group." Rey put the parts down and looked towards Jorian. "I personally don't want to get involved with those people. I just got out of one lousy business, and though I'm looking to do something new, it's definitely not that."

Jorian sighed as he paced around, his mind churning away at all the information El Capitan had just given him. Rey, on the other hand, looked at him curiously with a raised eyebrow and grinned to himself, wondering if he should relay the next piece of information, then decided to share. "I heard that to those that are suicidal or extremely motivated, there is a secret bounty on them. Well, not so secret, and not very well known either. The Asia sector put out a bounty for them and the bounty hunter guild, like any other, did their job and put it out there. Though a few years old already, the bounty is still very much active and other organizations have even added to the bounty.

"The guild lost a lot of good people and keeps the bounty somewhat hidden, making it almost obsolete. All that have gone after them, have never been heard of again. The ships and gear of those bounty hunters have served the mercenaries well and have swollen the Admiral's ranks and pockets. Like I said, the bounty keeps increasing, and though it's quite a fat purse, no one is going to touch it. That group of mercenaries will attack anyone for the right price, even the GDF themselves. No one would dare face them straight out," the veteran salvager said as a side note, then glanced at his friend. "Please let this one go."

Jorian sat there focused on putting something together, but his hands were doing the motions, while most of his thoughts were processing what Rey had told him. His mind was drifting away deep in thought. Then in a moment, like a rubber band snapping back, it all came together in his mind, he finished assembling the part perfectly. A sinister grin flashed on the young man's face as his eyes fell on his friend.

"Your smile scares me, Compai. Did you hear what I said about that group?" the man asked, concerned.

"I heard and processed every word, I had an eidetic memory when I was younger, before the military, since then, it has improved somehow. I heard your words and slowly processed them, as I watched the video again in my mind," Jorian explained.

"Ahh, then it would do you good to remember that those mercenaries use to be in special operations for a long time and still hold ties with the GDF high command. Not to mention they are extremely dangerous. Yes?" the former pirate reiterated.

"I heard you. I also heard you say they had a secret bounty on their heads. How much?" Jorian asked curiously.

"If my memory serves me correct, I believe the last number was three hundred and fifty thousand credits for the entire group, plus you keep one hundred percent of the salvage and it's all tax free. It is one of the guilds, after all," Rey replied.

After a few moments, Jorian spoke. "We can partner up and split it fifty-fifty. Like real partners."

Rey nodded as he chuckled. "I'll consider it, but I'll still advise against it."

The two continued working diligently and Rey continued speaking of forge printers and some of his escapades as a salvager, making the time go by quicker. Another few hours passed as they replaced all the worn parts and finished the upgrades, allowing them to prepare for the final touches, suddenly Rey noticed something.

"A-ha! Those savage idiots, they seemed to have snipped this wire when they pulled this part out," Rey said as he held a small component with various wires hanging from it. "This little guy causes more problems than practically the rest of the machine put together. This regulates heat and energy, with it, you get all the issues you were experiencing before you bypassed the cooling regulator with additional water from the ship's systems. Which was ingenious, by the way, but could severely damage the unit. Here's the funny part: we can fix this and reinforce it by just replacing the wire with a heavier gauge wire, and it's good as new," the salvager said as he finished tightening a screw.

They continued replacing parts, tightening a few more bolts, and finally the job was complete. Turning on the machine, it began its processes with some humming as its multiple systems and components began coming online. Rey stood from his stool and stretched, having been in that position for such a long time.

"My goodness, I feel so stiff. Mistress, how long have we been down here?" he asked.

"Well, Capitan, I hope you are not complaining about being stiff while turning me on." Mistress said shamelessly, then added, "But to answer your question, you have been down here for about ten hours straight. It is currently eight pm planet time."

"I see," Rey stated, stretching as he admired the work he had done approvingly. "Mistress, I would also like to inform you that the system is running better than when it came off the assembly line. I will make a test print and then program it to continue printing out the new valves."

"I see that, Rey, and confirm your statement. Thank you. Excellent work gentlemen, I shall inform the captain," Mistress said with a hint of glee.

"Ah yes, please do, then tell her that me and my Compai are headed to dinner."

Jorian surprisingly smiled. "My treat. I insist. You pick, but keep it under 300 credits, I don't get paid that much."

"Agreed," the other man happily stated.

The two washed their hands and El Capitan donned his long jacket, making his way to the door, with Jorian just a few feet behind. Rey stopped before he exited the ship, turning and calling out to Mistress, "Bonita, if you'd be a dear and send me a receipt of completion and a good rating, I would greatly appreciate it."

"It would be my pleasure, Rey, please have a nice evening," the ship replied.

"We shall, Bonita, we shall," the man replied as he adjusted his hat and exited the ship. "Come Compai, let's go and dine like kings. Yes!" Rey said and cheerfully put his arm around his friend as they headed off into the night. "Into the night we go, to face all madness and delight."

Chapter 15

A week later and the forge printer was spewing out parts, keeping Jorian busy swapping out valves throughout the ship. The working forge printer had brought new life to the ship, inspiring Ophelia and Emmy to invest some more time in other projects. Emmy began working in the ship's greenhouse, planting some new seeds she had found locally. Ophelia dove headlong into some long overdue programming of the ship's cleaning systems.

Everything seemed more productive, with schedules of exercise and work being added as they formed a daily routine. Even the fox had started training, as it played fetch with anyone who would toss a ball or a stick, but spent most of its time hunting rats that had somehow gotten into one of the food storages. The fox was a natural hunter with quick reflexes and a knack for stealth, but most impressive was its intelligence, as it proved an ability to learn and understand what Jorian and others asked of it. The animal showed a strong sense of loyalty to its owner, which was now clear to everyone to be Jorian as it followed him everywhere, even in the tightest of spaces.

One morning Brother Julius wandered by requesting some help to watch his grandkids, because of a high-profile surgery that required the utmost discretion. The crew of the Mistress split the chore with the girls taking Terri and Jorian taking Nate and the fox as his assistants. Nate acted like a first-rate assistant handing the technician tools or any other thing he might have asked for, and every time, the young boy was on point. Eventually, the group met for lunch, then watched a movie on the large screen in the lounge that left the two children mesmerized at the immersive technology of the video and audio.

The hours sped by, and the sun had retreated long ago as everyone onboard started getting concerned that the doctor was now long overdue. The children had not begun worrying yet, being so thoroughly entertained, but Ophelia and the others were quite concerned.

"Mistress, anything from Brother Julius?" Ophelia asked.

"Nothing Ma'am."

Ophelia sighed as she shrugged towards the others, showing a lack of response. Another few more hours had gone by and the port quieted down as the moon rose high in the night sky when Mistress broke the silence, announcing a visitor.

"Excuse me Jorian, Rey is outside and requesting your company," he says it's urgent.

Without a word, Jorian stood, glancing at Ophelia, who signaled him to go, taking the boy under her arm. The soldier hurried down the steps, reaching the entrance to the ship, where Rey insisted he wait inside.

"Rey, you all right?" Jorian asked as he rushed into the room expecting trouble.

"Aye, Compai, I am fine, but it seems we have unfinished business. The youngest son of the Empress has captured brother Julius. He has a handful of guards and has left the consortium in a tirade, seeking revenge. This needs to be addressed. I was thinking..." Rey was saying but was cut off.

"Let's go get him," Jorian replied without hesitation.

Rey was unaccustomed to people like Jorian, and though he didn't expect such a response, he had hoped for it. The salvager and the soldier headed out into the night, taking a transport to a deeper and more industrious section of town. The transport stopped two blocks away from their intended location at their request, allowing them to get off and walk the rest of the way, getting a layout of the building.

"What do you think, Compai?" Rey asked.

"We have to do this quietly. No blaster. They could be seen from far away in the darkness and draw a lot of unwanted attention. Do you have a knife?" Jorian asked.

"I do," Rey replied.

"Give it to me and take watch. I also need you to deal with the guards at the gate, leave the rest to me," Jorian instructed.

"Why don't I keep my knife and give you the one I brought for you, eh?" Rey replied, extending out something in a dark cloth.

"You should have led with that," Jorian stated, taking the item. "And why do they want the Doc and not me? I shot her."

Both men paused quietly at the thought of the statement, then Jorian turned his head slowly and narrowed his eyes at the former pirate suspiciously, "Wait, please don't tell me you brought me here to collect on some bounty or reward? Are you going to try to sell me?"

"Believe me, if I could, I probably would, but I had not thought of that as an option. I heard they got the healer and came to tell you," Rey paused, looking at his Compai, then at the compound as he scratched his head.

Jorian glared at his friend and shook his head in disbelief, "Really Rey! Come on, why would there even be a bounty on me?"

"This is the outer rim, my friend. Anyone could put a bounty or a contract on anyone if you will fork over the money. But do you want to try that angle? I'll split it with you eighty-thirty my favor," Rey replied with a cocked eyebrow.

Jorian eyed his friend and shook his head. "You really going to give me that as an actual good offer, I thought we were partners. I will counter," Jorian retorted as he studied the layout. "You know what, I'll go with your plan, but I want a night flyer suit and a better percentage."

"Really?" Rey replied, surprised, then added. "You're a worse negotiator than I thought, Compai. But I'll do forty since it's you."

"Yes, but remember, you need to get me a night-flyer suit on top of it. And a good one," Jorian restated.

"A Night-flyer what? Wait, first let me check if there is a bounty on you. And how much is one of those things?" Rey asked hesitantly.

"I don't know, I didn't do a lot of purchasing," Jorian stated as he undid the cloth and inspected the knife he was handed. "Let's do this."

"Do what?" Ophelia's voice said over his earpiece.

"What are you doing on this channel?" Jorian asked.

"I was calling to see if you are okay, and Mistress told me you are somewhere in the center of the city. What are you doing? Are you okay?" she asked.

"Some people have captured Julius; we are going to get him back."

"Do you have a plan?" Ophelia asked.

"Yes, Rey will distract the guard at the gate and I'm going in by the back," Jorian replied.

"That sounds like you're pulling it out of your ass," Ophelia complained.

"Without workable intel and time, it's all we have," Jorian replied.

"Come back, we can call the authorities," Ophelia stated innocently.

"This is Tersa 4, the authorities know who owns this and stay away from it. If we go back now, they would more than likely kill Julius, if he's not dead already," Rey chimed in, hearing her broadcast.

Jorian then insisted, "Let's go."

Having an impromptu plan, the pirate slowly made his way to the front of the warehouse while Jorian made his way to the rear of the property. El Capitan approached the guard house casually, giving the guard a friendly salutation that was hesitantly received. The two talked for a while, which was unfortunate for the guard, giving Rey's amazing ability to get people to say or divulge things because of his disarming personality. The guard seemed involved in what he was telling Rey, bringing the attention of another guard, within minutes four of the guards were talking with El Capitan, each providing their own input to the man.

Jorian saw the guards were engaged with Rey and took advantage of the opportunity, reconnaissance was vital to any operation, and this was their great opportunity. Turning to his IDP, he contacted Mistress, hoping to get a positive response by the ship.

"Mistress, do you copy?"

"Yes, Jorian, how can I assist you?"

"Mistress, how many words do you need someone to say to mimic their voice?" he asked.

"Technically one, but with one word, accuracy and how they say the word makes thing much more difficult. The more words, the greater the accuracy, and it's preferable for them to be in their normal tone. If the target is stressed, that will also reflect on the recording," the AI replied.

"I will not be responding so I'm not heard, just monitor and record," he asked.

"Yes, be aware that your IDP is a very basic model, and you will need to upgrade if you want future operational support," Mistress answered.

"We need to save Brother Julius and time is of the essence, I'm going in, just record the voices of all the guards you can, in case we need it for voice recognition or to report in," he said and began moving further away from the gatehouse and towards the corner of the warehouse that was opposite to where Rey and the other guards were standing. Spotting a lone guard in the shadows, Jorian hopped the fence near that lone guard acting as if he had not seen him and hid behind a crate looking out into the street, pretending that he was hiding from someone. The guard had seen him and approached him from behind, quietly stopping about two meters away, pointing his rifle at Jorian and charging the weapon. The weapon made a well-known sound, signifying it was charged and ready to shoot. Jorian froze and put his hands up.

"I want no problems with you, I am just hiding from some people coming after me. I thought this place was abandoned," Jorian said, acting scared.

"Well, it's not and you're trespassing. Move and I'll put a few holes in you," the guard said cockily.

Jorian quickly replied with a pleading sound in his voice, "Don't do that please, it's my first gig, and I messed up. Please, don't hurt me. Look, you can have what I took. Just let me go, please, mister. I don't want problems with you. I don't want to die," Jorian pleaded again, but more to the man's greed than his conscious.

The guard took the bait and quickly asked, curiously, "Hmmmm. What'd you take?"

"It's some sort of ceremonial knife," Jorian replied.

"A knife? What the hell do I need another knife for?" the guard replied, uninterested.

"No, no, no. Its' not just any knife. It's some sort of ceremonial thing, supposedly worth big money. Look, I'll show you," Jorian said as he acted, going for the knife.

"S-S-ssst. Don't move!" the guard warned, then asked, "Big money, huh?"

Putting his hands back up quickly, Jorian answered, "yeah, no, no, not moving."

The guard looked at Jorian sizing him up for a moment, "I could kill you now and take everything you have, why shouldn't I?"

"Look man, you shoot me. It draws attention; those guys are looking for me and they're a bunch of crazed zealots. You don't need any more problems, though you look like you can handle anything that comes your way. You also don't need to draw attention from anyone else, because they may want a cut."

"Fuck the others," the guard argued back, looking around but lowering his voice.

"Like I said, it's bad for everyone. I give you the dagger and you let me leave. You get rich and I live to see another day, that's a win-win in my book," Jorian quickly added.

The guard paused considering his prisoner's words, and looked around. He knew the other guards were engaged with El Capitan and believed he could make a quick profit at the expense of the young man in front of him. Having decided, the guard then told him. "Let me see it, slowly, with two fingers and keep your other hand up. You move too fast, you die!"

"Sure man, sure. Nice and slow," Jorian replied, seeming nervous.

Moving slowly and taking the cloth covered knife from his waist, he held it up with two fingers next to his head to show the greedy guard. His hand shaking to add to the effect of his story. The guard cockily grinned, seeing the young man tremble before him, looking around as if a cultist could approach or one of the other guards.

"There it is, take it. It's all yours, man," Jorian said nervously.

"That's a piece of cloth. You fucking with me?" The guard said, irritated, pushing the muzzle of his rifle into Jorian's back.

"Easy man, easy. You said two fingers it's in the cloth. I'm just trying not to get shot, okay?" Jorian answered in a low but agitated voice.

The guard adjusted his visor, allowing him to see better in the darkness. He could see the cloth and could make out the shape of the knife in it. Glancing around once more, seeing he had an opportunity to make some money, he took a step closer to get the item, but that was his mistake. Jorian could hear the man moving, his step on the ground, the gear shifting on his body, the clicking of the strap on the guard's rifle. The man's movement gave away his exact position, telling Jorian's sensitive ears how far the weapon and the guard were and publicized it was time to strike.

The Guard reached for the knife and as he grabbed it, Jorian turned with inhuman speed and attacked him. Grabbing the guard's head and turning it backwards with such force, shattering the man's neck, killing him instantly. Jorian held the body up to avoid any unwanted sounds, then putting the corpse down slowly and quietly just out of view.

"Mistress, were you able to record his voice?" The Ravager asked.

"Affirmative."

"If I link my IDP to this guard's unit, can you interface with his and gain access to their communications and possibly isolate communications?" Jorian asked, watching the area around him once again.

"Jorian, you are asking a lot of that calculator on your wrist, either way, connect me to the guard's IDP, let's see what I can do," Mistress answered, then took another jab at his equipment, "I do highly suggest that if you are going to be doing things like this that you upgrade your gear."

"I would love to, but have you seen my salary?" Jorian said as he hard-wired the two devices together.

"You know I'm the one keeping track of your wages, right?" the AI shot back.

"I know. Mistress, please be aware that you might also need to mimic his vitals, it's possible its being monitored passively or actively. When you are on their channel, patch me in so I can listen to their chatter. Get to work, I need to find a way up to the roof," Jorian instructed in a very serious tone.

"Jorian, this may take longer than expected," Ophelia interrupted.

"Ophelia, you're still on?" Jorian asked, surprised.

"Of course, I am. Not only are you my responsibility as a member of my crew, but I'm invested in your future," Ophelia replied, then added, "This may take more than a few seconds, that processor on your datapad may actually be slower than a child's calculator. As for the earpiece that goes with it, well, it's also subpar. FYI your IDP is a knockoff of a poor design to begin with, if that wasn't bad enough, it was made by the CCP sector, a much lessor competitor of Knightforge Technologies, and not one of the good ones. So, if you're lucky, you can get two meters of range. Can you take the guard's IDP?"

"Negative, it has a lock on it. I'll just leave the two connected, so you keep working on it. Remember, time is of the essence, I'm going to the roof to take out that guard, if you isolate the channel, get him talking, enough to mimic his voice and tell me where they're at as well. When he talks, I know you're done and I will eliminate the threat. Damn CCP crap," he grumbled with a small sigh and moved off.

Quietly making his way to an exposed pipe that went to the roof, Jorian tested the pipe to see if it would hold his weight. Looking around once more, he began his ascent. It was only three floors, but not an easy climb for most, not even for Jorian, who now missed some of the high-tech gear he'd used in the past.

Quickly, he moved hand over hand as he climbed the pipe. He had just pulled himself past the second level when he heard a door opening to his side. He slid down and leaped to grab one of the support bars that held up that balcony, and shimmied over just as the guard walked out. Jorian hung underneath the balcony, listening to the soldier's footfalls as he moved on the balcony. He heard a "click" coming from the soldier's direction, who then began sucking on an electronic device, letting out a distinct and powerful aroma as he exhaled. Jorian crinkled his nose, recognizing the odor from a previous mission on a drug smuggler's vessel.

Amirl-dream was the name of the latest synthetic narcotic ravaging the sector, it was supposed to elevate a person's mood, while the user experiences euphoria like sensations, mixed with chills and twitches which attempted to mimic an orgasmic experience. Though popular, long-term use could affect the nervous system. The drug normally took about a minute to take effect, but the sensation lasted for almost 10 minutes. A curse from the guard disrupted the moment and then a response to his comm device.

"Damn it! What is it! I'm here, but I'm on my break. Eagle can confirm, I'm on the south side balcony," the man said, irritated. Letting out a deep breath as he closed his eyes feeling the drug taking effect, he was breathing erratically and tried to shake it off, but could only control the sensation momentarily, not wanting to be seen using, while working and waiting for the guard on the roof to acknowledge his location. A few seconds passed and Jorian heard the guard say, "Hey," acknowledging the sniper on the roof.

"Fucking assholes," the guard grumbled as he returned to his original spot on the balcony, picking up the disc seeing if it still had serum left. The guard on the roof moved off in another direction, as one of their boots dragged over some rocks on the roof, demonstrating they had turned and were moving away. Looking back to the roof as he suppressed a twitch, assuring himself the sniper on the roof had left, he turned the disk to get the second dose.

"Oh yeah, two hits left, it's my lucky day. One now, and another one back at the inn," he said cheerfully, and just as he was about to click the disc, he let out another grumble, "What! I checked in already, leave me the fuck alone, I'm on my break!" he stated.

The message caught Jorian's attention, causing him to suspect that Ophelia and Mistress had been successful and could adjust somehow to his location. Jorian heard the click of the disc and the man sucking on the serum. A few seconds passed, and the man closed his eyes, tilting his head back, letting the sensation fill him, but instead got

Jorian's crushing hand around his neck, partially interrupting his high. This extra dose, with the previous dose, kept the man off balance and reacting slowly. He was shivering while gasping and trying to fight Jorian off unsuccessfully. The Ravager yanked the man over the railing, holding him by his throat, when he heard his earpiece come on.

"Jorian, come in. Jorian, come in, please! Eagle is returning. I repeat, Eagle is returning," he heard Ophelia's stressed voice in his ear and looked at the roof.

Knowing he only had seconds, he dropped down, grabbing the ledge with one hand, while still holding the guard in the other. Jorian strained as the jolt of grabbing the ledge with his and the guards combined weight coursed through his arm, but he suppressed it, allowing some of the rage to filter into his mind. He could feel his senses becoming more acute. As his heartbeat increased, so did the pressure in his hand as he crushed the man's throat. The guard jerked and twitched as he tried to grab for the hand that was killing him, but Jorian only squeezed more until the body went limp.

He could hear Ophelia on the earpiece again. "Do not let him go. The eagle is still near you and we're bouncing the signal off the IDP of the guard in your hand, if you let him go, we lose you."

Jorian looked down and shook his head, seeing that guard's feet were about two meters from the ground and sighed. Jorian waited quietly as the sniper above finished their inspection. The Ravager looked down at the suffocating and dying guard in his hand that drooled out of his mouth, with the stench of the serum on Jorian's hand.

A few moments passed when Ophelia's voice came back on in his ear. "Okay, she left."

"How are you seeing me?" Jorian asked in a forced whisper.

"Mini drones, we have five in the area. They are capable of 2-way communications and visuals in a variety of light spectrums. Why didn't you tell me what you are doing?" she demanded.

"Not the time. We'll talk when we get back. I promise," Jorian replied and dropped the body.

Letting himself down as quietly as possible, he moved over and repositioned the body so it would be hidden from view. Cleaning his hand on the man's sleeve, then looking up once again as Ophelia spoke in his ear, "Though it may be utterly disgusting, you can use this guard's datapad to keep communicating with us. Their systems have been overridden and are in our control."

"Copy that, heading to take out the eagle," Jorian replied.

Chopping the man's arm off and removing the datapad, he placed it on his belt pouch and began the climb again, reaching the top, he heard men talking in his ear and then identified Rey's voice. "You really think that, eh? Well, let me tell you this. I think she is much better than her alternatives, so much so that I would contract her as my sniper in a heartbeat. Heck, maybe I'll go up to your roof and offer her a job myself, and hope that she'll accept my offer for employment and leave you degenerates," Rey finished with a laugh and was joined by the other guards around him.

"Nah, you just like to look at her legs," another voice said.

"Can you blame me?" Rey chuckled. "She's very easy on the eyes, yes?" Rey nodded with a dismissive hand gesture, and continued. "Anyway, I'd rather look at her than you, but a man can only dream of her in their future, yes?"

"Good luck with that. She's a tough nut to crack and a good fighter, too. She'd probably kick your ass as quick as take the job," One guard added, laughing.

Rey's tone was one that everyone knew, he had a sly smile on his face as the others laughed around him. Jorian just shook his head, understanding the coded message. *As if this wasn't hard enough, now Rey wants the sniper alive. Damn, this makes things more difficult, especially if she's as good as Rey and the others say she is.*

"Rey's talking about her like she's a piece of meat or a dog on a leash and yet, you find it hard not to like the guy," Ophelia protested to Mistress.

Mistress promptly replied. "Did you consider that he is playing to the crowd?"

"I guess it's possible, but he says it so naturally," Ophelia replied.

"It doesn't matter either way, she will most likely be dead in a few minutes, anyway. Jorian is on the move. I am picking something up from the drones, it comes and goes?" Mistress replied.

"Comes and goes. Have the drones move in five meters," the captain instructed.

"It's tiny, and it seems to move with the guard on the roof, or at least in front of her," Mistress stated.

"Inform Jorian, tell him we are looking into it," the young woman replied nervously.

Jorian had just crawled up on the roof quietly next to a vent to hide his position when he got the message and froze, pulling his legs in with him. Taking a moment to think, then realized what it was. *Another drone,* he thought before answering. "Micro-drone, probably with a camera to see behind her so she's not snuck up on or surprised. Hack the feed and loop it for 20 seconds."

"Jorian, that's a high-end drone with barely a signature and if it's part of her datapad, it has an individualized encryption and security to avoid just that. I can't hack that! Not in this amount of time," Ophelia protested to Jorian.

"If you can't hack the drone, hack the output, coming into her visor, or just overload it. Just disable her feed and hurry," the operative advised.

Just then, El Capitan came back on the comm channel. "So that much you say, what if I can arrange it? I'd want immediate payment via transfer."

Jorian heard the guard's voice relay the same message over their voice channel. "El Capitan says he could arrange it, if we can pay him via immediate transfer?"

A few moments passed before the guard got a reply. "The boss says you bring that guy in and you'll get your immediate transfer."

"How about a side bet, yes? Not only will I bring him in, but I will have him come willingly," Rey said, spreading his arms out cockily.

"Bullshit!" Another guard replied.

"How much? 200 credits?" Rey asked slyly.

"I'm in for 500, no one comes in willingly to their execution," the first guard stated.

Other guards agreed as well, and each took the bet for 500 credits. Rey played the part perfectly and then surprised them all with his next comment. "I have a mistress that is running a courier operation and will send him right over since he is working for her, who knows, even on her sometimes," he stated, pausing and raising his eyebrows to imply a second meaning before continuing. "But I'm not greedy, I'll share," the former pirate captain said as he laughed, then pressed a button on his datapad.

Opening a live channel to the Mistress of Mayhem and placing it on speaker for all to hear. He signaled them to be quiet and then began his call. "Watch and learn."

Mistress's seductive voice came over the man's datapad. "Oh Don Capitan, what do I owe the distinct pleasure of this call to? Will you be coming by later?"

"Ah, Bonita, that voice of yours is like a Deluvian cherry on top of whip cream, yes?" The man said charismatically.

"Oh, Capitan, you do know how to talk to a girl. Are you coming by later? I'm lonely and I have no one to play with," the AI asked flirtatiously.

"Ah Bonita, it would bring me so much pleasure to see you again, but alas, I must finish some work. I could finish sooner if you sent me your tech to help me with something. What do you say, and I will bring the drinks?" Rey offered.

"They only thing a lonely girl like me could say. Send me the coordinates and hurry, I can't wait for you to put your hands on me again. You make me heat up so much I can melt metal. See you soon," the AI responded, blew him a kiss, and closed the call.

"NOOO!" two of the guards stated at the same time.

"This is good even for you, Capitan, almost worth losing the money," another one added, chuckling.

"Okay, Jorian, go. The signal has been interrupted, and she is out of sight," Ophelia instructed with a hint of anxiousness in her voice.

The Ravager stood, moving up stealthily from behind the sniper, ready to pounce. She was tall for a woman with long wavy hair that could be seen coming out from under her helmet and visor. She tapped the side of her visor, then briefly laid her rifle against the ledge and checked her datapad, verifying the link to her drone. She even made the micro-drone blink its lights briefly, which caught Jorian's eye as he closed in on her. Tapping on her visor once more before it went completely dark.

Annoyed, the sniper removed her helmet and visor to check the malfunction, when Jorian quickly recognized her, she had watched over him when he was a prisoner at the Pirate Consortium's base. She had brought him food one day and unlike the others; she didn't hurt him, but instead looked him over and gave him something to drink. Jorian realized that, unlike the other guards and mercenaries, she had a code of ethics and was much more of a professional than a hired gun.

What she had done had little barring to the soldier, she was just a target, but for a brief moment he was glad that Rey wanted her alive. With her helmet off and distracted with the malfunctioning visor, Jorian pounced, taking advantage of the opening, placing his powerful arm around her neck and pulling her back. Using a choke hold and his augmented strength, to pull her off her feet and subdue her quickly.

El Capitan was not being generous when he said she was a capable fighter, instead of acting defensively like most, she immediately went on the offensive, swinging her helmet back, hitting Jorian in the head hard. The impact hurt and even slightly dazed the young man, but he held on to his grip and squeezed tighter to incapacitate her quickly without hurting her as she clawed at his arm and hand.

Within seconds she was unconscious, her body went limp, dropping her helmet towards the ground. Jorian's training kicked in and by instinct, quickly stopped the helmet from hitting the ground with his foot. Placing the sniper down gently, he recalled the drone, folding it and replacing it back into her IDP.

The sniper had hit him hard, but fortunately, the impact had not drawn blood, but would most likely leave a giant welt at some point. Checking her pulse, he confirmed she was still alive. Convinced of her status, Jorian bound her hands and feet, then placing a gag in her mouth to make sure she kept silent. Grabbing her helmet, he reset it and placed it over her head with the visor down.

"Are you okay?" Ophelia asked

"I'm fine, and so is she?" he replied.

"Why didn't you kill her like the others? Is it because she's a woman?" Ophelia asked curiously and defensively.

"No. A combatant is a combatant. Did you not hear Rey's message? He wanted her alive to give her a job," Jorian responded calmly as he rubbed his head, confirming he had not been cut, then asked, "Ophelia, since you're hacked into the visor, place a message that she can read, telling her to stay down and stay quiet, if she wants to live, put Rey's signature on it, so it's well received."

Rey and the other guards were laughing it up as Jorian made his way down from the roof. Making his way quietly over the fence and around another building, he notified Rey of his location. The charismatic salvager played it until the end, urging the guards to quickly hide to not raise suspicion.

Jorian arrived greeting Rey, who just stood there leaning against the side of a small guard gate. Standing up strait greeting the young man warmly, astounding even Jorian how good El Capitan really was at selling an idea or concept.

"So, we meet again, eh?" El Capitan said with a lavish bow. "Well, I, for one, am glad you're here, so I can settle some accounts and get paid. Also, I need your help to take some cargo back to your facility for our lady friend, yes?" Rey stated plainly.

"Sure Capitan. I'm still on the clock. So, whatever you need, I'm happy to help." Jorian answered gleefully.

"Fantastic, let's go make some money this way," Rey said, leading the young man passed the guard shack and towards the building.

The other guards quickly came out of hiding with guns blazing, while shouting, ordering him to freeze and get down on his knees. One guard threw some binding cuffs at Rey, instructing him to bind the young man with his hands behind his back. Rey quickly followed the instructions, grabbing the cuffs and binding in place one of Jorian's hands, who looked at the guards with a confused expression on his face.

"Willing as promised, now pay up!" He told the guards.

"Damn you, Capitan, how many times are you going to sell me?" Jorian cried out angrily.

"As many times as I'll get paid for it. Don't take it personal, it's just business," Rey stated so convincingly that even Jorian paused and wondered. The former pirate captain smiled at the others as they all got a quick laugh at the reality of his comments and then, one by one, initialized payment for their loss in the bet. The guards gruffly grabbed Jorian, bringing him up to his feet.

"Easy boys, don't rough up the merchandise until I get paid," Rey told them.

"Don't worry Capitan, you'll get your money. The Prince wants this guy bad, "one guard added.

"Krenzky, you stay here. Everyone else report," the highest-ranking guard ordered.

Rey and Jorian grew in concern hoping that everything would be fine, when the leader asked everyone to report in and everyone did, even the dead and the unconscious thanks to Ophelia and Mistress's sophisticated systems that mimicked the voices perfectly. With everyone checking in, Jorian had an adequate count of the numbers they'd be facing, and the count was currently six guards and whoever else was with the young Prince.

"We are entering the building with the target," the leading guard said over the radio.

The group entered the building, with one guard in the front, followed by Rey, then Jorian with a guard pushing him from behind with a sidearm pointed at the Ravager's head. Behind them was the lead guard with a weapon at the ready and pointing it at Jorian as well.

Passing the first set of double doors and entering the building that seemed darker on the inside than the outside, the group continued down a long hallway. To the left stood an enormous set of doors that gave way to the main area of the warehouse. The building had various offices with a sizeable gap in the center that overlooked the center area of the main floor, while yet more rooms continued on the third floor. Jorian surveyed the main floor of the building as he walked inside, seeing Brother Julius beaten and tied to two beams with chains, arms spread out and naked. The old man looked up, his face full of blood, and peaked through a partially shut eye.

Julius could see the young man whom they called the Prince. He was about sixteen years of age, standing on a raised dais with a large wooden seat like a throne behind him. He had the sour glare of a pompous child that had been deprived of a toy. He glared at Rey, then looked to Jorian spitefully. Seeing Rey enter followed by a bound Jorian frightened the old man who thought immediately of his grandchildren, *If they're here, where are Terri and Nate? Wait, is El Capitan smiling? Did he sell me and Jorian out and why is Jorian looking around like that? Oh my God, please help me. Please help my grandchildren.* But all hope left the good doctor when he heard El Capitan speak.

"My good Prince, it is good to see you well. As you see, I have provided you and your family once again with great service. Though I believe that this will not end well for certain parties, eh? I would like to conclude our business, as I have other things to attend to that I have placed on hold, giving you priority."

The youth snickered, looking down at the group from his raised dais, "El Capitan!" He paused for dramatic effect, eyeing the salvager intently. "I wonder how much of this is all your fault by allowing my mother to die. Maybe I should have your head too. It seems all that you want is money, maybe you sold my mother out. How much did they pay you, I wonder?" The Prince said accusingly, with a pointed finger stretched out.

But Rey was well-versed and didn't lose a step. "My young Prince, your mother the Empress, God rest her soul," Rey said and quickly made a sign of the cross, before continuing, "shared with me an idea that profit is a profit, showing me new roads and possibilities. She gave me an opportunity which I cherished, but with her departure I feared the worst for the Consortium and left. Your mother was an amazing leader, but in her absence, I feared for the outcome of the group. To honor her memory and what we had built together, I did what I did to avoid bloodshed and the destruction of what we all worked so hard for these last few years," Rey replied with the most flamboyant of gestures.

"You can save it Capitan, my sources tell me you have been hanging out with the one who beat out my agent at the auction. And to add insult to injury, that you've been consorting with them and the doctor of your own free will. That looks pretty bad, wouldn't you say?" The young man paused, glaring at Jorian and Rey, trying to temper his anger before continuing. "I am not a little kid anymore; I see the world for what it is, and my mother taught me well. You, sir..." The young man was cut off by the former pirate captain.

"Yes, I can see that you are no longer a child. You have become a force of your own, and in your own wisdom, you have understood everything that has happened in the Consortium. You must also see that the sacrifice I made has led me to a lack of employment. I require employment to sustain a lifestyle that I enjoy. So yes, I have consorted with this swine's benefactor. Which has led me to a contract for work and more prospective employment. After all, he's part of Knightforge Technologies now. There is much profit in that, and your mother showed me so much, especially about how to make the best out of situations to make them profitable." Rey paused with a gesture of his head. "I understand that this may look bad, but I assure you, I am just keeping her memory alive, by keeping to her teachings and no more," Rey finished with a sincerity that would put so many others to shame.

"He killed my mother! The doctor killed my brother, and you defended him. How can I allow you to live?" the young man screamed.

"Yes, I defended the good doctor, not for loyalty to him, but to the Consortium. That man has tended to so many of us and was, and still is, most likely the best doctor on the planet, maybe even in this sector. I did not defend him, because of loyalties to him, but to the resource that kept the Consortium in business." Rey took a step closer with a deep passion in his heart. "I carried your brother to the table after he'd been hurt in that raid. There was little hope that he would survive. The doctor told me and your mother that all he could do was make him comfortable. There was no saving him. He had taken a hit from an explosion. Shrapnel had filled his body with cuts, there was so much blood everywhere. He was one of our best captains, and he deserved to go into the great empty in peace, even if it was too soon. Those last few

minutes, he was calm and at peace. What more can you ask of him?" El
Capitan argued back, stating the facts for the teenager.

"They need to be avenged!" the young man demanded

"You want to avenge your brother? Go after those that hurt him.
The Czar and his troops killed your brother. Please young Prince, be
better than all of them, you have the capacity and with the right
strategy you can take back the Consortium, it's your birthright," the
charismatic salvager stated passionately to the youth.

"I gave up my birthright for revenge, and I will have it!" The young
man retorted bitterly.

"Then so be it," Rey said, throwing his hands up. "I've done what I
could. I completed the contract and expect my payment, as promised
or did you give up your word too? Because a man without his word is
nothing," Rey shot back.

The guards all looked at each other questioningly, then at the
young Prince, who could feel their eyes on him. He did not want to look
weak, nor as a man without his word, leading to dissension and maybe
even betrayal by his own guards.

"No, Capitan, I am a man of my word," the Prince turned, calling
towards a side room. "Father, pay him and let him go on his way. He
has done his part," the young man ordered with a dismissive hand.

An older man, somewhat hunched over and with a slight limp
hobbled out of one of the side rooms, the sunken eyes on his face
added to his defeated existence. The older man had the look of a man
who had his will stripped from him long ago, along with everything
else. He was an empty shell and a sad one at that. What the Empress
hadn't taken from him, the young Prince had. The older man moved
over towards El Capitan with a device in hand and said in almost a
whisper, "Capitan please, link your device to the teller, direct payment
will be processed immediately."

Rey hard wired his datapad to the portable teller and placed his
thumb on the scanner confirming his claim. The old man did the same,
then walked to the Prince with the portable biometrics' unit for the
young man's confirmation. Once the transaction was completed, the
old man replaced two portable units into the portable teller device and
told the two in a slightly higher voice.

"The transaction is complete. We have transferred fifty thousand
credits from the Prince's accounts to yours, Capitan. Have a good day
and don't spend it all in one place," the old clerk stated as he

customarily did with any transaction he had ever done, ending with a defeated chuckle, before scurrying back to the room.

"I thank you my Prince, with our business concluded, I bid you farewell and wish you the best of luck, I see you have quite the night ahead of you," Rey said, bowing gracefully.

"Guards see him out," the Prince commanded out loud, with a shooing motion.

One of the guards' escorted Rey out, leaving behind four of the mercenaries; the two guards with Jorian and the two guards next to the Prince. Outside, there was one guard at the gate, plus the one escorting Rey, which was not a large number, but enough to complicate the situation. The Prince waited until El Capitan had left the room with the doors closing behind him, when he started yelling again, but this time, it was at Jorian.

"YOU KILLED MY MOTHER YOU FUCKING PIECE OF SHIT! I AM GOING TO MAKE YOU SUFFERRR!!!"

Jorian just stood there calmly as the Prince continued on with his rant, practically blaming Julius and Jorian for everything going wrong in his life. The sound diminished with the closing of the double doors as Rey exited the building, hearing nothing through the insulated walls by the time he reached outside.

"Sounds like he's pissed," Rey said, chuckling.

"You got lucky, Capitan. Do yourself a favor, don't come back around. You might not survive the experience," the guard escorting him said with hostility.

"Of course, thank you," Rey said politely, then turned to the guard at the gatehouse. "Krenzky, my weapon please, it's dangerous out there," he asked as he extended his hand.

"Sure Capitan. Don't charge it until you leave," the guard replied, handing back the weapon and the charge magazine.

Rey holstered his weapon and inserted the magazine. His weapon was unlike most weapons, having been modified a long time ago. It was an expensive modification that didn't require a manual charge, but instead self-charged upon insertion of the cartridge. Rey could still hear all the happenings inside through the open comm channel. Hearing the Prince yell and rant at Jorian spitefully, he finally asked the corporal, expecting the young man to beg for his life. "Do you have anything to say, you worthless piece of shit?"

Rey turned to leave the area when he heard Jorian's response to the prince through the open comm channel. "Fuck that bitch!"

Rey nodded to himself, wanting to say that to the woman for so many years and, with a smile on his face, told the two guards as he turned back. "Goodbye, gentlemen."

"Goo..." was the word the guards uttered when Rey pulled his weapon, shooting both guards dead, one in the back of the neck between the helmet and the armor, the other in the face. Both men dropped instantly, then Rey hurried, dragging the bodies out of sight and back into the building.

Releasing the bodies once inside the building and hurrying back towards the double doors, each step brought Rey closer to the sounds of combat in the room, which only got louder as he closed in on the double doors. Hearing blaster fire and screaming as if men were being torn apart by a monster inside the room, he tried to open the door as something heavy hit the door, forcing it closed, pushing Rey back into the hallway.

Rey pushed on the massive door, fighting against whatever was on the other side as the door slowly opened. The salvager froze, horrified at the scene before him. Looking down, he saw the mangled body of a dead guard he presumed had struck the door forcing him back. Now that man stared off into the distance with a look of agony forever etched on his face. Looking up, he could see the other guards' bodies broken, laying in pools of blood with limbs in awkward or unnatural positions with bones protruding through their skin. Jorian, wounded by laser fire, was walking towards the Prince, carrying one of the unfortunate guards in front of him and using him as a shield. The Prince trembled with fear, shooting his blaster in a state of panic towards the incoming Ravager but the Prince's shots missed or hit the body of the dead guard.

A blaster shot came from behind the throne, hitting the young Prince in the back, causing him to drop his weapon, gasping as he tried grabbing at his back. Jorian didn't hesitate tossing the body of the dead guard he was using as a shield to the side as he rushed the dais. With an open hand, he palmed the Prince's head and face, pushing it hard into the throne chair. The young man's eyes bulged out as he screamed at the top of his lungs, from the Ravager's crushing grip pushing in his skull. The red veins in Jorian's eyes reached across towards his pupils, increasing with every second that passed by, turning his head slightly to look at the young man squirming in pain from the force being exerted on his skull. A call came from a few meters away, Jorian's eyes darted up hearing the plea of the old clerk from behind the throne.

The old clerk hesitated, seeing the face of a red-eyed demon, and took a step back before he mustered the courage to repeat his statement. "Please don't kill him."

"What!" Jorian demanded angrily, in a guttural voice.

"Don't kill him, at least not yet. I need him alive for a few moments longer," the old man clarified.

Rey rushed towards the dais, his pistol in hand, and leaped up to the dais, his weapon leading the way, and pointed it at the old clerk. "Drop it!"

The old man quickly complied, releasing the weapon onto the floor, and placed his hands up. The Prince struggled to turn his head, with no success. As the old man approached, limping with his hands raised. Coming into sight, the Prince saw the old man and pleaded. "Fa-fa-fath-h-her."

"You are no son of mine. You came from some union between your whore of a mother and some bastard out in space. As for you! My son is dead because of you. I know the truth of how your stupidity caused your brother's death." The eyes moved from the Prince to Rey and they had a sudden pain that filled them. "He was getting out of this shitty life, he had a family, a good heart, and I held his secret, now all that I have left are my grandchildren and I won't let you squander what should have been rightfully his, for your petty bullshit. You will transfer all the money to my accounts and at least die with dignity for your crimes against your half-brother."

The soldier eyed the Prince menacingly, then changing his gaze towards the old man unconvinced and uncaring. Rey stepped up closer, coming into Jorian's line of sight with his weapon pointed at the old man. The Ravager's reddened eyes shifted towards Rey, acknowledging his presence, and then threw the Prince's body onto the floor at Rey's feet. "I'm here for Julius. You deal with this."

The old clerk quickly interjected. "I have access to the lock. It's a biometric lock. Allow me to release him. I hold no malice towards the good doctor. I know he had no hand in my son's death, if anything, I am grateful that he helped him not suffer."

Jorian moved to grab the Prince's gun, but Rey stopped him. "No, not that one, its booby trapped to his biometrics."

Jorian kicked the gun away, grabbing one of the guard's side arm's and escorted the old man to the doctor. Rey moved closer to the Prince, putting his weapon to the juvenile's head while patting the young man down for any other hidden weapons or treasure. Jorian followed the old man, who quickly released a badly beaten Julius, who would have crumpled to the ground had in not been for Jorian's strong arms supporting him.

The old man considered the doctor. "Julius, I have known you for a long time. I can't take back what she did or what's happened here today, but I promise you it ends here. From one father to another, I thank you for what you did for my boy," the old clerk ended with watery eyes.

Julius focused on the old clerk and nodded. The old clerk's eyes got red and watery thinking of his son, then considered the poor state of the man that had helped him not die in agony. "I have nothing else to offer you, but I ask that you accept being compensated for your time and expenses appropriately. A few coins is all I have left to give," the old clerk said as he dropped the last chain and stepped back.

Julius nodded and mustering all his strength to stand on his own and taking a step forward, his hand extending and clasping the old clerk's shoulder, "I understand the pain of a mourning, father. And I have and will continue to pray to the Almighty for your redemption."

Jorian looked at Rey as he grabbed Julius's torn and bloody robes. "I will get him back, then return when I can."

Rey nodded towards the Ravager as he draped the torn robe on Brother Julius and helped him through the door, carrying him by the time they exited the building. "Let's get you some help," Jorian told the doctor in the most encouraging tone he could.

"No!" Julius said, looking at him sternly. "Just get me to my clinic, I can fix this."

A voice suddenly came through his earpiece. "Jorian, there is transport in route to pick you up. Are you okay? I lost all communications when you went inside," Ophelia stated coming back on the comms.

"Yes, we are fine, it must have been some interference in the building. Can you meet us at the clinic?" Jorian asked.

"I'll be outside waiting," Ophelia replied.

Not a minute had passed by and a transport pulled up and parked, waiting for their fare. Jorian put brother Julius carefully in the transport vehicle, got in himself and closed the door, letting the transport speed off into the night.

At the warehouse, the old man sat on the throne and let out a deep sigh. "Capitan, I have gotten old, and all that I have left are horrible memories." The old clerk leaned back in the seat and took a deep breath. "Did you know I built this chair for my wife? I told her she was my queen, and I went down into the forest and cut down a majestic tree and built this throne seat for her. This throne spurred something dark within her and now, something that took everything from me." The old man chuckled to himself as he ran his hands over the armrests of the seat. "Did you know in all the years since I made this accursed thing, I never got to sit in it, and here I am finally?" the old man stated seeing all the dead bodies and the young man kneeling on the floor with a pistol to his head, then letting out a sigh stated, "What a waste of a magnificent tree."

"So, what now, Torvus?" Rey asked.

"Now, I will make you an offer, and let you decide my fate. I will take the money, except the expenses, and the portion I will give the good doctor. You can keep the assets of my company, heck, you can even have the company. I promise you, it is well worth it," The old clerk replied.

"All we have is our money and a few minor trinkets. What assets?" The Prince said from the floor.

"Shut it," Rey said, pushing the Prince's his head against the floor with his boot.

"Foolish boy, for decades, I've been hiding away things and moving assets from my wife, the Consortium, and countless others, even the Oculus. I know of things that no one else does. I hid it from her, from them, and from you. It was all for him and his dreams," he said, his thoughts moving to his lost son. "He had good dreams. Dreams that I can still give to my grandkids. Offer them the future I could not offer their father." The old man paused. "Rey del Castillo, is it?" Torvus asked.

El Capitan looked at the man and nodded.

"I know a lot of things, a lot of secrets, and I never shared them, they were not mine to share. As a clerk, I was privy to lots and lots of information. I know you wanted to open a bar. I heard you talking with my son one day, he liked you. He told me you helped him think of better things and even helped him get away occasionally. I thank you for that Rey. It meant a lot to him and to me," the old man said respectfully, then sighed, pausing as he took in another deep breath and gripped the armrest of the throne and looked at El Capitan with determination. "Rey, I have assets that will help you with your dreams, and much more, all that I ask in return is that you help me with mine. I want to take my son's remains off planet and give a life to his children, my grandchildren. Can you help me?" the old man humbly asked.

"You know, Torvus, I like you, too. You spent a lot of time speaking with your son and teaching him things in secret. I know because I saw you occasionally running off with him to one place or another and I could tell he loved you very much. I will not deny you your dream. I remember seeing you two once fishing. I liked how you tried to show him something better and let me tell you, it took." Rey paused and smiled. "Let us conclude our business, so you can follow what's left of your dream, yes?"

"Very well," the old man said as he stood.

Making his way over to the Prince, Torvus grabbed his hand and pushed his print against the portable teller machine. Once the ID was confirmed, he produced a recording that was the Prince's voice stating that he wanted to move his holding to a different account. Once again, the small device asked for confirmation and received it.

"The sum of twelve million credits has been transferred, we thank you for your business," the portable teller said and shut down.

"Twelve million! That's all? I expected you to have much more than that," Rey said, a look of surprise on his face.

"We did, but this idiot started burning through it as if it just magically appeared. But with what I know, I will make it grow and even if it doesn't, it is enough for a simple man like me to tend to his grandchildren. As for you Capitan, I thank you for your service and ask you to confirm your transfer. King's Jester Enterprises, am I correct?" the old man stated.

"You are," Rey said cautiously.

"I am aware you have others, but that one will do," Torvus added while pushing a few buttons on his datapad, the old man completed the transaction and presented the teller to Rey, who confirmed the transaction.

"Transaction complete. Assets and corporations transferred, list and receipt mailed to both parties. Thank you for your business," the device stated, and shut down.

"Capitan, it has been a pleasure to know you. I wish you the best. May I go?" Torvus asked.

"Of course you can, but you knew I would say that, since we've made a contract, and I'm a man of my word. But please allow me to wish you the best as well, Mister Torvus, and I thank you for your kindness." El Capitan nodded, then pointed to the Prince. "As for him, what would you like me to do?"

"Put him next to his mother, that will be my last gift to her, but please after I go. Oh, and destroy the chair. I would like to leave that darkness behind me, and here you will need these," the old man said, extending his hand to Rey, holding a set of keys.

Rey grabbed the old man's hand, shaking it, then took the keys the man was offering. "Thank you, Mr. Torvus, and be well."

"Thank you, Capitan. You will find her in the garage in the back," the old man replied as he winked and turned for the door.

The Prince called for his stepfather, but a quick kick to his gut silenced him. Rey waited for the man to exit, then turned his attention to the young Prince at his feet. The Prince started pleading and offering Rey other things that he swore were stored elsewhere and under different companies, but Rey didn't care.

"A contract is a contract, and my word is my bond, my dear Prince. And I don't need to be reminded of that. This sector is now free of your family's tyranny." Rey finished and pointed the weapon at the young man's head and silenced him forever. Two more shots followed for good measure. "Asshole."

Rey scanned the room, considering the mess and the bodies, then looked to the large throne chair as it enticed him to sit. He looked at it and was about to sit on it, then thought better of it. "Forget it, chair! You are bad news, I want nothing to do with you, but return you to the ashes you came from." Moving closer and pushing the throne over as he toppled an empire. Feeling a message come in on his IDP he scrolled down and realized it was the email he received with the list of assets. Studying it over, he nodded to himself.

"Impressive!"

The transport arrived at the port's Tower Gate and Jorian quickly rushed out carrying Brother Julius. The two guards saw him with the body and approached apprehensively with hands on their weapons.

Before they questioned him, Jorian addressed them first. "Medical emergency! Going to the clinic."

The two guards changed their demeanor and were about to offer them some help, when the young man just took off running at full speed carrying brother Julius as if he were a child. The guards quickly called over the radio and within a few seconds, other guards had shown up and were running down the tunnel, but Jorian was already turning, exiting the tunnel.

"Hold on, Julius," Jorian said between breaths.

The old man held on and looked at Jorian, "Slow down, remember what I said about keeping your abilities hidden."

"We're here," Jorian replied.

Making his way into the tented area, he saw Ophelia stand up and rush to them, he gently set the old man down. Julius leaned heavily against the door that scanned him, turning on the lights and unlocking the doors to the clinic.

"Welcome, Doctor Julius," the voice of the AI's clinic said over a speaker, as the door slid open.

"Jorian, is he okay?" Ophelia asked. "And why did you lose contact?" she demanded.

Jorian looked at her sternly. "You really need to learn when and how to ask questions, because your timing sucks."

"Jorian! You have better manners than that," the old man insisted with a reprimand.

"Yes, sir," the young man answered angrily.

"Take me to the last room. Ms. Knight, if you would please tend to the security forces that are following us. I will be okay. Let them know I was attacked on the way home by thugs and Jorian found me. Nothing more. Stick to the story. We know nothing," the old man said sternly, between pained coughs, then grimacing as he moved.

"Yes, Brother Julius," the young woman replied and turned to leave, but not before shooting Jorian an angry glare.

Jorian helped the doctor to the room and assisted him onto the bed. The old man groaned softly, holding on to his midsection. Now that they were under the bright light of the clinic, Jorian could see that one of Julius's hands was extremely swollen, bruised, and, most likely broken.

"Doc, my medical skills are very basic, I can't fix all this, and you don't look like you are in any condition, to do anything to yourself."

"Well, at least you are smart enough to know some limits. You are right, I'm really bad off. But I believe there is still time. Go over there to the closet, you'll see a fridge, open it and grab what's in the locked area. I'll give you the code," Julius replied through labored breathing.

The doctor straightened out on the table and order the AI to start a full scan. A robotic arm lowered and passed over Julius emitting a light showing where it was scanning, it made various passes and each time the light color changed. Jorian did as he was instructed and moved to the fridge, opening it, and saw a biometric scanner for a palm. "Um. This is a biometric scanner."

"Not really. Nurse, please activate the keypad for Cryostorage," the doctor said in a raspy, strained voice.

"Keypad activated," the AI replied warmly.

The old man laid as straight as he could and began rambling out, letters, numbers, and symbols to Jorian, who inputted each one of the 12-digit combination. As he was about to open the door, he could hear the motorized sounds of something turning inside the fridge unit, making him suspect that there was more than one type of storage unit that could be accessed.

"Scan complete. Cryostorage unit accessible," the AI said.

The two men looked at the screen as a series of images came up showing affected areas and the nurse listed all the injuries and physical trauma of the older man. The soldier turned back to the fridge and pulled open the door, which had a symbol indicating it was unlocked, as he pulled the drawer door, a series of vials filled with a blue gelatin like liquid were lined up followed by yellow ones, then green ones.

"Get two blue ones and a green one," the doctor said.

Jorian grabbed the vials and searched the drawers for a jet spray gun, and called out to the nurse, "Nurse patient status, please?"

"Patient Julius Orga, sixty-three-year-old, male, weight ninety-eight kilos. Multiple abrasions on face, back, legs, and torso. Various lacerations on head, face, back, legs, arms, and torso. Broken ribs at two, three, and seven right side. Broken ribs at three and four left side. Left hand, broken bones and damaged tendons. Right side dislocated shoulder. Bruised internal organs, punctured liver, severe injury to the lungs both left and right. Toxin found in the blood, organ failure in twenty-five minutes. Toxins found in the digestive track. Suggest immediate treatment or stasis, followed by spinal adjustment at T8 through T12."

"Doc, you're hurt bad, I don't think some antibiotics are going to help. I need to get you to a hospital," Jorian stated, concerned.

The old man grimaced in pain as he chuckled. "Don't make me laugh! I would normally agree but inject me with the green serum, four doses. One for each extremity. Forearms and thighs," the old man said through labored breaths.

Jorian grabbed the green serum and inserted it into the jet gun, adjusted the dose as instructed, and injected the old man. Stepping back, he swapped out the vial and inserted a blue one and approached the old man again.

"Now what?" Jorian said expectantly.

"Now we wait and hope it works. If it doesn't, Jorian the kids..."

"Quiet, old man, it has to. I'm not equipped for that; I am trained to survive and to kill. I wouldn't know where to begin," Jorian replied defensively.

The old man looked at the soldier and for the first time, the old man saw something he had not seen before in Jorian: fear. He saw the boy inside and smiled.

"Then you prepare them to survive and always hoping they're better than you. That is how our species thrives. When we remove pride and get out of our own way, the future is brighter. Take the blue ones, I made them for you. Take one save the other.

Go, finish the job and tell Ophelia to bring my grandchildren, if this is the end, I want to say goodbye properly," the old man said and laid back.

He asked the nurse for music and laid there as old soft jazz played. He thought of better times, of his wife and his daughter and stared off into the roof. Jorian looked at the old man and couldn't stop a tear rolling down his eye. Moving to another room, he removed his shirt, seeing the hole made by the blaster that had hit him and the multiple rips and blood splatters that stained it. "Nurse, do you recycle biomedical trash and waste?"

"Yes, we do Jorian, would you like to put something in for deconstructing and processing?" the AI replied.

A container slid out with the recycling symbol used since the 23rd century, with multicolored arrows spiraling in a circle. Jorian placed his shirt in the container then laid on the table.

"Nurse, initialize scan and process recycling immediately," Jorian instructed the AI and then called for his captain, with a sad tone. "Ophelia. Please call for the children, it might be Julius's last request. I'm signing off."

"I understand, I'll be inside in a minute," she replied.

Jorian paused for a moment considering the night's events, then looked down feeling the guard's IDP at his side and removed it, crushed it, and placed it in the recycler for deconstruction. A man's voice came from the door. "That is destruction of evidence, and that looks like blaster fire on your side."

Jorian looked at the Sergeant standing at the doorway and with a defiant expression, pushed the button for manual deconstruction.

"You a doctor?" Jorian asked the sergeant casually.

"No. But ..." The man was interrupted.

"Nurse, wipe screen," Jorian instructed, then turned to meet the sergeant's gaze. "Then this is privileged information."

"Jorian! Odis is only trying to help," Ophelia protested to him.

"Trying to help? With an accusation like that, for your information, Sergeant, I was disposing of my datapad because it failed me and was a sub-par module. The Captain can attest to that, she even mentioned I needed to get a new one." Jorian paused, taking a moment to collect himself. "So, Sergeant, what evidence are you talking about?" Jorian asked.

"The evidence is any forensic material; physical or digital that could assist us in catching the people who did this to the doctor and you," Odis shot back.

"Me?" Jorian asked, surprised, pointing to himself. "Nothing happened to me, I was walking down the street and saw Julius hurt and brought him back here. These injuries are old ones that opened up as I was rushing Julius back," Jorian replied.

"Yeah, what about that fresh bump on your head," Odis argued back angrily.

"What!" Jorian replied, touching his forehead and feeling the sting and the bump he'd gotten from being hit in the head with the helmet. "Oh, that. I hit my head when I bent down to get Julius. Anything else?"

Odis was visibly annoyed and took a step towards Jorian. When the two were interrupted by a loud groan by Julius, who sounded like he was in tremendous pain. Jorian pushed past the Sergeant and rushed to Julius with the others hot on his heals.

"Julius!" Jorian called out as he entered the room.

The old man was sitting up on the table as the automated arm placed sanitary adhesive in his cuts, sealing them shut. The old man looked over and seem in much better shape than he'd been when Jorian left him minutes ago. Jorian looked and immediately recognized the massive improvement in Julius's condition, having experienced it so many times before, and thought. *Nanites*, narrowing his eyes suspiciously at the old man.

"You scared me for a second, old man," Jorian stated.

"I'm tougher than I look, I was just a bit disoriented, most likely a concussion. I believe I will make a full recovery in a few days. Sergeant Odis, I appreciate your concern and that of your men. I will write a letter to your superiors about your supportive efforts."

Odis was confused, having heard the man was gravely injured and had a hesitation in thought. "Of course, doctor, thank you. But if you're up to it, I need to ask you a couple of questions about the incident?"

"Yes, of course, but I am afraid that there is nothing to discuss. I had an appointment earlier and when I left, I had decided to take a walk to stretch the old legs. I must have taken a wrong turn, because someone hit me in the head with, I don't know what." The old man shrugged. "I must have passed out, because when I came to, someone was rummaging my pockets, the next thing I remember was hearing Jorian's voice talking to me as he put me in the transport. Thank goodness he was there, but that is all I remember. I wish I could do more, Sergeant," the old man replied.

Odis looked at the doctor then back to Jorian, he didn't buy it, and knew there was more to the story but without evidence, he had nothing to go on. He looked at Ophelia, who was just staring at the old man, concerned.

"Well doctor, I guess there is nothing to report then. Jorian said he picked you up at, where did you say?" the sergeant asked as he turned to Jorian.

Jorian just looked at the man. "I didn't, because I don't know this city. I couldn't tell one street from another."

The sergeant sighed in frustration and was about to ask more when they were interrupted by the grandchildren calling for their grandfather and running to him. The old man winced as he hugged them and smiled warmly.

"Papaw is okay. Just a little bump," he said as he hugged them tenderly.

Emmy handed Jorian a fresh shirt after looking him up and down and winking. A gesture Odis did not miss. Turning to her, he politely asked, "Do you know anything about this?"

"Oh yes, Sergeant. Jorian is hot! Look at those muscles," she said, smiling.

The sergeant was about to protest when Jorian walked out of the room, Odis right behind him. "I'm not done!"

"I'm going to the bathroom. Do you want to hold it for me?" replied the Ravager defiantly.

"You have a problem with me doing my job?" Odis asked, stepping closer to him looking down at him being slightly taller.

Jorian stepped towards the man as well and whispered, "Nope! Just look in another direction, because all I did was help the old man."

"So why so defensive, huh?" Odis asked angrily.

"Because I couldn't get there sooner all right. Now just leave me be," Jorian shot back.

Ophelia stepped in between them, pushing them both back. "ENOUGH! Everyone is okay. That's what matters."

Jorian threw his hands up in frustration as he turned, walking off. Once in the bathroom, he started washing off his hands and face and everywhere else that had blood. He took the jet gun and injected himself with the blue serum; he had never seen the serum in blue but was willing to try it as long as it worked with no side effects.

He checked on the wound that was already almost healed and nodded at the effectiveness of the nano-serum. He put on the fresh shirt Emmy had brought him and hid the other vial in his pocket, then exited the bathroom. Looking down, he noticed his pants were stained too with blood, but the dark pants would hide the stains until he finished.

Jorian looked around when he exited the bathroom and took advantage of the opportunity that no one was looking and quietly exited the clinic to return to the warehouse and finish the job. The guards asked him about the doc, and he gave them the good news that he would recover and how minor it really was, then continued off into the night.

Looking at his watch and sighing, the former pirate stood and stretched, *I better get started,* he thought to himself, but as he was moving off, he remembered the sniper on the roof and a big grin came to his face. Whistling, he casually made his way up the stairs.

Once on the roof, he drew his weapon and looked around until he saw the woman lying on the floor tied up. Slowly, he approached and noticed she'd changed position, having heard his footsteps.

"Cariño, what are you doing here?" He told her.

The woman was trying to talk, but the gag muffled her words. She kicked and attempted to scream, but almost no noise was heard. Rey got closer, lowering his glasses, adjusting the lens to see in the dark, and zoomed in on the ropes that bound her.

"Cariño, El Capitan will free you, but please, don't attack me, I am only here to help you. Yes?" the man said with his heavy Hispanic accent.

The woman stopped struggling and stayed still, showing that she understood. Rey reached her, took off her visor and looked into her big green eyes and smiled.

"As lovely as ever, but Cariño, if you like being tied up you should have just told me, eh?" he said and smiled.

The woman just glared at him and turned over for him to undo her bindings. Rey untied her feet and then helped her stand, allowing him to finish undoing her hands. After she was untied, Rey stood up and took a step back, allowing her to finish taking off all the ropes and clapped. The woman stood and dusted herself off, then took a swing at the pirate, who leaped back ready to fight.

Fortunately for Rey, he was expecting her reaction and dodged the blow. "Cariño, I am not here to fight you, if I was, I would've just shot you while you were tied up. Please be sensible. Though I am surprised you can react so quickly after being tied up for so long. Eh?" Rey paused, letting his words sink in, then added. "I do apologize, I would have been here sooner, but I was preoccupied. But let me not ramble on and get to the point, yes?" Rey said as he kept his distance moving with the woman.

"I'm not letting you talk your way out of this," she said angrily and moved towards him.

"Fine, then I will just shoot, no?" the man said in a very casual voice.

With exceptionally fast hands, Rey drew his weapon and pointed it at the woman. The woman immediately stopped and put her hands up. Her eyes darted around, looking towards her rifle and then her pistol, that were sitting next to each other about three meters away. Rey noticed her eyes and blurted.

"Eh, eh, eh, don't be so foolish. You'll never make it, and you know it. Now please stop this foolishness and hear me out, okay?" Rey stated in almost a pleading voice. "I want to offer you a job. And since you're currently unemployed. I figure it was a good time to ask, what do you say?"

"Why? Do I no longer have a job Capitan?" she asked hesitantly.

"Because your benefactor is dead, and so is everyone else. Well, almost everyone else, the two at the inn are still breathing," he informed her.

"You did this, didn't you? Why?" she demanded.

"Come now Kassandra, you know better than to ask those questions. And if I did do this, it speaks volumes that I spared you, when everyone else is dead, no?" he said cunningly.

"I guess, but why me?" she asked, moving towards a vent and leaning on it, ending her hostility and showing she was listening.

"Well, you and I have history, and more than that, you are not like the others. You are smart and talented. I was hoping to spare you and save you from this life," Rey replied.

"I'm not a puppy, Rey, or is it El Capitan?" Kassandra said sarcastically.

"You sure?" Rey said as picking up the rope they had tied her with.

"Point taken, but any history we had ended when you left me to go mess around with that redhead. Yes, Rey, I heard, and I knew. I also know that it was a dick move. I deserved better," she stated, obviously bothered.

"Technically, I was messing around with you, on her, but that is neither here nor there. I apologize for my womanizing ways. I admit, it is one of my worst qualities, but we all have flaws." Rey shrugged before continuing, "The point of the matter is that I want to offer you some work and I will try not to flirt with you, but I make no promises. What do you say?" Rey expressed in a very sincere tone as he twirled his weapon, then returned it to his holster in one smooth motion. The woman cracked a smile, always having liked how good he was with his weapon.

"I believe you Rey, but let's go downstairs and let me see with my eyes that everyone is dead and confirm your story. If it is as you say, and I believe it is," the sniper paused, "we'll talk. What about the other two? They are still back at the hotel."

"As for your compatriots, they must be freed from their mortal bonds, yes?" Rey said and shrugged.

Shaking her head and letting out a breath, she replied, "I'm not doing it. They may be a pair of incompetent morons, but I don't betray my team or former team. You know what I mean."

The two continued some usual small talk as they finally reached the ground floor. Kassandra looked around in shock at the sheer brutality of the scene. She looked at all the bodies and then at the young man, that was once the Prince.

"Where is......"

"Gone, leave it at that. Now I will ask again. Do you want the job?" Rey said.

"Let's talk money. I want..."

"I will pay you fifty percent of your current salary. The Empress and the Prince were much higher value target than what or who you will be protecting."

"Fifty percent!" Kassandra said, outraged. "For that, you should have shot me on the roof. Ninety percent and a new suit of my choice. This scheme is horrendous."

"Maybe I should have shot you if I knew you were trying to rob me. After all, your team failed to protect their last two targets," the salvager said, shaking his head sadly, then looked at her. "Look, I will pay you sixty percent of your salary and a gear allotment, plus a percentage of the haul, a small percentage. Take it or leave it," Rey said, not wanting to argue.

"Fine, that's fair. When do I start?" The woman asked.

"Now. There are two bodies out back and two by the door, bring them in," Rey stated.

"I said I wasn't doing my team," Kassandra complained.

"You're not. They are already dead, you are just moving them so they are not seen," he replied.

"What a gentleman, Rey," she said sarcastically and moved off.

Rey smiled to himself and moved back to the dais to continue scrolling through his datapad. The list of assets he had gained was long and impressive, but he found the catch, and most likely the reason Torvus was so quick to part with it, most of it was off planet and spread out all over the place.

Being done perusing the list and knowing this was not the time to study it. He closed the file and moved over to the bodies, relieving them of anything that could be reused or salvaged. Armor, weapons, visors, and any gear that had value were placed in a pile. He then wandered the building, inspecting the merchandise still in crates ready for shipment or just being held in storage.

"Very nice," he said as he opened one crate.

Having a keen eye for fine things, the salvager dug through the crate and smiled victoriously as he picked up a bottle of Tenerian whiskey. Uncorking the bottle and smelling it, letting the aroma fill his nostrils, taking a swig from the bottle and thinking to himself, *This is uncivilized to treat such a refined beverage in this fashion, it deserves a glass. A glass that I will get later, but for now from the bottle will have to do.* Taking the bottle to his lips again and taking another drink, then letting out a sigh of relief as he savored the drink's aftereffects.

"Very smooth," he said out loud.

"That case belongs to the governor," Kassandra said as she brought in the last body.

"Well, then I better move it before he comes looking for it. I don't think the Prince will make his delivery," El Capitan said whimsically.

"This feels so wrong," the woman stated as she removed the gear off of one of her former teammates.

"That there is why I spared you. You have a sense of loyalty and duty, even to a bunch of hired guns and a piece of..." He stopped himself, then straighten his overcoat and continued, "Let's not speak ill of the dead, yes?"

"Rey, you are not like the others, how did you end up with the Consortium?" the woman asked.

The smuggler looked at her, then to the bodies, taking a moment to think back on that day so many years ago. Jorian had entered the room quietly and listened intently, having heard the question and was curious as his friend was about to divulge a bit of his past.

"It's not that complicated, much like your situation, I suppose. I was salvaging a destroyed freighter. When I returned to the ship, the Empress and her crew had boarded my ship and had killed a bunch of my crew, including my first mate, then executed a few more members of my crew and asked me at gunpoint to join her crew as one of her officers. I'd had some dealing with the Consortium in the past. She seemed very pleased with my performance and my ability to persuade people and get things done." Rey paused, shrugging. "Looking around my ship and seeing the outcome of the people that had refused or tried to resist them littered all over my cargo bay floor, I happily accepted. I could have chosen a different path, but I had a feeling that would have ended my career much sooner than I would have liked, no."

The man turned as he finished and was looking at the woman when he noticed Jorian standing there, listening. The woman paused, seeming somewhat offended and saddened by the former pirate's tale, and asked him.

"Rey, were you going to kill me?" she asked.

"Kill you? Why would you say such a thing?" Rey stated, pointing to Jorian that was now in the room. "I stopped him from killing you, I was hoping you would accept my offer of employment."

Following El Capitan's finger and seeing Jorian, Kassandra quickly twirled and reached for her sidearm. Jorian just stood there, taking notice of her reaction time and the way she pulled her weapon. Looking at the sniper, then to Rey, waiting for him to intervene.

"Kassandra, please, put down your weapon and don't point it at Jorian. He doesn't like it, plus, is that any way to treat my friend and business partner?" Rey stated passively.

"Friend? Rey, you don't have any friends," Kassandra retorted.

"Well, he has one," Jorian said firmly.

"Well, Jorian, let's see how good you are when I have a gun on you?" she said spitefully.

"I never had a gun on you, I choked you out. As for my odds, I like my odds, since Rey has his gun on you right now," Jorian replied calmly with a grin.

Partially turning her head to look at Rey and quickly noticing it was a rouse. Mentally cursing at herself for falling for the young man's trick, she returned her gaze towards Jorian, but he was gone. She scanned to either side of his previous location, knowing he could have been behind any of the stacks of crates in the area. Her eyes darted back and forth when she saw the movement of a crate sliding in her direction. Moving to the side, she aimed her gun and fired at the crate, putting two burn holes in the wood. Jorian popped out from behind some crates near her, hitting her weapon hand and possibly breaking it.

The sniper tossed the weapon to her other hand and pointed it towards Jorian, who slapped her arm wide, then with his foot, swept her legs from under her, making her crash hard onto the floor. She pulled the trigger once more, but her movement was too slow for the augmented Jorian and only ended up putting another hole in a crate. Kassandra tried to get to her feet, but Jorian had already positioned himself on top of her and had stripped the gun from her hand and placed his knife at her throat.

"Whatever you damaged is coming out of your salary, Kassandra," Rey said as he took another swig of the brandy.

"What!" the woman said, outraged.

Jorian leaned in closer, pushing the knife's edge slightly harder against her neck, and whispered in her ear, "You have bigger things to worry about."

The woman froze and stopped resisting, not wanting to push her luck anymore and understanding the severity of her situation with the knife biting on her skin. Jorian felt the need to control his urge to slash the mercenary's throat. Seeing the struggle inside of Jorian, Rey decided it would be prudent if he intervened.

"Compai, please forgive her, she's just feeling a little shaken because you got the drop on her twice this evening. I'm sure neither one of you is thinking clearly right now. Why don't you put away the knife, I'll take this gun and we can call an end to this? After all, we still have a lot of work to do this evening and she is now in my employment," Rey said extremely passively.

Jorian pushed the knife down a little harder, then slowly retracted it. Rey grabbed the pistol, engaged the safety, placing it at his waist. The woman was about to resist when Rey stopped her from committing a fatal mistake.

"Kassandra, Stop! Enough of your foolishness. He has spared you twice this night, I don't think there will be a third," Rey said seriously and sternly.

The mercenary got a glimpse of the monster being held at bay and released her hands, throwing them up, showing she was done. An action that Jorian understood but would not accept. Something inside of him wanted more, that same something would only accept her submission and asked, "You done?"

Through gritted teeth, Kassandra finally relented, growling, "I'm done!"

The young man released her and stepped back, but ready to pounce. The woman pushed herself off the floor and got to her feet. She grabbed at her hand that she knew might be fractured from the impact of Jorian's attack. Cupping the bad hand with the good one. "You broke my hand."

"Consider yourself lucky," Jorian replied coldly.

"Do the two at the inn know you had Julius?" Rey asked her.

"Yes. That's where the trap was set. They invited the doctor to attend to a fake person. They took him from there and brought him here." Kassandra paused, studying Jorian's face. "Wait a minute, you are the one who killed the Empress and the Consortium champion. I didn't recognize you with all that clothes on and with no blood on your face." She paused and looked at Rey. "Didn't you sell him at auction?" she asked, then turned to face Jorian. "How does he do that to you, and you still call him a friend? Friends don't sell each other to slavery," the sniper stated.

Rey quickly interjected. "He is my friend. We made a deal and both of us held up our end of the bargain. Most importantly, he is no longer a slave, except in his own mind. But enough with the question's lets clean this mess and finish our work." Rey let out a frustrated breath and asked, "Kassandra dear, if we call the others and tell them to check us out of the inn and bring everything here, would they?"

Sighing, she replied, "Yes Rey, they would."

"Then make the call Kassandra, consider it as you making up for the indiscretions again Jorian and me," the former pirate instructed.

"You! What did I do to you?" the woman asked.

"You are on the clock, under my employment, and you go off fighting, after I introduce you to a friend and business partner of mine. That was rude to him and me and I cannot, and will not, accept that type of behavior. You had your conditions for employment, and I have mine. Now make the damn call," Rey finished, obviously bothered.

The woman muttered in frustration, but finally made the call. Giving the right codes and commands, the other two guards emptied the room and walked into their deaths as Jorian and Rey ambushed them upon entering the building. With the work concluded, any possible loose ends to Brother Julius or Jorian himself disappeared, they were free to complete the transfer of goods and begin the clean-up.

El Capitan made a call through his datapad and a short while later, a small group of medical techs and cleaning droids, that made house calls for the right price, showed up with a portable bio-deconstructor to dispose of the bodies. Rey insisted they wait outside under the watchful eye of Kassandra as he and Jorian threw the bodies into the machine, breaking the bodies down to individual elemental particles that were saved in a container.

Once the bodies were disposed of, the throne chair was dismantled and deconstructed as well. At that point, the group was allowed inside to sanitize the building, cleaning any remnants of blood on the walls and floors. When they had finished, the two teams of forensic cleaners for hire exited the building and waited for the medic.

Jorian just looked at the device and studied the use of it in this particular situation. He looked at Rey, then back to the device as it processed the bodies. Rey could see the young man's confusion. "What's the problem?"

"This device. What stops just anybody from having one and sticking someone in there?" Jorian asked inquisitively.

"Well, that was understood a long time ago, but there are security protocols that are installed in the programming of these machines or others like this that forbid processing a live being and/or biomaterial without a license. There are the strictest of protocols being used to keep these machines safe. Fortunately, there are people that have skills in bypassing those protocols or have acquired licenses and have people that can circumnavigate the process for profit," Rey replied.

"What, you live in a bubble all these years?" Kassandra asked sarcastically.

"Pretty much," Jorian answered sincerely.

The sniper grunted in disbelief as a medic injected her with some pain meds and finished bandaging her hand. The medic looked at Rey and stated, "It's not broken but severely bruised, some ice and rest and it should be fine in a couple of days. She was fortunate to have the armor gauntlet that covered her hand, or it would have shattered some bones. We have sent the bill to your account Capitan. Good luck and thanks for the business."

"Thank you, my dear," Rey told the young woman with a grateful smile and a wink.

Having finished the disposal of the bodies and the sanitation of the building, the medic and her staff exited the area. They jumped into their vehicles and disappeared into the night, leaving the trio in the building. El Capitan walked through the rows of boxes, inspecting the manifest that he had found and matched it to the list he had on his datapad, while Jorian studied the room, then looked at Kassandra.

"Did you hurt Julius?" he asked her in a level tone.

The woman hesitated for a moment, then replied, "No, I had nothing to do with that, I was on the roof the whole time. I got paid to guard, not torture. Did I torture you when you were imprisoned?"

"She is correct Compai, Kassandra is a hired gun, not a pirate. They contracted her through the mercenary's guild and had stipulations as to her contract. Why do you ask?" Rey interjected

"Because if she was civil to Julius, he could treat her in the future. After all he is the preferred choice when it comes to doctors on this planet, and it seems that she will be with us for a while. I was curious if that was an arrangement that would work," Jorian stated as a side note.

"Let's get one thing straight, I work for Rey, not you," the woman said spitefully.

"Whatever," Jorian replied dismissively.

The woman took a step towards the young man, but Jorian didn't even turn around, he just continued to look at the warehouse and all the crates full of cargo. "You going to process this today?" Jorian asked.

"No," Rey replied and took Jorian to the side, whispering, "the old man made me an offer, he traded me a few moments to make a transaction for over a hundred million credits in cargo and land. The catch is that most of it is on other planets or stations. Here on this planet, there are only two buildings, this one and another one. Compai, thirty percent is yours."

"Forty," The young man countered.

"Ah, yes. Forty," Rey corrected.

"Why are you telling me this, Rey? You could have kept it all," Jorian asked.

"Because we are friends and friends don't betray each other, no matter the price. But now we are more than friends, we are partners. You told me to take care of it and I did, plus twenty thousand credits for turning you in, we are on our way, Compai. We are on our way," Rey said excitedly.

"That's what, six thousand credits for me? Nice, all I had to do was kill most of the people and get sold to a psychotic teenager by my only friend. I live a charmed life," Jorian said sarcastically, shaking his head.

Rey hesitated and almost accepted the young man's misunderstanding of the situation, but decided against it, since it involved Jorian. and chuckled, shaking his head in disbelief. "No Compai. I got fifty thousand credits for you, your cut is twenty thousand plus another fifty million credits, give or take a few thousand credits after we collect all the cargo in the sector."

Rey actually hugged Jorian and put his arm around his neck excitedly. Being unable to contain himself, Rey whispered to Jorian, "Partners, Compai! Our adventure together will take us all over the sector and then some, and it's profitable. The deal I made with Torvus will be worth over one hundred and thirty million credits and then some. You know what this means? We are rich Compai, Rich!" He finished in a hushed voice.

Jorian and Rey started walking back to the center of the room, the soldier had a smile on his face thinking of the chance of going on an actual adventure. *I've always wanted to go on adventures as a kid, now I might actually get the chance.*

Rey showed the young man the email on his datapad and scrolled through the list, "This is all ours, Compai, ours."

Jorian didn't really care about the goods. The thought that Rey, for all his antics was honest with him, even when he was not around. He knew Rey must've been tempted to keep it all to himself and could have, but was truthful and honest, made Jorian feel fortunate, realizing he had a genuine friend, even if he was an odd one.

"That sounds like fun, Capitan. I think I would like that," the young man said.

"Of course it will be Compai. Now we celebrate. Let's go to the parlor and get massages, yes?" the former pirate said as he raised his eyebrows. "Women always make celebrations better."

Jorian hesitated and somewhat blushed, remembering the last time they went. The salvager looked at the young man and laughed. Kassandra, who had walked close enough to hear the last statement, rolled her eyes and scoffed. Rey looked at her and smiled. "You know, you can join us, Kassandra, my treat. They have male masseuses too."

Kassandra looked at the sly, smooth-talking man and grinned. "Well Capitan, who said I needed a male masseuse? But if it's your treat, then I must, but don't be getting any funny ideas, Rey."

The trio locked the building, changed the alarm code and reengaged the system, walking off into the night.

Chapter 16

Rey sat back in the bubbles of the hot water puffing on a cigar, he was staring at the roof and could think of nothing else but the massive bounty that they had just acquired, but after the excitement had set in, his mind quickly moved to the logistics of the project. Some planets were war torn and very dangerous, and though profitable, these excursions would be costly.

Jorian exited the room with a relaxed expression and wearing nothing but a pair of trunks. Seeming almost sleepy as he walked into the relaxation area. The man smiled at his friend and looked behind him as the ladies exited the room Jorian had just come from and winked at El Capitan.

"Excellent! Yes, Compai?" Rey asked.

Jorian once again blushed averting his eyes and hesitantly replied, "Oh, yeah, it was great, thanks."

A few moments later Kassandra exited her room, with a towel wrapped around her, and made her way to the spa. The woman let out of breath of relief, turning she thanked the man and woman that exited her chamber. Reaching the spa, she looked at the other two and removed her towel, displaying her naked body. Rey looked and smiled while Jorian averted his face and eyes, a response that caught Rey's and Kassandra's attention.

"Something wrong? You never seen a naked woman before?" the woman defensively snapped.

"You must forgive our friend; he is a bit modest. He is inexperienced," Rey said politely.

"He's a virgin? But we're at a parlor, he can get whatever he wants here," she said, implying the absurdity.

Jorian stood up and was about to leave when he looked at Kassandra in the eyes. "You must have spent too long amongst pirates. Excuse me for not knowing being respectful was so wrong. You have an exceptional physique, I advert my eyes to not be rude, at least I still have manners."

"Look at me. Look-at-me," she demanded. "Do I look ashamed or bothered? I am an adult and if I wasn't ready for others to see me and not make a big deal out of it, I would not be getting into the water naked. Either we're adults or we're not."

Rey just scratched at his face and sighed before attempting to intervene. "He was somewhat isolated for those last few years, in a highly structured group. Cut him some slack or teach him something better."

Jorian turned, making his way up the steps to get out of the water, when the woman embraced him from behind. Her firm, supple breast pushed against his back. The young man froze, not knowing how to react. Rey looked up somewhat surprised, his jaw dropped not suspecting this type of action from the woman, being so unlike her personality. She leaned close to his ear and whispered, "How does it feel? Do you like it? Does it feel good?"

Jorian swallowed hard, being caught by surprise and not knowing what to do. He hesitated, his limbs frozen in place as the woman continued nudging his ear with her nose and continued whispering in his ear as her hand caressed his chest and made its way up to his face.

"Lesson one, be honest with yourself and what you want. Up on the roof earlier, when you grabbed me and pressed me hard against your body, did you know what you wanted? Then have the same presence of mind now," she said and rushed her hand up, putting him in a choke hold.

The young man went from being aroused and insulted to his survival instincts, in a flash of movement, grabbing at her arm. To minimize the squeezing of his arteries on his neck. His instinct was to hurl her over his shoulder, but he could seriously hurt her.

"How do my tits feel on your back now?" she said as she squeezed with all her might.

"They feel nice!" he muttered back and started pushing against her arm.

She kicked him hard behind the knee, making it buckle, and pulled him back to keep him off balance, but got more than she bargained for, not suspecting him to weigh so much. Jorian started pulling her arm from his neck, surprising the mercenary of his raw strength, and immediately understood it was not luck back at the warehouse that had given him his edge.

Rey shook his head as he shifted further away from the two, keeping his cigar and drink from getting wet. Jorian and Kassandra wrestled some more as she tried to get the upper hand. She was relentless, and no matter how many times Jorian pushed her off, she would quickly jump on him again. At one point he had grabbed her ass tightly without even knowing raising her up over his head, annoyed.

"Compai, don't hurt her, she's a proud woman, and you wounded her pride by besting her in combat, two, no wait three times if you count now. But please stop spilling water all over, you are going to ruin my drink, eh?" Rey stated being tired of the fighting.

"You don't seem to have a problem grabbing my ass, huh?" the woman stated, trying to turn, but his grip was like steel.

"Kassandra! Enough already, bed him or leave him be, but enough," Rey interrupted, irritated, then added, "She's attracted by physical prowess, even more so in combat. The more she struggles, the more aroused she gets." Rey looked at the woman, then to Jorian's perplexed face. "You're making her horny."

"What?" The young man said, confused, tossing the woman to the side.

"She's troubled. What can I say?" El Capitan replied and shrugged.

Jorian threw his hands up exasperated turning for the exit but Kassandra leaped for his legs, tripping him and was quickly on him again, whispering in his ear, "Let me make you a man." Jorian pushed her off and exited the room as fast as he could.

Rey grumbled. "Why did you do that?"

The woman rolled to her feet and returned to the pool casually. "Does it bother you, Rey?"

Rey just shrugged. "He's my friend, it's not appropriate."

"Shut it, Rey, you would probably bed my sister if she let you," the woman retorted.

Rey conceded, agreeing to the point, and replied. "You have a sister?"

The woman glared at him. "Don't even think about it. I will cut your nuts off."

"You brought it up," the man said defensively.

"Excuse me. Is everything okay, or would you like something else?" A seductive female voice said, interrupting the two.

"Everything is delightful, but could you please send one of your ladies to bring back my friend? And could you send for his clothes, please?" El Capitan asked.

"Of course, right away, Capitan." The woman bowed her head slightly and exited the room.

"You are different with him. I've never seen you this way about anyone. You really like him," Kassandra told Rey.

"He's my friend, I have not had one of those. And yes, for all of his stubbornness and moodiness, he is quite likeable and very smart," Rey replied sincerely.

"If he's so smart, why is he still hanging around with you?" the woman asked as she took a sip of Rey's drink.

Rey just gave the woman a sideways glance. "There is an innocence to him, but he is true to himself, despite of everything he has been through. I respect him for that. Now, if you could please be civilized and stop this foolishness, I would greatly appreciate it. Be nice to Jorian, you may be working with him a lot," the former pirate said, grabbing back his drink and taking another swallow. "Now, if you don't mind, I'd like to relax before I go back to the room."

"Where am I staying?" the sniper asked.

"After the way you've behaved, I should make you sleep at the warehouse, but fortunately for you, I will let you sleep on the couch in my room, until we make arrangements for you," Rey answered.

"That's a threat either way," the woman said, chuckling.

The hostess returned and addressed Rey. "My apologies, Capitan, he would not return. He asked for his clothes and left. I even tried to entice him with another massage or anything else, but he just wanted to leave. Again, I'm sorry."

"Don't worry, I'm sure he'll be fine, thank you. I know you tried your best. I will return to my room soon, send my clothes there, I will wear this robe up. By the way, is there any other room available?" he asked.

"Once again, my apologies, Capitan. Since the auction, all of our rooms have been booked. Is your room not to your liking?" the woman asked, concerned.

"Yes, very much so, but the young lady over there will stay with me for the night. If you would be so kind, have some more pillows and blankets sent up, and have the couch prepared for her."

"Of course, Capitan, it will be taken care of right away," the woman replied graciously.

Rey smiled at the attention and rested his head back, letting all the other thoughts go away.

A few days had passed, and no one had seen or heard from Jorian. Ophelia knew he could take care of himself, but anything could happen in this city. Being out there alone, with no datapad, ID, or money, was not a good thing; she worried whether he had run off.

It was the middle of the afternoon on the fourth day, when the doctor's medical bag appeared on his desk and the healer caught a glimpse of Jorian walking out. "Stop! Come back, please."

Jorian turned and walked back to the clinic where the man was working. The old man sized him up, nodding his head as a series of thoughts ran through his mind, but finally made a statement. "It's good to see you Jorian, how are you?"

"I'm fine, thank you. I guess congratulations are in order."

"What do you mean?" Brother Julius asked, confused.

"By the looks of you, it seems that you somehow duplicated the healing serum, and it worked wonderfully. I suspect your success came from analyzing the nanites from my blood work?" Jorian replied.

Looking at him from above his glasses, the healer grinned. "I did, and it's truly ingenious and dangerous if overused. The results are amazing though, I feel better than I did 10 years ago," the old man replied, then extended his hand. "Thank you, Jorian. You saved my life."

Jorian looked at the old man's hand and took it, shaking it. "It was nothing, but I wasn't the only one, if Rey and Ophelia hadn't helped, I may not have been able to pull it off."

The old man looked at him and made a face. "That's horseshit. What I saw you do should not be possible, but I can't deny it. Without them, you would have just massacred everyone. Maybe even me."

"I'm not proud of that, and I wasn't in full rage. I do what I need to. I don't take pleasure in it, or pride. It's just what needed doing, so I did it," Jorian replied flatly.

"I'm not judging you. And though it may not be right of me to say as a clergyman or a doctor, I am glad you did, and even if they don't know, I'm sure Nate and Terri are too. But it was you who saved me. Rey told you where I was, and he helped. As for Ophelia, I'm sure she provided some support, but it was you who put his ass on the line. It was you who ran with me to get me here. It was you that made it possible for me to make that serum," the man stated as his eyes got a little watery thinking of what he almost lost, then asked, "after everything that's happened, why did you?"

"Doc, I lost everything as a youth and your grandchildren have lost enough. I didn't want them losing you, too. Children too often pay the price for the actions of adults, if it makes you feel better, just consider it unfinished business, that is now concluded," the young man said with finality.

"That it is, and with that done, I would like to compensate you if it wouldn't offend you. What ever happened after we left, I suddenly got much richer a few days ago. I'm sure that was Rey's doing, that man has a way to make things profitable. But I think he likes you. Be careful, your friend is dangerous, and not a trusting man, but he trusts you. Guard that friendship well because a genuine friend in this universe is hard to find. Except in GOD who is always there. And just so you know, you have one in me, too," the old man said, smiling.

"Thank you, Julius, but I don't need a reward. Instead, make me some more vials of that healing serum, then talk to Ophelia about joining us on the ship. It is getting dangerous out here for you and your family. This planet may not suit you anymore," the young man replied.

"I will consider it. If I may, would you allow me to do some follow-up tests on you? No straps or anything like that, I just want to understand you better, in case anything happens someday, good or bad, we can be ready, plus it will allow me to continue to tweak the formula for the serum," the healer stated his thoughts openly with no hidden agendas.

"I have nothing to hide, as long as we are open with each other about it. In truth, I can use a doctor that understands my special circumstance and you seem like the perfect candidate. Maybe you can even find a way to cure me of the rage someday," the soldier replied.

The old doctor smiled as he nodded. "That is a very tempting offer, but that is for your captain to decide. I will consider it. Thank you again, this bag was a gift from my wife and daughter some years ago." Julius started turning back to his desk and pausing as he looked into his bag. "You need to talk to Ophelia, she's worried and upset, maybe even feeling a little betrayed. Think about that when you go talk to her. She's been by here every day looking for you. She's a very bright young lady, give her a chance and this time try talking to her. You two always seem to be at ends." The old man finished as he shifted through the items in his bag, then looked up, suddenly adding, "Oh, and the fox is here. Do you want to take it with you?" the old man said, but it was too late, the fox was already sitting at Jorian's side.

"Forget it. It seems like the little critter already knows," Julius said, chuckling.

Jorian smiled, bent down and picked the animal up in his arms and began scratching the back of its ears as he turned to leave. "I'm glad you are still with us. See you later and thanks for the advice," Jorian said as he left.

"Give that poor thing a name already," Julius stated loudly behind the soldier as he made his way down the hall.

Jorian exited the clinic and looked up to the sky, quickly dismissing his thoughts, then turned his gaze towards the ships at the port, finally resting his eyes on Mistress and her dirty copper colored exterior that desperately needed to be cleaned. The large port was such a dry area of the city, with lots of dust, sand, and wind that could commonly be found making a mess of everything, giving the multitude of ships a powdery cover of dirt.

Having made his way to the ship, Jorian paused in front of her, taking in her massive bulk and sleek lines. The young man paused there for a few moments, just staring at the ship and considering his life. For all his abilities and augmentations, he felt small compared to the large ship, but knew that the ship was infinitely smaller compared to the vastness of the universe. *Can we really make a difference? Can we even get her parent's back? Would she forgive me if she found out that I put her parents in a pod and jettisoned them into space three years ago?* Sighing and having no solution for his contemplations, he proceeded to the docking panel.

"Welcome back Jorian, playing hooky huh?" Mistress said, greeting him.

"You look embarrassing, let's get you washed," he answered as he and the fox stepped on the platform of a washing unit. "I am going to clean you from top to bottom, if the others want to know so bad where I've been or what I'm doing, tell them to get on a washing unit and have them come help me. Let them know I am here and ready to work."

"Of course, Jorian, and thank you, I like a man's caress. It shows me he cares," Mistress said in her sultry voice.

Jorian's unit floated up to the top of the ship and with the push of a few buttons, a series of automated scrubbers dropped from the platform and began spraying and scrubbing, then polishing the ship meter by meter. Various times Jorian jumped off the platform with a power-brush, hitting some spots again before moving to the next area. "Mistress, send me one of your drones to record the exterior of the ship in detail. We need to assess the damage for repairs."

A short while later, Ophelia and Emmy were outside hitching a ride with another floating disk. They noticed the process Jorian had chosen would take hours, but they didn't mind since it was more thorough than letting the automated system do it, and knew it was necessary to properly assess the damage to their home.

Ophelia and Emmy saw him power-brushing another area and jumped off their platform. Both had power-brushes in their hand and came up quietly next to him. A glance and a nod were the only exchange between them as they started scrubbing, and not a word was said.

Chapter 17

The sun had gone down, and it was late into the night when they finally finished. The ship looked immaculate, gleaming in the moonlight.

"She looks amazing, we did a great job," Jorian told them.

Finished, the three headed back into the ship, exhausted. Jorian suddenly turned towards Ophelia, that was a few steps behind him. "I have invited a few guests over for dinner. If that's okay? I will cover the cost of the food. If you want to talk, I'll talk. How about after dinner?"

She hesitated, caught by surprise. "I have a date tonight, but I can move it back or cancel it. This is more important, plus I don't like strange people on my ship."

Jorian grinned at the response, appreciating the gesture made by his captain. "I appreciate that, thank you. And you know most of the people I would invite. One hour at the mess hall, after dinner, the three of us can have a chat?" Jorian said.

"What?" Emmy said hesitantly. "No offense, but I don't want to get between the two of you again, it's very uncomfortable."

"We all need to talk, and we are going to do that, just talk. After that, Emmy, unless the captain needs you for something, you are free to go. Is that acceptable?" Jorian asked.

Everyone agreed as they entered the ship. The three were hesitant about what was to come, but willing to take part. Each person went to their rooms and made their calls as Mistress made dinner for eight and set the table.

Jorian entered the conference room; it was a room set up specifically for nicer meals and meetings with guest or dignitaries. It was mostly for the use of the captain of the ship, but given their few numbers, Ophelia didn't mind. Believing he was the first one there, Jorian moved towards the window, but a glimpse of color and movement caught the corner of his eyes, and he turned, prepared for a confrontation.

Quickly, he got himself together, realizing that it was Ophelia who had first arrived and had been sitting quietly in the chair waiting for him. He scanned the room once more, as if waiting for creatures to jump at him from the ceiling, before moving towards a seat.

"Are you always on edge?" she asked curiously.

"Somewhat," he replied.

"Your intensity is exhausting. I don't know how you keep that up without burning out," she told him in a sympathetic tone.

"I would apologize, but it's how I survived all these years, I can't let it go," Jorian said as he selected a chair.

"That would be inappropriate. If we have guests, you should be next to me as should Emmy. It's the proper protocol. I'm just saying. You can sit wherever you want," the young woman said cautiously, not wanting to get into an argument with him.

He, too, wanted their talks to be successful and responded openly to her suggestions. "Please tell me where, I am not completely familiar with this arrangement."

"You would be on my left and Emmy on my right, being the science officer, she would technically out rank you, but if you were of the same rank, it would be by time in-service. Which, in this case, she has been with me longer, so she still would be on my right," the young woman replied.

Mistress politely interjected, "Normally true, but Emmy still has not finished her contract with the Galactic Defense Force, so Jorian would technically be your highest-ranking and only crew member on the ship, so he should be on your right. It's a technicality, but important. Emmy is still not an official member of the crew, so she should never sit on your right at a formal table."

Ophelia quietly sighed, shaking her head, bothered at getting something else wrong, then took a breath and looked at Jorian. "Please excuse me Jorian, it seems that you would sit at my right."

Jorian noticed Ophelia's reaction and quickly replied to be supportive. "Captain, I'll sit outside if you want me to. It doesn't make much of a difference to me. You tell me where, I will sit there."

"It's okay, Jorian, I am not a stickler for it as much as my mom was. She had it down to the millisecond," Ophelia said tenderly.

"She sounds strict," Jorian replied.

"She could be, but she was great, she could juggle so many things, I thought she was amazing. I miss her so very much. I just wish I knew something, anything, about what happened," the young woman stated.

"I'm sure she'll turn up soon enough, both of them will," he said, with a softer kindness.

"Thank you, Jorian," she answered with a hint of a smile.

A moment of silence began, but Ophelia wasn't going to let it grow and stale their conversation. "Can I start, please?"

"Sure," he replied.

"Are you okay, you were gone for almost four days and then just show up out of the blue. You had no datapad, ID, money, or anything. We and I—I mean... We all were getting worried, we thought something had happened or worse." Ophelia paused, and in a moment of honest sincerity, added, "I thought you might have been killed or had run off. Are you okay?"

"I won't leave you. Or run off or whatever. I promise," he told her, his eyes fixed on hers. "I'm okay now, thanks for asking, but I needed some time for myself. In my unit, after we'd gone on an operation, it was customary for us to level off before we would overview what had gone right or wrong during the mission. Mainly to learn from mistakes or see other avenues the next time and use the practical experience of others as additional learning resources. I needed to clear my head because I was feeling overwhelmed. I needed a cool-down period," Jorian replied evenly.

"So why don't you cover that with us, so we can learn, too? It is a great idea. It would allow us to better support you in the future," she asked.

Jorian hesitated as he searched for an answer. "I never led a post operation evaluation, I only provided feedback."

"We probably have never been in one, so anything you do is most likely better than nothing. Jorian, we need to start somewhere."

"You have! I saw the logs. You and Emmy have both continued your training and have shown some improvement in your strength and stamina," Jorian said.

"What do you mean, I don't see anything that looks like progress?" she said, reviewing her data on her IDP, not seeing anything jump out at her. "I still don't see it."

"Because you are looking in the wrong place. Observe your recovery time between exercises, you have improved your rate and have improved your recovery time by a few seconds, but those few seconds are multiplying and you fit in another exercise over here. That is one of the most important parts of all this, in another week or so, if you push, you can shave off another minute easy. Those seconds go building up as you develop and get better. The more you do it, the more you improve, and the faster the next lesson comes," he answered.

"Are you going to attack us again?" she said hesitantly.

"Eventually, but I'm not attacking you. I am training you. I would not attack you," Jorian said plainly.

"You threw us in the pool, then set off and an electrical charge almost drowning us," the young woman snapped back.

"You weren't prioritizing the most important thing for your survival. That is not something you teach, it is something you must experience," Jorian started arguing.

Ophelia took a deep breath to gain control of herself and the conversation before it got away from them. "Wait! You don't seem to get my point, and I am not really making it either. Why Jorian? Why did you do that? You said you were training us, for what exactly that would require that kind of training?"

Jorian paused, his eyes full of sincerity. "To help you achieve what you asked. You want to take the things taken from you on that raid. In your shape and combat skills, you'll be dead, maybe even all of us. I'm not only committed to our deal, but I care about you... I mean, about the success of your objective. I train you like that because that is what we will face, or worse. You need to understand the gravity of your request, and I am showing you the gravity of your request, but I know you can do it. You just have to step it up."

Ophelia huffed and asked, "did they do that to you in your training?"

Jorian hesitated, but spoke, "In our training, they worked us hard, constantly placing us in life-threatening conditions. After a week of those drills, then starving us for three days, they took us over to this massive body of water. Inside were keys that would open lockers with food. We had to dive into the water and retrieve a key. The problem was, every time someone grabbed a key, anyone with a key would get shocked. The keys were shocking us, so we'd drop the keys. Over and over. Some people got smart and waited outside, attacking the people that managed to retain the key and exit the pool. I am the smallest member of my unit, I learned that day, that I had to be smarter and more determined to survive. Twenty-two people died that day, some were eventually resuscitated."

Ophelia gasped in horror, "that's just inhumane."

"We are not going up against college kids, we are going up against, murders, thieves, killers, pirates, hackers, specially trained soldiers, terrorists and they all will want one thing: Everything you have!" Jorian's eyes fell to the floor as he shook his head, taking a deep breath and then meeting Ophelia's gaze once more. "Don't you get it? It's not them you are going after. It's their greed, their ambition, their perversions that have led them to a point where they have no conscious, no pity, or remorse. They will exploit your weaknesses just to get what they want and by whatever means necessary. And we are not ready yet," he finished, direct and to the point.

Shaking her head, not wanting to hear those words, she tried to change the direction of the conversation. "The other day you raided that warehouse and then vanished for days without a word, then you just show up out of the blue. How can we ever build trust if I have to find out that you are doing something highly illegal, even if it's for a good reason, because I was concerned and happened to catch part of your conversation? What you did was highly illegal and now we are technically accomplices. How does that build trust?" she retorted.

"I was trying not to include you to spare you from that," Jorian answered.

"How? You are part of my crew and like it or not, I am invested in you and what happens to you affects me, and matters to me, and it's not about the money, or not completely at least. I saw you kill that man. Correction two men, assault a third and lord knows what else." Her voice suddenly softened. "Did they really have to die?"

"Yes! It was unfinished business and to get a clean cut away from what I had done before, I had to eliminate them. You got on the comms, and you started asking questions. I had to tell you it wasn't the time. When people are not focused on the mission, the operative dies because they're distracted. That is why I tried entrusting it to Mistress. Sometimes you need someone to just follow instruction. And to your credit, you finally did, but I did not want you involved. In the end, though, I am glad you were, because I noticed you have real potential, and also needed you to see what is required to achieve what you have asked for, in getting your revenge and finding your parents," Jorian replied in a more agitated tone.

"Jorian, I know we are not you, but who is? What I saw you do with that man on the balcony, I still can't believe it. You held yourself up while strangling another man in midair with one arm. That should be statistically impossible. Yet somehow you did it. If you expect us to be at your level, I don't think that is possible. You are... You are the most dangerous man I have ever met, and you scare me," the woman finally admitted.

Jorian's shoulders fell, saddened when he finally replied, almost ashamed. "You are right to fear me, but I do not want to scare you. I like you and hold you with much regard."

"Jorian, how are we going to build trust if you don't give us the opportunity? Give us a chance; we are going to make mistakes. We are ignorant, not incapable," she stated, then added. "Just teach us."

"Ignorant is much more dangerous, because mistakes can cost lives and we don't have lives to spare. You did well that night. Quick on your feet, and decisive in your actions. That is what I needed from a field support person. It is sometimes disregarded, but they are critical personnel. It takes time for teams to work together, and you surprised me every time you step up, which allowed me to trust you more." He paused briefly, watching another ship take off through the windows, then turned back to her. "Understand that I'm not talking about the attack. I'm talking about the other day when you helped me with the pipes. You put our petty bullshit aside and did the job. That opened a door for me to give you the benefit of the doubt while on the raid. I need someone I can trust with my eyes closed, not to have an agenda and that trusts me to get the job done. Someone who is watching my back, like with the drone, or the transport, even by just picking up the tool and doing the job. If that job is turning a screw, or picking up a blaster and shooting someone. I have to be able to trust you will."

"Shooting someone?" she said with a momentary hesitation. "I don't know if..."

Jorian interrupted her. "That hesitation right there, right now, in your voice. That's what gets people killed out on the field. You want to stop and cry about it? Fine, after the mission. I'll even lend you my shoulder, but on mission, you must be clearheaded, not thinking about the ship, or going out with your boyfriend. You think about the mission." He was saying when she cut him off.

"Boyfriend? I don't have a boyfriend. You mean Odis? No, no, he is a distraction, someone with whom I have shared some moments together. I've been feeling overwhelmed lately and instead of killing people, I enjoy going out, because it helps, and he's a nice guy."

"He's an asshole," Jorian interjected.

"Moving on." she sighed. "Truth be told, Jorian, that night on the mission, I was terrified. Mistress contacted me, informing me of your location, and I expected her to need my permission to hack and override systems. She needs my authority to execute certain programs. It's a protocol for safety, to avoid incidents. My mother programmed various safeguards into Mistress. She was the real genius when it came to programming. I may have majored in it, but I didn't even finish the cleaning programming for the ship. Truth is, I barely graduated. The only reason I got my degree is because I had a double major and had taken so many extra classes. After my parents disappeared and everything that happened with the company, the lawyers, and the government entities that came after me. Me!" Ophelia paused to collect herself before looking at Jorian again. "The reality is, I-I threw myself into piloting and ships to just leave. I am not an expert, I'm just barely getting by, I'm just a fraud," the woman answered shamefully.

"I wouldn't say that," he said with sincerity and respect. "I would say you have a broader range or that you are multi-talented. Ophelia, no one is born knowing, it takes time and dedication. Every hobby, every interest, any profession, they all have one thing in common: they all take time and dedication to be good at it."

"Thank you. Those are kind words," she replied, giving him a small smile.

"I'm sorry, I should have been more open with you. I know I have trust issues, and for good reason. I know they have ingrained my issues in me, but it's not your fault. When I was in special operations, I trusted my datapad more than I did my unit. That's not normal. In the military, your unit is supposed to be a family. Half the time, I felt like that family was trying to kill me, the other half I felt they were trying to sabotage me.

"So, I dove into augmenting my technical and infiltration skills. I practiced with the use of an AI as a partner. That night you did well, but you need to understand that we don't need you to be the best at everything or at any one thing, just to be at your best." He paused, staring at the wall and taking a deep breath before continuing. "The training is to teach you to push past your mental limits, push your body to new limits, and help you prioritize objectives. If we can condition ourselves properly, we can have the focus of working as a unit, and if we work as a unit, we become more and more efficient, which should result in greater success. That is difficult to get and if you want to get better, stop expecting things to happen and make them happen.

"Read everything you can get your hands on because the more you know, the more experiences you have to refer to when making a decision. They don't have to be your experiences for you to take advantage of them. That will help you be a better person and a better captain."

A voice from the door interjected, "Balance! A good captain must have a balance in their life, in their heart, and in their mind. When a person loses their balance, they become either fixated or rudderless. It is easy to lose sight of anything and everything, but if you live a balanced life and hold that balance, things will eventually go in the direction you want," Rey said as he entered the door, nodding to the two. "But please excuse me for interjecting, I was not trying to be nosey. I just happened in on the conversation. I have brought some wine for dinner, and it's good stuff."

"It's okay, Capitan, those are wise words, and appreciated from an experienced captain like yourself. Thank you," Ophelia replied.

"It is my pleasure. I, too, would also suggest you read everything you can, old tales have lots of wisdom, if you can see it. Videos sometimes are cumbersome, and everyone makes one, but every little thing you expose yourself to could be the thing that saves your life, your ship, or that of your crew. Wine anyone?" Rey stated as he opened the bottle, letting it breathe.

"Yes, please!" the young captain said, taking a glass.

"Me, too," Emmy said from behind him as she entered the room.

Behind the scientist entered a female guard. Her outfit was a charcoal color that matched Rey's jacket. It had a dark stripe going down the sides and around the wrist, ankles, and neck. She had a patch with an insignia no one recognized on her lapel and dark leather-like boots, gloves, and accessories that finished out the outfit. Her hair was nicely done, a visor was sitting on top of her head at the moment. She wore a little makeup, augmenting some of her attractive facial features and augmenting her light-colored eyes and dark tanned skin. She was an attractive woman, and tall at just over two meters in height. Her form was athletic, and the tailor-made outfit accented her curves, but most of all was the confidence she walked around with that was truly inspiring.

"Captain Ophelia, Emmy, may I please present to you, Kassandra. She is working for me now," Rey stated as the woman came into the room. Ophelia immediately recognized the woman as the sniper, restraining herself from gawking at Rey, then shifting her eyes to Jorian confused as to her presence.

"I see you are confused, Captain, I have known Kassandra for quite some time, and I asked Jorian not to eliminate her that night," Rey began and Jorian finished, "Because he wanted to employ her and knew that after that night, she would be free of her commitments, mainly because there would be no one to pay for her contract anymore. That's why he said what he said on the comms."

"As a guard, she is of the highest quality and extremely professional, also she is good people," Rey finished and noticed Jorian's facial expression at the comment. "Well, at least most of the time, we all have our off days, no?" he said, chuckling.

Kassandra noticed Jorian's face as well, then extended her hand out to Ophelia and Emmy and spoke in a very professional and sincere tone. "It is a pleasure to meet you both, you have a lovely ship and I thank you for having me over."

Emmy shook the woman's hand and gave Rey a kiss on the cheek, then took her glass and took a sip as she sat down at the table. "Ooh, this is good."

"Nothing but the best for you. I also will have some crates delivered here tomorrow, it is your cut Compai, and Ophelia's, but I will let you guys sort out the details of your agreement. There will be other things to come later. We are still processing the items at the warehouse," Rey stated in his usual flamboyant style.

"Ms. Kassandra, it is very nice to meet you formally and welcome aboard," Ophelia stated gracefully.

"Thank you," Kassandra replied formally.

"I must say, I love your outfit, Kassandra, and your gear," Emmy stated.

"Thank you. Rey got it for me. It's my new uniform. I must admit, as far as men go, El Capitan is one of the few on this planet that actually has taste and some common sense as to function and design."

"What can I say, I would not have Kassandra dressing in some garbage from her last job. She is no longer a contract worker; she is my employee and crew member and I want everyone to know it," Rey stated with authority and pride.

Jorian stayed away from the woman, though he tried not to make it obvious. Kassandra was talking and being social with the others, but slowly making her way towards Jorian. Two children rushed into the room as the young girl called for Emmy and Jorian, and quickly hugged them both. Brother Julius followed behind with a casual smile, greeting everyone, including the guard.

"Greetings, Ms. Kasandra," Julius said in a proper tone.

Jorian and Ophelia held their breath for a moment uncomfortably as the old man greeted Kassandra. Returning his greeting, the two turned again, seeing the pause in the room and the reaction of the others that were expecting something by far worse. Julius chuckled and clarified. "Worry not you two, I have known Ms. Kassandra for quite some time now and she is a professional. I am aware of her past affiliations, but she had nothing to do with the leadership of that group, it's intentions, or decisions. If anything, our interactions have always been pleasant. There is no need to stop now, is that not so, Ms. Kassandra?"

"This is true, Brother Julius. As a matter of fact, I still use some of the jokes you have told me in the past," the woman said light heartedly.

Soft music was playing in the background as the group continued talking and enjoying themselves. The fox darted into the room, nudging Jorian, who kneeled to pet it, and then rushed off to tug at the young boy's pants, wanting to play. Jorian found the fox's approach amusing and stared for a moment longer before standing back up to see Kassandra standing before him. His face changed immediately to the seriousness she had seen before; he shifted his stand, letting her know he was already on the defensive and prepared to defend himself.

Kassandra stopped her forward progress and spoke almost in a whisper. "Can we please talk? Outside the room. No tricks."

Jorian just looked at her warily and pointed with his hand for her to lead the way. The woman graciously accepted and excused herself, heading for the door. Jorian followed, which caused Rey and Ophelia's eyes to follow, then looked at each other. Rey shrugged and took another sip of his drink.

Once in the hall, Kassandra leaned against the wall, trying to show no hostility. "Thank you for talking with me, I understand your hesitation and can't blame you. But I just wanted to apologize about the other night. The first time at the warehouse I was upset you had bested me so easily and my pride got the best of me, but what I truly want to apologize for are my words and my actions at the parlor. I was out of line, the alcohol mixed with the pain meds put me in a mental state that allowed me to act like an ass. Jorian, I'm sorry. I am much more professional than that and my actions were inexcusable."

Jorian looked at her and studied her up and down, then accepted her sincerity. "Buy me lunch and we'll call it even," he stated, wanting to move on, though he still felt odd befriending someone who was an enemy a few days earlier.

The woman looked at the young man, noticing there was something different in his eyes. He had clarity and purpose, with no internal struggle or redness in his eyes. *Was he on some sort of drug that night?* She instantly knew that the person before her now accepted the apology, but would attack her without hesitation or doubt. His demeanor was like that of a tiger, relaxed but ready to strike, which made her cautious and aroused.

"Agreed then, a meal at some point, on me," she stated, and walked back to the room. She glanced back and smiled, seeing that he was looking at her walk off, though he quickly averted his eyes.

The woman reentered the room first, then was followed by Jorian a few seconds later. Holding himself back to regain his thoughts and continue calculating his plan that he was about to share with everyone. The people in room continued talking and laughing as they awaited their meal. Ophelia made her way to her crewmate and whispered in his ear, asking about Kassandra. "Can you explain later, and is it safe?"

Jorian sensed her trust and need of his support at that moment and he gave it to her with a nod, which visibly put her at a greater sense of ease, though still somewhat alert, which he also noticed and grinned, thinking, *She's learning!*

The group moved to the table and sat ready to enjoy a meal prepared by Mistress. Once seated, a pair of automated arms came down from the ceiling and served each guest their plate, as the arms glided up and down the table with ease and finesse attending to each person individually.

When it was his turn, Brother Julius studied the hands intensely and confirmed his suspicion. "These are surgical hands, no wonder they move so gracefully."

"Why thank you doctor, it's good to be stared at, it makes a woman feel appreciated," the AI replied cheerfully.

Everyone at the table laughed, except the children that didn't get the joke fully, but shrugged and kept eating. While the fox complained to the hands for not giving it its meal, which caused the table to laugh again. The fox looked at the group oddly, then back to the automated hands, complaining until it had its meal.

The group had finished their meal, and once again, the automated hands came down from the ceiling and cleared the table, leaving only the drinks. The group conversed some more and then moved to the upper deck library, where the room was more comfortable and inviting. Along the way, Jorian moved next to Ophelia and asked her discretely. "Do you trust me?"

The question caught the young woman by surprise and for a moment she hesitated, and gazed at him, her eyes fixed on his for a second and for once in a long time she could see and feel hope. Her eyes never left his and nodded as she whispered, "Yes."

Jorian whispered back, "Go with it and we will discuss it in depth later, okay?"

Taking a leap of faith, the young woman nodded, placing Jorian in the driver's seat for whatever was going to happen next. The lights came on in the media center, and everyone was awed by the décor and welcoming nature of the room. There were old books that lined the shelves and elegant paintings along with other art objects that filled the walls, giving the room a sophisticated feel, while the extremely comfortable furniture gave it a sense of home.

The group paused as the seats shifted into a better grouping for conversation and interacting. The group took a seat as Jorian looked at each person. Taking a sip for courage, he then raised his glass of wine.

I hope this works. It has to, it's the only way.

"A toast, please." Everyone turned surprised and starred at him expectantly and filled with curiosity. The group raised their glasses, awaiting his words. "To the end of an old chapter and the excitement of the next page. I asked you all here today, to extend to you an invitation. An invitation to an adventure that will take us across this sector and possibly beyond." Jorian stood, seeming confident, but his stomach churned with anxiety. "Soon, the Mistress of Mayhem will depart from this planet to complete a prearranged stop. From there, we will plot a new course and I hope that everyone here will be on this ship as we depart. Brother Julius, our travels will take us all over and we hope you will join us as our medical doctor. While Kassandra joins us in upgrading the ship's defenses, weaponry, and providing combat training of all on board. Children, you too will have duties and responsibilities as part of our crew. Dr. Emmy Kricay is our residing science officer and botanist. I take faith in our journey and in the guidance of our Captain Ophelia Knight, who has allowed me to present this offer." Jorian paused, nodding to Ophelia who faked a smile surprised by his words and what they meant, and nodded in return.

"But let us not be selfish in our words and offer tribute to the one that is making this happen, our patron and my friend El Capitan, Rey del Castillo." Jorian smiled at the salvager, who had a smirk on his face as he eyed Jorian, who turned towards the rest continuing. "I ask you to raise your glass and join me on this adventure as the crew of the Mistress of Mayhem. Join us as we cause a little 'MAYHEM' all over this galaxy." Jorian paused, raising his glass higher. "To adventure!"

A moment of awkward silence filled the room and everyone eyed Jorian suspiciously as he had sprung this news on them, but two of the attendees quickly jumped up, raising their glasses. The grandchildren of Julius quickly raised their glasses and the young girl said loudly and excitedly, "TO ADVENTURE!"

Everyone got a chuckle at the young girl's reaction and then Brother Julius stated comically, "I guess I have no say in it. To adventure?"

Ophelia raised her glass and, with apprehensive support, replied, "To adventure!"

Emmy, who already had too much to drink, smiled and quickly joined in raising her glass, "To adventure!"

Rey smiled as he looked at Jorian intently, considering the young man until Jorian mouthed one word "PARTNERS!" Rey jumped up excitedly and raised his glass. "To adventure."

"To adventure!" Kassandra replied supportively on Rey's nod.

The group finished their drinks and celebrated the surprising news. Rey approached Jorian quickly and embraced him, laughing. "You and me, Compai, we're partners!"

"My fellow crew members, I know this is a bit of a surprise, but three weeks is not much time to get everything together for an extended campaign. We need various meetings to plan, strategize, and most of all to prepare everything for our expedition. Now let us enjoy the rest of the night and I expect you all here tomorrow to begin enacting the plan. You can start moving in as soon as tomorrow evening, welcome," Jorian stated and returned to his seat.

Ophelia was in complete surprise, and poured herself another drink. She was on her ship, but felt like she was the one being taken for a ride. Chugging her glass of wine and pouring herself another. This is not what she had set out to do, but had somehow agreed to support him. As a child she longed for adventure, always curious and always wandering, she would get herself into all kinds of trouble, but she was not a child anymore.

The young woman put a smile on her face, but felt betrayed inside, felt as if Jorian had and was using her to get what he wanted instead of what she did. It felt like the nicest mutiny in the galaxy, and she was being allowed to watch. The despair and negativity were filling her when the young man was suddenly standing next to her and whispered in her ear.

"This might just work, we just might be able to get your stuff back and find your parents," the young man said supportively, and squeezed her hand gently.

All she could do was stare at him, confused, after the words woke her up from her nightmare. The young man looked back at her and smiled with a childish grin before moving on.

Jorian walked his friend out after the night had ended. "You know Compai, I'm glad we are doing this together, but next time please, give me a heads up, eh?"

"You're right, Rey, but it's the only way it could have worked. You'll see, it will all be for the best," Jorian replied with a hopeful grin.

"I'm sure it will be. Good night my friend and we need to talk soon, I have a line on your suit thingy, it's not cheap, but I will keep my part of the bargain. Can you tell me what you want it for?" the former pirate asked.

"Sure, but how about if I show you tomorrow instead?" the young man replied with a mischievous grin.

"You know, when you smile, I'm happy, when you grin, though." Rey pursed his lips and shook his head. "When you grin, I must admit, I do get a bit concerned," Rey replied.

"Tomorrow then, my friend," Jorian said sincerely.

"Tomorrow then, Compai," El Capitan answered warmly.

"Oh, by the way, Rey, you are our supply officer, so be ready. There is just no one better in the whole... Anywhere."

"This is true," Rey responded with cockiness and sincerity as he walked off with a wave and whistling a tune.

"Good night Jorian. By the way, you know I work for Rey, right?" Kassandra said as she glared at him, stating more than asking.

"I do, but you know we are partners, right? So technically, you work for us. We'll clear it up later, but mess with my ship and I'll push you out of an airlock. Guaranteed! Good night, Kassandra, sleep well," the young man stated calmly, but with a chilling smile. Oddly enough, the woman smiled back, somewhat aroused.

Brother Julius followed, saying his farewells to the others carrying the sleeping boy on his shoulder, with the young girl beside him. "Good night Jorian. I hope we have a greater chance to talk tomorrow, but let me ask you, how did you know I would agree?"

"Well, I hoped, but I didn't expect you would pass an opportunity to get the kids off this cesspool of crap called a planet, nor the opportunity to monitor me and run tests with me willingly. I figured one or both would work," the young soldier replied with a chuckle.

The old man grinned as he exited the ramp, with Jorian waving from behind them as they left, before the young man turned, returning to the ship. Ophelia and Emmy waited at the door waiting for him. "Let's go back to the study. I still need to talk to the two of you."

"Jorian, please don't mess up my buzz," the scientist uttered in protest.

"No Emmy, this needs to be taken care of tonight, given the time frame we have," Ophelia said supportively.

"What, you are on his side now?" the scientist complained once more.

"We can go back to the gym if you'd like?" Jorian stated.

"Nope! To the library it is," Emmy said with a fake smile, taking another sip of her wine.

The trio sat once again on the comfortable furniture and looked at each other in a moment of awkward silence. The fox entered the room and hopped on Ophelia's lap, waiting for her to pet it, to which she complied, shaking her head. A few moments passed when Ophelia looked at Jorian and chuckled.

"Are we really doing this?" she asked, somewhat hesitantly.

"We are, and this is going to help us get ready to complete what you have asked for and getting Mistress back together, not to mention getting revenge for what those pirates did to you, but that will be later, much later, but I promise it will happen," Jorian said with conviction.

A smile danced on the young captain's lips as she gazed at him, sensing the strength of his will and the depth of his character. She could feel his passion and noticed the clarity in his thought. She had begun to understand after the rescue mission that Jorian was a person of deep loyalties, even if he didn't say it. It was a realization that had helped her put faith in him, or at least give him the benefit of the doubt.

"Jorian, this is your plan and I trust you, even if you didn't talk with me first, which I expect you to in the future with anything that involves this ship," she stated in a reprimanding tone, then continued supportively. "Now, lay it out for us and what you need us to do."

Emmy's jaw dropped as she looked at Ophelia and her recent and sudden change of attitude towards Jorian after four days of moodiness and complaining about the young man. She welcomed it, but was still waiting for an argument to ensue, an argument that never came. The only thing she received from Ophelia was a relaxed smile, but the fear was still in the captain's eyes.

"Emmy, you are a botanist," Jorian began. "I want you to prepare an area for a full hydroponics and aquaponics operation. This will assist us in keeping the crew sustained for longer periods of time, even if we can't resupply. Aim to sustain from fifty to one hundred people."

"Fifty to one hundred people!" both women exclaimed simultaneously, then laughed.

"Yes, fifty people and with the possibility of expansion to one hundred down the road. It's not that we need that amount, but if an emergency arises, that we help some people or break down along the way, we'll have the ability to sustain ourselves for long periods of time. You will work with Julius's granddaughter, Terri. She is reliable and will make a brilliant assistant."

Emmy just nodded and took another sip.

"Remember, she is learning, teach her as much as you can. I will take the boy with me, he can be my helper. When he is not studying and only for things that are not dangerous," Jorian finished, seeing Ophelia was about to complain.

"Ophelia, you are the captain and need to assign rooms schedules, oversee supplies, cargo and any other details that will need to be taken care of on the ship, as you coordinate our departure. I need a thorough check on all systems, so I can try to fix everything before we go. We will need to do a test flight or two which needs to be arranged with the dockmaster, Tower, or whoever."

"Mistress, please scan everyone that will be on the ship. We are going to need new uniforms," Ophelia ordered with a flustered sigh.

"Emmy, questions?" Jorian asked.

"I will get with you later with my list of adaptations to the room and will have a list of seeds and other things I may or will require in a few days. With that, I say good night," the young woman stated, and patted Jorian on his head as she walked out the door. "Good job, this is going to be fun."

Jorian looked at the young woman, perplexed as to her actions and then at Ophelia for clarification. "She's been drinking, a lot," Ophelia stated guessing.

"Where does this leave us?" Jorian asked Ophelia.

The young captain pursed her lips as she looked over, waiting for the door to close behind the scientist. "I don't know, but it feels like you're taking over the ship and, to be honest, it's a little uncomfortable."

"Okay. Let's talk about it some more, if you're up to it," he said nicely.

The young woman considered it, and though hesitant, nodded her head in agreement, pressing some buttons on her datapad, rearranging the seats so the two faced each other. The room was much quieter, as it was only them. Jorian offered her some hydration fluid, which she gladly accepted. Once again, the automated arms came down, providing them both a bottle of the tasty liquid.

"So, do you want me to talk first, or would you like to share with me your hesitation and concerns first, and we can discuss those?" he asked, not wanting to mess up the progress they had made that night. "Or we can just watch a movie as your mind processes your thoughts," he added, to relieve some tension.

"Let's do that!" she quickly stated.

The two rearranged the seats again and sat quietly after selecting a movie. The lights had dimmed slightly, as the film began on the large screen. Eventually, the two started talking about the movie and its premise and slowly made their way around to the topic of each other, which quickly changed when Ophelia turned to him.

"Are you trying to take over my ship? Why would you do all this and not even talk to me? Or discuss it with me? Or share with me in the planning? How am I supposed to learn?" she retorted, but more hurt after their earlier discussion.

The question caught him by surprise, but he had expected that question long ago. "No. But I am trying to help you learn how to plan an expedition, a mission, or an extended campaign, while providing time, experience, and profit. Time for everyone on board to get ready and eventually face the pirates that attacked you. Experience so that when we do face problems, we are better prepared to face them. That is where El Capitan and Kassandra come in, he is an experienced captain, and she is an experienced soldier that can help you train at your level. The good doctor is just that, a good doctor and has a mountain of experience."

"That's all nice, but that is all logistics and common sense. Why did you not include me in the plans?" she demanded.

"Because this was the only way this could have happened. The way it had to happen. Not you and Rey thinking about pros and cons, considering it, arguing over percentages or what not. This step had to be pushed through, so I pushed it. We need all the time working together as we can muster. Please believe me, I just want you to succeed," Jorian told Ophelia honestly as he grabbed her hands and looked deeply into her eyes. "I want this to work. I promised you that, and I fulfill my promises."

His heart fluttered for a moment as he looked into her purple eyes, being lost in them once again. The young woman looked back at him, feeling safe with her hands in his. The two looked at each other and gravitated closer, unknowingly. About a foot was between the two when she asked. "How am I going to pay for all of this?"

Jorian grinned and explained to her the nature of the arrangement between him and Rey and how it came about. He described to her of the deal that was made, and the estimated value of the items involved. Ophelia's jaw dropped at the enormous figure, sensing a surge of reassurance and hope, with something tangible to work with on this so called "Adventure."

"What about your contract?" she said, suddenly pulling back from him again, fear creeping into her mind once more.

"What about it?" Jorian asked.

"At the rate you're going, you will have paid it off in no time. Will you abandon me then, and where will that leave me?" she asked.

"I will see it through. When my contract is complete, we will make a new contract. Except this time Rey will negotiate for me," he said with a chuckle. "But I will be with you until we find your parents. I promise," he said with conviction.

"What happens then?" she asked.

"I don't know. We will deal with it then. Let's just focus on getting your parents back, and I promise you, we will find them," Jorian replied supportively, his eyes never leaving hers.

On an impulse, Ophelia leaned forward and kissed Jorian's lips. It was simple but genuine, even if it lingered for just over a second, then hugged him tightly, whispering in his ear, "I'm scared and I'm putting my faith in you. Please don't let us fail."

Jorian embraced her in his powerful arms, surprised at being kissed on the lips for the first time in his life, and he was glad that it was Ophelia. She was the woman of his dreams since the day he first met her five years ago. A surge of emotions filled him, she was his savior and his tormentor, but he wanted more, more of her lips, more of her.

But that scared him, feeling his hands tremble and hearing his pounding heart that sounded like a war drum in his chest. A sensation too close to what he felt when the rage was about to overtake him, and he tensed. Fear filled him now. The woman he had wanted for years, the woman whose eyes he saw when he was in the direst of circumstances, had just kissed him. Restraining his desires to kiss her again—and possibly more—he focused on answering the question. "We won't!"

He released her, leaning back to finish the movie, feeling attracted to the young woman and wanting to kiss her again, but scared of what could happen with the rage demon inside him. Ophelia looked at him for a moment longer, then cuddled into the crook of his arm.

He had tensed after the kiss and moved back, leaving her unsure of her next action, but her thoughts went to the moment they shared under the water. The image of the boy in the stockade came to her again, but she pushed it away. Her emotional outburst that spurred her to kiss Jorian, embarrassed Ophelia, but it felt so natural. Add the thought of finding her parents, the emotions of her dreams becoming a reality, and the nightmare finally ending, overwhelmed her. Sinking deeper into him, thinking of everything that transpired, and during all this, she never let go of his hand.

I don't know how, or why, but for the first time since I got on Mistress and started down this road, I feel something. I feel a sense of hope, and it's all because of him. A stranger I accidentally bought as a slave. I feel like I know him, like if we're somehow connected. I know he's dangerous, but I feel safe with him, and even though he's very different to anyone I've ever met, in my soul I feel like I can trust him, really trust him, and I haven't felt that in a very long time.

The end of Book I of the Mistress of Mayhem series
Thank you for reading it and sharing in the adventure.
An adventure that will continue...

~J.A. Ramirez

<u>About the Author</u>

J.A. Ramirez has loved a good story since childhood. Growing up, he enjoyed listening to his father's captivating tales on his days off from school; on other days he was enchanted by his aunt's folklore. As he grew, his passion for storytelling deepened through television, books, and video games.

In his late teens, J.A. Ramirez joined the stage combatants at a Renaissance fair, where he discovered a love for performance and creativity.

An animal lover and adventurer at heart, J.A. Ramirez dreams of creating his own video games, animations, and audio fiction series. He invites readers to join him on his imaginative journeys through the cosmos and fantastical places.

Find Out More

To learn more about the author, his books, and other projects by J.A. Ramirez, visit us online at our iMAGITECH website. Share in our adventure with cool swag, merchandise, and stay tuned on future projects at www.iMAGITECHMEDIA.com.

Coming Soon

Mistress of Mayhem

Book 2

Echoes of The Avalanche

Fantasy Series

The Rising Flame

Book 1

Embers of Hope

www.ingramcontent.com/pod-product-compliance
Lightning Source LLC
Chambersburg PA
CBHW020333180626
46812CB00001B/186